SUNRISE
OVER DISNEY

by Bert

L.N. Smith Publishing
Madison, Wisconsin

Published by:

L.N. Smith Publishing
3818 Birch Avenue
Madison, WI 53711

The cover art was derived, in part, from NASA images, courtesy of World Wind and nasaimages.org.

The photograph on page 432 was taken by Joseph W. Jackson III and published in the *Wisconsin State Journal* on April 30, 1982.

The Preamble to the *Constitution of the Communist Party USA* was supplied courtesy of the Reference Center for Marxist Studies of the COMMUNIST PARTY USA.

The Statement of Principles for the MOTION PICTURE ALLIANCE FOR THE PRESERVATION OF AMERICAN IDEALS was furnished by the Academy of Motion Picture Arts and Sciences—Fairbanks Center for Motion Picture Study.

This book and its author and publisher are not affiliated with or endorsed by the Walt Disney Company.

Dedicated to
Uncle Albert

Contents

PART I

The
Wish

CHAPTER 1

The Holiday Gathering

All is right with the world; I can feel it. It is the first holiday season of the new millennium, and I'm full of optimism.

As always, Mom and Dad are hosting tonight's Christmas Eve celebration in their 1850s farmhouse—a survivor of the Chicago suburbs and also the backdrop for my childhood memories. It swells with the return of my two sisters, our three spouses, the six children, and my wife's Uncle Albert.

Each of the children is camped out on a floor upstairs: three in my old bedroom, two in Elsa's, and one in the hall closet. Meanwhile, their elders are at work on the floor below, planting the evidence of Santa's visit. Mom and Uncle Albert prepare a ham to be discovered baking tomorrow morning; Mary and Ferguson shovel a Christmas snowfall and create hoof prints on the rooftop; and the remaining five of us occupy the living room—preparing presents, nursing drinks, and watching *It's a Wonderful Life*. As tradition dictates, tonight's film is the one we view when the year is an even number. Next year, in 2001, we'll watch *A Christmas Carol*.

Dad kneels beside me on the carpet, reading the assembly instructions for a bookshelf. He turns his face toward his son-in-law, Tom, who is deaf. "Hey, Tarzan," he says. "Make yourself useful. Hand me the slot."

Tom is an excellent lip reader. He squats beside the open toolbox and withdraws a phillips-head screwdriver. He holds out the implement to Dad, who studies it with a look of displeasure.

"Okay, Mrs. Tarzan," he says to his oldest daughter, who is standing beside Tom. "You're a women's libber. What's this tool?"

Despite all of our exposure to the tinkerers on Dad's side of the family, Jane has no idea what to call the screwdriver. She shifts her weight to her other foot, causing her drinking-arm to swing like a gate away from her face. Her blood-red fingertips disappear behind the blood-red wine in her glass. She stares down her nose at her father. "I *hire* my help," she says.

Elsa—the middle child—sits beside the fireplace, wrapping presents. She pauses in her work to enjoy the home-spun entertainment.

Dad leans toward me, as if to speak confidentially, though he's careful to make sure his mouth is clearly visible to Tom. "Three college degrees between them," he says, "and they're lost in a paper sack. College is a racket, Bert. You were wise to skip it."

"I didn't skip it," I say, but my words are drowned out by a conspicuous tearing of wrapping paper. Elsa crumples a wad and throws it at Jane.

"Remind me again, Janey," she says. "Who gets the bookshelf? Isn't Angelica *your* daughter? I hope these fine gentlemen are on your payroll."

"Ha...ha," says Jane, "very funny." She takes another sip of her wine, then casts a scornful eye upon me. "I suppose Mary goes another year without a diamond," she says.

A second wad sails her way, this one bouncing off her head.

I bury my amusement and manage to drone out a weary reply. "It must be hard for you," I say. "Can you possibly accept that Mary doesn't actually want one?"

"False," says Jane, and she switches her glass to her other

hand, exposing the diamond ring and studded bracelet that form the knob and chain of her left-handed gate. "What's wrong with you, Bert?" her voice squeaks like a rusty hinge. "Are you afraid of a jewelry store? Step outside your comfort zone just once. . . . Tell him, Elsa."

Elsa is a research psychologist with three college degrees all her own. But just as important at this moment, she is wearing a diamond ring on her finger. These are the credentials Jane is trying to use against me.

"Jane's right about *some* things, you know," says Elsa. "It *is* a good idea to step outside of your comfort zone once in a while."

As usual, I deflect the topic of diamonds. "Mary's wishes are much simpler," I say. "She wants to see the solar eclipse tomorrow. So that's what I'm giving her: a clear day."

"A clear day," scoffs Jane.

Tom hides his smile behind his drink.

"Someday," says Jane, "she'll leave you, Bert. Then you'll be sorry."

"Oh, I'm sure he's sorry right now," says Elsa, "—to be in this conversation. Don't listen to her, Bert."

Tom turns and walks quickly away toward the front entry hall. A familiar creaking sound on the stairwell then alerts me to the wall-hanging that's already been swinging. A child is coming down.

I scramble for the afghan and drape it over the bookshelf. Dad rolls himself in front of the Christmas tree to shield some unwrapped presents. Elsa stashes her work-in-progress behind the couch. And Jane kicks the two wads of wrapping paper under a chair.

Tom opens the stairway door and closes it behind him.

"I'm freezing!" comes the muffled voice of his stepdaughter, Angelica. "Tell the idiots to turn up the heat."

Only murmurs are heard after that, as the two climb the stairs.

"That's funny," says Dad, "I didn't hear a thump. That's what she needs, you know."

"So why haven't you bought a furnace?" says Jane. "Lord knows you can afford one."

Dad looks across the room at Elsa, who is already caressing the masonry bench beneath her.

"Now-now, Ketchell," says Elsa to the family fireplace. "You just ignore Big Bad Jane. We would never replace *you.*"

Jane turns away and closes her mouth. I'm sure she doesn't want the lecture she's provoking.

Our house was built by a German immigrant who constructed it around a massive stone kachelofen. Of course, Mom and Dad couldn't pronounce this German word on the real estate listing, so Ketchell Oven became its nickname. The oven's flue gases travel through a maze of passageways in the chimney, which warm the masonry surfaces that face into each room. One hot fire a day is all it takes to heat the first floor.

"I'm doing my part for global warming," says Dad, and he grabs for Jane's ankles. "Why aren't *you?*"

Jane eludes his hands and remains speechless. She really can't deny the paradox that she and Tom present to him.

Dad is a firm believer that global climate change is a hoax—a scare tactic of the Democratic Party—which makes it all the more ironic that he has conserved more fossil fuel than anyone I know. Every outside wall of his house is double-thickness and super-insulated, and he keeps the second floor unheated and sealed off by a door. The only concession he has ever made was to Mom, who wanted a bathroom added upstairs. Yet even then, Dad managed to avoid installing auxiliary heat. He cleverly placed the bathroom over Ketchell

Oven and exposed it to a chimney wall. Dad argues, to this day, that *thrift* and *comfort* have always been his motivation, not the environment. *"Why should I believe in global warming,"* he insists, *"when the one true expert in my family lives in a mansion and keeps it air-conditioned even when nobody's home?"* Dad's remarks are leveled at Tom, who works as a climatologist for Argonne National Laboratory and who routinely warns us of impending cataclysms.

A subject change is in order here. "How could Angelica have been cold?" I say. "I'm sure Tom will have her settled in no time."

Dad takes over the completion of the bookshelf, and Elsa returns to her wrapping. Jane pours herself another glass of wine, and I kneel at the coffee table to clean up some puzzles that have been scrambled together.

When the bookshelf is done, Dad carries the toolbox from the room, and the breeze he creates on his way past the Christmas tree liberates a cool fragrance of evergreen. My attention then drifts from the puzzles to my favorite scene of *It's a Wonderful Life*.

The film's character, Mary, has just locked eyes with George Bailey across a crowded gymnasium. Her gaze is one that always stirs my emotions, reminding me of the way my own Mary looked at me some fifteen years ago across Uncle Albert's parlor. I yearn to see those eyes again, but I don't think the gift of a diamond is going to conjure them.

Dad returns to the living room and pauses beside the Christmas tree, snatching up an unwrapped tee-ball set. "No Barbie for MJ," he snickers, and he carries the toy across the room.

Dad places the ball on its tee and takes a practice swing. "Pinch run for me, Bert," he says. And he points the bat at the far doorway.

Whack! Dad smacks a line drive, which corkscrews past Jane and just misses my mom's nose, as her face appears in the doorway from the kitchen. The ball strikes the Christmas tree and catapults a silver bell from one of its soft branches. I dive across the floor in an attempt to catch the fragile ornament.

"Will he beat the tag?" says Dad.

The bell hits the floor and smashes to pieces.

"Out!" says Jane.

I slide up to my knees and hover over the silver fragments. "Nice going, Dad. You'd've slugged me for that one."

"Just great," says Elsa. "Now we'll never know if Clarence gets his wings or not." She's referring to the film on the television.

Dad ignores his peanut gallery and focuses on Mom, who is waving an angry finger at him.

"And I'd do it again, too," he says.

Mom reaches into the hall closet and removes a broom. "The snacks are almost ready," she says. "Are Mary and Ferguson still outside? Do be a dear, Janey, and call in the help, won't you?"

Jane is oblivious to Mom's sarcasm. She pivots on her heels and struts across the living room like a fashion model on a runway.

Jane's figure is conventionally attractive, I'll admit, though it suffers in my perception from her need to flaunt it. Mary's body is equally fit and trim, further benefiting from five years less wear and tear and from skin that's been spared the abuses of year-round tanning. Mary could easily trump my sister in that cocktail dress, but Mary doesn't play that game.

Jane lowers her chin and watches herself walk into the front foyer. She seems to have heard Tom's footsteps on the stairway because her path is swinging wide to make room for the door. But she's failing to notice that the front door is now opening to her right.

"Jane!" I call out. But too late.

The front door clips her heel and collapses her to the floor like a folding chair. Somehow, though, she manages to prevent her drink from spilling.

Ferguson steps inside and discovers Jane. "Sorry," he says, "let me—" And he bends over to help her.

"No!" she cries.

Ferguson is built like a bison. In fact, we're suspicious that his Native American blood was commingled with that of a Viking somewhere in the distant past. He can comfortably seat Jane and Elsa on his two bench-like shoulders, and these shoulders, at this particular moment, are covered with snow. He unleashes an avalanche into Jane's lap.

Ferguson straightens quickly, then just as swiftly launches a stiff-arm toward the stairway door. He prevents Tom from clobbering Jane on the head with it, but releases another deluge of snow onto her from his coat sleeve.

Jane preserves her drink through this second ordeal and earns the applause of her spectators.

Tom squeezes past the partially-opened door and helps Jane to her feet. The two of them brush the snow off her dress.

Dad and I hurry into the foyer and scrape up the fast-thawing remains. We each pack a snowball and head outside onto the front porch.

The evening is a frigid one, and the only packing snow is the stuff in our hands. Swirls of powder take flight from the eaves, and the rain barrels sit buried under sculptures of ice. There's a golden glow from the windows behind us, though it fades to a steely blue beyond the railing. I squint into the darkness and find Mary.

Her cloaked figure leans on a shovel at the end of the driveway. "Are you here to help?" she shouts.

The work is obviously done, so neither Dad nor I respond. Instead, I take aim and heave my snowball at her.

Mary catches my throw easily with one hand, then repacks the snowball. "Come on, Gramps," she says. "Let's see what you've got. Show me some pepper."

Dad turns away and eyes the old oak tree—the one that saw soldiers off to the Civil War. He pitches his snowball and misses the trunk. "Ah!" he says. Then he turns back to Mary. "I don't throw at women."

Mary crosses her arms. "Oh, pl-eease," she says. "Spare me your *Greatest Generation* fantasy. You might not throw at a woman . . . but people of color, look out. You're priceless, Duke-ee-doo."

Dad manages to chuckle at Mary's remark. I can't believe the things she can say to him without making his blood boil. Dad seems to adore Mary to such a degree that he can excuse almost anything she says or does . . . and that's plenty. Mary challenges almost every one of his preconceived notions about women, even more so than his own daughters do.

Mary turns and fires her snowball halfway across the yard, smacking the trunk of the old oak tree dead center.

Dad smiles. "It's time to come in," he says. "We need your heat in the house."

Dad returns to the front door, and I remain on the porch to wait for Mary. She is quite a sight in Dad's oversized trench coat and galoshes, and I can't help but think that this is the closest thing to a dress and sexy boots I've seen her in since our wedding day. But I guess that's not exactly true. She didn't actually wear boots to our wedding, and her summertime swimsuit cover-up is essentially a dress.

I descend the steps and block her path along the front walk.

Her dark hair supports a veil of glistening ice crystals, and the plastic strap of her earmuffs carries a crown of snow. I don't dare call her a princess, though.

I wrap my arms around her and press my warm face to her cold one. It seems I live to touch this woman, and this might just be the only real purpose to my life.

♦ ♦ ♦

Elsa is on her hands and knees drying the foyer floor when Mary and I enter the house. The television set is off, and Dad is walking toward us through the living room.

"Everyone to the table," he says. He crosses the front hall and opens the pocket doors to the dining room. The table has been set for a special occasion.

The down-light of the chandelier bathes an array of carefully arranged porcelains, silvers, fabrics, and flowers. Votive candles float in a bowl on the buffet, and the shelves within the china hutch glow beneath hidden lamps. Steam rises from a kettle, and the air is sweet with coffee, chocolate, molasses, and nutmeg.

Uncle Albert teeters in from the kitchen carrying two bottles of liquor by the neck, swinging them like holiday geese. One is Irish cream, and the other is rum. Mom and Jane file in behind him with platters of treats, while Dad brings up the rear with nothing but a freshly-opened can of Budweiser. He finds his place at the head of the table and waits for the rest of us to sit down.

Albert, Mary, and I complete one side of the table. Ferguson, Elsa, Tom, and Jane complete the other. Mom takes her seat at the far end.

"Looks like the Scrabble game is off this year," says Mary, and she hand-signs her comment to Tom.

"What a shame," says Tom. "I guess you brought your book-locker for nothing, Uncle Albert."

"Oh, to the contrary, my boy," says Albert. "That crate keeps the train on the tracks. . . . And who doesn't love the suspicion that I'm hauling a dead body?"

Dad scoots his chair to the table and clears his throat. Soon, the room is a whisper of clinking tableware and darting eyes. The last time we were assembled in this way was two years ago at the annual Labor Day picnic. Dad had just sold the business and was hiring an estate planning attorney to draw up his and Mom's documents . . . and everyone else's too. This well-intentioned gift, however, caused some hard feelings. It ended up that Jane's name didn't appear as an "alternate guardian" for any of the children. And to make matters worse, Elsa and Ferguson actually listed Mary and me as their first choice.

Dad swallows a mouthful of beer and gestures with his hand. "We've brought you in here tonight to make a special announcement. We're taking all of you to Disney World . . . Albert too."

If the room wasn't perfectly quiet before, it certainly is now. Elsa and Jane look horrified.

"You're kidding, right?" says Jane.

"Nope," says Dad.

Jane raises a piece of fudge and holds it before her mouth. "You can count me out," she says, and she stuffs in the cube.

Dad smiles, then turns his attention to his nearer daughter, Elsa, who forces a pleasant look onto her face.

"Perhaps a weekend trip to the Dells could be just as good," she says. "The twins aren't even three yet. I don't want to lug them all the way to Florida."

"Good news, then," says Dad. "The trip's not for two years. The boys'll be—"

"Wrong," says Jane. "I'm not pulling Angelica from school, and we've got vacations planned for the holidays."

"Make it two and a half years, then," says Dad, "—the summer of 2003. The kids'll be on break, and the twins'll be five."

Jane plunges an empty spoon into her coffee and stirs it with a maniacal fury. She's a tempest of dark lipstick and long fingernails who's about to explode. "Disney is a culture-eating monster!" she says. "I won't feed the beast."

Uncle Albert reaches across the corner of the table and takes hold of my mother's hand. His face beams as though a chorus of holiday carolers is singing at our table. "Your preparations have been exquisite, my dear," he says. "Dare I say, great thanks to the East India Companies."

"But think of Angelica," says Dad to Jane.

"I am," she fires back.

Albert's remark dissolves into the shadows of the room as if it was never spoken. But I heard what he said, and his message isn't lost on me.

I remember the name *East India Company* from my grade school history lessons. It was the name of a shipping enterprise—or perhaps several—that engaged in global trade across the seven seas. Everyone at this table, including Jane, is entirely guilty of homogenizing the world's cultures; the evidence is right in front of us. The colonizing of the planet was motivated by consumer demand for things like coffee, sugar, chocolate, spices, and Jane's precious diamonds. Leave it to Uncle Albert to bring meaning to a mundane fact. I wish all of my college professors had been like *him*.

Elsa leans forward. "I really have to say that I agree with Jane on this one. What about a trip to Sea World or Busch Gardens? Does it have to be a Disney vacation?"

Mom and Dad stare across the table at one another, and in this moment of pause, I notice the gentle sound of music seeping in from the living room. The song now playing is one I know by heart. It's called *Little Wooden Head*.

When our daughter MJ was three years old, she and I checked out a Disney sing-along video from the library. Of all the songs on the tape, she somehow chose *Little Wooden Head* as her favorite. She instructed me to play it over and over again until we could sing every word of it without the music. This was the first of many songs she mastered in this way, and it remains one of my fondest memories of her early childhood. We passed countless hours at home and in the car singing these songs together.

Dad raises his beer, as if preparing a toast. "My condolences, boys." He nods to Ferguson and Tom. "Coffee-house intellectuals, both of them." Then he turns to Mary and lifts an eyebrow. "So how do you suppose baby brother weighs in? No doubt stranded on the coffee-house fence."

I can feel the eyes upon me as I study the crumbs on my plate. I have no idea what to say.

Mary and I spent three days of our honeymoon in Disney World in 1991. The stop had been my suggestion. I had hoped that Mary and I would experience some of the famed Disney Magic—the kind I remembered as a child—and I believed it might be possible. I believed that the Disney Magic was akin to the Holiday Spirit: a good feeling born of desire and favorable circumstances. The Holiday Spirit was a good feeling I could revive each year by watching *It's a Wonderful Life* or *A Christmas Carol*. I thought surely a honeymoon trip to Disney World would offer a similar rejuvenation: a refreshing escape to the innocence and optimism of childhood to start our marriage. But our Disney "escape" produced no moments of enchantment. The pixie dust of Disney missed us entirely. I concluded that if the Disney Magic and the Holiday Spirit were like sugar bowls to a tea set, then the

Holiday Spirit was made of sterling silver, and the Disney Magic was plated chrome. Both could sparkle in the firelight of childhood, but only the Holiday Spirit bore the richness of material to charm an adult.

I no longer believe in the Disney Magic, though I can't deny that I felt it as a child. And what of our daughter MJ and her love for *Little Wooden Head?* I think there are children in this equation who aren't being represented here.

"Don't be a fool, Bert," says Jane. "What's there to think about?"

I pry my eyes off my plate and lock them onto hers. I then scroll them sideways to meet with those of her husband.

With all the compassion I can muster, I repeat the words of my father. "My condolences, Tom."

During the laughter that follows, I rise from my chair and let my feelings flow into words. "Don't you remember, Janey?" I say. "We used to make pizzas on Sunday nights and eat them in front of *The Wonderful World of Disney*. It makes me warm just thinking about it. And don't you remember the big man himself, Uncle Walt? I always sensed there was something genuine about that guy."

I spy the sugar bowl on the table and lift out its spoon, hauling up a cargo of sweetness. "Maybe I'm a fool," I say, "but I want to go to Disney World . . . if not for myself, then for my kids. The pixie dust is real to them . . . as real as this sugar."

I drizzle the white crystals back into their bowl and return to my seat. I wonder what Mary must be thinking of me right now. A few years ago, the two of us rejected the idea of ever taking our children to Disney World. But now, without even consulting her, I've done a wholesale reversal on that position.

"Well," says Jane, "that's an interesting vote of one. How about you, Elsa? Surely you're more sensible."

Elsa refrains from comment. Instead, she makes a peculiar study of the table, eventually seizing a nutmeg cookie and feeding it to her colossal husband. She then raises his napkin and uses it to dab the corners of his mouth. "I'm just a kid at heart," she says. "Please pass the sugar, Bert."

I hand Elsa the sugar bowl and watch her heap a spoonful into her Irish coffee.

"We're all adults here," she says. "*We* control the pixie dust now. I dare you to put a little magic in your own vacation. Thanks for the idea, Bert." She then turns to Jane. "There's your interesting vote of two. I'm standing outside my comfort zone, can you see?"

Elsa sets down the bowl in front of Dad, who is shrewdly hiding any signs of his apparent victory. He tops off his teacup with beer, then hoists up a load of sugar and peers at it through crossed eyes. He lets it rain down into his drink, where it forms a froth that spills over onto his saucer. He gathers up another spoonful and holds it out to Mary. "Some, Miss?"

"I'll do it myself, thank you." And she takes her own serving before passing the bowl along to me.

"Well," I say, "how can I refuse? It was my idea, wasn't it?" I drop some sugar into my spiked eggnog and forward the pixie dust to Albert.

"Hupp," he chirps, "you're all too kind to me. But two and a half years is a long time at my age. I'll need some extra help." Albert deposits two and a half spoonfuls of sugar into his already-sweetened coffee.

Mom takes her turn, then sets the sugar bowl in front of Jane, who merely glowers at it.

"You're all making a big mistake," she says. "But what choice do you leave me? Angelica can't be the only grandchild not going. Therefore, I accept on one condition . . . that we don't tell the children about the trip until it's almost time to go. Maybe you'll come to your senses by then—"

"A surprise vacation!" says Dad. "Jane, you're a natural. What a great idea."

Jane purses her lips. "You can keep your silly sugar."

Tom reaches for the bowl and serves himself two scoops while rubbing Jane's back. "I guess we're a hard sell for a free vacation. Thanks for the gift, Mom and Dad."

Jane remains quiet, as the rest of us move on to other topics of conversation. She rejoins us at the mention of New Year's Eve.

Jane and Tom intend to celebrate the first years of the new millennium with twelve vacations at casinos, each one coinciding with a lucky date on the Christian calendar: 01/01/01, 02/02/02, 03/03/03, and so on until 12/12/12.

As she bores us with the details of each trip, I imagine a cartoon Mickey Mouse strutting across the table. He snaps his fingers and winks at me on his way past my plate. He then approaches Jane and boldly hops onto a *Balance Scale of Moral Depravity* that has magically replaced the platter of treats in front of her. But despite all his jumping and pounding on his pan of the scale, Mickey can't seem to counter the burdensome poker chips piled into the other tray . . . that is, until Jane's hand reaches out and pulls him down. The image pops like a soap bubble, as Jane carries a cookie back to her plate.

"So, Bert," she says, "how's the *Oddball* coming?"

"You mean, *Wobble-bearing*?" I correct her.

"Whatever you're calling the blasted thing. Will it be your job next Fall when Michael starts school?"

Jane's attack is a cheap shot. She knows that my latest invention is barely off the drawing board. It's a quirk of geometry that rolls like a ball when sandwiched between two surfaces, but that won't roll away when set free. I'm still searching for a use for it.

I lean back in my chair and place my hands behind my head. "Let's see, now . . . next Fall. I think I've got a well-earned vacation from child-rearing coming, don't you? Maybe I'll take the year off."

Mary erupts with a theatrical cough.

"I mean . . . I'll get a job, of course. What else would I do?"

I'm well aware of the many opinions around the table as to what my future should hold: Mary, Elsa, and Tom want me to return to college; Dad wants me to find a construction job; Jane thinks I'm worthless; and Ferguson doesn't think about me at all. Mom and Uncle Albert are the only two who seem to support me no matter what I do. The one consistency among us all, however, is that nobody thinks my inventions hold much promise.

The hall clock begins to chime the hour of eleven, and Mary raises her hand. "I've got a joke," she says.

A groan rises from around the table, and I warn everybody that she probably heard it at work.

All but Tom stand up to leave.

"How does the Man in the Moon cut his hair?" says Mary. She waits. *"—Eclipse it."*

Dad signals to Ferguson, and the two men head for the hallway. "I've got a new brand of smokes for us to try," he says.

Tom raises a finger to get Mary's attention. "Here's one. Watch this."

I remain in the kitchen doorway to witness just how painful this might be.

Tom elevates his eyebrows, causing the skin of his forehead to crease into horizontal lines. "Cartesian coordinates," he says. Then, he makes a minor adjustment to his eyebrows, realigning the wrinkles into arcs and radials. "Polar coordinates."

"Excellent," says Mary. "Here's another one."

"God, no," says Albert. And he hurries from the dining room with another load of dishes.

"What did Adam say on the day before Christmas?"

"Somebody shoot her," says Jane from the kitchen.

I lift Mary from her chair and carry her into the front hallway.

"It's Christmas, Eve," she finishes her joke over my shoulder.

In the foyer, I hold Mary under the mistletoe and prepare to keep her quiet with a kiss on the lips. But when Dad and Ferguson enter the hallway, she flees from my arms and scrambles up the stairs.

"Atta boy," says Dad. "That's showin' her who's boss."

Dad and Ferguson put on their coats and head out the front door with their cigars.

Before the door is closed, a train horn blares across the road. The 11:02 from Chicago is right on time, slowing into the Western Springs station. I hope this enchanted sound finds its way into the dreams of three sleeping children upstairs.

At bedtime tonight, I read *The Polar Express* to MJ, Michael, and Nellie. With any luck at all, the children are now boarding an imaginary train bound for the North Pole. Perhaps Santa will ask one of *them* to choose the first gift of Christmas. I hope he selects MJ this year.

◆ ◆ ◆

I return to the kitchen and help with the cleanup. Mom and I then set the table for breakfast and are the last two to retire for the night.

In the hallway outside of Jane's bedroom, I overhear her talking with Tom, "She was *where*?"

I hurry past to the end of the hall and clasp the glass doorknob to the front bedroom. I know just how to turn it so that it doesn't squeal.

A pale luminescence greets me from within the familiar space. Three tall windows let in the nighttime glow from the lights of the train tracks, and each window wears a covering of frost that's been etched by the fingers of three young children and one loving adult. The backward-printed letters all read with the same message: "I believe."

I step carefully around the sleeping bags and climb into bed beside Mary. She is reading by flashlight, and her book is a biography of Albert Einstein. I pull up next to her and rub my hands across her legs, hoping to interest her in something other than her reading.

"Did you know that Einstein's wife was a physicist too?" she says. Mary closes the book and turns off her flashlight. "He essentially abandoned her, leaving her to raise their two children by herself."

"Mmm," I say, and I wonder if Mary can see the parallels with her own life. Sometimes I feel like a single parent too, left solely responsible for the care of MJ and Michael. Mary has become an inattentive wife and mother, so much so that even now, during this Christmas holiday, she is knee deep in her self-imposed research. It's hard for me to imagine that she won't someday regret not having participated in our readings of *The Polar Express*. Surely her heart would bleed if she knew the extent to which MJ has been wishing for a small miracle from Santa Claus—that he might somehow find a way to soften Mary's insistence that MJ not wear her hair long.

Truth be told, though, I'm sort of glad Mary excuses herself from this holiday ritual. I'm not so sure she could prevent herself from questioning the children about a train that travels all the way to the North Pole and back in a single night.

And how could she possibly refrain from comment, when oily fingers press themselves against windows? Yet, even if she *could* manage to hold her tongue, her mere presence in the room would almost certainly supply the same tensions. Perhaps Mary's subconscious mind knows all of this and covertly banishes her from the event.

I stare beyond her at the shaft of light coming in through the window. I wonder when she's going to ask me about my Disney defense.

Mary extends her left hand into the stream of light and puts a shine onto the simple gold band I placed on her ring-finger nine years ago. "Was it Jane or your father this year?" she says. "I hope you told them you're my diamond in the rough."

"I used that line last year," I say. "It was Jane this time."

Mary sits quietly, then sinks down under the covers and places her mouth beside my ear. "What did you do with Angelica?" she whispers.

I explain to her that our obnoxious niece was on her fourth complaint before I had even finished setting up the mattresses: *the room's too cold; this sleeping bag's too thin; I need more space; who put you in charge?* I couldn't let her ruin the bedtime story for the others, so I pulled her aside and told her of a secret warm place in the closet beside the chimney, adding that it was only big enough for one person. She immediately grabbed her bedding and left the room without saying a word.

◆ ◆ ◆

I lie awake until Mary has fallen asleep and the house is quiet. Then, I sneak from the bedroom and tip-toe down the stairs, careful to avoid the creaky step.

I grope my way into the living room and plug in the Christmas tree, then bury myself beneath blankets on the couch. I restart the film *It's a Wonderful Life.*

The opening credits take me on a trip down Memory Lane.

When I was a boy, my father sat me down to watch the movies of John Wayne. Wayne became an instant role model to me, and I was the king of the playground when I copied his behaviors. But then, upon entering middle school, another actor won my attention—one with Wayne's cool and confidence, but one who could also be tender and self-effacing. His name was James Stewart, and his films, like *It's a Wonderful Life* and *Mr. Smith Goes to Washington,* soon became my favorites. And now, as I've advanced into my thirties, I've grown to identify ever more closely with Stewart's character, George Bailey, in *It's a Wonderful Life.*

Like me, George Bailey longs for a college education. He dreams of making a difference in the world, but how can he do it from such a no-nothing town as Bedford Falls, and without a college degree? Fortunately for George, though, he has a guardian angel to relieve him of his despair. I, on the other hand, am not so lucky.

When Michael enters kindergarten next year, I'll be faced with a new chapter of my life. My babies will have flown, leaving me with a large chunk of time to fill each day. Should I risk a second failure and return to college, where I'd be studying to begin a career at mid life? Or should I find a job that eases Mary's burdens and lets her spend more time with our children? All I know is that I can't rely on one of my inventions to pay off.

The film ends, and I gaze hopefully into the twinkling lights of the Christmas tree. Only one thing about my future seems certain: the entire family is going to Disney World in two and a half years, and Elsa has challenged us to put some magic into that trip. Magic is something I think I can do.

CHAPTER 2

The Surprise Announcement

Today is Friday, July 11, 2003, and we leave for Disney World on Sunday. Uncle Albert's health has remained good, and Jane, by some miracle, stopped grumbling about the vacation several months ago. We've continued, however, to honor her request that the children not be told of the trip until shortly before departure.

MJ, age nine, and Michael, age seven, know nothing of the plans as they travel behind me on their bicycles. We are cruising along the sidewalk of Old Sauk Road under the noontime sun, leaking with perspiration as we go. But relief is just ahead with our first water-stop.

I bear down on my pedals and climb the short rise, then park my bike and trailer along the thin terrace of grass next to the road. The view from this spot is magnificent.

The Wisconsin State Capitol building is more than five miles away from this point, yet it remains clearly visible through the summer haze. Its dome floats over Madison's downtown like a tethered balloon, beckoning us homeward. Although the kids don't know it, the dome holds even greater significance for us today; it signals the arrival of a carnival designed just for them. Tonight, Mary and I will take MJ and Michael on a special dinner outing, where we'll announce the Disney vacation. We'll be walking in the shadow of that dome.

MJ's platform sandal slips off her pedal, stalling her bike in front of Michael's. He tries to swerve around her, but his front wheel rolls off the sidewalk, causing him to tumble into the weeds.

"Hey!" he shouts. "You did that on purpose!"

"Did not," she says. MJ walks her bike the rest of the way up the hill and accepts my water bottle, guzzling from it until it's nearly empty.

"Give it here," says Michael, and he rips the bottle from her hands. He runs behind me for protection, then drinks what's left of the water before tossing the empty container into my trailer.

"Don't *I* get any?" I say. "Next time, you guys can pack your *own* waters."

Michael hops onto his bike and pushes off, attempting to go first down Roller Coaster Hill.

"No!" screams MJ, who's never been denied the pole position.

I hurry my bike and trailer in front of them and order them to negotiate. However, neither child is in the mood to compromise, so the demands they make of each other are completely unreasonable. Each of them seems determined to argue.

I lower my kickstand and take a step back for another look at the Capitol building. This time, the dome sends me a different message: it tells me of a goal I'll never reach.

When Michael entered kindergarten two years ago, I didn't return to college, and I didn't get a construction job. Nor did I find a use for my Oddball. Instead, I took a job as a substitute teacher for the Madison Public School District. And the hours, as it turned out, proved so steady that I finally persuaded Mary to reduce her workweek beginning this Fall. But now, after the letter I received this morning, everything is about to change.

I pull the letter from my pocket and read it one more time.

> Dear Bert,
>
> Please accept my heart-felt regret at the news I must share with you today. (I couldn't bear the thought of sending you the form letter.) The district-wide shortage of substitute teachers has ended. So, beginning this Fall, only candidates with proper accreditations will be hired.
>
> It is my sincere hope that this setback won't keep you out of the classroom for long. I've nominated you for a "returning adult" scholarship with the hope you might pursue a teaching degree. (It's no secret that many of our faculty list you as their first choice for a sub.)
>
> We need more teachers like you, Bert. Best of luck.
> –Rose Iverson, Superintendent of Schools

So why couldn't this letter have arrived *after* our vacation rather than *before*? The last thing I want to do is fret about my future while I'm trying to have fun. And to make matters worse, I've already arranged for a Disney surprise I can now ill afford. Though I suppose there's still time to pare it down a little. The costumed guards are sounding rather silly to me now anyway.

But there's no denying the bright side to this turn of events. If the letter had arrived tomorrow—on Saturday—then Mary would have been home to find it. At least now I can keep the news a secret from her until we get back from the trip.

"Dad, we need a coin," says Michael.

I stare at him blankly, and he gets annoyed.

"*Pleeease,*" he says. "Can we *please* have a coin?"

"Sure," I answer.

I pull a quarter from my pocket and hold it while the two of them decide who will be *heads* and who will be *tails*. "I have an idea," I say. "What if today's winner goes second down the hill next time?"

"No way," says MJ.

"No way," says Michael.

Both of them would rather risk losing twice than to concede a single victory to the enemy.

I toss the coin and watch it roll across the sidewalk before rendering its decision. MJ is the winner, and she celebrates her victory with a small dance over her bicycle. "Oh yeah . . . oh yeah . . . it's my birthday . . . it's my birthday."

Michael suppresses his resentment and yields to the authority of the coin. He takes his place behind MJ, and the three of us are once again on our way.

As we cruise down Roller Coaster Hill, I marvel at the two primitive minds stuck within the helmets in front of me. My children are ruled by their emotions, often blind to the very facts that would give them better outcomes. I see such blindness all the time among the students in the middle and high schools. It seems that the ability to miss evidence is a strong characteristic of young people. Yet, I've also discovered an interesting trick for bringing such evidence into the limelight. It seems that stories, rhymes, anecdotes, and analogies have the power to charm emotion, illuminating information and giving it ready access to the brain. In fact, a story is the very tool I plan to use tonight, as I deliver my first dose of magic to the family. I'll be reading a short story at dinnertime, with the purpose of bringing a little education and meaning to our trip. I composed it last summer with the hope that I might forget enough of it to derive some magic from it myself. Lord knows I could use some today.

♦ ♦ ♦

The kids and I reach Birch Avenue and spy Mom's car in the driveway. She is almost never home early from work, and she certainly never makes it a surprise when she is. I check my pocket for the note and make sure it's safely hidden.

MJ passes me in the grass with Michael right behind her. They are in a race for our house.

Michael accelerates past MJ, whose shoes are barely suitable for walking, let alone pedaling.

"Cheater!" she shouts, and she flips her sandals at Michael.

Her two plastic bricks tumble through the air and fall harmlessly to the ground, though I recognize that they've at last found a valid usefulness.

Michael lays down his bike on the front lawn and bolts toward the side door, but his progress is slowed by his own clumsy flip-flops.

MJ ditches her bike in the neighbor's yard and runs swiftly in her bare feet. She reaches the side door just ahead of him.

But not to be outdone, Michael grabs MJ by the head and yanks her backward, tearing off her helmet and her elastic scrunchy. MJ's hair falls instantly over her eyes.

"No fair," she yells, and she kicks at Michael through the open doorway.

MJ remains outside with me to retrieve her hair band and to place it back in service. Meanwhile, I park my bike and notice a stream of condensation running beneath the car. Mary has just gotten home.

I hold the door for MJ, and the two of us enter the kitchen, where Michael is sitting on the floor, showing Mary his grass-stained knee. Mary has already changed her clothes and is now wearing a t-shirt and capris.

"Maryjane pushed me off my bike," he says. "It's bleeding."

Mary dampens a washcloth and cleans the bloodless wound.

"I need a Band-Aid," he says.

"Well," says Mary, "I guess we can't go to the pool then."

Michael's eyes light up. "All better," he says. "See?" And he slaps his knee as he dances around the kitchen.

"A miracle," says Mary.

"Clean livin'," I say.

In the short time that Mary has been home, she has not only changed her clothes, but she has also gathered our swim gear and prepared us a lunch. She is one of those rare individuals who can take the same number of steps as the person next to her but somehow do three times the work.

"Eat up," she says. "Remember, no Snack Shack."

MJ and Michael grouse, as they poke their forks into their left-over stir-fry. They eat just enough to satisfy their parents, then declare themselves ready for the pool.

The four of us return to the driveway and load up the trailer, then wait for Mary to get her bike.

She climbs the driveway to our detached garage, which is a decrepit old stable with a swayback and a permanent lean. Its overhead door just barely hangs together as she opens it, and the entire structure is long overdue for a rebuild.

Mary lowers the door, sharing with us her look of stunning empathy for it, then she joins our lineup at the sidewalk. She places herself between the children, who can't seem to keep their tires from rubbing each other. I hope their attitudes improve once we announce the dinner plans.

At the pool, MJ and Michael refuse to share Mary in a game of catch, prompting them to ask for another coin toss.

"Talk this one out," says Mary, denying their request.

MJ then grabs a plastic ring along the gutter and tosses it into the pool for herself to fetch. Michael does the same with another he finds, and their dispute is over and forgotten.

While the kids play cooperatively, Mary and I retreat to a pair of deck chairs in the sunshine. I strategically take the farther one so that I can stare across her legs while we watch the children. She's wearing her usual swimsuit cover-up—the closest thing she has to a little black dress.

"Don't forget the scrapbook tonight," she says. She is peering at me over her sunglasses. "I've added truth to her story."

"When *haven't* you?" I say.

Her mention of the scrapbook is a yearly occurrence, and it indicates that we'll be stopping beside a statue tonight for a short visit.

◆ ◆ ◆

The pool clears for Adult Swim, and MJ and Michael hurry to our chairs for their towels.

"Can we go to the Snack Shack?" says MJ.

Mary and I exchange glances, bewildered that our child can be so tirelessly testing of her parents.

Mary inspects MJ's face. "Excellent disguise," she says, "but the *real* MJ knows the Snack Shack is off limits. You must be an impostor."

I pull MJ onto my chair and tickle her aggressively. "Confess," I say. "Who are you *really*?"

"Can we go to the Snack Shack?" says Michael.

Mary inspects him too and determines we have another impostor on our hands. I pull him down next to MJ and subject him to the same tickle-torture.

Old habits die hard, as the kids remember fondly the days when we used to visit the Snack Shack regularly. But then, about a year ago, Mary experienced a health crisis that changed our whole perspective on nutrition. We have subsequently overhauled the daily menus, and the children continue to bemoan the new diet, which eliminates gluten and minimizes the consumption of junk meat, fast carbs, dairy, and other delectables. MJ and Michael voice their grievances to whoever will listen, portraying me as an unfit parent who uses strange words. And their greatest ally, it turns out, is my sister Jane, who works as a nutritionist for a hospital. She is the expert they call upon to discredit me, and she hasn't disappointed them yet. She refers to me as *The Food Nazi* and presumes that I don't know what I'm doing. She refuses to listen to any of the evidence I furnish for her, especially when it contradicts what she already believes.

"How about dinner at a restaurant tonight?" I say.

The kids stop squirming and study my face to see if I'm serious. Dinner at a restaurant is a cherished prize. It means that *junk meat* will substitute for *clean meat* and that almost every other food restriction will be relaxed. They never refuse an offer for dinner out.

"Let's go," says MJ, no doubt trying to seal the deal.

She and Michael pick up their belongings and walk briskly to the dressing rooms.

♦ ♦ ♦

Our one-bathroom house has a broad mirror over its sink and toilet. The four of us stand in front of it wearing our polos and khakis, and we resemble the cars of a circus train: Mary is the gleaming steam engine up front; MJ is the attached coal tender packed with fireworks; I'm the boxcar carrying the tents and supplies; and Michael is the friendly caboose. I detach from the train and move through its vapor trail, sucking up the fumes of lotions and body sprays. I have an idea.

Tonight's announcement of the Disney trip comes in the form of a letter from Grandma and Grandpa, and I've just thought of a phrase to put on the outside of the envelope. The phrase will help me to initiate a discussion about *luck,* where my hope is to introduce the children to the concept of *cunning* as a superior alternative.

I print the Disney phrase, then double-check my bag for the items I'm to bring on tonight's outing: two envelopes, Mary's scrapbook, and my surprise story for the family. Now, all that's missing is the cooperation of the children; I can hear them arguing in the living room.

"I get to sit next to Mom," says Michael.

"Nuh-uh," says MJ.

The kids continue their squabble all the way to the bus stop and onto the bus. But the quarrel proves pointless when we find five open seats across the back, meaning both of them are able to sit beside Mary.

"Can we switch seats, Mom?" says MJ. And she stands up as though expecting Mary to slide over without giving the idea a second thought.

Mary doesn't budge. "You need to sit down," she says.

"But Dad's too close to me," adds MJ.

Michael grabs Mary by the arm. "But *I'm* sitting with you," he says.

I offer a friendly suggestion. "What if I sit beside Michael instead of MJ?"

"No!" says Michael, and he stands up too.

"Both of you need to sit down," says Mary.

"I've got it," I say. "Let's put Mom on my lap. Then *neither* of you will be closer to me."

The kids and Mary ignore my proposal.

"You can sit *there*," says MJ, commanding me forward to an empty seat beside another passenger.

"That's enough," says Mary. "I'm pulling the cord."

Mary reaches over to the window and grabs the yellow rope, though she doesn't pull it far enough to activate the chime.

The kids know this is serious; we've stopped the bus before and walked home. But tonight needs to be different. My story at dinner demands a certain setting—the one we've selected. I don't want our plans aborted.

The restaurant Mary and I chose for tonight's announcement is one of the first places we discovered after moving to Madison some twelve years ago. And since then, this restaurant has become home to some of our more enduring memories. It was there that we celebrated Mary's new job—the one that brought us to Madison in the first place; it was there that we fretted my sudden layoff while expecting MJ; it was there that we decided I would stay home with the babies while Mary took on the role of sole breadwinner; and it was there that Mary and I have celebrated nearly all of our wedding anniversaries since then. Thus, this restaurant in the former Fess Hotel was our first choice for tonight's outing. Yet, there was another reason to select this location over any other: it is the home of *Our Little Friend.*

Our Little Friend is a mouse who lives on the restaurant's patio and who occasionally visits with Mary and me while we dine. We've been telling the children about him for years, so I hope he makes an appearance tonight, because my story ends with his renaming.

"Wait!" I say, looking from Mary to the kids. "Think of the french fries you'll be missing."

Mary relaxes her hand. "And I was planning to buy you guys some ice cream."

The kids ease back into their seats and accept their relative proximities to me. They then turn their attention to the windows and look outside as we ride along Regent Street.

The sight of Randall Elementary School launches MJ into a tall tale of her life as a former third-grader.

Michael—the former first-grader—pays no attention to her and instead points to construction equipment, also noting our momentary glimpse of the State Capitol building on the horizon as we pass the university's football stadium. Once again, it speaks to us, this time announcing the destination of our bus ride.

The Capitol building is the centerpiece of Madison's downtown: a glistening white temple that calls to the faithful along some sixteen streets and pedestrian malls that lead to it. Its skyward dome serves as a beacon to those at great distances, glowing gently through the night and welcoming weary travelers still miles from home. I can't fully explain my affection for this building, but it is entirely real. I'm always glad when my circumstances bring me near it.

Our bus reaches the State Street Mall for its final approach to the Capitol Square. This mall is a pedestrian-friendly roadway that limits wheeled traffic to buses, service vehicles, and human-powered conveyances. The street is lined by buildings and trees, which grant cameo appearances of the Capitol dome along its axis.

On this particular evening, the last block of State Street is barricaded to keep traffic away from the Concourse, as organizers prepare for the annual *Art Fair on the Square.*

While our driver awaits his right turn onto the outer loop, Mary directs our eyes forward to the western corner of the Square. "There she is," says Mary.

Ahead of us, standing above a stone stairway, is the statue for which I've packed the scrapbook tonight. The sight of her

initiates a family ritual that is almost as old as the children.
We each cup a hand behind one ear and recite in unison, "I
can hear her talking. She has a story to tell."

♦ ♦ ♦

The patio of our chosen restaurant is an urban garden walled
by century-old buildings of brick and stucco. Vines climb
these textured surfaces, and trees put a canopy over our heads.

MJ and Michael investigate the plant bed next to our table,
but find no sign of Our Little Friend.

The drinks arrive, and the waitress leaves with our orders.
It's time for the first envelope, so I place it on the table.

"This is for *you* guys," I say. "Mom and I already know
what's inside. Now it's *your* turn to find out."

"I want it," says Michael, and he seizes the envelope.

"He can have it," says MJ, avoiding his call to battle.

"But wait a second," I say. "Before you tear into it, check
out the writing on the outside. It says, *When you wish upon a
star.* What do you suppose that means?"

Michael pauses, but when no answer is forthcoming, he
goes ahead and rips through the paper. He discovers a printed
card inside and hands it off to MJ for reading. She relays
that Grandma and Grandpa are inviting us to join them in
Disney World.

It takes a moment for the news to sink in, but when it
finally does, she and Michael begin to shriek. Seconds later,
they are bombarding Mary and me with questions about the
trip: *When are we going? How are we getting there? How long will
we stay? Will our cousins be there? Will Uncle Albert be there? Does
the hotel have a pool? Will we be eating in restaurants for every meal?*

Mary explains the details while I retrieve the second envelope and rock it on the table. MJ is first to notice it.

"This letter came in the mail *today,*" I lie. "But we couldn't
let you open it until now . . . and here's why."

I show them the return address on the outside of the envelope, which is written in unmistakable handwriting and reads *Mickey Mouse*.

The kids share the duty of opening it, and again, it is MJ who reads the note within.

> Dear Michael, MJ, Mary and Bert,
>   I can't wait for your visit. Please come find me in my Toontown home on your first morning in the Magic Kingdom.
>   —Mickey Mouse

The kids set the letter aside and return to their fantasizing about the trip. Perhaps I should have waited a little longer before delivering the second note.

I collect both letters and their envelopes, careful to preserve the *When you wish upon a star* scrap for later use, then place them back in my bag.

Our food arrives, and the table becomes quiet. There's a faint rustling in the ivy, and we discover that Our Little Friend is making his way down the garden wall.

"The mouse," whispers Michael.

We watch Our Little Friend descend into the plant bed and find the french fries that MJ and Michael have tossed in for him. Our party of four is now a party of five. It's time for my story.

CHAPTER 3

The Story of Walter

"Hey there, little mouse," I call into the planter. "I've got some news for you today. It's about your great-great grandfather."

Out of the corner of my eye I can see that MJ and Michael are watching me. I ignore them and open the stapled booklet in my hands. I then begin reading to the mouse.

> Once upon a time there was a boy named Walter. Like every other child in the world, Walter was born one day, lived his life, and then died. Just imagine his life as the pages of this book: the first page tells of the day he was born; the last page tells of the day he died; and all the pages in between tell the story of his life. . . . And see if you don't agree that Walter's story is exciting from the beginning to the end.
>
> When Walter was very young, his family moved from a city to a farm. Walter loved it on that farm: he loved the pigs and the cows, and he loved the horses and the chickens. In fact, he loved the animals so much that he wanted to draw them.
>
> But Walter had a problem. You see, Walter's parents didn't have much money, so they didn't think they could spare any of it to buy him some paper. So how could Walter draw his favorite animals without paper? Well, I'll tell you.

Walter was resourceful—a word which means *he
didn't give up when faced with a problem*. Walter's solution
was to use a stick and draw on the dusty ground . . .
or to use a pencil and draw on the family's toilet
paper . . . or to use black tar and draw on the family's
white house. (You might have guessed that Walter
and his younger sister Ruth got in a lot of trouble
for putting tar on the house.)

But Walter was also lucky. He had an Aunt Mar-
garet who learned of his love for drawing, and she
bought him some crayons and a real pad of paper.
Walter practiced his drawing for hours and hours. He
even took art classes whenever he could. His dream
was to be a cartoonist for a newspaper.

Yet some dreams are not meant to come true, and
this was certainly the case for Walter. He couldn't
find a job at a newspaper.

So, what do you think Walter did? Did he crawl
into a closet and cry himself to sleep? Of course not.
Remember, Walter was resourceful. He searched for
other work as an artist, and you'll never guess what
happened: Walter's dream actually changed. He
found a job making cartoon films for a movie theater
and never again wanted to work for a newspaper.

Walter worked hard at his new job, and he came
up with lots of ideas he wanted to try. But Walter's
boss was not an adventuresome sort of person, meaning that he didn't allow Walter to test his ideas. So
what do you suppose Walter did *then*? Did he give up
on his ideas and feel cheated? Absolutely not. Walter
left his job and began his own company, finding
business to be good for a while . . . that is, until the
autumn of 1922.

In 1922, Walter's company began to run short of
money . . . so short, in fact, that he couldn't actually keep any of his employees. And by wintertime,
Walter was so broke that he couldn't even afford a
place to live. He slept in his office and ate canned
beans.

Now, how do you suppose Walter took a bath
while living at his office? Well, once a week, Walter
walked the frozen streets of Kansas City to the train
station, where he could bathe for a dime.

"Ewe," says Mary, holding her nose.

MJ and Michael copy her behavior, though I'm not so sure
they fully appreciate that Walter wasn't bathing very often,
given their own lax standards for personal hygiene.

After his bath, Walter spent a few minutes on
the station's platform, staring along the tracks. He
longed for the company of his parents, his sister, and
his favorite brother, all of whom had boarded trains
and moved away during the prior two years. Walter
was just twenty-one years old. He was all alone and
struggling to make it. He couldn't possibly know that
he was about to make a new friend.

On a bitterly cold winter's night, as Walter worked
late at his drawing table, all was quiet until a sound
from the wastebasket caught his attention. Walter
knew that sound well. He walked to the basket and
lifted out a mouse, then carried it back to his table,
where he placed it in a cage with some others he had
found. Walter soon discovered, however, that his
new captive had an interesting personality—warmer
and more outgoing than the others'. Walter freed

this little fellow to roam his tabletop, and soon the two were pals.

Walter named this mouse Mortimer, and the two comforted each other during those long winter months. Eventually, Walter set Mortimer and the other mice free, but Walter never forgot his little friend.

During the summer of 1923, Walter boarded a train and left Kansas City, bound for California, where he reunited with his favorite brother Roy. Again, Walter entered the cartoon business.

Within a few years, Walter had created a cartoon character that promised to make him rich and famous. The character's name was *Oswald the Lucky Rabbit.* But you've probably never heard of Oswald before, and I'm about to tell you why.

Walter and his wife Lilly took a train all the way across the country—from California to New York—to collect more money for Oswald. But *Oswald the Lucky Rabbit* wasn't really so lucky after all. Walter and Lilly discovered that their New York business partner was actually a pirate dressed in fancy clothing and carrying a briefcase. He took Oswald away from them using nothing more than a pen and paper, and there was nothing Walter or Lilly could do about it.

"No," says MJ. "He couldn't steal Oswald with paper."

"Oh yes," I say. "He did."

"It happens all the time," says Mary. "Pen and paper beat guns and swords."

"Right," I say. "In the grown-up game of Rock-Paper-

Scissors, Paper is the all-time winner. Paper beats Rock *and* Scissors."

> Walter was very sad when he and Lilly left New York City. So, what do you suppose Walter did during that three-day train ride back to California? Did he cry *boo hoo* all the way home? Of course not. Remember, Walter was resourceful; he never gave up when there was a problem to solve. He was determined to create a cartoon character even better than Oswald.
>
> But what kind of critter should this new character be? What should it look like? How should it act? Walter drew many pictures, but none of them were quite right. Then, he remembered his little mouse friend back in Kansas City—the one who had helped him through that tough winter. Walter produced some more sketches, and soon he had one that he liked. He explained the new character to Lilly and told her its name: *Mortimer Mouse.*
>
> Lilly liked the drawings and the character's spunky personality, but she didn't much care for the name Mortimer. She proposed, instead, to call him Mickey. So that's what Walter did; he named his new character *Mickey Mouse.*

I lift my eyes from the page, expecting to see glows of recognition on the faces of my children. I've just given them the critical clue for deciphering the true identity of the Walter in my story. But their faces remain blank; they've made no real-world connections. I'm just grateful they're still listening.

> When Walter reached California, he went straight to work making Mickey Mouse cartoons. And

audiences loved them. Walter had at last become rich and famous.

Now, perhaps you're thinking that Walter's story is almost over . . . or that maybe the rest will be boring. Not so. Even though Walter's dream of making popular cartoons came true, he never stopped dreaming. In fact, his life's story is far from over and far from boring. The pages of his book will be exciting all the way to the end.

Walter had more ideas he wanted to try, and a few of them were going to set some new world records: he created the first *sound* cartoon; he created the first *color* cartoon; and he created the first *full-length animated feature* cartoon. But even more important, Walter's cartoons were so extravagantly beautiful that some people actually cried as they watched them.

So tell me this: was Walter done dreaming *now*? Of course not; he was *never* done. His next dream would be the biggest one yet.

Walter had visited amusement parks with his daughters and had been disappointed: he found the parks to be dirty and of little interest to parents. So, he set out to design a new kind of park that would be clean and fun for the whole family. When his park finally opened in 1955, it was a dream come true. People—even kings and queens—traveled from around the world to see it. Walter had never imagined that his pile of money could grow so enormous. What could he possibly do with it all?

"Buy more clothes," says MJ, "and a bigger house."
"Yes," I say, "but how many pairs of pants can you wear

at one time? And how big of a house do you really need? Walter had a lot more money to spend than that. He could dream much bigger."

> Well, as you know by now, Walter was never short of ideas. He planned to use his great fortune to build a second, much larger amusement park on the opposite side of the country.
>
> . . . But now, tragically . . . Have you noticed what page I'm on? It's almost the last one. And you know what that means.
>
> Walter became sick and died before he could ever build his second park. Yet, the happy ending to this story is that the people who loved Walter carried his dreams into the pages of their own books. They built that second park, opening it in 1971 and calling it Disney World. That's the place Grandma and Grandpa are taking us on this vacation.
>
> Can you guess the last name of the famous Walter in my story? You've heard it many times.

MJ and Michael are surprised by the question: they had no idea there would be a quiz. So I read on.

> Very few people called him Walter. Most people knew him as . . . Walt.

I can practically hear the levers tripping in their brains. "Walt Disney!" they say simultaneously.

> That's right. Walt Disney was the Walter who grew up to do all of these great things. And Disney

World is the park he was dreaming about when he died.

But before I can finish this *Story of Walter*, there's one more thing I have to say.

Walter was a person who was not afraid to chase his dreams. And by chasing his dreams, he made his life so interesting that we still tell of it today. I think there's an important lesson here.

Each of us is writing a book right now. How will it sound when it's finished? Will it be exciting from beginning to end, like Walter's? Will it tell of a person who overflows with fun and energy, and who works to make the world a better place? Or will it tell of a person who is angry and lazy—someone who infects the world with pain and misery? I ask this question of you now: Which story would you rather write? Which story would you rather read?

And *you*, MJ and Michael. You sit in the best positions of all. Your books are mostly unwritten at this point, waiting for you to fill the pages. You have the most time to plan what those pages will say. So plan carefully, and start writing. What are you waiting for?

I close my book amid pangs from my final remarks; my own life's story is adding up to less than I had hoped. I'll be forty years old on my next birthday, and I have yet to find my mission in life. And now, as my teaching job comes to an end, an old demon has reawakened and is daring me to enroll at the university. I can hear my clock ticking—the boring pages of my life flipping past. All I know is that Walt Disney had it right. He set his goals high, always aiming to do the extraordinary . . . the truly remarkable. He never let up. And I intend to follow his example.

—But for god's sake, can't it wait just a week? I've worked so hard to prepare for this vacation that surely I deserve a break. Maybe a distraction is what I need, and I think I know just the thing.

My *Story of Walter* was a cursory look at Walt Disney's life. I had bypassed the full biographies in favor of the watered-down children's versions while doing my research. Perhaps a closer look at this man's life could do me some good.

I close my booklet and proceed to the finale. "Our Little Friend has been without a real name for a long time. Let's give him one tonight."

I lift a french fry off my plate and level it like a sword over the plant bed. "Hear ye, hear ye," I say. "Arise, Our Little Friend. Today, I dub thee Mortimer Mouse . . . in memory of your distant relative who inspired Walt Disney all those years ago. Without *you*, there would be no Mickey Mouse."

CHAPTER 4

The Indelible Words

Long shadows blanket the ground in front of the restaurant, and the Capitol building looms across our western path like a giant ice cream cone. The dome is the vanilla scoop, and it wears a halo of sunshine from the State Street side. Birds soar in silhouette above it, making me envious that we, too, can't cross so directly. The Capitol Square, it turns out, plays host to a second of our Alfred-family's downtown rituals: the embarrassing one. I've been hoping to avoid it tonight.

Like the other entrances to the Square, King Street is blocked off to traffic this evening, and the Concourse is bustling with vendors setting up for the art fair. Workers hammer on pipes to erect tents, while others drag supplies through the streets on noisy carts. Organizers patrol the area in golf carts and draw chalk lines on the pavement to mark off stalls. A restaurant's mobile grill has been fired up and is serving the pre-fair clientele.

When we reach the corner with the Square, I'm relieved to see that a beer caddy is blocking our view along Pinckney Street. Perhaps the kids won't notice the fountains.

I should know better, though; the kids instinctively seek them out.

MJ and Michael steer us around the caddy until their eyes have locked onto their targets. There's now no stopping the phrase that will spill from their lips—the phrase that will make every woman in earshot look my way. I can only hope that the noise level of the street is enough to drown out their voices.

MJ and Michael point at the fountains and turn to me. "Hey, look!" they shout. "Boobs, Daddy!"

Mary raises an eyebrow—as is customary—and I play the whole situation cool.

The two matching fountains ahead of us on the sidewalk are half spheres made of brick. Though they don't actually look like a woman's breasts in the summertime, come winter, when each one is capped by a metal dome, they can easily cause such an association. They did in *my* case, anyway.

Two years ago, on a fall outing with the children, I muttered the word "boob" in reference to the fountains, and MJ obviously heard it. She selected out the fun-sounding B-word and spontaneously spun it into a humorous phrase, even playacting the delivery. It was impeccably cute, and I couldn't help but laugh at this first performance of "Hey, look! Boobs, Daddy!" And that was all it took, of course; my laughter put the stamp of approval right on it. Michael quickly joined in, and the two of them now repeat this performance whenever we encounter the fountains.

The introduction of the word "boob" into the children's vocabulary prompted Mary and me to evaluate carefully the limits we might set regarding the kids' use of language. Our own childhood experiences were vastly different in this regard. In Mary's case, her parents were careful to model proper English for their children at all times, prohibiting the use of any crude or profane words. My parents, quite to the contrary, spoke freely, often finding fun in naughty words. My mom still tells the joke, "What happened to the girl who backed into the airplane propeller? Dis-ASSed-her!" And my Dad, whose disrespect for architects and engineers is monumental, is always quick to refer to them as "draw-rers" or to reclassify their college degrees as "B.S. for *bull shit,* M.S. for *more shit,* and Ph.D. for *piled higher & deeper.*" But despite these differences in our upbringings, Mary and I both favored my family's relaxed style: language should be fun, and it should be tailored to one's audience. Mary relishes her role in my family as the *more shit* engineer willing to get her hands dirty re-shingling Dad's roof, and we never refer to my parents' fireplace, Ketchell Oven, by its nickname Catchya Lovin' in the company of Mary's parents. So the boundaries we settled on for MJ and Michael were similar to those of my own childhood. We decided to do as little policing as possible, instead concentrating on good coaching about *when* and *when not* to use certain words. The kids know that even *my* parents don't want to hear the word "boob" uttered by a child. We instruct them that "bosom" is an acceptable substitute, but that avoidance of the reference is altogether their best alternative.

The kids race to the first fountain and place their hands against the bricks, letting the cool water run between their fingers.

"Nannah's boob," says MJ, referring to Mary's mom. The kids slap the bricks, laughing at their own mischief.

I scratch my head and lean with my other hand against the fountain. "Nannah's *what?*" I say.

"Eewe," says Michael, "your touching it!"

"Nya!" I yank my hand away, and the two kids laugh again.

Mary stands off to the side with her arms crossed and her foot tapping impatiently. She wears a look of phony disgust.

"You'll see," I say. "Someday, I'm going to make Boobs Daddy mean something. Then you'll—"

Mary's foot stops tapping, and her eyes flash with alarm.

I've stumbled onto a secret, so I gamble that it's a surprise for me.

"Yeah," I say, "I've seen what you're hiding."

"Desk or dresser," she snaps.

She's trying to trick me. "Closet," I answer.

Mary's whole body relaxes; I've obviously answered incorrectly. She moves beside me and places both of her hands against the fountain, keeping her eyes fixed on mine. This is not the Mary I know. She's never touched the fountain before.

The Mary I fell in love with eighteen years ago had the disposition of a lion tamer: cool and calculating. She governed her pride of men with a whip and a chair, and her only real friend during graduate school was her dear Uncle Albert . . . until I came along, that is. I was the clown, with my silly bass drum and cymbals, who scattered Mary's lions. My arrival partly disarmed her, causing her to exchange her whip for a feather. But Mary held fast to the chair and still carries it today—some Victorian holdover that stifles her freedom of physical expression. Mary is not comfortable being affectionate or in any way sexual in public: she won't hop on my lap in a bus or wear a fancy dress on an outing . . . and she's not inclined to touch a fountain that's been compared to her mother's breast. Her voice is free to speak as it pleases, but her body is not.

So how am I to interpret her hands on this fountain? She seems to be changing right before my very eyes, and I can't help but think that her story at the statue is somehow responsible. It seems to be coaxing the chair from her hand.

Mary lifts her fingers and flicks some water into my face. "*Desk* was the correct answer, Bert. Now you're going to pay. The truth I've added to her story will just have to wait until Disney."

◆ ◆ ◆

We cross the street onto the Capitol Square, where MJ and Michael run ahead of us onto the terrace that surrounds the base of the Capitol building.

Mary and I stroll behind them, enjoying the carnival atmosphere and picture-perfect scenery.

"Your *Story of Walter* was excellent," says Mary. "The kids were listening the whole time. . . . I've made a decision; I'm giving up my search. You'll have me back by liftoff on Sunday."

I've been waiting a long time to hear these words: that Mary will stop adding to her story at the statue. But now that they've arrived, I'm not so sure I like the way they sound. Mary is closing a chapter of her own life—a chapter that has fueled her passions for seven years and perhaps worked a subtle magic to change her. Ironically enough, she is declaring this end in almost exactly the spot where it all began: on the western sidewalk of the Capitol building.

When MJ was two years old, Mary and I were at a farmers' market on the Capitol Square. Mary was instructing MJ to return to the stroller, but our defiant little girl was not in the mood to cooperate. She escaped to a nearby stairway and held tight to a stone pedestal rising from it. The aggravated Mary strode toward her, intent on plucking her away, but she didn't. Instead, Mary sank to the steps and tenderly explored the raised letters of the pedestal's plaque.

FORWARD

WISCONSIN•WOMENS•MEMORIAL

OF•THE

COLUMBIAN•EXPOSITION

1893

The statue recalled in Mary the memory of an elderly aunt from her childhood—a favorite aunt who had forged a special bond between them. When Mary was seven years old, the aunt shared with her a scrapbook and told her its wondrous story—a story that ended by naming the greatest educator of all time. This aunt, known to the family as

Poppi, passed away shortly thereafter, and the scrapbook was packed away in an attic.

This statue in Madison reawakened Mary to these shadows of her past. She returned home for the scrapbook and has been reconstructing the lost tale ever since, hoping to somehow uncover the forgotten name. Mary's first five years of study focused on the Columbian Exposition and the model town of Pullman. But then, about two years ago, her efforts broadened to encompass the history of amusement parks and model cities. Mary has continued to pile up the details, turning Poppi's story into an untenable mess. And meanwhile, our garage and screened-in porch take on more water, waiting for her to help with their redesigning and rebuilding. "Just one more year," Mary pleads at each birthday.

And now, she is finally making good on that promise, though the news is bittersweet. Mary's scientific mind has been softening, and it became apparent last Christmas when she actually waxed poetic to me, saying, "The details I'm charting—like stars—will one day reveal a beautiful constellation."

I don't want Mary to surrender her search if it means forfeiting the changes I've noticed. I guess I don't really want her to end the project after all.

"Take whatever time you need," I say. "I'll bet the porch and garage can last another ten years."

Mary doesn't answer.

We catch up to the children along the western sidewalk, where they are sitting on a low wall and tossing leftover french fries down to some sparrows. Mary and I sit on a bench nearby.

"I'm afraid more time won't help," she says, and there's surrender in her voice. "I've done all I can do. . . . It's up to *you*, now."

I don't like the sound of *that*. "*What's* up to me?" I say.

"Poppi's story. Just look what you did for Walter's. If *I* had written his story, you wouldn't have recognized it; I would have gummed it all up with the facts. . . . And a *point*? *What* point? It wouldn't have had one. Don't you see, Bert? If anyone can make Boobs Daddy mean something, it's you. If anyone can unlock the secret to Poppi's story, it's you."

"Wow," I say, "you'll go a long way to give a guy a compliment. But I'm undeserving. I knew full well the point of Walter's story before I ever began writing. *Your* work's been just the opposite: a story in search of a point. I'm not even sure that's possible."

"Be that as it may, Bert, Poppi needs you. You're her only hope."

I sit quietly, unsure how to respond. Does Mary really think I can add anything meaningful to her seven years of research? Or is her true motive far sadder? Maybe she simply can't bear the thought of abandoning her story so completely, so she's heaping the bloated corpse onto me just to keep it close by. All I know is that the situation is also rather comical. If Mary only knew of the letter from the school district today, this conversation would seem like a clever ploy to get me back into college; I'd do just about anything to avoid ownership of Poppi's story.

CHAPTER 5

The Story of Poppi

Poppi was born in 1876 in London, England. Her given name was Mary, and she had a brother eight years her senior. Poppi's father was a kind and gentle man who made his fortune manufacturing umbrellas and carpetbags. Poppi's mother was a self-assured woman who worked tirelessly for the causes of racial equality and women's suffrage.

Poppi grew up in the care of a nanny but spent every hour she could in the company of her father. She tagged along with him to lectures at London's Royal Academy, and she became his nighttime helper in the family's crow's-nest observatory on the rooftop.

In 1893, when Poppi was seventeen, she and her parents boarded a steamship bound for America. They were headed for Chicago to attend the World's Columbian Exposition and to tour the nearby model town of Pullman. Poppi's father wanted to build such a model town in England to relieve the miseries of his workers then living in London's slums. He had already visited the English model towns of Port Sunlight, Copley, Akroydon, and Saltaire for ideas, and he had even crossed the channel to study Guise, France and Essen, Germany. He envied his friend, George Cadbury, who was already planning to build an ideal community of picturesque villas, cottages, and gardens around his chocolate enterprise. Poppi's father staunchly rejected the theories of Marx and

Engels, which called for the violent revolution of the working classes as the essential next step in society's evolution.
Instead, Poppi's father believed it was possible for change
to happen peacefully, as explained by the early industrialist,
Robert Owen, who founded the model town of New Lanark,
Scotland in 1816. Poppi's father was a collector of Owen's
writings and shared them with Poppi during their voyage
to America.

But Poppi's own interest in the vacation was far from high-
minded. A friend of hers had returned from the Fair and
told her that the Midway Plaisance was much better than
advertised.

Though it was originally billed as an educational area to
showcase world cultures, the Midway was actually a place of
exotic sights, sounds, and smells that had to be experienced
to be believed.

Poppi was determined to explore the Midway during her
visit, but she also knew that her parents wouldn't be willing
to spend much time there. So Poppi studied her friend's map
and devised a plan for separating herself from them. She
ultimately deceived her mother at the Palace of Fine Arts
and was nearly discovered shortly thereafter while en route
to the Midway. But she ducked into the Wisconsin building
before being detected, which is where she met the statue now
on display in Madison—Ms. Forward.

Poppi stowed her hat and umbrella near the statue, then
unpinned her hair and let it down for a disguise. She must
have been quite a sight to behold—a strikingly attractive
young woman wearing a well-tailored street dress but with
wild flowing hair. She spent that afternoon in the Midway.

It was during Poppi's return to the Wisconsin building
that she had her first of countless episodes.

At the entrance to Hagenback's Menagerie, a small dog was performing tricks for its trainer. The rhythmic pattern of its somersaults coincided with a string of audible words that replayed through Poppi's mind: "flips, flips, flips . . . flips, flips, flips . . . all day long it's flips, flips, flips . . . I'd like to see *him* try." Poppi laughed out loud at this feat of ventriloquy, but soon realized that no other bystanders were hearing it.

Poppi hurried away, confused and completely unaware of the mental condition overtaking her. When she made it back to the Wisconsin building, it was the statue, Ms. Forward, who spoke to her next.

Poppi returned to London and received medical attention. But according to the doctors, she did not need treatments or hospitalization because the voices in her head were not commanding or threatening. In truth, Poppi's voices were actually quite friendly and encouraging, such that she grew into a woman of sparkling intelligence and unshakable confidence. She lived quite normally in the home of her parents.

Like her mother, Poppi championed the causes of equal rights for women and minorities . . . at least, for a while. Eventually, however, Poppi grew frustrated with the slow rate of progress, concluding that there must be a faster way to spur change within a society. She based this conclusion on the words of Robert Owen:

> . . . instruction to the young must be, of necessity, the only foundation upon which the superstructure of society can be raised.

Poppi disengaged from the causes of her day, leaving her mother and friends feeling betrayed. But Poppi's father understood her motives perfectly. He helped his daughter secure positions as a nanny for London's most prominent families, for it was *their* children who would one day grow into the positions of wealth and influence.

Poppi became London's most famous nanny, far surpassing even her own ambitions to merely help children. Poppi discovered she had a knack for changing the behavior of parents as well. She could enter a household and turn everything higgledy-piggledy, then leave having somehow inspired every member of the family to see the world a little differently. Poppi could strengthen an entire family in a matter of weeks, then move on to the next.

For twenty-three years, between 1895 and 1918, Poppi worked her magic as a nanny. And during this time, her episodes of dementia grew ever more fanciful: she hallucinated extravagant fairy-tale adventures; she talked to a growing list of animals, furnitures, and figurines; and, most remarkable of all, she believed she could sail through the sky under her umbrella. Poppi's reputation as London's premier nanny became legendary.

But the direction of Aunt Poppi's life took a dramatic turn in 1918 with the death of her father from influenza. Poppi's grief was so debilitating that she could no longer work. She spent her days in her room sobbing and her nights in the crow's-nest observatory searching the heavens for some sign that her father was still with her.

In the spring of 1919, Poppi's mother persuaded her to accompany a scientific expedition to Brazil, with a stopover in North America to visit her brother. Poppi never returned to England.

While staying in Chicago, Poppi made two disastrous discoveries. She revisited the town of Pullman, where she had stayed with her parents in 1893, and found that it was no longer a countryside paradise. Rather, it had become engulfed by the city of Chicago and was now a poor, run-down, inner-city neighborhood with overcrowded tenements, vacant homes, and trash-littered streets. How could such a beautiful and uplifting town decay to such a degree in such a short time?

Poppi then ventured to the site of the World's Fair, where an even greater trauma awaited her. Every major building of the White City was gone except for the Palace of Fine Arts—the one building that had served as her accomplice in the deception of her parents all those years ago. Poppi was devastated by the symbolism. Why was *this* building chosen to remain as the only monument to the Fair?

For the first time in Poppi's life, the voices in her head became punishing. Poppi fell to the ground, weeping, until another voice—one she had missed for so long—came to her rescue. The voice that rang sweetly into her ears was that of her deceased father, delivering words of comfort and protection to her.

Poppi was hospitalized in Chicago for several months, then released into the care of her brother. For the rest of her life, she held odd jobs and moved in and out of institutions.

Then, in 1963, when Poppi was 87 years old, she learned of her niece's new baby granddaughter, named Mary. Poppi was excited to meet this new namesake, and upon their first encounter, Poppi was so smitten that she retook her psychiatric exams and won another release from the county home. Poppi moved in with her niece and made regular visits to see Mary.

On Mary's seventh birthday, Poppi gave her the 1893 scrapbook and told her the story that went with it. She ended that story by naming the greatest educator of all time.

Within days of the gift, however, Poppi's health began to fail; a blood vessel broke in her head, damaging part of her brain. But oddly enough, even Poppi's decline was somewhat high-spirited. The loss to her brain affected only her spoken words, so she remained fully capable of singing songs and reciting poetry. Poppi and Mary spent those final days on a roller coaster of emotions, singing and chanting Poppi's favorite verses at the piano. The only time in my life I've ever heard Mary crying was recently when she was listening to an old recording of the song *After the Ball*.

The Ms. Forward statue in Madison inspired Mary to reconnect with her Aunt Poppi and to contemplate that this dear relative may have known something important—some shred of wisdom sorely needed in a troubled world. Mary made it her mission to reconstruct the story and to search for the missing name.

But Mary's progress has been flagging for years. Poppi's story is an aimless ramble that tallies to nothing, which is why the version we share with the children is so radically truncated. The full story is a *Who's Who* of historic figures, naming scientists like Thomas Edison, Albert Einstein, Benjamin Franklin, and Eadweard Muybridge . . . and entertainers like Buffalo Bill Cody, Annie Oakley, and Eugen Sandow . . . and reformers like Thomas Macaulay, Frederick Douglass, and Ida Wells. The project has been languishing, and I sincerely hope that Mary doesn't press me to take it on.

CHAPTER 6

The Talking Statue

Michael finds a garbage can and discards his empty dinner container. He and MJ then walk along the top of the seat-wall toward the street corner, eventually noticing the statue perched on the last stairway. They run to stand in front of her.

"Please Mom, please," says MJ. "Tell us her story."

We catch up, and Mary surveys the area, taking stock of the many vendors and pedestrians around us.

Mary crosses her arms. "You want *what?* I have no intention of making a spectacle of myself."

This is all part of our act; it's *my* job to get her motivated.

"All right then," I say, and I take a step toward the statue, rubbing my hands together. "I'll do it myself."

"Do *what?*" says Mary.

"Talk to the statue."

I gaze up into Ms. Forward's face and nervously peer over my shoulder at Mary and the children. I take the official storyteller's seat beside the pedestal, then close my eyes and wait for the friendly voice of the statue to emerge. My eyes remain closed for a long time.

"Bert, what utter nonsense!" says Mary. "Why do you always complicate things that are really quite simple?"

Mary takes a giant step toward the pedestal, which is my signal to return to the children. The kids and I know that Mary is the only one who can channel the statue.

Mary seats herself on the steps and closes her eyes. The kids and I take our places at her feet.

When Mary's eyes reopen, they are somehow kinder and more patient than her own. Her voice is sweeter too, and her usual economy of words gives way to great flourish.

"Well, hello my favorite family," she says. "I'm so glad you've come to see me. And might I say, you all look scrumptious tonight. Could it be that you've come to hear the story of your delightful Aunt Poppi? —You know how I love to tell it. I'll get started right away.

"As you probably remember, I met your Aunt Poppi when I was a new statue, in 1893. I was originally made of clay and positioned far from this spot—at the World's Columbian Exposition in Chicago . . . in the Wisconsin building, to be exact—and that's where I met your splendid Poppi.

"Ahh, the Columbian Exposition: it was a grand affair. It was, in fact, a *World's* Fair. People from all over the world came to see it, and Poppi and her parents were three of those people. They traveled for ten days—seven by steamship and three by train—all the way from London, England.

"Four years earlier, in 1889, the family had attended the World's Fair in Paris. It was there that they had marveled at the tallest iron structure on earth, built by Gustave Eiffel."

"The Eiffel Tower!" the kids and I reply on cue.

"But the Chicago World's Fair," Mary continues, "offered a heavenly marvel of its own—a giant wheel built by George Ferris."

"The Ferris Wheel!" we reply.

MJ and Michael turn to me, anticipating that I've properly prepared for this visit with Ms. Forward. I don't disappoint them. I reach into my bag and pull out the tattered box containing Aunt Poppi's 1893 scrapbook. I untie the shoelace and lift off the fragile lid, then lay the book open across my lap.

"Remember the Woman's building?" says Mary with her regular voice. She is pointing to the photograph on the current page. This is her segue into the *Marian Shaw Resuscitation*—a spoken passage during which Mary attempts to recite two unbelievably long sentences in a single breath.

"I learned something new about this building since our last visit," she says. She is deviating from the script. "There were three marble sculptures at the main entry . . . but there should have been four!"

Mary rolls her eyes in a wide circle, then fixes her gaze upon MJ. "We hold these truths to be self-evident," she says, "that all men *AND WOMEN* are created equal."

Mary has made another addition to her story, and I happen to know the basis for this one.

Back in February, Mary and I watched a documentary about Elizabeth Cady Stanton and Susan B. Anthony—two of the matriarchs of the Women's Movement. It was Stanton who first voiced this revision to the Declaration of Independence.

Mary turns her face skyward. "Oh where was Sojourner Truth?" she croons.

Mary then gives me a quick grin and points into the book. "Next page, please."

I guess that's all I'm going to hear about the *truth* Mary added to her story, at least for now. The name Sojourner Truth means nothing to me.

We continue turning pages until a certain snapshot launches the next routine.

Mary puts her finger beside the picture of a small building in the Midway, where Aunt Poppi met the famous photographer, Eadweard Muybridge. "Hey," she says, "that's Zoopraxographical Hall."

"Zoopraxographical Hall?" I parrot her with practiced speed.

"That's right," she says.

"Are you sure it wasn't Stroboscope Hall?" I say.

"Quite certain."

"How about Zoetrope?"

Mary shakes her head.

I count down on my fingers. "Mutoscope? . . . Phasmatrope? . . . Kinematoscope? . . . Phenakistoscope?"

"Certainly not!" says Mary. "Even the kinetoscope wasn't at the Fair."

Michael stands up and moves to the bottom of the steps, impatient to begin the next performance.

"Can I be the belly dancer?" he says.

MJ is more than happy to take the less animated role of the camel today. She has become more self-conscious over the past year. She positions herself at the top of the stairs and hides behind the pedestal.

I put the scrapbook away and join in Mary's humming of the tune *Dance of the Snake Charmer.*

Michael gyrates his hips and waves his hands over his head. His eyes remain focused on MJ, whose job it is to sneak up behind us.

Right on schedule, MJ produces the sound of a giant loogie being disgorged over our shoulders.

I leap to my feet and face our offender, only to discover it is a humpbacked camel.

MJ returns to her seat, and I join Michael at the base of the steps. It's time for the crazy camel rides, and I'm the first one to go.

Michael prepares an invisible pillow for my camel to kneel upon, while I suppress my nervous jitters. I pet the camel's neck and throw my leg over his back, then ready myself for his climb from knees to feet.

First, one of his legs straightens . . . then another . . . then another . . . and one more. With each lurching movement, I chirp in distress and tip from side to side. Michael then leads me in a circle around the flower bed, returning me to the cushion for a reversal of the boarding procedure.

Michael's turn is next. He climbs quickly onto the back of the camel and instantly commences with a vaudeville extravaganza, which includes galloping across the plaza, veering into the grass, striking a tree, rolling on the ground, and then stumbling back to the stairway to our applause.

Mary then closes her eyes and ushers the return of the statue's voice. "While Poppi stood before me, pinning up her lovely hair, I told her how radiantly beautiful she was with it down . . . and do you know what? SHE HEARD ME! I couldn't believe it; no one had ever heard me speaking to them before.

"Poppi and I talked for several minutes that afternoon, and then again in the days that followed. She shared with me her discoveries of molasses-covered popcorn, hamburgers, and Wrigley's Juicy Fruit gum. And she couldn't wait to return home and experiment with the new piano sound she had heard—the one that put rhythm on its head, with *ragged time*.

"Ragtime!" the kids and I shout.

"But most of all," Mary continues, "your Aunt Poppi wished I could meet her boys from the Midway, Edward and George. She claimed to have practically kissed them at the Blarney Castle when she touched her lips to the kissing-stone just after *they* did. Poppi's eyes filled with tears when she told me of their final goodbyes.

"And her farewell to me was equally sweet. Poppi thanked

me for listening and told me I was beautiful, too." Mary sighs. "From that day forward, I held out hope that she and I would one day meet again. But that day never came. I waited a full century for another person to come along who could at last hear me speaking. And that person was *you*, my darling Mary. You are the one who hears me now."

Mary closes her eyes slowly, then reawakens to her normal self. She stands up and stares into the face of the statue. "Thank you for those kind words, Ms. Forward. I'm quite fond of you, too. And thank you for tonight's *Story of Poppi*."

The four of us line up in front of the statue and complete tonight's visit with her. "Goodbye, Beautiful," we say in unison.

These final words of farewell were chosen by Mary long ago in this ritual, and they stand in stark contrast to her alleged beliefs. Near the start of our relationship, I once called Mary *beautiful*, and boy did I take a beating for it. *"Looks shouldn't matter,"* she said. *"Beauty is only skin deep. Your attraction to me better be more than physical."* I apologized unrelentingly and have never again called her beautiful, but I can't say that I've ever come to agree with her position on the matter. Beauty is definitely real, and it extends far beyond the skin. The beauty I saw in Mary—and still see in her today—involved the whole package, not just her looks. In fact, her defiance of gender inequalities and the spirit of that earlier revolt are a big part of what I love about her. Yet, here we stand today in front of this bronze effigy of a woman, labeling her as beautiful. It's a disconnect in Mary's behavior that I've never been able to reconcile.

Michael takes Mary by the hand. "Does the statue really talk?" he says.

It's the same question every year.

CHAPTER 7

The Madison Midway

The four of us weave between tents and equipment as we cross the Concourse. It then dawns on me that this little slice of Madison is similar to Poppi's World's Fair.

According to Mary's research, the rebuilding of the Wisconsin State Capitol building, which began in 1906, was practically a reunion of the artists and architects who designed the Columbian Exposition. *"This is the White City in miniature,"* Mary had said, pointing to the Capitol Square. But now I see that the parallels extend even further: Ms. Forward stands in the place of the Woman's building, and State Street is clearly the Midway Plaisance at her feet.

State Street is a commercial playground that caters to the full cross-section of Madison's residents—from the loftiest of professors to the lowliest of the disenfranchised. Each group exists here peacefully, side by side, and their blend is such that the place enjoys a wild vitality . . . an exuberance . . . where people seem less hesitant to converse with those of a different social stratum. And it's my understanding that the Midway of 1893 was likewise a place of uncommon diversity.

The Fair's Midway was divided into themed regions, just like our State Street is divided into blocks. The first on today's route is the Museum Block.

Mary points down at the street as we walk. "I bet you

didn't know that the sanitary sewers under our feet are a century old. The 100 Block gets reconstructed next summer."

Mary is an engineer with the City of Madison, and she often shares with us the details of her work.

"You're going to like the new lampposts," she says. "The banners will be color coded for each block: purple for the 100 Block, green for the 200, olive for the 300, "—She lists them all.

At the first intersection, we cross onto the Theater Block, where dueling movie palaces, dating back to the Roaring Twenties, face each other across the street. The one to our left, the Capitol Theater, is currently fenced off, as a 200 million dollar performing arts center is built around it. The one to our right, the Orpheum Theater, is newly restored and showing films that are listed on its marquee. I notice that a certain new release—*Pirates of the Caribbean: The Curse of the Black Pearl*—is not showing there tonight.

My sister Jane and her husband Tom fashion themselves as amateur movie critics. They take it upon themselves to screen anticipated blockbusters on opening night and then send out a review by e-mail the next day. *Pirates of the Caribbean* premiered on Wednesday, so their review reached my computer yesterday. It wasn't what I expected.

The *Pirates* movie is a Disney production, inspired by the amusement park attraction of the same name. Jane's been bashing the film ever since its early hype of last year, making her opinions from yesterday that much more surprising. She called the film "groundbreaking" and raved of the brilliant acting. It seems that the Disney monster won a temporary reprieve for creating such a great film.

The next intersection we come to has two cross streets, which meet at odd angles. Wedge-shaped buildings rise from the corners, and one of them is spilling with music. The song now playing is *Fly Me to the Moon* by Frank Sinatra.

We cross the street, where I stop us under a sign that carries a strange message. "*World Famous Triangle Market*," I read. "*Tours Daily . . . Free Admission.* Hmm. Do you suppose they sell gum in there? Let's take a look."

"But stay close," says Mary. "We don't want you getting lost."

The Triangle Market is about the size of a rich-person's walk-in closet. MJ is the first one to get the joke, and she explains it to Michael. The kids then select their favorite flavors of bubble gum and take the necessary five steps across the store to reach the cash register.

Returning outside to the 300 Block, Mary leads us to the curb and points down. "State Street has storm sewers in every block except *this* one. Any guesses why?"

I study the street for some unique characteristic that might single out this block, but my attention is caught by a pair of bloodshot eyes that are fixated on my beautiful Mary.

"Woe," comes a tired voice from the mouth below those eyes. The man staggers to his feet and approaches us. He is grungy and thin, with the emaciated look of a skeleton draped in tattered clothing. "You wanna know what's under the street?" he says. "*I'll* tell you what's under the street. Tunnels, man. I've seen 'em."

The man extends a grimy finger toward the tiny restaurant beside us, named Himal Chuli. "I used to own that," he says, "—Good News Bakery." He lowers the aim of his finger to the wooden panel beneath the window. "See that blue? I painted it every day. The police stopped me. They took my brush."

"Oh, I'm sorry," says Mary. "Did you say there were tunnels under the street?"

"Woe!" he says again. "Bootleggers! Shatki's basement."

Shatki is the name of the bookstore next to Himal Chuli, and the two storefronts share a building.

Our Good News Bakery Man turns slowly and looks out across the street toward the intersection of State and Gorham. "Over there, man. *Five floors down!* . . . I was *in* there."

"Can you show us?" says Mary. "Take us to the spot where it's five floors deep."

The man leads us across the street. "Al Capone, man," he says. "The Bush was all Italians . . . *Sicilians!* . . . the bootleggers. They bulldozed it to clean 'em out. Ha! . . . That was the sixties for ya."

We follow him around the corner and stop beside the busy patio of Quinton's Bar & Deli.

"Right here, man," he says, "five . . . floors . . . down."

"Did you ever come out of the tunnels here?" says Mary.

"Woe," he says. "Barrels of beer—"

"You saw barrels?" I say.

"No, man. People lived down there. You never saw 'em."

"Was your store the only way in?" says Mary.

"It was Shatki's," he says, "—a crack in the wall."

I can see that Mary is now content. How can this man possibly be sure of the precise location of a subterranean world if he never actually emerged from it to see where he was? His story is almost certainly untrue.

From across the street, a friendly voice hails in our direction, and the Good News Bakery Man shouts a reply: "Mother Fucker! What's up?" He moves away from us as though we never existed.

His sudden outburst of profanity draws attention from the people around us. MJ and Michael study our faces to see how their parents will react.

"*Boobs Daddy* doesn't look so bad now, eh?" I say.

Mary shakes her head.

We return to the corner, and Mary asks the children if they believed the man's story. The very nature of her question telegraphs the answer she wants, so I decide to muddy the waters.

"I think his story is true," I say. "He certainly knew a lot of the details." I rub my chin, trying to look thoughtful. "And Mary, didn't you say the 300 Block never had storm sewers? . . . and that the rest of the piping is a century old? This pavement hasn't been touched since the bootleggers. Those tunnels could be right under our feet."

"Well . . ." says Mary.

I close one eye and open the other one wide. "Woe," I grumble like a pirate. "This here be the block of yore . . . Bootleggers Block!"

"Cute," says Mary. "But we won't have to wait long to know the truth. This block gets reconstructed in 2006. If there are any tunnels, we'll find them."

We cross over to the 400 Block and travel a short distance before stopping in front of a handsome house built of cream brick and sandstone. This structure is an anomaly of the State Street storefronts, and we took note of it last year for the first time. We were curious to know what was sold there, but the glare off the picture window prevented us from seeing in. Our only clue was the sign above the door, which read *Sacred Feather* and featured a drawing of a swashbuckler's hat stuck with a plume. Michael immediately guessed that the store sold hats, and he was proven correct.

"What do they sell there?" I point to the house.

"Hats," says Michael, and he smiles proudly.

Three doors down, we come to another test of our wits, where a vacant storefront is being remodeled, and the sign in the window says, *"Coming Soon, Cold Stone Creamery."* We've never heard of this business before, but it's not difficult to deduce its merchandise from the graphic on the sign, which shows an impressionistic rendering of an ice cream cone.

"Mmm," says Mary. "Ice cream. I believe I owe you guys some."

She delivers us across the street to a building with a completely unambiguous sign: the words *Ice Cream* are printed right on it, and the logo shows a cow licking an ice cream cone. We enter the *Chocolate Shoppe Ice Cream Parlor* and return to State Street with our prizes.

"Ice cream was Walt Disney's favorite treat," I say, boasting of what little I can remember from last year's research. "And guess what. The day we fly to Disney World is the day Walt and Lilly were married—July thirteenth."

"How do you remember such things?" says Mary. "Do you recall the year?"

I think for a moment, but I have no idea. "I'm guessing the 1920s," I say. "But ask me tomorrow; I'm getting a Disney biography."

I attempt to redeem myself with one last fact. "Did you know that Lilly giggled throughout their entire wedding ceremony?"

The four us share smiles, all of us knowing the story of my and Mary's wedding, where laughter played a significant role.

The 500 Block of State Street is twice as long as the others—the Double Block. Its transition to the 600 Block coincides with *Old Vienna* of the Fair's Midway. And the Alpine-looking restaurant to our left has a name that is sure to fool the children.

"Okay, Hansel. Okay, Gretel," I say. "You two brats better behave or you'll be the dinner at that restaurant over there. See the sign? *State Street Brats*."

"Move along," says Mary.

The children know we're just kidding, but they pick up their pace anyway.

We cross Lake Street and step onto the plaza that carries State Street for its final two blocks to the base of Bascom Hill. This simple loss of the curbline changes the entire feel of the street. In fact, coupled with the forsaken architecture of the buildings at its entrance, this 700 Block of State resembles a gully of sheer-wall concrete that's been gouged by window sockets. Even the gully floor provides nothing to soothe the senses—an unimaginative paving scheme made worse by poor repair. My Madison Midway ends here.

But why is it that I'm comparing Madison to the Columbian Exposition anyway? I didn't accept Poppi's story, so why do I seem to be working on it? There's no point in searching for meaning where there's none to be found.

CHAPTER 8

The "Wish Upon a Fountain"

The university's Memorial Library is one of the concrete fortresses at the entrance to the 700 Block. We enter it for a pit stop.

While I'm waiting in the hallway near the men's bathroom, I notice a bulletin taped to the wall beside the drinking fountain. It's an announcement for a lecture series on the topic of human origins.

I'm about to take a closer look at it when, from around a corner, a little old woman, with fly-away hair and gypsy-like clothing, enters the hallway and shuffles in my direction. She's either a retired professor or a homeless person—it's hard to tell which.

She steps toward the drinking fountain, and as she does so, her eyes meet with mine, sending sparks to my toes. "Excuse me," she says. Her voice is clear and bright.

She bends to the fountain, and a well-worn leather shoulderbag falls to her side. Its monogram reads *L.N. Smith*.

I step away to give her more room.

When she finishes her drink, she pauses at the posted bulletin, though she reads it for only a moment. "Nonsense," she says, and she proceeds to the north doors.

What did she find to be nonsense, I wonder?

I return to the bulletin, expecting it to endorse some pseudoscience, like *intelligent design* or *creationism*. But it doesn't. In fact, this announcement is entirely dry and scholarly, embracing the hard science of Darwinian evolution. Where's the nonsense in *that*? What was it that this woman was reacting to?

A sick feeling creeps over me. What if college is not as true an education as people think it is? What if the professors don't really know what they're talking about? I would hate to come away from the university dumber than when I started; an empty chalkboard is far better, in my opinion, than a hopelessly scribbled one. How can I be sure that what I'm learning is not nonsense?

Our family reconvenes in the hallway and returns outside into the warm evening. We've walked onto the Library Mall, which is an attractive plaza tucked between the buildings of the 700 and 800 blocks of State Street. It is centered by a circular fountain.

MJ and Michael race to the fountain's parapet wall and are excited to see so many coins littering the bottom.

"Can we get them?" says MJ, and she places her foot on the wall as if ready to jump in.

"Wishful thinking," says Mary. "It's not a wading pool."

MJ brings her foot back to the ground and leans over the wall, reaching into the water for the coins. But they're farther away than they appear.

"I know," says MJ, "let's make wishes. Who's got pennies?"

"Hmm," I say. "Are you telling me you didn't bring any, just in case something like this came along?"

MJ shrugs her shoulders. She's certainly not interested in hearing my standard lecture on personal responsibility. "I thought . . . well . . . maybe . . . 'cause it's a special occasion and all . . . you might—"

"Cough up some coins?" I hurry her to the point. "Well, today's your lucky day."

Her suggestion of making a wish has given me an idea—another chance to discuss the phrase on the envelope from dinner.

I pull out the scrap of paper along with four coins. "*When you wish upon a star,*" I say. "It's the title of a song. Do you know what movie it's from?"

The children ponder the question, but it's Mary who gives them the vital clue. She hums the familiar tune, and they know the film right away: *Pinocchio.*

"So, what are the words telling us?" I say. "What does it mean to *wish upon a star?*"

"You can't," says Michael. "You'll burn up."

"No," says MJ, "you don't sit on it. That's—"

"You're both right," I say. "*Wishing on a star* is like *wishing on a fountain*. You don't actually get in."

"And it's the same for your birthday cake," says Mary.

"Right," I answer. "Think how messy *that* would be."

The kids laugh, and I note this unexpected turn in my discussion. Never before have I considered the similarities between stars, fountains, and birthday candles when it comes to making wishes. Perhaps this line of conversation will lead somewhere.

"Why stars?" I say. "Why fountains? Why birthday candles? Why do these objects get our wishes and not others?

Why don't we make wishes on cars, or noses . . . or butts?"

The word *butt* is a guaranteed laugh for our children. It is also a word that is acceptable to my parents but disliked by Mary's. Her parents prefer us to use the word *fanny* instead.

Our discussion digresses into a long list of outrageous things to wish upon, like bathtubs, toilets, and underwear. Eventually, though, I bring us back to the question at hand: why do certain objects get our wishes, and not others?

But no one offers an answer, so it makes me wonder what the little old woman in the library might say.

I return to my original presentation. "Okay then, so how does wishing on a faraway star . . . or tossing a coin in a fountain . . . or blowing out the candles on your birthday cake actually make a wish come true?"

"It can't," says MJ. "It's just superstition."

Michael nods, though he doesn't try to say the difficult word.

I then pose a follow-up question. "So, what does it mean if you make a wish and it really *does* come true? How do you explain *that*?"

"Just luck," says MJ. "—*Luck* made it come true."

But Michael's face turns grave and serious. "Maybe the wish really *did* work," he says.

I ignore their responses and offer a third possibility. "Have you ever heard of the saying, *when preparation meets opportunity*? It means that pursuing a wish with all your heart gives it a better chance of coming true. It means—"

But there's no point in my continuing; I've committed a fatal leap into the abstract. Leave it to a grown-up to make things complicated.

MJ pries open my fist and takes out the coins. She passes them around, then the four of us stand beside the wall of the fountain to fashion our wishes.

To my surprise, I'm not stuck there trying to conjure up a phony wish. In fact, there's one ready and waiting on the tip of my tongue. I don't know where it comes from, but it surfaces in an upswell of tears. I want to recapture the Disney Magic—the magic I remember as a child. How I yearn to feel this vacation like the eight year old I once was. Can I please get lost in some magic just once? That's all I want. Is it too much to ask for?

I toss in my coin, startled by this tide of emotion. My wish has appeared out of nowhere, yet I can't deny that I'm grateful for it. I love my wish; I love everything about it. To rediscover the Disney Magic as an adult would be a dream come true.

But what of my lecture to the children? How can I preach of *preparation meeting opportunity* when it comes to the fulfillment

of a wish for the Disney Magic? There's no way I can deliberately *prepare* myself for an *opportunity* to feel magic; it has to
just happen on its own. Thus, it seems that my wish presents
a blatant contradiction to the axiom I was just professing.
Perhaps the kids were wise to tune me out. Maybe *I* should be
listening to *them*—putting my trust in MJ's luck and believing,
as Michael suggested, that wishes really do work. My own
advice seems little better.

"What did you wish for?" says Mary. "I'll tell you mine if
you tell me yours."

The children and I keep quiet. We know that a wish has
a better chance of coming true when it's kept secret.

♦ ♦ ♦

The university's carillon tower rings the eight o'clock hour,
and the sun's rays are fast disappearing. We walk to the bus
stop and catch our ride home.

It's been an eventful evening for the children. They've
enjoyed junk meat, fast carbs, ice cream, and some exciting
news. And now, right on schedule, their behavior is beginning to unravel. Mary and I wrestle them home and into
their beds, where Michael falls asleep quickly and MJ stays
awake to create a packing list for the trip.

Mary retreats to our screened-in porch with her computer
and resumes working on another of our surprises for the
children—a collection of Walt Disney quotes she found on
the internet. She says she's preparing them in a special way
as a gift for me too, so I'm forbidden from peeking over her
shoulder.

I enter the kitchen and begin cleaning the day's dishes.
Foremost on my mind is my wish at the fountain.

My two internal appraisers, Logic and Reason, once
convinced me to discard the Disney Magic. I chucked its
counterfeit sugar bowl out the window and never looked back.

But little did I know, the betrayed child within me saw the sinister deed. He crept out under the cover of nightfall and retrieved it, carrying it back to his room, where he locked it in a trunk for safekeeping. And now, here I stand, gazing at that trunk, knowing I've just wished for the key to open it.

But even if I should find that key during our trip, I can't imagine that the sugar bowl will ever win its return to my parlor downstairs. The Disney Magic is a lower quality of tableware than the Holiday Spirit; it is unworthy of adult display. It is doomed to remain in the tower of my childhood for all time.

CHAPTER 9

The Indelible Pictures

We awaken to a warm and sunny Saturday morning. Mary makes the breakfasts and doles out the chores, and I promise the children a movie-night if all the work gets done.

By mid-afternoon, we're in good shape: we've been to the library, we've done all the laundry, and we've packed our suitcases. The kids are now playing in a wading pool with their young neighbor Andrew, and Mary is working beside them in the garden.

This is my chance to phone Disney, though I'm now waffling on my decision to cancel the costumed guards.

Mary is fully aware of the romantic dinner I've scheduled for the two of us at the Cinderella Castle on our first day in Disney World. But what she *doesn't* know is that after our meal, she and I are to be escorted away by two castle guards to an intimate alcove overlooking the moat. There, under the nighttime glow of the castle walls, Uncle Albert is to lead us in a renewal of our wedding vows. The service will end with our coronation, as Albert places crowns on our heads and gives us the keys to the kingdom. I created the ceremony as much for Albert as for Mary.

It was Uncle Albert who introduced me to Mary back in 1985. And it was he, six years later, who made our wedding day so memorable. His contribution began tame enough—just a quiet wheezing from within the center seats. But before long, his wheezing had escalated into hissing and fizzing, and he struggled to quell the chirps and squeaks that were then erupting from his face. All eyes turned to watch the spectacle as Albert finally exploded into laughter. And his behavior proved contagious, spreading quickly throughout the hall. Tissues and handkerchiefs, thoughtfully packed for the happy sobbings of a wedding, were called upon to soak up tears of another kind. When the free-for-all finally ended, and the ceremony resumed, the occasion had a whole new atmosphere.

But Uncle Albert was terribly embarrassed by what had happened, and he regrets to this day that he didn't excuse himself as soon as he felt the episode coming on. In fact, each year at the family picnic—which jointly celebrates our wedding anniversary and Albert's birthday—he reissues the same apology to us.

Mary and I have tried to convince him for twelve years now that we are actually grateful for the disturbance he caused. But he simply doesn't believe us. And furthermore, he blames the incident for causing him to lose the toast he prepared for our reception. *"I worded it so perfectly,"* he says, *"I could never replace it."*

It took a lot of cajoling on my part, but I finally persuaded Albert to conduct our Disney ceremony. *"But what if it happens again?"* he said. *"All the better,"* I told him.

I decide to keep the plans as Albert is expecting them and to merely confirm my arrangements with my Event Manager. I ring Merryweather's phone, but I'm forwarded to her voice-mail, where I disconnect rather than leaving a message because I don't want to risk getting a call-back while Mary is at home. Maybe I'll try phoning again tomorrow.

◆ ◆ ◆

After dinner, we leave the mess in the kitchen and enter the living room for our movie-night.

Mary and the children find their usual seats on the couch, and I stand before them like a Master of Ceremonies, hiding a DVD case behind my back.

"Remember my *Story of Walter*?" I say. "It was the story of Walt Disney—the man who created Mickey Mouse."

I show them the DVD case. "In my hand is the cartoon that started it all. The year was 1928—seventy-five years ago. Uncle Albert was just five years old, and Grandma and Grandpa hadn't even been born yet. It's the first cartoon in history to have sound."

MJ and Michael scold me for ruining their movie-night. They can see from the picture on the cover that the film is in black and white.

"Remember Charlie Chaplin and Buster Keaton?" says Mary. "You liked *those* films . . . and *they* were black and white . . . and silent, too."

"Hold on," I say. "Don't worry. The film is only seven minutes long. It's called *Steamboat Willie,* and it was created in 1928 by Walt Disney. If you listen carefully, you'll even hear his voice playing the part of Mickey Mouse."

I take my seat beside Michael and start the player.

The cartoon is screechy and crude-looking, but MJ and Michael endure it without complaint.

The screen goes dark, and I retrieve the disc. "That was 1928," I say. "But Walt Disney didn't just sit around making Mickey Mouse cartoons. Nine years and a month later, in December of 1937, Walt Disney released the first ever full-length cartoon movie."

I reach into my paper bag, but I don't pull out the DVD case just yet. "People thought Walt Disney was crazy," I continue, "because even short cartoons, like *Steamboat Willie,* required thousands of hand-drawn pictures. But a feature-length film would mean *millions* of such pictures. He was taking a big gamble. If people didn't like his movie, his business would fail and he would lose all his money. Though perhaps you can guess that the film was a success. In fact, it was the most popular movie of its time. Can you tell me the name of it?"

The kids list some current Disney titles, like *Aladdin, Beauty and the Beast, The Little Mermaid,* and *Pocahontas.* Only one of their guesses even lands in the correct era: *Pinocchio.*

I withdraw the box and show them the picture on its cover. They know the cast of characters right away—Snow White and the seven dwarves—but they've never seen the film. I load it into the player and take my seat.

The movie opens with the jealous queen talking to her mirror and asking it to name the fairest maiden in the land. "Snow White" replies the mirror, and the scene moves outdoors to the walled garden of the castle, where Snow White is washing the stone steps. She empties her pail and walks to the well for more water, where she speaks to a flock of doves that accompany her.

> Want to know a secret?
> Promise not to tell?
> We are standing by a wishing well.
>
> Make a wish into the well.
> That's all you have to do.
> And if you hear it echoing,
> Your wish will soon come true.

A well! Of course. Why didn't I think of it yesterday? People make wishes to wells, too.

◆ ◆ ◆

The film is, for the most part, fine family entertainment. The four of us laugh at the slapstick of the dwarves and at the antics of the forest animals. And Mary and I get an added chuckle when the dwarf named Doc says to Snow White, "What *are* you, and *who* are you doing?"

But the movie is also frightening for Michael, who burrows his face into my arm. The first such instance owes to the huntsman, who, with crazed eyes, sneaks up behind Snow White and raises a gleaming knife to attempt her murder. Next, it is the images of Snow White fleeing into the dark woods, where menacing eyes study her from the shadows; where rock formations loom over her like skulls; where floating logs snap at her like alligators; and where angry trees claw at her with tentacle-like branches. But by far the toughest images for Michael to take owe to the wicked queen. He cringes at her gruesome transformation into the old hag, and he cowers at the pure evil of her deception of the innocent Snow White. It is not until the queen is on the run from the seven dwarves that Michael's eyes return to the screen to feast on the grim spectacle of her death. I worry that the film is going to give him nightmares.

Once the kids have gone to bed, Mary again retreats to the back porch with her laptop for one final night of work, and I remain inside to clean the kitchen.

Before long, I'm lying alone in our bed, reading the Disney biography I checked out of the library today. I'm just starting page five when Michael's face appears in the doorway.

"Dad?" he says, and he squints into the light. "I'm scared."

I beckon him over to the bed and click off my lamp. "Was it the movie?" I say.

He nods. "The queen."

I assure him that the images in his head can't hurt him.

"It's just your imagination," I say. "Try to think of something happy instead."

I walk Michael to the bathroom and wait for him outside the doorway. Meanwhile, my mind replays my words of comfort to him. They were almost an exact recording of the words my mom told me when *I* was having nightmares. And as I recall, they didn't work very well; they didn't chase away my nightmares like they were supposed to. But why not? Even then, I knew that the images in my head weren't real, so why couldn't I simply command them away? Perhaps my mom needed a better strategy.

I tuck Michael back into bed and wait for him to fade off toward sleep. I then whisper into his ear, "The next time you see something scary, look to the side . . . because that's where you'll find *me*. I'll shout, *Go away you nasty picture! Leave my Michael alone!* Then, I'll pull out my big eraser and I'll wipe that ugly picture away. There's nothing to fear; Dad is here."

I repeat my message several times, hoping it will somehow penetrate his subconscious mind and grant him relief.

I return to bed and reopen my book, though I'm unable to concentrate on my reading.

Where do dreams come from, I wonder? They seem to appear out of nowhere—just like my wish at the fountain did—rising up from some deep well of thought beyond any conscious observer. I stand at the top of this well, like Snow White, sending down my pail and pulling things up through the darkness. I've pulled up a wish to feel the Disney Magic, and now I'm relying on some hand of fate down there to put the key in my bucket that will open the trunk in my tower. It hardly seems possible.

I close the biography without moving my bookmark, then turn off the light and roll over. Mary is still away at her computer.

CHAPTER 10

The Priceless Gift

Sunday arrives, and it's another gorgeous day. We bike to church, return home, and then wait for our departure for the airport. I'm glad we're leaving on a Sunday.

Sunday is the most relaxing day of the week for me. It's the day we slow our pace and try to do more things as a family. Sunday is also the day we turn the dial of our radio to a station that plays the music of a bygone era. Sometimes we opt for classical or early rock 'n' roll, but more often our choice is *The Tux*—WTUX—for its vintage blues, jazz, swing, and old show tunes. It's the music Mary and I heard as children when in the company of our parents and older relatives.

Benny Goodman is the artist on tap at the moment. His clarinet rises on an updraft of saxophones.

I call Mary and the children onto the screened-in porch, informing them that I have presents to share.

My invention for this trip is called the *Flume Shooter*. It's a store-bought watershirt onto which I've sewn slippery pads behind the shoulders. Wearers can achieve top speed on a water slide by arching onto their heels and shoulder blades, also enjoying the protection these pads provide against the seams of the tube. The shirts I'm supplying are prototypes for us to test in Disney World.

The kids are excited by the shirts, and they hurry inside to pack them. I follow to make sure they don't upset the ready-to-go suitcases, and Mary takes the opportunity of their absence to leave for the print shop, where she'll be completing her Disney quote book.

As the kids return outside to play, I pick up the phone and dial Merryweather. Yet again, I'm forwarded to her voicemail, though this time I listen to her greeting all the way to the end before hanging up; I'm entertained by her scripted farewell: "Have a magical day."

I return to the back porch and call in the children for another activity. I spread out two Disney World maps on the table and ask MJ to reread Friday's note from Mickey Mouse.

> Dear Michael, MJ, Mary and Bert,
>   I can't wait for your visit. Please come find me at my Toontown home on your first morning in the Magic Kingdom.
>   —Mickey Mouse

"It's your job to get us to Toontown," I say. "And here are the maps."

Michael scans the transportation map, but MJ walks away. She opens the porch door. "Come on, Michael. Let's go swing." And the two of them resume playing in the back yard.

I repack the maps, then enter the house to begin preparing lunch.

Soon, Mary returns home. She dashes through the kitchen and grabs her plate off the counter, telling me our bedroom is off limits.

"So, what *else* is new?" I say.

She then locks herself into our room and doesn't reemerge until our ride to the airport is waiting in the driveway.

◆ ◆ ◆

Madison's regional airport is lightly traveled. We enter through its doors around noon and find that the interior feels more like a hotel lobby than a transportation hub. The kids run free across an acre of carpet, playing tag between potted trees. Their giggles seem remote in the vast open space.

This is my favorite moment of any vacation: the moment when all possible outcomes are condensed into a single anticipation.

We deposit our luggage at the ticket counter and move through security to Gate 3. Large windows overlook our airplane, and the kids kneel beside the glass to watch service crews do their work. Mary and I settle into a pair of chairs behind them, and I pull out my Disney biography.

The book I'm reading was published in 1976 by an author named Bob Thomas. I was hoping to find a more current title, but yesterday's trip to the library left me with only this option.

I return to my bookmark at page five, where I soon encounter the following passage:

> . . . he [Walt Disney] had an uncanny capacity for reaching the human heart, hence causing nervous-ness and distrust among intellectuals.

What a curious assertion this is. The author is saying that Walt Disney made intellectuals uneasy . . . and I can imme-diately think of two sisters who might agree with him. But I can also hear my dad. He'd say, "Show me an intellectual. They're a myth." I wonder how the old woman at the library would comment.

A small object falls into my lap, and I set the book aside. Mary has given me a slender piece of paper with printing on it.

"What's *this*?" I say.

"Just a bit of magic."

I lift the paper and read its note.

> Dear Bert,
>   I wanted to buy you the perfect book about Disney
> World, but it hadn't been written yet. Oh well . . .
> just more work for me. I hope you enjoy this price-
> less gift. I love you.
>
>   —Mary

Mary takes the Bob Thomas book from me and replaces it with a homemade paperback—complete with a card-stock cover and glue-tape binding. The picture on the front is of a city at night with a single high-rise tower at its center. The book's title is *The Disney World Dream,* and its author is Mary.

I bounce the book in my hands, as if to judge its value by weight. "Feels like two years," I say.

Mary nods. "Two and a half."

I thumb through the book and discover it to be rich with pictures and sidebars on a wide range of topics. But by and large, this book is a biography of Walt Disney—my *Story of Walter* times a thousand. Mary has surely read the Bob Thomas book and every other biography on the shelves. No wonder she was so distraught on Friday night, comparing my *Story of Walter* to what *she* might have produced. She *did* produce it. And there's no question that her work is not a story; it's a reference document all the way.

Each of us has our strengths, and Mary's is her knack for doing research. She can sift through volumes of information and somehow pluck out the important facts. She admittedly goes a little overboard with the details, but that's a small price to pay for such streamlined learning.

"I can't wait to read it," I say.

"Then don't; Gift Two. I'll entertain the kids while we travel today."

I kiss Mary on the cheek.

"But there's more," she says. "The book can't tell it all. Some things are better told at the park. Gift Three: your tour."

I kiss Mary again, but this time it's not for joy; I'm actually speechless. I can't think of a worse gift for her to be giving me while I'm trying to feel the Disney Magic. Her tour will surely fill my head with facts to the exclusion of all else.

But how can I refuse such a gift—one invested with so much of her personal time and energy?

Mary moves to the children and invites them on an excursion in search of bathrooms and a drinking fountain.

I open her book to chapter one, *The Context of History*.

Her account begins in the mid-1800s—during the industrial revolution—and tracks Walt Disney's ancestors as they adapted to a changing world. I'm fascinated to learn that Walt Disney's father was a construction worker for the 1893 World's Fair in Chicago, and also that there was a very good reason Aunt Poppi couldn't find Thomas Edison's kinetoscope at the Fair. But most beneficial to me is Mary's setup of the conditions that will shape Walt Disney's upbringing.

Walt Disney was born at the turn of the twentieth century, at a time of accelerating social change: the wealth of the industrial age was trickling down to the masses and launching a consumer revolution. But Walt's parents didn't like the way the changing world was affecting their Chicago neighborhood. So, in 1906, when Walt was just four years old, the family moved to a farm near the small town of Marceline, Missouri. They remained there until the summer of 1910, when they relocated to Kansas City.

I close the book at the end of chapter four.

"It's tremendous," I say to Mary. "It's . . ."

"Perspective?"

"Exactly. Nobody really knew what was happening. . . . Like the *lightning sketchers*. They had no idea that a simple chalkboard trick was leading them to cartoon animation."

"Right," says Mary. "Who would have guessed it?"

A voice announces the boarding of our plane, so we gather our belongings and head for the jetway.

Chapter 11

The Flight to Chicago

At the precise moment of liftoff, the kids administer their bubble gum and chew it swiftly. The ground falls away, and the four of us study our home city from this new and ever-changing vantage point. We're on the first leg of our journey—the quick hop from Madison to Chicago.

MJ sits beside me, staring out the window and listening to the music on her headphones. I return to Mary's book at chapter five.

Walt Disney's formative years coincided with the rise of film cinema as the world's first form of mass entertainment not requiring literacy. I'm impressed by Walt Disney's personal drive to be the master of his own destiny. He is a relentless learner, despite his abbreviated formal education, which ended after just one year of high school. It seems he took every opportunity to gain new knowledge and new experiences. At the age of sixteen, he joined the Red Cross Ambulance Corp and served as part of the clean-up crew for the First World War. Upon returning home, he entered the workforce as a commercial artist, opening his own art studio soon after. He then found a job with a Kansas City firm that made short animated commercials for movie houses, and this new work sparked his interests. Walt committed his evenings and his weekends to the study of animation by visiting the library and by frequenting movie theaters. He was determined to learn the techniques of the New York animation houses. Walt became the golden boy of his employer, though his ambitions soon outstripped those of the owner. At the age of twenty, Walt Disney rounded up investors and opened his own animation studio.

I think back to my *Story of Walter* and to the little mouse that kept Walt Disney company in Kansas City. It was this very same studio he opened in 1922 that would fail a year later. And it was Mortimer Mouse, and the other mice on his desk, that saw him through that tough winter.

In the summer of 1923, Walt Disney climbed aboard a Kansas City train bound for the west coast. He was intent on finding a new career because he believed he was too late to make it in animation.

I close the book and note that our plane is now descending on Chicago. The skyscrapers of the downtown are visible through a ring of haze.

I point out the window. "The World's Fair was just beyond those buildings," I say to MJ.

Mary's head pops up over the seat in front of us, as does Michael's.

"Did I hear someone say *World's Fair*? Can anyone guess why the Palace of Fine Arts was the only building left standing when Poppi returned? Was it really there just to punish her?"

Once again, Mary has telegraphed the answer she is looking for.

"Of course not," she continues. "The truth is, the Palace of Fine Arts was the only building made to last. The rest were more like sculptures . . . which burned quickly during the riots of 1894."

Mary sits back down, no doubt hoping the children will react to her dramatic final remark. But the kids remain quiet, so I give her some assistance.

"Did you say riots? Tell me more."

Mary pops back up and hands out pencils and Sudoku puzzles to the children. She then reads to us from a sheet of paper.

George Pullman wanted to make the world a better place to live. He built a beautiful town and a beautiful factory for his workers, then invited people to see his creation. Poppi and her parents were three such visitors who stayed in the town of Pullman during the 1893 World's Fair.

It was around this same time, however, that George Pullman was under a lot of financial pressure. He had reduced the wages of his workers in response to a national recession, though he hadn't likewise lowered their rents on his properties. The workers complained that they couldn't afford to live in his factory town, but George Pullman wouldn't listen to them. He believed that laborers had no right to organize and demand higher pay or lower rents. *Capital,* he believed, was fixed and inflexible, while *labor* could move and adjust as necessary. So, Mr. Pullman refused to negotiate with his workers, prompting them to call a strike.

Oddly enough, though, this model town of Pullman managed to host a model strike. The workers were determined to keep things peaceful. And to prove it, three hundred of them took turns standing guard outside the locked factories, night and day, to prevent vandalism. And the town's great fame as a social experiment meant that news crews came from far and wide to report the unfolding story.

This concentration of suffering families won the

sympathies of many people in Chicago and around the nation. Food and supplies were rushed in.

But the strike was not destined to end well. Thousands of railroad workers across the country joined the town's cause and refused to handle trains carrying Pullman cars. Train service in twenty-seven states and territories was affected. Tensions soon mounted and violence erupted. The worst of the destruction was in downtown Chicago, where hundreds of freight cars were looted, derailed, and burned over the course of a few days. It was during this violence that many of the buildings of the World's Fair were set ablaze. By the end of the strike, about a dozen people had been shot dead, and many more were injured.

George Pullman—the man who had devoted his life and fortune to improving the human condition, and whose name meant "unsurpassed quality" to so many people of his time—was destined to be remembered by this bloody strike that would bear his name. Few people remember the philanthropist, George Pullman. Instead, his legacy continues to punish him for the Pullman Strike and for his segregation of workers into "factory-whites" and "porter-blacks."

The kids remain busy with their puzzles, seemingly oblivious to whether or not Mary is still speaking. The seat-belt sign comes on, and Mary returns herself and Michael to their seated positions.

I wonder what error was made in George Pullman's upbringing that left him so ill-prepared to deal with the concerns of his workers. I think he genuinely felt justified in his actions. The outfall, however, was that he lost his opportunity to win the affections of future generations.

And what about Walt Disney? Like Pullman, Disney prepared for his adulthood without any compass to guide him, yet the Disney name continues to enjoy wide acclaim. It seems Walt Disney did *not* miss his opportunity to impress future generations.

People truly are flying blind. They navigate their lives on a wing and a prayer, hoping they've "prepared" properly for the "opportunities" they'll encounter. And for those who fly at the front of the flock, like George Pullman and Walt Disney, the consequences for their actions can be extreme. They boldly lead us into new territories and are then reviled or celebrated for where they've ultimately taken us. It is far safer to fly in the middle of the pack.

Our plane touches down at O'Hare International Airport, and we taxi to the gate.

Chapter 12

The Layover

Ninety minutes is the wait until our 4:30 flight. Mary has just left with the children on an expedition to explore the airport, leaving me behind in the boarding area to guard our bags.

I return to Mary's book at chapter nine, *The Rise of the Disney Studio*.

Walt Disney's 1923 train ride took him from Kansas City to California, where his brother Roy lived. The two of them then teamed up to begin the Disney Brothers Studio. Fate seemed to favor this hard-working pair, who, by a twist of good fortune, saw their Disney name become more than just a footnote in history. As it happened, Mickey Mouse became a smashing success because (1) his sound was well-synchronized, (2) he had a charming personality, (3) he got his debut, and (4) the reigning animated film star of the day, Felix the Cat, belonged to a studio that was refusing the switch to sound film. Mickey Mouse had a clear road to the top. In the 1930s, during the Great Depression, Walt then daringly risked the survival of his studio to attempt a filmmaking first in America—the creation of a full-length cartoon feature. In 1937, the Disney studio premiered *Snow White and the Seven Dwarfs*. The film captivated audiences and refilled the company's coffers, financing the go-ahead for four more long films heading into the 1940s—*Bambi, Pinoc-*

chio, Fantasia, and *Dumbo.* By 1941, the Walt Disney Studio was the world's standard for quality animation.

I close Mary's book and stare blankly into space. She and I each researched the life of Walt Disney, yet our results were miles apart: Mary's book is a serious compilation of facts, while my *Story of Walter* is now exposed as a comedy of errors.

Mickey Mouse was not entirely a creation of Walt and Lilly's 1928 train ride back to California. In truth, Mickey look-alikes populated many of Disney's and other studios' earlier cartoons. Even Walt's own *Oswald the Lucky Rabbit* bore a resemblance to Mickey. Likewise, *Steamboat Willie* was not officially the first sound cartoon. Nor was *Snow White and the Seven Dwarfs* the world's first animated feature.

I dig into Mary's bag for the Bob Thomas book and return to page five of the foreword.

> . . . he [Walt Disney] had an uncanny capacity for reaching the human heart, hence causing nervousness and distrust among intellectuals.

I wonder what Walt's secret was for reaching the human heart. Did he use half-truths and omissions, like my *Story of Walter* did? If so, I can understand why "intellectuals" might have mistrusted him, because even *I'm* feeling rather disturbed by my own spread of misinformation. With just a little more care, I could have created a story that was both inspiring *and* accurate.

Upon Mary's return with the children, I grant her some much-deserved satisfaction. "I think I'm beginning to remember now," I say. "Walt and Lilly were married in 1925."

"Are you sure?" she says.

"As sure as *you* are."

Michael takes my hand. "Come on, Dad. You gotta see."

He leads me away until we reach a display of dinosaur bones in Concourse B. It is a fully reassembled Brachiosaurus standing four-stories tall and 72 feet long. We walk beneath it several times, then stop at a bookstore on our return.

Michael surveys some picture books about dinosaurs while I look up the word *intellectual* in a Webster's dictionary. I find several variations, but only one definition strikes a chord with me.

> Intellectualize *v.* To examine rationally or objectively, especially so as to avoid emotional involvement.

Hmm. An intellectual is someone who silences their Emotion and listens to Logic and Reason. I guess it's a cinch I'm no intellectual then. Emotion has sent me on a quest for a Disney sugar bowl, and I'm blindly obeying against the good counsel of Logic and Reason.

Michael wanders across the store, attracted by a lava lamp, where he pauses and stares into its circulating wax. I join him there.

"What's it for?" he says to me.

"Just for fun," I answer. "Don't you see? There's Mickey's head." I point to three balls of wax that have come together to make two ears and a head. "The lamp knows we're going to Disney World."

Michael gives me a strange look, so I mess up his hair.

"Just kidding," I say. "It's only a lamp, don't-you-know. But it *is* kind of fun to find shapes in it, don't you think?"

Michael and I continue to watch the lamp until another recognizable figure develops. This one is an oblong bulb that stretches and tears, forming the likeness of a hot-air balloon with a hanging basket. Mary and I took just such a balloon ride over Disney World on our honeymoon, and the lamp seems to know this too.

♦ ♦ ♦

We return to the waiting area, where Mary sees us coming and reaches into her bag.

"Wanna do some gambling?" she says to MJ and Michael. She invites them to sit on the floor next to her, then gives each of them twenty pennies and a dice.

"Now," she says, "you're going to take turns, and if you roll a five or a six, I'll give you another penny. But if you roll anything else, I'll take one away. Do you want to play the game?"

The kids do, but it doesn't take them long to become upset that their piles of money are dwindling fast. So Mary makes a rule change. She switches the winning numbers to one, two, three, and four, effectively reversing the odds.

The kids now generate easy money, and their piles grow quickly.

Mary then changes the rules again; this time, the kids get to choose their two winning numbers ahead of each roll. She has cleverly restored their losing odds while giving them the illusion of control over the game. The kids are excited by the change.

Once again, Mary siphons away their coins, but this time the kids are frustrated rather than angry. They are actually feeling responsible for their own losses, blaming themselves for not being able to choose the correct numbers in advance of each roll.

Mary ends the game by letting the kids exchange their few remaining pennies for a shiny quarter. She then summarizes their experience and compares it to the real world of casinos and lotteries. It's comforting to hear them reply to her with statements like, "That's crazy!" and "*Who* would do *that?*"

Mary returns the dice to her bag and withdraws a small piece of paper.

"Do you know what I'm holding in my hand?" she says. "It's a Wisconsin lottery ticket that cost me a dollar . . . and we have virtually no chance of winning. So why do you suppose I bought it?"

"To teach us a lesson," says MJ.

"No," says Mary, "—*the lottery dream*. What would *you* do with fifty million dollars?"

We pass the remaining time in the waiting area describing how we might spend our winnings. Among the ideas: MJ and Michael would build a water-park around our house, and Mary and I would buy a second home down the street to get away from it. Mary would quit her job and become a stand-up comedian, and I would buy a college diploma online.

CHAPTER 13

The Flight to Orlando

The airplane to Florida is larger than the one to Chicago; it has three seats instead of two on either side of the aisle. Michael and I share a row with an elderly man, while Mary and MJ are alone on the three seats behind us.

As boarding continues, I entertain Michael by giving him spelling words. *Hat, belt, socks,* and *shoes* come to mind first, inspired by a passenger stowing his bag in the overhead compartment. Next, I look out the window and turn my mental dictionary to the transportation page, finding *truck, train, plane,* and *car.* Sight, it seems, is a conjurer of words, and although I'm using the trick on purpose right now, it seems to also work when I'm not really trying, like when I'm answering a question for my son about the purpose of a lava lamp.

Our plane backs away from the gate, and the seat beside Mary and MJ remains empty. Mary invites Michael to join them, and he scrambles around to fill the vacancy.

I return to Mary's book at the start of chapter twelve—*The Creation of Disneyland.*

Walt Disney lost interest in his studio during the 1940s because of a union battle that led to a troubling strike by some of his employees, and also because of a financial crisis that forced him to accept outside investors. Walt took time off to pursue new interests, and one of these interests was the notion of creating an amusement park.

But the investor-owned Disney Studio would not back
Walt's proposal to build a new and lavishly expensive kind of
park. So Walt went out on his own. He seeded a new company
and started planning his park. Then, he boldly embraced a
new medium, called television, to secure his financing and to
exploit the marketing potential it seemed to offer. His weekly
series, named *Disneyland,* reached millions of Americans in
their homes and was a free advertisement for his coming
amusement park. When Disneyland finally opened in California in 1955, it became a stellar success. And although it
was television that introduced the park to the masses, it was
the quality of the park itself that kept them coming back.

Walt and his designers had done their homework. They
had pored over every detail to ensure that their park could
achieve all that they had hoped: it functioned smoothly
without compromise to beauty; it harnessed exciting new
technologies to support attractions both thrilling and enrich-
ing; and, above all, it met the high Disney standard for clean
family fun.

I turn the page to the next chapter: *The History of Amusement Parks.*

The Columbian Exposition of 1893 was at the forefront
of a major social change in America. Its Midway Plaisance,
which was the first of its kind to be financially so successful,
spawned the development of amusement areas around the
country, like Coney Island in New York. These parks were
a sanctuary from the strictures of Victorian etiquette that
pervaded American culture at the time. The mechanical
rides put men and women into close physical contact, jostling
them around and giving them reasons to cling to one another.
This controlled carnival setting drew people into lively social
interactions and provided them with a safe venue for meeting
strangers and for experimenting with new roles for themselves.

They, in fact, became part of the show, moving from "spectator" to "spectacle." My favorite example comes from Coney Island's Steeplechase Park, where couples exiting one of the rides had to cross a stage, where a dwarf clown shocked the man with an electric cattle prod and where an air jet beneath the floor elevated the woman's skirt. The embarrassed couple then joined the audience to laugh at the next unwitting pair.

As the plane's dinner cart approaches, I finish Mary's chapter and set the book aside. My meal tray includes a small bag of Cracker Jack—the molasses-covered popcorn that Aunt Poppi discovered at the World's Fair.

Our beloved Poppi, of age seventeen, was not the only one experiencing her adolescence at the turn of the last century; in fact, a large contingent of the industrialized world's population was doing the same thing. Maybe *this* is the meaning to Poppi's story. Perhaps the magic it has performed on Mary has to do with the adolescence she never completed.

Mary is the oldest of two daughters who grew up as polar opposites. Mary's sister is delicate and feminine, like her mother, while Mary is athletic and more masculine, like her father. Mary grew up playing boys' soccer and boys' baseball. And she followed in her father's footsteps upon entering college, choosing the male-dominated discipline of engineering for her degree. And now, in her career with the City of Madison, she sits across the table from contractors and developers—most of whom are men—who treat her differently than her male counterparts, often trying to bully her or to dismiss her knowledge of construction. Mary's life has been a long battle against gender biases, and there's no doubt in my mind that she's won it . . . but at what cost? Deep down, Mary is injured.

Mary once remarked to me that she had postponed her adolescence until college. "That's when I bloomed," she said, then she showed me the pictures to prove it. Mary was an eye-popper when she wore makeup and short skirts. "I had the pick of the litter," she said, "which scared the good ones away, of course. Then one boy broke my heart, and I went back to wearing jeans and baggy sweatshirts."

I pour some Cracker Jack into my hand and peek between the seats at Mary. Her t-shirt and pants can't hide the raw beauty of her form, and I can't help but wish I could meet that party girl in the photos.

The final chapter of Mary's book is titled *The Search for Disneyland East.*

Within five years of opening Disneyland in California, the Disney corporation began shopping for an eastern location to site a second park. Walt was intent that the new park should be much larger than Disneyland so that he could protect it from unsightly commercial development that would inevitably crowd its borders. Walt chose swampland near Orlando, Florida, and quietly made his purchases, surprising even his own project team when he continued to buy options long after reaching the company's target of twelve thousand acres. By the time Walt revealed to the press that Disney was the buyer of all this land, the company held rights to over twenty-seven thousand acres. Walt had big plans for his property, including more than just a large amusement park. He intended to build a model community—one that would demonstrate solutions to the problems that were then plaguing the inner-cities of America.

Mary's book ends with a note, instructing me to ask her for the video camera.

"It's all cued up and ready to go," she says, handing me the camera before I can even ask for it. "This is the film Walt created to explain his plans for Disney World."

I insert the ear-buds and tilt out the screen, then press play.

The film opens with footage of Disneyland in California, set to cheerful music. A narrator welcomes me to this *Disney dream come true* and boasts of Disneyland's worldwide appeal. He then reads the park's dedication plaque.

> To all who come to this happy place: welcome. Disneyland is your land. Here age relives fond memories of the past, and here youth may savor the challenge and promise of the future. Disneyland is dedicated to the ideals, the dreams, and the hard facts that have created America, with the hope that it will be a source of joy and inspiration to all the world.

The narrator credits the park's remarkable success to the integrity and skill of Walt Disney and his imagineers—the talented team of artists, architects, and technicians who blend imagination with engineering. He then cites a speech from the 1963 Urban Design Conference at Harvard University, where the keynote speaker, James W. Rouse, made the following statements.

> I hold a view that may be somewhat shocking to an audience as sophisticated as this: that the greatest piece of urban design in the United States today is Disneyland.
>
> If you think about Disneyland and think of its performance in relation to its purpose—its meaning to people...more than that, its meaning to the process of development—you will find it the outstanding piece of urban design in the United States.
>
> It took an area of activity, the amusement park, and lifted it to a standard so high in its performance—in its respect for people . . . in its functioning

for people—that it really has become a brand new thing. It fulfills all the functions it set out to accomplish . . . un-self-consciously, usefully, and profitably to its owners and developers.

I find more to learn in the standards that have been set and in the goals that have been achieved in the development of Disneyland than in any other single piece of physical development in the country.

The film's short introduction ends with the narrator announcing that Disneyland was *yesterday,* ". . . tomorrow, a project so vast, it has been called a brand new Disney World."

The picture changes to a large office with maps and drawings covering the walls. Walt Disney, wearing a gray suit and black tie, sits on the edge of a table holding a long pointer. He speaks to the camera and welcomes viewers to his California studio, where the plans are being made for the Florida property. He explains that the details he will present are "a starting point"—a preliminary plan for what he feels to be "the most exciting and challenging assignment" his company has ever undertaken. He assures his viewers that, although the details will surely change as the planning proceeds, the overall philosophy will remain much the same.

The camera isolates a small region on a colorful map, and Walt explains that Disney World will have its own amusement park area—like the one in California—but that this new one will be five times larger. Then, as the picture zooms out, Walt is shown standing at the base of a fourteen foot tall map, revealing that the amusement park is just one small element of his vast Florida holding. Several nodes of development proceed along a tidy line up the center, flanked on each side by swamps that will protect the property from trespassers, according to Walt.

The amusement park is at the top of the map, and an "airport of the future" is at the bottom. The airport is set among neighboring buildings, "where all visitors will enter Disney World," and a high-speed train connects this point of entry to the three other regions of development: the one-thousand acre industrial park, the amusement area at the top, and an unnamed development lying between them.

The camera returns to Walt, who then introduces "the most important part" of the Florida project—"the heart of everything we'll be doing." Walt Disney intends to build an *Experimental Prototype Community of Tomorrow,* named Epcot.

Walt moves across the room to a detailed map on the wall and uses it as his backdrop while he explains the plans.

Epcot will be a "showcase" city, employing the latest technologies and the best thinking that America has to offer. It will aim to solve the problems of modern cities, not by "curing the old ills of old cities," but rather by "starting from scratch on virgin land and building a special kind of new community." The city will be "dedicated to the happiness of the people," and it will serve as an ever-evolving "blueprint of the future, where people actually live a life they can't find anyplace else in the world."

Walt concludes his visionary overview from a chair, inviting viewers to spend the next few minutes exploring the preliminary plans for Epcot.

The image changes to a familiar one: it's the picture on the cover of Mary's book—a city skyline with a single high-rise tower at the center. The narrator's voice returns and explains the design for Epcot and the industrial park.

The film ends with a few closing remarks by Walt Disney. He says that no single company can make Epcot a reality, but that his hope is to "bring together the technical know-how of American industry and the creative imagination of the

Disney organization" to create "a showcase to the world of
the American free-enterprise system." He believes that Epcot
"can influence the future of city living for generations to come."

The picture fades, and I flip the viewer closed. Walt's
layout for the Florida property looks nothing like the map
I've seen of the modern-day Disney World. The current
property is a tangle of roadways and widely scattered development—hardly the simplicity of Walt's original design. And
I also remember visiting Epcot on our honeymoon; it was
nothing like the city described in the film. It was just another
amusement park.

I remove the ear-buds and hand the camera back to Mary.
"I had no idea he was dreaming of a model city when he died."

"And did you notice the similarity to Pullman?" says Mary.
"—A rich and famous guy . . . intent on solving social problems . . . secretly buys *virgin* land for a model town . . . —each
perfectly confident that beauty and technology can lift the
human spirit."

"Yeah," I say, "but only one got built."

"And what a pity," says Mary. "Did you see the great genius
of Walt's plan? —Disney World could have been the next
Columbian Exposition. Walt was going to put his model city
between an entrance complex and an amusement park: he
was going to put his White City between the train station
and the Midway. Millions of Disney visitors would have had
no choice but to experience the look and feel of a model
city and a model industrial park, all from the comfort of a
smooth-running electric train. I wonder how this might have
changed the course of real cities."

Mary returns to her card game with the children, and I
stare out the window.

I can't help but feel a sense of loss that the Disney World

of today is almost nothing like Walt envisioned. The only region that even remotely resembles his original plan is the Magic Kingdom area at the north end of the property.

♦ ♦ ♦

Puffy clouds drift below the plane in a bath of scattered sunshine. The local time is 7:30 pm, and I reset my watch accordingly.

"Hey," says MJ, "there's a turtle."

"Yeah," says Michael, "and a cat."

The two children are studying the cloud formations outside.

"—A cat's *butt*, maybe," says MJ.

"You mean *fanny*," corrects Michael, and the two kids laugh.

"Hey, look," says MJ, "it's Donald Duck."

I look out my window to confirm the sighting, and sure enough, two clouds create an excellent likeness of Donald. The first cloud—his head—is the more convincing of the two. It features his bill, hanging slightly open, and two tall eyes below a tuft of feathers. The second cloud forms his body, though its connection to the head is barely a wisp. Donald's arms and legs are tucked beneath him.

"I bet we're going to see Donald in Disney World," says MJ.

"And Mickey too," says Michael. Then he recounts his sighting of Mickey in the lava lamp.

"Do you think we'll see more than just his head?" says Mary.

Apparently, the three of them have not combined the two clouds as I have done. They talk of seeing Donald's head over a fence or as a balloon in a parade.

I resist the temptation to join in their conversation and point out the second cloud, which is now even more separate than before. I don't want them dreaming up ways to see Donald Duck with a severed head. I do, however, hope we encounter him during our visit, because I'll be interested to see if they relate that experience back to this sign from the clouds.

But what am I saying here? Omens are just the sort of nonsense people use to select their lottery numbers and their dice rolls. Such a fortune-telling activity is easily on par with visions seen in a lava lamp and wishes made beside a fountain. What kind of irrational behavior will I engage in next? Shall I track down our horoscopes to plan our week? Or maybe I should seek out Mickey Mouse in his role as the Sorcerer's Apprentice and ask him for the scroll that explains all superstitions and games of chance. At least then I'd be learning something. All I know is that Logic and Reason are looking more competent to me now. Mary's book has revealed to me the many weaknesses in my *Story of Walter*; she has shown me that facts are king.

Yes, *facts*.

Children are ruled by their emotions because they can't yet cope with the many facts that bombard them. They *feel* the Disney Magic because they are unable to organize the details that would ultimately dispel it.

This is my first clue to finding the key to the Disney Magic: it is hidden among the smartly-crafted details of Disney World. There's no need for a hand of fate to put a key in my bucket; the burden of locating that key is all mine. I must dip and fish the pail around to capture it for myself. Mary's tour might actually hold the answer.

I scoot to my knees and lean over the seat. "I can't wait for your tour, Mary."

"Oh," she says, "I wasn't sure."

"Promise me you won't skip anything."

Our children insert more wads of chewing gum as the plane descends on Orlando's international airport.

Mary points out the window to what looks like a sprin-
kling of shiny raindrops on the ground. "Do you see those
lakes over there?" she says. "One of them is the Seven Seas
Lagoon, and its neighbor is Bay Lake. Mickey lives right
between them in the Magic Kingdom. That's where we're
going first thing tomorrow morning."

PART II

The
Magic

CHAPTER 14

The Port Orleans Homecoming

We arrive at the baggage claim and find my mom and dad waiting there for us.

"Maryjane!" says Dad. "Michael!" He scoops up his two grandchildren and carries them around like grocery sacks. "Where's your dress?" he says to MJ. "Who untucked your shirt?" he says to Michael. Then he sets them down on the luggage carousel for a ride.

"Herbert!" says Mom. "Get them off of there."

"Oh, you're no fun," he says.

He returns the kids to the floor, then gives Mary a devilish grin. "You're next, sweetie," he says.

He advances toward her, and she scuttles around behind me for protection.

Dad laughs. "What's pip-squeak gonna do?"

I keep my eyes on my father and reach blindly behind me. I grab Mary by the wrists and pull her forward, pinning her against my back and extending her hands toward Dad for his inspection.

"Hmm." He studies them.

Mary wiggles her ring finger. "Oh darn," she says, "I must have left it on the counter after I mowed the lawn."

Dad shakes his head.

"No," I say. "You were up on the ladder cleaning the gutters, remember? The ring's on the tool bench."

Dad knows that Mary does many of the "manly" chores around our house . . . and that *I* do the dishes. He also knows I've never given Mary a piece of diamond jewelry, and he still refuses to believe she doesn't truly want one. He's offered to help us with the financing for one, but each time he does, Mary tells him she's not interested. Dad interprets these rejections as evidence of her steadfast loyalty to her husband. *"You're even more deserving,"* he tells her.

Dad leans over and kisses Mary's hand. "I hope this is the one you hit him with."

◆　◆　◆

As we pass through the airport's doorway to the parking ramp, a faint glow of twilight lingers in the sky. The day is still warm, and the breeze feels moist and tropical. It gradually seeps through my clothing and flushes out the cool air trapped against my skin. I'm not used to being in so much air-conditioning, though I know my current thaw is only temporary.

Mom and Dad are climate-control junkies. In fact, scheduling this vacation during the heat of summer was a big concession on their part. I can guarantee the windows of the van will be closed for our ride to Disney World.

During our walk to the van, MJ and Michael determine our seating arrangement. They put Mary alone on the middle bench and themselves on either side of Grandma at the back. As for *me*, I'm placed as far away as possible in front with Grandpa.

Dad's computerized dashboard indicates that the outside air temperature is 81 degrees and that the indoor temperature is set at 72. "It'll feel cooler," he assures me, "once the compressor cuts the humidity." He always says that.

Road construction at the airport's exit forces Dad to make

a quick decision, and we soon discover that we're traveling in the wrong direction.

I open Dad's Florida map and take the role of navigator, choosing a new route to Disney World: one that will show us a bit of Orlando.

Like many travelers to the area, our original plan was to make a bee line for the Disney property along State Highway 528. We had no intention of seeing anything else . . . and for good reason. Our extended drive reveals that Orlando is *anywhere USA,* made extreme by the trappings of a tourist town. It's a madness of hotels, time-shares, and, according to Mary, more than eighty "fun-zones." We find glaring lights in every direction, showcasing strip malls, parking lots, driveways, security fences, utility wires, and billboards. I've seen more than enough of this in my lifetime. Orlando is a super-sized Wisconsin Dells.

Yet, soon enough, and without warning, my spirits get a lift. Forward of the van, a smooth and colorful sign arches over the roadway, welcoming us to Walt Disney World. The visual clamor of Orlando dissolves into the visual calm of Disney.

Roadside greenery lies under a blanket of darkness, yielding to the warm accents of distant lights trained on architecture, fountains, and gardens. Artistic road signs sprinkle the parkways, offering information only where necessary. And the park's utilities must lie underground because I don't see any wires or poles against the sky. Words like *soothing* and *intriguing* cycle through my mind, as we make our way to the French Quarter of Port Orleans—our resort.

The drive has taken longer than expected, and Michael is fast asleep. MJ is just now nodding off against Grandma's arm.

Grandpa stops at the gatehouse, then pulls forward to the canopy at the resort's main entrance. He asks Mary and me to check ourselves in.

I remember this canopy well. It's the same canopy Mary and I parked under twelve years ago in a rented convertible on our honeymoon. However, I recall that experience feeling much better than this one. Perhaps it was the fresh air of riding with the top down.

I open my door and step from the van. Once again, I'm warmed by a tropical breeze, but this time the cleansing comes with a jazz accompaniment. My years melt away, as I take my bride by the hand. We glance into the van at our two sleeping children and I wonder, *Can they really be ours? We're so young.*

In line at the registration counter, the background music changes to a new song—a familiar one: *When the Saints Go Marching In.* Mary stares straight ahead, and I'm strangely sensing she's about to cry.

When I step to the counter to take our turn, Mary doesn't step with me. Instead, she turns and heads toward the door without saying a word. Her eyes remain focused on the floor.

Mary truly *has* changed. If one of us should be getting sentimental at this return to Port Orleans, it should be *me,* because *I'm* the emotional one in our relationship. It was *me* who cried on our wedding night, and it was *me* who cried at the births of our children. So I'm just not sure how to interpret this new behavior, though I have to confess it pleases me greatly. I feel the promise that I'm going to be loving my wife even more than I already do.

I complete the check-in and find Mary back in the van. She seems more composed now, but she continues to avoid eye contact with me.

We take the short drive to Building One, and the four of us make two trips up the outside stairway to get our luggage and children to the room. Mom and Dad have a connecting door with our accommodations, and they offer to watch our sleeping children if we'd like to go out.

Mary rinses off in the shower, and I take my turn after her. She is no longer in the room when I emerge.

I step out onto the balcony hallway and spy her in the courtyard of our complex. She is sitting alone on a bench beside a loud fountain, and I manage to get quite close to her before she notices me approaching. She is on the verge of tears, and they begin to flow as I reach her.

For ten minutes at least, Mary convulses in my arms, heaving with the sobs of a thousand unspent emotions. "Thank god you defended Disney," she says. "You were the right one to stay home with our children. . . . You saved my life last year. . . . What did I ever do to deserve you? . . ."

I wipe Mary's tears and supply her with the tissues she packed for herself. And I can think of no greater gift of magic she could be giving me right now. She is allowing me to be her strength—the shoulder for her to cry upon and the arms to enfold her. There's nothing quite so sweet as the fulfillment of a desire you didn't even know you had.

Mary's outpouring subsides, and she asks me to take a walk with her. We stroll arm in arm through our New Orleans setting, following the music toward the center of the resort.

"Do you know why I almost started crying in the lobby?" she says.

Mary explains that the registration counter's artwork included musical notes that matched the melody of *When the Saints Go Marching In*—the song that was then playing. "I'm so pathetic," she says. "Here we are, in the place of our honeymoon, and the one thing that makes me nostalgic is a stupid detail. I almost want to start crying again."

The Dixieland jazz gets louder, and soon we've reached

the resort's pool area, known as Doubloon Lagoon. The pool features a giant serpent, which coils in and out of the deck and has a stairway up its back and a water slide down its tongue. Stationed around the pool are human-sized alligators made of green fiberglass that stand on their hind legs while squirting water instead of notes from their musical instruments.

Mary and I take a few minutes to get reacquainted with the players in the clamshell-bandshell, then head over to the pool-side bar, *Mardi Grogs.*

"I detect a biblical theme," I say. "This isn't New Orleans; this is the Garden of Eden."

"Well, then," says Mary, "I guess this calls for biblical drinks. I wonder if they serve a *Forbidden Fruit* cocktail."

"Or the *Tree of Carnal Knowledge,*" I say.

We step to the counter and order ourselves *Strip and Go Nakeds.*

Our twin beverages arrive with little plastic straws and white paper umbrellas inserted. Mary removes her umbrella and holds it out in front of her.

"Are you trying to fly?" I say.

"Yes, but I know it won't work."

"Too small?"

"No. Wrong color. Poppi's was black."

We carry our drinks to some lounge chairs, where Mary plops down beside me in the same recliner, despite the many eyes that can see us. We sip our tasty potions and let them cast their happy spell.

"So," says Mary, "do you think the blacks should have boycotted the World's Fair . . . or should they have attended in large numbers—you know, to show their civility?"

I think back to Poppi's story and the unsuccessful struggle of black Americans to gain recognition and find employment at the Fair. "I don't think it mattered much *what* they did," I say. "People don't change their minds that easily."

"True," says Mary. "We know that firsthand, don't we."

The Golden Rule is something we've been trying to teach our children since they were born, yet they still can't seem to fathom the difference between how they treat others and how they want to be treated themselves.

"But," says Mary, "there was one person doing her part to change a few minds . . . and long before the Fair. Her name was Sojourner Truth. Do you recognize it?"

"Only from the other night," I say.

"I didn't know it either until a few months ago. That's when I saw it in MJ's homework. It upset me that I'd never heard it before, so you can probably guess what I did."

"Went to the library."

"Right."

Mary pulls the straw from her drink and flicks some lemony droplets into my face. "Sojourner Truth was my addition to the Women's Movement in Poppi's story. It was *she* who deserved a sculpture beside the other three matriarchs at the entrance to the Woman's building. Did I mention she was black? I'm sure I didn't need to."

Mary then tells me the tale of Sojourner Truth. It's a genuine Cinderella story.

The slave girl, known as Belle, was thirteen years old when she was sold for the third time. She entered the household of a New Yorker named John Dumont—a man whose general cruelty toward her was surpassed only by that of his wife and one of their white servant girls. While Belle boiled potatoes for breakfast one morning and was out doing the farmyard chores, the white servant girl swept up ashes and deposited them into the kettle, where they discolored the potatoes. And each time this happened, Belle was soundly punished. But the true culprit was finally revealed when the Dumont's own ten-year-old daughter plotted and successfully exposed the guilty servant girl. As the years then passed, Belle eventually gained her freedom and became a public speaker, changing her name to Sojourner Truth. She traveled the northern states, telling the story of her life and challenging people to consider the notion that women and minorities might deserve a fuller measure of the nation's liberty.

Mary pulls a folded sheet of paper from her pocket. "I've got the meaning of your *Boobs Daddy* right here," she says. "I was keeping this in the desk."

Mary reads to me a letter dating back to 1858, recounting an incident from one of Sojourner's speeches.

> FRIEND W. L. GARRISON:—Sojourner Truth, an elderly colored woman, well known throughout the Eastern States, is now holding a series of anti-slavery meetings in Northern Indiana. Sojourner comes well recommended by H. B. Stowe, yourself, and others, and was gladly received and welcomed by the [F]riends of the [S]lave in this locality. Her progress in knowledge, truth, and righteousness is very remarkable, especially when we consider her former low estate as a slave. The border-ruffian Democracy of Indiana, however, appear to be jealous and suspicious of every anti-slavery movement. A rumor was immediately circulated that Sojourner was an impostor; that she was, indeed, a man disguised in women's clothing. It appears, too, from what has since transpired, that they suspected her to be a mercenary hireling of the Republican party.
>
> At her third appointed meeting in this vicinity,

which was held in the meeting-house of the United
Brethren, a large number of democrats and other
pro-slavery persons were present. At the close of the
meeting, Dr. T. W. Strain, the mouthpiece of the
slave Democracy, requested the large congregation
to 'hold on,' and stated that a doubt existed in the
minds of many persons present respecting the sex
of the speaker, and that it was his impression that a
majority of them believed the speaker to be a man.
The doctor also affirmed (which was not believed by
the friends of the slave) that it was for the speaker's
special benefit that he now demanded that Sojourner
submit her breast to the inspection of some of the
ladies present, that the doubt might be removed by
their testimony. There were a large number of ladies
present, who appeared to be ashamed and indignant
at such a proposition. Sojourner's friends, some of
whom had not heard the rumor, were surprised and
indignant at such ruffianly surmises and treatment.

Confusion and uproar ensued, which was soon
suppressed by Sojourner, who, immediately rising,
asked them why they suspected her to be a man. The
Democracy answered, 'Your voice is not the voice
of a woman, it is the voice of a man, and we believe
you are a man.' Dr. Strain called for a vote, and a
boisterous 'Aye,' was the result. A negative vote was
not called for. Sojourner told them that her breasts
had suckled many a white babe, to the exclusion of
her own offspring; that some of those white babies
had grown to man's estate; that, although they had
sucked her colored breasts, they were, in her esti-
mation, far more manly than they (her persecutors)
appeared to be; and she quietly asked them, as she

disrobed her bosom, if they, too, wished to suck! In vindication of her truthfulness, she told them that she would show her breast to the whole congregation; that it was not to her shame that she uncovered her breast before them, but to their shame. Two young men (A. Badgely and J. Horner) stepped forward while Sojourner exposed her naked breast to the audience. I heard a democrat say, as we were returning home from meeting, that Dr. Strain had, previous to the examination, offered to bet forty dollars that Sojourner was a man! So much for the physiological acumen of a western physician.

As 'agitation of thought is the beginning of wisdom,' we hope that Indiana will yet be redeemed.

Yours, truly, for the slave,

WILLIAM HAYWARD.

♦ ♦ ♦

Mary and I finish our drinks and walk to the far end of the pool, where a dark riverwalk borders our resort. We stop at the nearby gazebo and look out over the water.

A second Disney resort stands across the way, almost hidden by a line of trees. I recall this resort as being under construction during our honeymoon.

"Hey," I say, "isn't that Dixie Landings?" I'm proud to have remembered the name.

"Well," says Mary, "not exactly. It's now Port Orleans – Riverside. Any guesses why the name changed?"

Mary explains that the word *Dixie* belongs to the song *I Wish I Was In Dixie,* which became an anthem for the South during the Civil War and then again for angry whites during the Civil Rights Movement of the 1960s. The resort's plantation-style mansions, with their pre-Civil War splendor, don't need any help finding an association with slavery.

I stare through the trees, noting the glow of the white columns as they reflect themselves across the jet-black water below.

"Eve," I say to Mary, "the time has come for us to leave the Garden of Eden . . . for we possess the knowledge of good and evil."

CHAPTER 15

The Opening Curtain

It's a little before 8am when I open my eyes, and I'm huddled along the edge of the bed that I'm sharing with Michael.

Mary is already up and dressed, and she is assembling a quick breakfast.

The children and I arise, and before long, Mary is brushing her teeth and I'm packing the day's gear. The children are standing by the door, arguing quietly.

MJ then raises her voice and pushes Michael. "You're lying. I get to go first," she says.

"But it's *my turn!*" he shouts back.

"Quiet," I say, "—both of you. We're in a hotel."

I order them to stand apart, then tell them I'm not interested in their problem. But Michael seems compelled to plead his case anyway. He explains that he should be the first one out the door because MJ got to sit next to Grandma last night in the van.

His reasoning makes no sense to me; he and MJ *both* sat next to Grandma last night.

Such ludicrous arguments are a daily occurrence in our household. Uncle Albert calls them "poetic debates," referring to the Greek philosopher, Plato, who described two kinds of truth: *poetic* and *literal*. Michael wants to be first out the door—his *literal* truth—so he gushes with the words and actions that he hopes will secure this outcome. Like a seasoned politician or a savvy advertiser, Michael says and does whatever it takes to win the moment. These behaviors are his *poetic* truth. Yet, Michael's poetry misrepresents many of the facts. So Mary and I share the unpleasant responsibility of mentoring him, pointing out the honesty of his *literal* truth while exposing the lies of his *poetic* truth.

"Mmm," I say, "I really don't want to hear—"

"No!" screams MJ. "You always take his side. I hate you. Why can't you let *Mom* stay home?"

MJ's flare-up is nothing new or shocking. It, too, has components of *literal* and *poetic* truth. The *literal* truth is that she doesn't really hate me. Rather, her hostile words are a mere poetry born of her need to break a parental bond—a critical phase of her development, according to the parenting books. Her struggle is one that Mary and I take very seriously.

MJ's outburst continues, turning into a laundry list of my shortcomings as a parent. I stand there, taking the barrage, working hard to prevent the sort of reaction I know I'll regret. So far, though, I'm successful at warding off my smile.

But seven-year-old Michael is not so mature. He grins ear to ear, reveling in his sister's distress. Then he sticks out his tongue at her.

MJ's reaction is swift and decisive. She erupts with a shout into his face, then quickly returns to my flogging.

I can't keep my composure any longer, and I burst out laughing.

And to MJ's own surprise and horror, she laughs too. She immediately covers her face with her hands.

In the heat of the moment, I bring my face close to hers and swing her hands open like window shutters. I chirp into her face, then slam the shutters closed.

Now *everyone* is laughing, including Grandma and Grandpa, who have just entered our room through the adjoining door. They are ready to drive us to the Magic Kingdom.

In a satisfying twist of irony, we don't actually leave our room through the coveted main door. Instead, we pass through the grandparents' room and head out *their* door. The fight is over and forgotten, and MJ and Michael revert to negotiating the new seating arrangement for the van, ultimately settling on exactly the same scheme as last night.

Our plan is to ride to the Magic Kingdom this morning by automobile rather than Disney shuttle. According to Mary, the resort buses drop visitors off at the amusement park's main gate—a rather lackluster approach to such an enchanted land. Mary wants our initial encounter to proceed more as Walt Disney had originally intended it. Our ride with Mom and Dad will get us no closer than the distant shores of the Seven Seas Lagoon. This was the site Walt Disney planned as the main entrance to the amusement area of his property.

"Winds shifted overnight," says Dad. "—The pressure's falling. We might be in for some rain later today."

Dad knows the gravity of his news, because *he* is the person responsible for getting Uncle Albert to the castle on time for tonight's ceremony. He is also aware of the backup plan in case of rain, which is to hold the service inside the restaurant beside the windows overlooking Fantasyland.

"Let's hope for clear skies," he says, giving me a wink. Then he merges the van onto World Drive.

We cruise beside the Magic Kingdom's mammoth parking lot, then turn at the Transportation & Ticket Center for our drop-off. Mom and Dad will not be accompanying us into the park this morning because they are off to the Amtrak station to pick up Uncle Albert and then back to the airport for two more installments of family. The plan is for everyone to meet up later today at the hotel, at which time Mary and I will prepare for our evening out and leave MJ and Michael with the rest of the family for a visit to the MGM Studios.

We thank our chauffeurs and climb from the van.

♦ ♦ ♦

The Transportation & Ticket Center begins under a canopy that extends across our path. It shelters a host of ticket booths, where hordes of people now stand in line, waiting to purchase their park passes.

I pull four cards from my bag and show them to Mary and the children. "We can forget the lines," I say. "Follow me."

We pass under the canopy and enter an outdoor plaza. Music fills the air, and the tune that is playing seems destined to become the anthem for our vacation. It's the theme song from *Pinocchio:* "When You Wish Upon a Star."

Mary drops to one knee and takes hold of our children, instructing them to look forward.

Beyond the plaza, and across the Seven Seas Lagoon, rise the towers of the Cinderella Castle on the horizon.

"That's where we're going," says Mary, "and we have two ways to get there: the boat or the train. Let's take a vote. Kids first."

MJ and Michael both want to ride the boat, so Mary and I make the decision unanimous. We head in the direction of the dock and bypass the crowded ramps that lead up to the monorail stations.

On our way to the boat launch, Mary points to several objects hidden in the plant beds. "Do you hear that melody?" she says. "Outdoor music is— . . . Oh, how rude of me."

Mary faces me and shakes my hand. "Hello," she says. "My name is Mary. I'll be your tour guide today as the kids allow. Welcome to this private exploration of the Disney Magic and my salute to Walt Disney. We've now entered the

north end of his property—the area that developed somewhat according to his plans. It's no accident that we can see
the castle from here; Walt knew how to put visual charm
into a scene. It sends us a long-distance invitation to come
for a visit, just like the Capitol building does back home. It
compels us to risk the unknowns and to make that fateful
journey . . . to embark on an adventure even sweeter and
more fulfilling, perhaps, than our actual arrival. This is the
Disney Magic all around us. I've done a little homework and
can tell you about it."

"I bet."

Our ferry appears between two islands in the center of the
lagoon, and before long, it is docked at our plaza.

"Do you know what Disney calls its employees?" says Mary.

"No. Don't tell me. Associates? Representatives? Partners?
Customer-Care Specialists?"

Mary shakes her head at each answer. "And not *Operatives*
either. —That's what Pullman called them. Here in Disney
they're called *Cast Members.*"

"Of course," I say. "They're performers . . . and we're the
audience, right? Do they call us *Audience Members?*"

"Well," says Mary, "actually, we're the *guests.* But if it's any
consolation, each and every one of us is a *Very Individual Person,*
or *VIP* . . . well, unless of course you're a *real* VIP. Then the
designation is *PX,* where the P stands for *priority* and the X
stands for . . . well . . . *X.*"

The line reaches the boat, where a cast member gestures
us to board. Mary whispers as we pass him: "Did you see
his hand, Bert? He was using the Disney two-finger point.
He could have used the three-finger or the four-finger or the
open-palm point . . . but he didn't. Maybe he's a rookie. So
perhaps you've already guessed it," she says normally. "Disney
dictates the pointing techniques of its employees. Strictly

barred is the single-finger point, considered rude in some cultures. We *could* pretend to be members of Disney's *Fox Squad* and try to catch an unwary cast member in a breach of protocol. Pullman had such spies too, calling them *Spotters*."

Mary goes on to explain that cast members follow many rules, and that some of these rules involve their appearance. For instance, cast members cannot have visible tattoos or dye their hair unnatural colors. They can't outfit themselves in sunglasses that hide their eyes, and they can't wear more than one ring on a hand. Females, specifically, are expected to have "natural-length" manicured nails and are limited to one set of non-hoop-type, non-dangly earrings. Their male counterparts are prohibited from having earrings altogether, and their hair cannot be long. For most of the park's history, even male facial hair was not permitted. However, due to a labor shortage in the year 2000, Disney relaxed this long-standing policy and allowed male cast members to have neatly-trimmed mustaches, as long as they were grown while on vacation.

We follow the kids to the boat's upper deck and find a position along the port-side railing.

Mary executes an open-palm point to the west side of the boat. "On that shoreline beside the launch is one of Disney World's original resorts: the Polynesian. It opened in 1971 at the same time as the park, and like so many other places on the grounds, it features outdoor speakers. However, Disney took this design element one step further here, installing speakers into the walls of its swimming pools so that bathers could listen while under water.

"And note the tall building at the center of the complex," she says, "—the one with the crisscrossing rafters. That's the Great Ceremonial House. Please commit it to memory, Bert, for later reference. And, as you can see, the resort has a multitude of longhouses, each one paying tribute to a Pacific island in the South Seas. They're named Pago Pago, Maori— . . . Oh wait. Sorry. Those are the former *ficti- tious* names. Remember Dixie Landings? The Polynesian is another Disney resort that's been 'politically corrected.' In 1999, the buildings were renamed to better reflect a map of Polynesia. Samoa became Tuvalu, Hawaii became Samoa, Tonga became Hawaii, et cetera."

"No way," I say.

"Believe it. What a nightmare for Guest Services."

Mary taps on the children's shoulders. "Now, listen up," she says. "The beaches over there used to have wave machines. Just imagine it, you could have played in a roll- ing surf there. But guess what. It turns out that man-made waves are just as effective at eroding a beach as real ones are. Disney had to scrap the machines. . . . But take heart; the beaches were doomed anyway. Why do you suppose there's no one swimming over there? It's because swimming isn't allowed in Disney's lakes anymore, though I'm not sure why."

As our ferry reaches the lagoon's two central islands, we notice an unusual watercraft anchored nearby. The craft is staffed by three men, all of whom are wearing safari gear and trying to capture a very large alligator.

"Are they cast members too?" I say.

"All but the alligator," says Mary. "Is anyone ready to guess why the beaches are closed?"

When our ferry clears the islands, Mary performs a flaw- less three-finger point off the starboard bow toward a giant concrete building. "That behemoth is Disney World's other original resort: the Contemporary. Its futuristic theme fea- tures an eleven-story atrium, with two monorail tracks that pass through the center. Its architecture is *retro-tomorrow*—"

"Like the 700 Block of State Street," I say.

"That's right. It's the *Jetsons* meet the *Flintstones* . . . as seen through the eyes of *Mr. Magoo*. And note the waterway running beside it. It's actually a water 'bridge' connecting Bay Lake with the Seven Seas Lagoon. Hats off to Mr. Disney for solving so many problems at once, and without compromise to aesthetics."

As our boat approaches the dock for the Magic Kingdom, Mary teases the children about choosing the ferry instead of the train. "The lagoon is quite shallow," she says. "Boats can, and do, get stuck out here. We could have been stranded for hours."

"Leave the safety of the monorails for the less daring," I say. "You kids have guts."

MJ and Michael peer over the side of the boat, trying to see the bottom through the murky water.

We file off the boat and are once again immersed in the music of an outdoor sound system. Music is clearly an ingredient of the Disney Magic. I have my first clue of the day.

We're moving along with a crowd that joins two others: one from the bus terminals and the other from the monorail platforms. We all converge on a waterfront plaza that sweeps gently upward toward the gates of the Magic Kingdom. And directly behind those gates is a three-story building across the park's entrance, effectively blocking our view inside. We make our way through security and the turnstiles, then approach this architectural barrier.

Mary draws my attention to some framed posters lining the wall of this building. "What do those pictures remind you of?" she says.

"A box office," I answer.

"Correct. The Magic Kingdom is a theater; do you smell the popcorn? We're about to enter the lobby."

The *lobby* is a series of vaulted hallways that offer strollers and lockers for rent, as well as concessions. Mary veers us into the center aisle of the hallways.

"It's almost show time," she says. "Watch the forward archway as we approach it: it will appear to lift like a curtain, revealing Disney's lovely first scene."

CHAPTER 16

The Stroll Up Main Street

The "show" of the Magic Kingdom begins in a quaint downtown square, where a street leads away from it to the Cinderella Castle. The castle itself is the show's main feature, and although it stands nineteen stories tall, its designers employed a Hollywood trick to make it appear much taller. The secret to the illusion involves the proper sizing of the castle and also of the buildings that approach it. First-story façades along the street are scaled down to ninety percent, while each successive story shrinks by about an eighth. Such reducing, when applied to the castle, brings the tower-tops to about half scale. Every brick, every window, every balcony, and every decoration is scaled down accordingly. This alteration exaggerates the effects of perspective, causing the castle to soar.

Mary notes that some Disney enthusiasts falsely overstate the company's use of this *forced perspective*. They suggest that Main Street not only shrinks with height, but that its roadway actually narrows toward the castle to make the fortress seem farther away and thus larger. Not true, says Mary. Main Street is the same width all the way along.

"And no expense has been spared to keep this 'city' beautiful," says Mary. "The Public Works crew is divided into specialties, with one group doing nothing but changing light bulbs."

"You're kidding," I say. "Taxes must be high here."

"The highest."

We loop the square and turn up Main Street, joining the migration of happy taxpayers.

We stop for a street performance of the barbershop quartet called the Dapper Dans, then Mary points with an open hand toward the rooftops. "Each peak has an American flag on it," she says, "because every day is Independence Day here on Main Street USA. But how do you suppose Disney raises and lowers all of those hard-to-reach flags each day, in accordance with proper flag etiquette? The answer is, they don't. Each flag is a forgery of misplaced stars and stripes, allowing Disney to sidestep the rules."

"A Disney poetic truth," I say.

"And appropriately so," adds Mary. "After all, it's a cartoon world. See the credits rolling by while we walk?"

The second-story windows of Main Street are stenciled with the names of Disney designers and executives who helped to create the park. Walt's name appears twice: once for the studio bearing his name, and once for his role as the director. His mentions appear on the two venues he loved most: the train station and the ice cream parlor—both enjoying the honorary distinction of facing the castle. Walt's brother Roy, the financial mind of the business, faces the other way in the Town Square.

"But keep looking up," says Mary. "What color is the street?"

I answer *dark gray*, assuming it's made of asphalt.

"Right," says Mary. "Now what color is the sidewalk?"

"Hmm," I say. "Sidewalks are usually concrete, so I'll say white."

"Wrong. Not even close. Take a look."

To my astonishment, the smooth surface beneath my feet

is a pale brick red. Mary explains that Disney and Kodak carefully selected this color to make people and objects stand out in pictures.

Halfway up the street, there's a crossroad that forms an intersection, though the crossroad itself comes to an immediate dead end in both directions. MJ and Michael stop us there to watch a horse-drawn trolley go by.

"Check out that corner window up there," says Mary.

Printed on the glass overhead are some names I recognize from Mary's book. They belong to the dummy corporations Disney used to acquire the Florida property. They are listed as subsidiaries of a business called *M.T. Lott Real Estate.*

The children now tug on our arms, wanting us to move toward a fragrance of chocolate chip cookies that is wafting our way. An upcoming bakery must be venting its ovens to the street.

"That aroma comes in a can," whispers Mary. "—Another Disney poetic truth."

"Who cares?" I say. "Let's pick up a canister *to go.*"

At the top of Main Street, Mary instructs me to look back across the storefronts we've just passed. "It's just a strip mall with a fancy veneer," she says. "Walt was an early adopter of a new trend, and some say he *set* the trend. Don't let anyone tell you that the street-scape doesn't matter."

Main Street ends at the Central Plaza, where sidewalks radiate into the themed lands around it. It is centered by a bronze sculpture of Walt Disney holding the hand of Mickey Mouse.

"If the sidewalks are like the spokes of a wheel," says Mary, "then the Partners Statue is the cap on the axle."

"Does the statue talk?" I say.

"Don't they all?"

The kids pull us past the sculpture toward the handsome

landmark we've traveled so far to see: the Cinderella Castle. I look at Mary for her commentary, but it is not forthcoming. Instead, she stands quietly, staring at the castle, and I sense she's becoming emotional again.

"Oh, Bert," she says at last, "I'm ruining this for you."

"No-no," I say. "Really, you're not. The tour's great. I want the whole thing."

But Mary looks unconvinced.

"Well," she says, "it's *me*, then. Do you mind taking a rain check?"

"Actually, I do," I reply. "—Can you believe it? Please tell me something about the castle, even if just a little."

Mary smiles and arranges her fingers to form an "I love you" in sign language. She then aims her hand at the castle for a mixed-finger point and gives me the highlights.

The Cinderella Castle is a sculpture of concrete, steel, plaster, plastic, and fiberglass that borrows its look from eight centuries of European architecture. It's essentially a medieval fortress piled high with Gothic and Renaissance features, patterned after the palace from the film of its namesake: *Cinderella*. Even the castle clock remains faithful to the film, adopting the use of the alternate Roman numeral four—IIII instead of IV.

We enter the hallway, which runs through the center of the castle, and Michael points up, asking if we can go inside.

I give him the bad news—the same news my parents gave me—that there's no way to go exploring within the castle. There's only a restaurant inside, and it requires a reservation.

"But, hey," says Mary, "we have an appointment to keep with Mickey Mouse. Which way to Toontown?"

The kids have no idea which way to go; they didn't study the map, and they have no intention of doing so now. They lead us in exactly the wrong direction—toward Adventureland.

CHAPTER 17

The Spin Around the Park

Near the bridge to Adventureland, Mary stops us for a photograph. She finds the perfect place for us to stand . . . under a sign.

As we resume walking, Mary explains that each themed region of the Magic Kingdom is separated by landscaping or buildings, with the most notable separation being the castle across the entrance to Fantasyland. "But themes have a way of jumping," she says. "The Great Ceremonial House of the Polynesian Resort is supposedly visible from somewhere in Adventureland, mirroring the South Seas theme across the lagoon."

But we find no sight lines through the vegetation on our left, and even our climb to the top of the *Swiss Family Treehouse* produces no view of the Polynesian.

We continue through Adventureland and come to a small plaza, where a conventional amusement park ride spins at the center. It's called the *Magic Carpets of Aladdin,* and it features robotic camels that spit water at guests. MJ and Michael take a ride on it, hoping to get wet in this semi-reenactment of their skit from Aunt Poppi's story.

"Hey," I say to Mary, "since when is Arabia in the South Seas? I'm sensing a theming violation."

"Very perceptive," says Mary. "Adventureland's theme is actually *Exotic*. —You know, anything non-European."

The four of us move past a popular attraction, known as the *Jungle Cruise,* and the kids don't even notice its entrance. It's just as well; I remember this safari-type boat ride as rather slow, especially for children.

The next two rides, the *Pirates of the Caribbean* and the *Enchanted Tiki Room,* are equally well-disguised and elude the children's detection.

Before long, we're out of Adventureland and into Frontierland, where the background music has switched from bongo drums to the raucous fiddles of a hoedown. Once again, the details of our surroundings have changed to match a new theme.

"Welcome to the American Old West," says Mary, "Disney-style."

According to Mary, Frontierland offers a glimpse into the profoundly noble history of the United States—where misdealings and massacres, and acts of prejudice, are refreshingly overlooked just this once. *Why not* celebrate the great white male?

MJ and Michael pause at a railing and watch passengers scream down *Splash Mountain* from within dark brown logs. We enter a cavernous hallway and join the queue.

Our line's progress is exceedingly slow, however, while an open aisle beside us has people moving easily by. We discover, to our disappointment, that we are the *standby* guests, and that those boarding without waiting are users of the *fast-pass* system.

A fast-pass is a ticket stamped with a return time that guests can acquire from a kiosk outside the entrance of a ride. The guests now moving past us approached *Splash Mountain* earlier this morning and have been enjoying other attractions rather than suffering this line.

When it's finally our turn to board, we occupy the center and back rows of a log, behind a pair of young women in the front.

"Keep your eyes open for Br'er Bear," says Mary, "—especially his hairy bear butt."

MJ and Michael giggle.

"Some people call this *Butt Mountain*," she adds.

Mary is not exaggerating. Br'er Bear's hairy bear butt confronts us at almost every turn.

When at last our log reaches the top of Chickapin Hill, MJ and Michael raise their hands over their heads and scream during the plunge. The two female passengers ahead of us do the same, but with a slight variation: instead of just raising their hands, they raise their shirts as well.

Upon our exit from the ride, we encounter a series of television monitors that display the photographs taken during the great drop. One screen, however, is pictureless and carries a message: *Sorry, your picture has been washed away.*

The attendant on duty informs us that our photograph is not available for viewing or purchase because the riders in front of us violated Disney's *nipple policy*. "They're being escorted from the park as we speak," she says. "But lucky *you.* . . . *You* get to ride again without waiting."

We are ushered back to the boarding area and seated in the next available log. We joyfully rename the ride *Flash-&-Splash Fanny-Mountain*, then relish the fact that our second photo hasn't been washed away.

Returning park-side, the kids lead us to the nearby roller coaster, called *Big Thunder Mountain Railroad*, where I pick up four fast-passes stamped for noon.

A loud steam whistle draws us to an adjacent railing, and we discover we're on an overlook for a waterway, where a paddle-wheeled boat is coming toward us.

"Rivers of America is the barrier between Frontierland and Liberty Square," says Mary.

The three decks of the Liberty Belle riverboat are laden with passengers, and we wave to them before taking the path toward Liberty Square.

Mary stops us along our way at a small stretch of wooden planking that crosses our route. "I bet you can't guess what runs beneath this bridge," she says. "—It marks the divide between East and West. Give up? It's the Little Mississippi River. Goodbye Frontierland. Hello Liberty Square."

A fife and drum corps performs under a large tree, and the flowers all around us are red, white, and blue. We stay along the riverbank and swing left toward the *Haunted Mansion,* which Mary characterizes as a spooky old manor-house on the Hudson River.

"Legend has it," she whispers, "that a young bride was murdered there . . . thrown from an attic window by her insane husband . . . who hung himself, of course."

"Of course."

"Nine hundred and ninety-nine ghosts haunt the place," she continues, "meaning there's room for one more."

I raise my eyebrows and curl an imaginary mustache. "Young bride, you say? Thrown from a window? . . . Will you marry me?"

"Too late for *that,*" says Mary. And her casual response seems like a good indication that she's not suspicious about tonight, when *she'll* be the new bride in town.

We move past the *Haunted Mansion* and climb a steep walkway, which passes beneath the second floor of a building.

"Welcome to Fantasyland," says Mary, "where details reign

supreme. This breezeway is the cross-dissolve between scenes, taking us from *colonial America* to *storybook Europe*."

The kids' faces brighten as we enter this new land.

Mary explains to me that this region is a village within the fortress walls of the castle, where hints of the walls are visible over the rooftops.

It's funny; I've been to Disney World two other times in my life, and I've never before noticed these upper walls. Or *have* I? Maybe my peripheral vision saw them and worked them into my experience. Perhaps such details, like music and the smell of popcorn, play a subconscious role in generating good feelings. This seems like another clue to the Disney Magic.

According to Mary, Fantasyland's architecture ranges in style from Gothic to Alpine to English Tudor, and its colorful canopies lend the area an atmosphere of *medieval tournament* and *Renaissance fair*. Traditional carnival rides provide the all-important *kinetics*, and by far the greatest relic of Disney World is centered behind the castle—*Cinderella's Golden Carrousel*. It's an heirloom from the heyday of amusement parks, serving two tours of duty before falling into disrepair and being rescued by Disney. It dates back to 1917 and was originally nicknamed the *Spinning Lady*.

MJ and Michael are enthusiastic about the "kinetic" attractions. They vow to ride *Dumbo the Flying Elephant* first thing after we see Mickey Mouse, when they're hoping the line will be shorter.

We pass the twirling teacups of the *Madhatter's Tea Party* and at last come to the shady pathway that leads into Toontown. We pause alongside a nearby railing and watch young drivers on *Indy Speedway* finish their races and line up for the pits. MJ and Michael now decide that *this* will be their first stop after visiting Mickey.

We resume our walk into Toontown, and I notice that

Michael has been engaging in a curious behavior. He has been occasionally looking over his shoulder, and I can only guess it has been for glimpses of the castle; I've been doing it too. It's as if we're both back in Madison trying to catch sightings of the Capitol building. Is this another clue to the Disney Magic? Why do these two buildings attract our attention?

Toontown was originally called Mickey's Birthdayland. It was built in 1988 as a one-year attraction to celebrate Mickey's 60th birthday, but its popularity convinced Disney to revamp it and make it permanent. It's now the official home of Mickey and Minnie, who reside in separate houses, of course.

We pass Minnie's house and Goofy's roller coaster, where MJ and Michael make it their latest vow to ride the roller coaster first thing after seeing Mickey.

We enter Mickey's house and join the line that crosses his backyard and which flows into a circus tent, where the greetings take place. Once inside, the line weaves back and forth in front of a movie screen that shows early Mickey Mouse cartoons in black and white. I hear no complaints from the children.

When our turn arrives to see Mickey, we are directed into a reception room, where the famous mouse and a photographer stand waiting for us. I give the kids the drawings they made for Mickey on the airplane, and they make their deliveries.

Mickey pantomimes his jubilation over each piece of artwork, then summons us all together for a group picture. Before we know it, the four of us are standing alone behind the tent.

As we follow the sidewalk around, I sneak an envelope from my bag. "Look what Mickey gave me," I say.

MJ and Michael whip around, but they quickly lose interest when they discover I'm holding a mere envelope. They hurry on toward *Goofy's Barnstormer.*

Once we've entered *Goofy's* line, I open the envelope and pull out a stack of activity cards I made. The top one contains a note from Mickey Mouse, and I read it aloud.

> Hi guys,
>   Welcome to my home. I'm so glad you're here. Please have fun . . . and never forget that every step is an ADVENTURE.
> >   —Love, Mickey
> Oh, the cards? . . . Just do the activities and show them to your hotel clerk before you leave.

The kids scan the cards, then hand them back to me. They have no interest in doing word searches and playing "I Spy" when there's so much else to see and do around them. I return the cards to my bag, feeling the small bite of my failed attempt at some magic.

The loading platform for *Goofy's Barnstormer* is a full story above the walkways of Toontown, and it is from this elevated perch that I hear the faint cry of a train whistle. Soon, a locomotive is chugging into the Toontown Station below, where it stops to let off its passengers. But none of the people arriving finds anyone to greet them there. They all just drift off into the walkways.

"That's such a sad sight," I say, voicing my romantic notion that all of life's journeys should end in the arms of a loved one.

"Yeah," says Mary. "It really was nice of your parents to be there for us at the airport."

♦ ♦ ♦

We exit Toontown by the same route we came in—along the fence beside *Indy Speedway.*

"Are you ready?" says Mary. "—Because *Tomorrow* is just around the corner. And you're about to see why Walt Disney was the master of theming."

As we enter Tomorrowland, the futuristic Contemporary hotel looms large on the horizon outside the park. It is a theme that has successfully made the jump.

We join the line for *Indy Speedway,* where we meet a middle-aged couple who are always on the lookout for Hidden Mickeys. I ask them to explain the term.

"A Hidden Mickey is an outline of Mickey's head found somewhere unexpected," says the man. "The imagineers put them everywhere—"

"To *plus* our experience," says the woman.

"They owed their jobs to a mouse," he adds, "and Walt didn't want them to forget it."

Mary pulls out our camera and displays the photo she took earlier under the Kodak *Picture Spot* sign, where the kids and I have our heads held close together. "A *fleeting* Hidden Mickey," she says.

◆ ◆ ◆

The scalding-hot engines and sun-baked pavement of *Indy Speedway* render us pining for some respite in the shade. We find it under the canopy of the *Tomorrowland Transit Authority,* where an outdoor escalator carries us up to a revolving platform that is bordered by empty vehicles.

"There's no waiting for a Wedway PeopleMover," says Mary. "This is a scaled-down version of Walt's transportation system for Epcot."

Our gondola-shaped car exits the turnstile and picks up speed along the track. It carries us through a darkened building, where we pass an illuminated model of Walt's dream city. We're then returned into the daylight and again plunged into darkness. This time, we're given a glimpse inside of *Space*

Mountain—Disney's dark indoor roller coaster. To our surprise, however, the lights have come on, and we are gazing upon an eerie tangle of steel framework and suspended cars. I can't help but imagine the sorts of debris that must be scattered across the floor down there.

"Is that a wig?" I say.

"Where?" says MJ.

"My teeth!" says Mary.

MJ gets the joke and grabs the waistband of her shorts. "My pants!" she says.

"My butt!" says Michael.

Upon our exit from the *Transit Authority,* we travel to the counter-service restaurant, known as *Cosmic Ray's,* and pick up a rotisserie chicken along with some soft drinks and sides. We carry them to the Central Plaza, where a performance is about to begin on the castle's forecourt stage. We find a place to sit on the lawn and enjoy our picnic and a show.

CHAPTER 18

The Cinderella Castle

The noontime stage production is a classic tale of good and evil, where *good* is in the hands of a beautiful princess, and where *evil* is in the hands of a sorceress queen. What more does a story need? Well, it needs Minnie Mouse to get frightened; it needs Mickey Mouse to be courageous; it needs Pluto to be loyal; and it needs Goofy to make mistakes. And there's one more member of the cast, though he's hardly worth mentioning. The handsome prince appears just briefly for the finale, and he says not a word. He simply stands there like a statue.

MJ and Michael are spellbound by the performance, and so too, it seems, is Mary. Upon its conclusion, Mary turns to me with starry eyes. "Oh, Bert, how I love happy endings."

I smile and nod, but I have no idea why she's saying this. Since when has Mary ever cared about a happy ending? The only romance novel she's ever read, as far as I know, was published in 1894 and had the Chicago World's Fair as its setting. It was simply more research for Poppi's story.

"Did you notice the prince?" I say. "He just stood there, posing like a trophy."

"Take the hint," says Mary.

The four of us set a course for Fantasyland, intent on finding a drinking fountain before heading to the *Dumbo* ride. The fastest route there is through the central corridor of the castle, but due to the stage show, the entrance ramps are currently closed. I direct us to the right for an alternate way around.

Mary points with an elbow toward the castle stage. "The lights and speakers are clearly visible," she says, "but where are the technicians who control them?"

I look around, expecting to see cables on the ground that will give away their position, but I don't find any.

"Give up?" says Mary. "They're hidden on top of the concession stands."

Michael then points into the air at a wire stretched far overhead. "Is that where the electricity runs?" he says.

He is pointing at the cable that carries Tinker Bell on her nighttime flight from the tallest castle tower to a rooftop in Tomorrowland for the kickoff of the fireworks show. Mary and I saw the stunt performed on our honeymoon, though I hope Mary doesn't spoil the surprise for Michael.

"That's a good question," says Mary. "I don't know."

I lead the family across a bridge and onto a narrow path that climbs toward the castle. Connecting to this path is the small alcove that will serve as tonight's site for my wedding service with Mary.

"Donald!" shouts MJ.

MJ and Michael race ahead and dart into the alcove, where they peer down through the railing at the bridge we just crossed. There, the costumed character of Donald Duck has just arrived, and a long line of guests has already formed to greet him.

"Remember the cloud?" says MJ. "It's just like we saw."

"And we're above him and everything," says Michael.

It amuses me that they've conveniently forgotten that they were only supposed to see his head.

While MJ and Michael revel in their sighting, I step over to the adjacent railing and take in my favorite view of the park.

This alcove sits on a sleepy knoll beside the castle moat, where water stretches through an open glen of grass and trees, and where birds glide easily across walls that climb from earth to sky. It's the perfect setting for tonight's ceremony. Uncle Albert will stand where I am now, with his back to the railing, and Mary and I will face him from within a chapel of flowers. Two castle guards will cross halberds at the alcove's entrance to keep our service private.

Giggles from the children turn my head, and I see them tossing potato chips down to the birds. Before I can react and stop them, however, a cast member kneels behind them and touches them on the shoulders.

They wheel around and meet this new acquaintance.

"Do you want to try for a magic coin?" she says. "If you're brave, truthful, and unselfish, one will appear for you."

I'm familiar with these words—*brave, truthful,* and *unselfish.* They come from the film *Pinocchio.*

Pinocchio was a wooden puppet in the home of a kindly woodcarver named Geppetto, who wished that his puppet could be a real boy. One night, while Geppetto slept, a fairy came down from the stars and brought Pinocchio to life. She promised to make him a real boy if he could prove himself brave, truthful, and unselfish. Yet, even with the help of Jiminy Cricket as his conscience, Pinocchio struggled to demonstrate the virtues demanded by the fairy. His problem was not a lack of integrity, however: Pinocchio's intentions were innocently pure. Rather, his problem was a lack of ability. Pinocchio could not detect the lies and deceptions of the scoundrels he befriended. Honest John Foulfellow lured Pinocchio from his route to school by promising him "the easy road to success" as an actor. Honest John's true motive, however, was to sell Pinocchio—this magical marionette without strings—to Stromboli, the greedy puppeteer. Pinocchio was easily manipulated by Honest John's kind words and friendly gestures; he could not see the *literal* truth through John's veil of *poetic* truth. Consequently, Pinocchio found himself in a predicament he could not have anticipated: he found himself locked in a bird cage in Stromboli's wagon and headed out of town. When the fairy came down to rescue Pinocchio, she first asked him to explain the events that had led to his capture. But this request put Pinocchio in something of a bind. His conscience, Jiminy Cricket, advised him to state the facts. Yet stating the facts meant taking responsibility for the situation, and Pinocchio was not responsible; he couldn't be. To state the facts, then, would be somewhat of a lie. So, Pinocchio argued his innocence as best he could. He told the fairy that two monsters tied him in a sack and chopped him into firewood. Pinocchio's nose grew longer with each of his factual errors, prompting the fairy to explain, "You see, Pinocchio, a lie keeps growing and growing . . . until it's as plain as the nose on your face." It was Mary and I who concluded that the Blue Fairy was holding Pinocchio to a standard of truth he had not yet mastered. She was expecting this newly-alive puppet to be more skilled at telling the literal truth than our seven-year-old Michael. We thought it unfair that Pinocchio might be denied his boyhood based on a condition he couldn't satisfy. But the fairy ultimately recognized the truth of Pinocchio's innocence. She freed him from Stromboli's bird cage and granted him another chance to prove himself.

I return my attention to the children and wonder what standard of truth their new friend will use for deciding whether they deserve magic coins. I suspect their status as fully-paid guests will be enough.

The cast member places her hands above the children's heads and recites a short rhyme. She then brings down her fists and uncurls them, revealing a copper coin in each palm.

"Congratulations," she says. "Your parents must be very proud." She stands as if to go. "But just one more thing. The magic of the coins wears off when you feed the birds."

We exit the alcove and resume our walk up the path, which brings us to the rear courtyard of the castle. A short distance away, the calliope of *Cinderella's Golden Carrousel* whistles with *Hi Diddle Dee Dee,* and we find four drinking fountains to our left, perched on a wall at the base of a statue. We line up there and wait for our turns to drink.

"Look," says MJ, pointing at the statue, "the crown goes on her head."

The statue behind the fountains is of Cinderella in her work clothes, and painted on the wall behind her is a crown that hovers over her head . . . at least, it hovers if you're *my* height. But at MJ's height, the crown nestles onto Cinderella's head.

"From rags to riches," I say. And I yank MJ's bandanna from her pocket and wear it like a crown.

MJ steals it away from me and soaks it in the fountain, then returns it to my head, where the cool water runs down my face and neck. "Ahhh," I say. "It's good to be king."

MJ takes back the crown and recharges it, then she and Michael switch off drenching themselves. I use this short recess to study the back of the castle.

The first story is a solid wall, except for the passageway cut through the center, and the second story is spanned by columns and leaded glass, giving it the look of a gothic cathedral. There's also a balcony wrapping this upper story, which ends at a turret, where a stairway performs a switchback down the castle's rear wall. At the base of the stairs hangs a chain with a sign, declaring it an emergency exit for the restaurant.

"We'll be eating at Cinderella's Royal Table tonight," says Mary. "But the restaurant hasn't always been called that. It used to be King Stefan's Banquet Hall. Do you see the problem there?"

I shrug.

"King Stefan was Aurora's father in the story of *Sleeping Beauty*. But *this* is the Cinderella Castle. It only took Disney twenty-six years to make the correction."

"It's expensive to print new napkins," I say.

Mary then explains that the castle has become home to some persistent myths. For instance, there's the notion that the interior of the castle, most of which is off limits to guests, holds a water tower to deliver pressure to the park. Not so. And some authors claim that the pinnacle of the largest castle tower can be unscrewed like a bottle top for removal ahead of severe storms. Again, not true. But the granddaddy of the castle's lore—the urban legend truly worthy of the Disney name—involves Uncle Walt himself. It goes like this. Buried deep within the castle, in a secret chamber, lies the dead body of Walt Disney, frozen in liquid nitrogen, awaiting the day that technology can revive him and restore his good health.

I then raise my hand with a question. "What's this stripe beneath our feet?" I say.

Mary looks thoughtfully at the pavement, noting the swath that leads away from the castle stairs. It is slightly smoother and shinier than the other surfaces around us.

"Hmm," says Mary. "I don't remember reading about this."

We complete our water break and form a family huddle. I pull out the four fast-passes and share the bad news that they've expired. I then suggest to Mary that she and the children go over to the *Dumbo* ride while I make a quick confirmation of tonight's dinner reservation.

We part company, and I approach the castle hallway, where a receptionist stands ready to serve me from behind a counter outside the restaurant's entrance. "Hello, My Lord," she says. "How may I help you today?"

"I'm here to check on a reservation. Alfred's the name."

The cast member spends a few moments at her computer. "I'm sorry, sir," she says. "I don't see a dinner reservation for you. But there *is* a note from Merryweather that says you have some papers to sign."

"What?" I glance over my shoulder to make sure Mary's not around. "You're kidding, right? I completed the paperwork months ago. There must be a mistake."

"Just a minute, please," she says. And she makes a phone call.

She hangs up and apologizes for the confusion. Then she tells me to step through the doors and meet Merryweather in the restaurant's lobby.

I don't have time for this; Mary will get suspicious if I'm gone for too long. But what's my alternative? I don't want to risk my plans falling through, even if it means spoiling Mary's surprise. I do as I'm told and march through the doors.

The restaurant's lobby is a windowless two-story room, completely removed from the dining room. Its walls are bordered by upholstered benches and dark wooden panels, and Cinderella's throne resides at the near end. The far wall has a built-in spiral staircase, and there are about a dozen people sharing the room with me.

A female cast member descends the stairs and reads from a notecard in her hands. "Whitbourne-Allen," she says. And she leads a party of six up the stairs.

A pit forms in my stomach. I must have missed some detail

in my planning. How appropriate, since details are the things I get wrong. If only I had pressed a little harder to reach Merryweather on the phone these past few days, I might have averted all this.

The center column of the staircase, it turns out, is an elevator shaft. Its small wooden door slides open, and out steps a middle-aged woman. She is dressed differently than the other cast members of the restaurant.

"Mr. Alfred?" she says. She's not reading from a card.

"That's me," I say.

"It's so nice to finally meet you, Bert." She shakes my hand. "I'm Merryweather. Sorry for the miscommunication. Please follow me and I'll explain everything."

Merryweather ushers me into the elevator and pushes a button. The door closes, and we begin to rise.

"The note on the computer was an old one," she says. "I forgot to delete it. —You have no papers to sign. . . . And your dinner reservation is a special one, so it doesn't appear on our computers. Please rest assured; everything's in order for your perfect evening."

"So where are you taking me?" I say. "Mary will be wondering about me."

"Oh, this won't take long," she says. "Since I've got you here, I thought I'd run an idea past you—a *plussing* of your plans . . . compliments of Disney."

The elevator stops, and we emerge into the restaurant's dining room, where Merryweather hustles me along the back wall.

"Which table is ours?" I say.

But she turns through a doorway, and I follow her.

We enter a staging area for the restaurant, where the smell of grilled steak and steamed vegetables fills my nostrils.

Another elevator stands open, and we take it to a lower

floor, this time passing through a full kitchen to reach a concrete hallway. Merryweather then brings me to a room filled with costumes and holds up a heavy white robe for me.

"Would you like your uncle to wear this?" she says. She then sets down the robe and lifts up its accompanying head-piece and scepter. "He could be your royal cleric for the coronation. How about it?"

"Thanks, but no thanks," I say. "I'm trying to keep things simple. The castle guards are more than enough costuming."

"Very well," she says. "Let's get you back."

We return to the hallway, and Merryweather takes a phone call.

"Well?" she says into the handset. There's a long pause. "Great! I'll ask."

She turns to me. "Where can we find Mary and the kids?"

"The *Dumbo* ride," I say.

"Dumbo," she says into the phone. "Get 'em on, then get 'em to City Hall. I'll meet you at Stairway 19."

Merryweather ends her call and takes a deep breath. "Everything's set," she says. "Just tell Mary we lost your reservation and took you to our offices to get it back. You'll be a hero in more than *that*."

"Huh?"

"Disney's making this up to you, Bert. And you'll see what I mean in about half an hour. . . . By the way, do you have any idea where you're standing right now?"

CHAPTER 19

The Unexpected Tour

According to Merryweather, this concrete hallway is the utility corridor that runs beneath the Magic Kingdom. It's a nine-acre backstage that ensures the quality of "guest experience" up above. Not only does it handle garbage collection and store deliveries, but it also prevents violations of Disney theming. "No one wants to see a silver-clad cast member from Tomorrowland going home along historic Main Street. Cast members are required to come and go discreetly from this lower level, which exits at the back of the park."

The hallway is well lit and spotlessly clean. Lockers line one wall, and the ceiling carries conduits of every size and type. Traffic is light, consisting mostly of cast members on foot—some with pushcarts—and there's an occasional electric vehicle. I wonder when Mary was going to tell me about *this* place.

"It's called *Utilidors*," says Merryweather, "and it's the reason we're in no hurry to get to City Hall. Mary and your children will be contending with the crowd on Main Street, but you and I are just minutes away. Shall I give you a tour?"

Merryweather explains that Utilidors is referred to as the first floor of the park. Guests walk outside on the second floor, except for in Fantasyland, where they are actually on the third floor. The only region not served by the corridors is Mickey's Toontown Fair, which was added to the park later.

This mile-and-a-half of hallways connects to kitchens, wardrobes, dressing rooms, storage rooms, computer command centers, and a cafeteria. There's even a payroll office. And the passages are color-coded to help cast members find their way around to the numerous stairways and elevators that lead to restaurants, shops, and attractions. "If you ever see an unmarked door up there, it probably comes down here."

Our conversation is interrupted by a noise developing on the ceiling. One of the pipes has begun to rattle, sounding like an ice machine dispensing its cubes. When the clatter eventually subsides, Merryweather informs me that the park's garbage is shuttled at high speed through vacuum tubes to a processing station behind Frontierland's famous water ride. "When the wind is just right," she says, "you can smell it from *Trash Mountain*."

Merryweather and I move easily through the central corridor, dipping beneath the castle's moat and cruising under Main Street. There's a pushcart up ahead, and the sight of it halts me in my tracks when I realize what it's carrying.

The head of a Donald Duck costume is riding on it, and the neatly folded suit for his body is tucked right behind. This is exactly the vision I had from the airplane. I can't wait to tell Mary and the children about it.

"Kids under sixteen aren't allowed down here," says Merryweather. She must be reading my mind. "And this is why. A sight like this could easily spoil the magic for them."

We enter Stairway 19, and I ask her a question: "Is Mickey allowed to talk?" I say. "We met him this morning, but he didn't say anything to us."

"Right," says Merryweather. "*Headed* characters aren't supposed to speak, though some of them can make laughing and kissing sounds. They're also not supposed to walk backward, because they're half blind in those costumes. If the head pops off, *boing*, you're fired."

At the top of the stairway, there's a cast member waiting for us. His name is Oliver, and he carries a plastic bag filled with Mickey baseball caps. He is drenched in sweat.

"Is this the lucky fella?" he says.

"Yup," says Merryweather. "But why all the hats? You only need four."

Oliver laughs. "Fifteen, you mean."

Merryweather shakes her head. "I'm gonna catch hell for *this* one. Oh, well. Never a dull moment here in Disney."

She turns to me and shakes my hand. "It's been a pleasure meeting you, Bert. Oliver will take you the rest of the way. Have a magical day."

CHAPTER 20

The Three O'clock Parade

Oliver opens a steel door, and my eyes have to adjust to the bright sunlight. I step outside and am blasted by hot air, reminding me that I've been in air conditioning for the past forty-five minutes. My skin is instantly clammy-wet.

"This is the backstage area of Main Street," says Oliver. "The parade lines up behind City Hall. And you're in it!"

Awooga! Awooooga! An open-air motorcar rolls into view from behind a building, and it is overflowing with the members of my family. Dad and Tom stand on the running board beside the driver, and Ferguson is their counterweight on the opposite side. The rest of the family is piled into the seats like puppies.

Awooga! Awoooga! Dad plays with the horn over the driver's shoulder, as the car slows to a stop.

"Just look at the trash Mary picked up on Main Street," says Dad, and he jumps down. "I see you didn't waste a minute, Bert. We just get here, and you've already got the magic on tap."

Ferguson hops down, and the whole car recoils, tossing its contents like a salad. He opens the passenger door and helps Mom and Uncle Albert from the front seat.

"Thank Disney," I say. "They're the ones who screwed up."

"You got that right," says Oliver. "But no time to explain. You guys have a parade to catch."

"Lemme out," says Angelica.

My eleven-year-old niece noses her way through the other children and pounces to the ground like a Rat Terrier. Her behavior goes unscolded by her parents, Jane and Tom.

"Comin' through," says MJ, and she tries to follow her alpha dog.

"Not so fast," says Mary, who grabs MJ's arm. "Mind your manners."

Nellie and Michael are now clogging the doorway, attempting to coordinate a piggyback ride that we don't have time for. MJ gets impatient and climbs out over the side of the car.

To expedite matters, Elsa puts Michael on Nellie's back and helps them to the ground.

The last of the young pups to exit the car are the twin pugs, Dorsey and Sanders. Ferguson reaches in and lifts each boy out by the nape of the shirt. He then hands one off to Dad.

As Elsa and Mary step from the car, Jane remains behind as its sole passenger. She stretches out in the rear seat, looking like a warm-weather Cruella De Vil, in her tuxedo-white tank top and candy-apple red shorts. The only thing missing is her long cigarette.

"Take her away," says Dad, and he gestures to the driver.

"And miss this parade?" says Jane, standing up. "Not on your life." She struts to the open doorway and lowers her long legs to the ground. Each of her ten toes has at least one silver ring on it.

"Follow me," says Oliver, and he hands out the baseball caps while we walk. He then reaches out to Uncle Albert. "Would you like to be a Grand Marshal?"

"Oh, me!" says Angelica. "Pick me!"

"You get to ride instead of walk," he says to Albert, ignoring the young girl who has her hand in his face. "And I can arrange rides for you, too," he informs my parents.

"No thanks," says Dad. "We're skipping the parade."

"Oh really?" says Elsa. "Who's *we*? Maybe Mom would like to speak for herself for a change."

"Yeah," says Jane. "What do *you* want, Mom?"

Mom smiles sweetly at Dad. "To be with your father for ever and always," she says.

"Okay, it's settled then," says Oliver, and he leads us past a building to where the pavement changes color, again matching the black roadways and red sidewalks of Main Street. A gate to our left stands partially open, revealing a sea of spectators waiting in Town Square. Ahead of us are the first entries in the parade—a four-seated buggy for the Grand Marshals, the Disney World marching band, and a horse drawn stagecoach.

Oliver hails to a cast member beside the gate. "Take these two into the square."

"Make it three!" says Mary, and she steps away from our pack to join Mom and Dad.

"No, no," says Dad, "you're *in* the parade."

"So why aren't *you*?" she replies.

Oliver hurries Albert to the blue buggy and places him in the front seat beside the driver.

"I'm doing the filming," says Dad.

"You'll get a better view from in the parade," I say.

Jane laughs. "Don't you get it? He's afraid to be seen with stuffed animals. Heaven forbid if Winnie the Pooh should give him a hug. Admit it, Dad."

"I admit nothing," he says.

Oliver returns. "It's now or never, folks. Gate's opening."

Everyone—including Mary and my parents—rushes to keep up with Oliver, as he leads us alongside the participants of the parade.

A musical broadcast fills the Town Square behind us,

announcing the start of the parade. Albert's car rolls forward, and the drummers of the marching band begin their cadence.

The backstage road turns a corner, and the first entry along our path is a peculiar wheeled contraption pushed by two cast members. Its framework holds a banner with the name of the parade—*Share A Dream Come True*—and its front podium supports an actor portraying a young Walt Disney seated at his drawing table. There's no sign of Mortimer Mouse, however.

Beyond the bannered vehicle is the first float, appropriately titled *It Was All Started By A Mouse*. Mickey stands on top in a clear ball, and he places his hand over his mouth as we run by, as if to giggle at our tardiness.

Mickey's float is followed by five of the walking broomsticks from the Sorcerer's Apprentice, but I don't see any scrolls to consult with about superstitions and games of chance.

"Your with the Alice crew," says Oliver. "Break into family units and hold hands. No dancing with the characters unless invited."

The second float also features a clear ball on top, but this one has Pinocchio standing inside. On the lower platform in front of him are Geppetto and the Blue Fairy, while his ne'r-do-well influences—Honest John Foulfellow, Gideon, and two of the donkey boys—lead the way on the ground. The float is named *Wish Upon A Star*, and we, as fate would have it, are slated to follow.

The rear half of the Pinocchio float is built with a balcony and stairway facing backward. Snow White and two of her seven dwarves are stationed on the platform, with the remaining five dwarves walking behind. The *Alice in Wonderland* crew comes next, followed by the cast of *Winnie the Pooh*, with Pooh himself seated on the next float.

"Oh, there's Pooh," says Jane. "Go get your hug, Dad."

Dad mumbles something to Ferguson, and the two men laugh.

Oliver delivers us to Alice and the Mad Hatter, who introduce themselves to us.

"And where are you all from?" says Alice.

"Chicagoland," says Jane.

"*Well*," roars the Hatter, "could that be somewhere near Wonderland?"

Tweedledum and Tweedledee approach Elsa's family and pantomime their similar twinlyness to Dorsey and Sanders. The two characters then lock arms and dance away.

Dad is already filming as we enter the Town Square, and Mary squeezes my hand, giving me a nod toward Jane.

Jane is winking at the parade-watchers and mouthing secret messages to them. She then steers her family to the sidelines and shakes hands with people.

"She's the Queen of Hearts," says Mary.

"Yeah, but with an extreme makeover."

We loop through the Town Square and watch Pinocchio perform gestures inside his bubble. His movements are synchronized to a recording of his voice.

"Have you ever had strings on you?" he says. "Just like my friend Jiminy says, *Always let your conscience be your guide. . . .* Have you ever wished upon a star? . . ."

The parade is halted at the corner with Main Street, and the surrounding cast of characters move to the audience and invite guests to dance. Merryweather was right; the characters wearing headed costumes are careful not to move backward.

I see Angelica tug on Jane's arm, and I feel a similar tug on my own.

"Can I dance with Alice?" says MJ. And she steps forward as if I'm going to say yes.

I keep hold of her hand. "Remember what Oliver said? —We have to be asked. Isn't it great that we're in the parade?"

But MJ doesn't see things this way. We've already been given the parade. Now she wants more.

In a way, MJ is just like Pinocchio—a marionette without strings—and I'm her Jiminy Cricket, serving as the conscience that keeps her in line.

Angelica, unfortunately—as the daughter of the Queen of Hearts—has no such conscience to guide her. Jane releases Angelica's hand.

Angelica moves forward and horns her way into a dance between Tweedledum and a little girl. Tweedledum does his best to accommodate the added partner, and Angelica returns to her family's line without being reprimanded.

During a later stop at the Central Plaza, the *Alice* characters finally invite our families to dance. Dad avoids his own participation by working the camera, and Jane is overly energetic with the Mad Hatter, twirling rapidly under his arm.

We return to our ranks and move past the castle into Liberty Square, where the parade stops again to engage the audience in dancing.

This time, both Angelica and Jane hurry forward and intercept two of the dwarves before they've reached the sidelines. Angelica finds Dopey, and Jane finds Sleepy – or Sneezy, I can't tell them apart.

Jane is an accomplished ballroom dancer, yet she is failing to appreciate the clumsy footing of her cloth-padded partner. She moves too deftly and uses steps that are too complicated.

In the wink of an eye, one of her toe rings snags the soft

costume of her dwarf. She swings off balance, and I'm on the run immediately.

Jane clings to her partner rather than letting herself fall. But it's clear to me that she's going to fall anyway.

She blind-sides poor Dopey on her way down, chopping him at the knees and collapsing him onto Angelica, who exhales with a withering scream. But lucky for Dopey, his head doesn't hit the ground, though I'm fearing Jane's dwarf might not be so fortunate.

Jane is lying on her back with her arms extended, bracing herself for the full impact of the dwarf. She could easily push off his head.

I'm there just in time to sweep down Jane's arms and place a protective hand over the dwarf's head. He crushes down upon her, and the two of them emit disturbing groans. But his head remains in place.

Cast members descend on us quickly, untangling the dwarves from the maidens. There's laughter in the crowd, and I hear someone say, "I think he sneezed on her on the way down."

Jane and Angelica are fuming. They look upon the intervening cast members with hostility, and they grudgingly return to Tom. We are all instructed to hold our ranks until the end of the parade or be ejected.

At the far end of Frontierland, the road climbs into a woods—another backstage area. We're dismissed at this location and reunited with Uncle Albert.

Dad is grinning ear-to-ear and patting his video camera. "Got the whole thing on film," he says.

CHAPTER 21

The Change of Plans

It's nearly four o'clock when the final float of the parade rolls through Frontierland and the roadway becomes passable. Mary and I need to be returning to the hotel now to prepare for our evening out, and the rest of the family decides to join us to ready themselves for MGM.

Along Main Street, many of the dispersing parade-watchers are heading for the exit too. And an army of uniformed cast members swarm around us, cleaning up the litter left behind by guests. We cross the Town Square and pass through the main gates.

Elsa's family and Uncle Albert follow Mom and Dad to the monorail platforms, where they'll be traveling back to the parking lot and taking the van to the hotel. My family and Jane's will ride the buses.

We walk to the shelters, where the many canopies are overcrowded with people. I pull out my transportation map and search for another option.

"Let's take the monorail to Epcot," I say. "From there, it's just a stone's throw to Port Orleans."

"Don't be an idiot," says Jane. "Wait for the shuttles."

"We'll make it a race, then," I say. And I hurry Mary and the children away before there's time for debate. We cross the plaza and climb the ramp to the express monorail, boarding the second train into the station. Our car is standing-room only, and we huddle at a pole in the middle. The train heads due west from the station.

"That's the Grand Floridian," says Mary, referring to the resort along the first curve. "Its Victorian architecture matches that of the two white summer houses beyond it."

Mary explains that the two summer houses are Disney's Fairy Tale Wedding Pavilion and Brides Vestibule. They share their own private island in the Seven Seas Lagoon, and hundreds of couples tie the knot there each year, posing for photos at the island's Picture Point, where the Cinderella Castle is stamped into every wedding album. "But couples needn't feel trapped by such branding," says Mary. "Disney tailors plans to suit. Services can be arranged almost anywhere on the property . . . even within the theme parks."

I listen closely for any clues that Mary is wise to my surprise for her. She's talking all around the subject.

Mary goes on to say that private weekday services begin at $3,000, but that costs mount quickly, with dinners at $120 per plate, live music at $6,000, themed topiaries at $820, character appearances starting at $600, and an exclusive carriage ride for the bride in Cinderella's glass coach at $2,500. Mary then notes that couples willing to shell out more than $42,000 qualify for a ceremony in the Magic Kingdom after closing time.

Mary's last remark is a strong indication that she doesn't suspect anything for tonight. I would never spend $42,000 on a wedding service, even if I could afford to. My private ceremony is a special arrangement I pitched to Disney as a possible new offering to its Fairy Tale lineup: a guestless service in the Magic Kingdom during park hours. I'm being charged $3,000 for the whole shebang, and Merryweather's offer to put Uncle Albert in a costume probably means that

Disney likes the idea and wants to promote it by making the service more conspicuous.

"The wedding planners will even arrange stag parties for the bride and groom," says Mary. "For the gentlemen, it's pints of soda and high-fives all around with Mickey and his gang. For the ladies, it's tea on the knee with the princess collection and a visit by the original Chip 'n' Dale dancers."

Passengers around the car chuckle at Mary's comments. She then points with two fingers toward the eastern shore of the Seven Seas Lagoon.

"The Wilderness Lodge Resort features a man-made geyser. Early on in the resort's history, guests complained of the geyser's spray reaching their balconies and entering their rooms. But no problem is too tough for Disney. With a little technology, and some creative imagination, the imagineers applied a wind gauge to adjust the height of each eruption."

Mary pauses, then turns and faces the opposite direction. Heads in our compartment turn along with her.

"If you look there to the southwest, you might just catch a glimpse of the Shades of Green Armed Forces Recreation Center. In 1994, the U.S. government leased the property for the private use of military vacationers. Then, two years later, the government actually *bought* the resort for forty-three million dollars. According to the Department of Defense, the resort pays for itself. It surely *must!* It's currently closed for a fifty-five million dollar expansion. Just leave it to Uncle Sam to be the greatest hotel operator ever. The rooms are among the largest here in Disney World, while the rates are among the lowest. Guests even enjoy discounted park passes and a pardon from the usual state and local taxes. Note to self: contact Uncle Sam for best travel deals . . . but only to Disney."

Our train swings past the Polynesian resort, then arrives at the Transportation Plaza. The doors slide open, and we walk to the adjacent platform for the monorail to Epcot. We squeeze onto the first train, and are soon cruising along the elevated beam.

Our car is cramped, and the air-conditioning system isn't keeping up. Then, there's a loss of power, and the train glides to a stop.

For the first few minutes, eyes glance anxiously around the compartment. The air temperature rises quickly, and the windows are the kind that don't open. Sweat begins to accumulate on every face.

But despite our flushed cheeks and soggy clothing, attitudes in the car remain cool. Mary and I open the overhead escape hatches to let in some fresh air, and MJ teams up with a fellow passenger to soak her bandana and pass it around.

Finally, after about fifteen minutes, our train is on the move again, though not by its own power. Another vehicle is pushing us along the beam; I can see it as we round the first curve. We're delivered, quite slowly, to the monorail station at Epcot.

It's now five-thirty, and Mary and I are beginning to feel the pressure of time. We were hoping to walk or jog from here to our resort, but a cast member informs us that there's no way to get there on foot. We'll have to take a bus or call for a ride.

We manage to fit ourselves onto the second shuttle that arrives, though we soon learn that our French Quarter destination is the last of five stops. We estimate our arrival to the room at about six-thirty, meaning we'll have less than ninety minutes to shower, dress, ride a bus back to the Magic Kingdom, get through security, and make our way up Main Street to the back of the castle before our eight o'clock reservation. I can't imagine we'll be there on time, and the last thing I want is for this evening to be stressful. So, I develop a plan.

I'll phone my Event Manager while Mary is in the shower and arrange for us to arrive at the restaurant just in time for our escort to the alcove. Then, I'll lie to Mary that our dinner reservation has been changed to nine o'clock. We'll simply eat somewhere else after the service.

". . . It's where your father and I stayed after our wedding," says Mary. She is discussing our connection to Port Orleans with the children.

"Tell us again how you met," says MJ.

"Well," says Mary, "I was a senior in college at the time."

"And *I* lived in the college town," I say. "I was a handyman for Uncle Albert, and I was on a ladder in his parlor on the day your mother walked in. I nearly tipped off when I saw her."

"I had a standing date for tea," says Mary, "—the first Friday of every month. But I knew something was up when I saw the third place-setting at the table. Uncle Albert introduced me to your father, referring to him as his *resident artist and philosopher.* To which your father cleverly replied, *Please forgive him, Miss. He's confusing me with my twin brother—also named Bert.*"

"Albert then introduced your mother to *me*," I say, "calling her his *devoted student of science.* To which she corrected him, *Oh, pay no attention. There are far too many Marys in the family for him to remember which one I am.*"

"I was a bit cold to your father that day," says Mary, "but it ended up being a fine tea. And Uncle Albert continued to schedule Bert for Fridays, always asking him to join us at the table. . . . That is, until one special Friday—"

"The greatest Friday of them all," I say.

"Bert was working in the basement when I arrived, and Uncle Albert sat us down to tea without him."

"And I could hear their conversation through the ductwork,"

I say. "It was Mary who spoke up. *Where's Bert?* she said. *Why isn't he here? Is everything all right?* Those were the sweetest words I had ever heard."

"And it was that very same afternoon," says Mary, "—Albert's birthday in fact—that the three of us got to laughing so hard that we didn't come down for hours. We left Albert's house after dark, and your father walked me home."

"Funny thing," I say, "it was the first time we had ever been alone together, and the talking came easy. Soon, we were dating."

"Good old Uncle Albert," says Mary. "Six years later—to the exact day—we were married."

"On a Friday, no less. And Port Orleans is the place we stayed on our honeymoon."

Our bus enters the resort and passes the gatehouse.

"What's a honeymoon?" says Michael. "Is it like a honey stick? Can I have one?"

◆ ◆ ◆

Dad is waiting for us beside the bus shelters, and he is standing with his arms crossed. He is no doubt agitated that we've taken so long to get back. He escorts MJ and Michael to the food court, where the rest of the family is now eating, then he finds me in our hotel room during Mary's shower. I've just gotten off the phone with Merryweather.

"The plans have changed," I say. "Albert needs to be at the alcove by nine-thirty instead of nine, and we'll be eating in the castle *after* the service instead of before."

Dad notes the revision and exits the room.

I enter the bathroom and share the good news with Mary. We now have an extra hour and a half to get to the castle.

While I'm taking my turn in the shower, I'm surprised to hear the sound of a blow-dryer coming from the area of the sinks.

When I shut off the water and reach for my towel, I catch a glimpse of Mary standing outside the bathroom in front of the mirror, and I can't believe what I'm seeing.

I never gave any thought to what Mary might be wearing tonight. I assumed it would be her standard fare of preppy, boyish clothing.

But the Mary who stands before me now is something else completely. She has sheathed herself in a pink and white cocktail dress that is artfully torn off one shoulder and tattered at the knee. Her hair is wild and wind-blown, and her legs are bare down to her burgundy sandals. The only remnant of the former Mary is her exclusion of jewelry, nail polish, and lipstick. She is taking a gamble . . . so I will too.

"Mary, you look beautiful."

She doesn't flinch. "Do you really think so?" she says. And she holds her gaze in the mirror.

"Cross my heart you do. Like the day I met you."

"This was your *Boobs Daddy* in the dresser, Bert. I'm your poor-girl tonight. Some help with my cologne?"

I wrap myself in a towel and accept the cheap bottle of suntan lotion she hands to me. I apply its coconuty cream to her neck and shoulders.

With plenty of time to spare, we decide that a bus ride is not to our liking tonight. Instead, we plan to walk the length of our resort and cross over to the Fort Wilderness Campground, where we can catch a water shuttle to the gates of the Magic Kingdom.

We grab a quick snack in the room and then head out the door.

Chapter 22

The Peaceful Journey

Mary and I step outside into a warm summer's evening, where the lingering heat of the day is no match for the cool starts we've been given by our showers. We find the carriage path along the waterway and follow it across the resort.

As we walk past the pool area, jazz music christens our journey, and I can't help but wish I could follow us from about ten steps behind and ogle Mary.

At the first parking lot of the French Quarter's sister resort, Riverside, I finally ask Mary the question I've been saving all afternoon. "When were you going to tell me about Utilidors?"

"Oh," she says, "I wondered how you got to the parade. I was going to tell you at dinner tonight. What was it like down there?"

I describe the hallways and then relate to her my sighting of Donald Duck on the pushcart. "And I was above him and everything," I say.

It's a long walk through the parking lots of Riverside, but we eventually reach the far end. From there, though, our route is less certain.

A plant bed stands in our way, followed by a ring-road for the resort. There are no stepping stones or stop signs to help us across, and beyond these obstacles, there's a pond surrounded by lawn. We'll have to trudge beside the busy

Bonnet Creek Parkway without the benefit of a sidewalk. If Disney has an out-of-bounds, we're surely about to enter it.

"Shall we risk it?" says Mary.

"Sure," I say. "I want to see you in handcuffs."

"Fur-lined, I hope."

We step through the plant bed and dash across the ring-road, then follow the grass field along the curbline of the parkway. I carefully avoid eye contact with drivers and keep my gaze forward to the intersection ahead. The ground under our feet is soft, like it's never been tread upon, and I know we must look horribly out of place. I'm just grateful that no one has stopped.

"Honk, honk." A vehicle draws up beside us, and it's Dad in the van with Uncle Albert. The passenger-side window has been lowered.

"Get in," yells Dad from across the seat.

Mary and I climb in and close the back door.

"What the hell are you doing?" says Dad. "Are you too good for the buses? All you had to do was ask and I'd have given you a ride."

"Thanks for stopping," I say. "Can you drop us at the entrance to Fort Wilderness?"

"I should drop you on your head is what I should do," he says.

Dad checks his side mirror and accelerates into traffic. He then turns left onto Vista Boulevard.

Albert beams at Mary from the front seat. "Well, bless me, bless my soul," he says. "You look radiant, Mary." He raises an empty pill bottle to his lips. "Charmed is my life, I guess—ran out just in time. Your father's so kind to me, Bert."

Good old Uncle Albert, ready with an alibi at a moment's notice. Mary will never suspect that Dad is actually delivering him to the Magic Kingdom for a wedding ceremony . . . albeit quite early, though. Maybe Albert really *did* run out of pills.

Dad enters the Fort Wilderness parking lot and lets us out at the information center. "Get a map," he says. "Don't be late for dinner."

♦ ♦ ♦

Dusk has settled across the floor of this 640 acre wood, though the treetops remain bathed in a golden sunshine. We open our map and find the trail that crosses the center of the campground.

"We've had two brushes with danger today," says Mary.

"Huh?"

"The first was on the monorail this afternoon; the second was just moments ago on our walk beside the parkway. But fear not, Ivanhoe; we've never been in any *real* danger. Perhaps you're not aware of it, but death is forbidden in Disney World."

"Can they do that?"

"Oh yes," says Mary. "And even in extreme cases . . . like when limbs have been severed, or when critical body parts have been scattered in all directions . . . the official declarations of death have patiently awaited the proper authorities outside of Disney."

"Excellent," I say. "We should retire here . . . and live forever."

"My thoughts exactly. And what better place for Poor-girl to shack up than in a trailer park."

At the campground's first intersection, we take a detour and scout for retirement properties.

The evening air is heavy with humidity, and there's a gentle breeze that circulates the scent of grilled foods and cigarette smoke—a combination that always puts me in a festive mood. These fragrances remind me of childhood block parties and large public events. And when a third aroma is added to the mix, I'm actually propelled to an exact place and time: Chicago's Wrigley Field during the summer after my fifth grade year.

My friend's father took us boys to watch a Cubs baseball game. I was impressed by the field and the players, all appearing much larger in real life than on television. I remember vividly the crack of the bat and the roar of the fans and the melodies from the Wurlitzer organ. And I'll never forget the spellbinding charm of that stadium filled with people singing *Take Me Out to the Ball Game* with Jack Brickhouse during the 7th inning stretch. But what's most compelling to me now is that this entire recollection is indexed to the flavor of pipe tobacco my friend's dad was smoking that day.

As our walk nears the campground's Meadow Trading Post, we see families and cast members gathered around a bonfire and singing Disney songs. Two costumed characters are on hand as well: Chip and Dale.

"There's your bachelorette party, Poor-girl."

"Yeah," says Mary, "but no Princess Collection for *me*."

We return to the main trail and reach the marina on Bay Lake, where a water shuttle is just now making its way to the dock.

The sky remains clear above us, but the western horizon has grown thick with heroic clouds. The sunset splays from behind them and sends up shafts of light, while the entire skyward scene is mirrored on the water below.

We board our boat and are soon motoring into the twilight.

At the narrow channel between Bay Lake and the Seven Seas Lagoon, a daisy-chain of lights sails into view from the trees on our left. It is a monorail train, gliding smoothly overhead and into the atrium of the Contemporary hotel.

At the channel's accompanying water bridge, Mary and

I watch, with great pleasure, as cars and buses race beneath us. We've avoided a rat race tonight and chosen a different destiny for ourselves. Each of us breathes a sigh of deep satisfaction for our current peaceful circumstances, as we cruise out onto the lagoon.

Night has finally settled over Disney World.

CHAPTER 23

The Wedding Ceremony

As we step onto the dock beside the Magic Kingdom, I check my wristwatch. It is five minutes to nine, giving us just over half an hour to enter the park and walk up Main Street to the castle. No problem.

We breeze through security and cross the turnstiles, both of us eager to experience the nighttime version of the opening curtain. But it's not to be.

Town Square is packed with guests, and they're stacked all the way back to the breezeway openings. We can see little more than the rooftops of Main Street and the higher elevations of the castle. The first float of a parade is rolling by, and Mary and I quickly realize that our route to the castle is blocked by spectators filling the sidewalks.

Mary and I look at each other with disbelief. Our destination is right there—only a few hundred yards away—yet we seem to have no way to get there.

I suppose I could find a cast member and plead for access to the Utilidors, but I know I'd have to ruin Mary's surprise in doing so.

"I've got it!" says Mary, "—the Main Street shops. They're all connected inside. We can at least get to the Central Plaza."

"Lead the way," I say.

But before either of us can take a step forward, a voice speaks to us from behind. It's a familiar one.

"You look trapped by this parade," says Merryweather. "Can I make a suggestion?"

"Please do," says Mary. "We're trying to get to the castle."

"Follow me, then," she says. And she leads us back into the breezeway and points to a stairway. "Take the train to Toontown. That's the fastest way."

"Of course!" says Mary. "We're standing under the train station."

We thank the cast member and hasten up the stairs.

The deck on top provides an overlook of the Town Square, though its railing is currently crowded with parade-watchers. Beyond them, the castle glows in a rainbow of pastel colors.

The Main Street Train Station is at the opposite end of the deck, and its platform is almost empty. Once again, we're dodging the masses.

Mary and I enjoy this semi-private perch over the park's main entrance, where we gaze out over the Seven Seas Lagoon and watch the lights of a dozen Disney conveyances circulate in the darkness. At the lagoon's far shore, a procession of lighted sea creatures makes its way toward the Fairy Tale Wedding pavilion, granting us a quiet substitute for the boisterous parade behind us. And on the near-western shore, the Grand Floridian resort dominates the skyline, bearing a rooftop that is traced by popcorn lights, just like the buildings around us. Yet again, Disney is carrying a theme both inside and outside the park—a Victorian one this time. The look reminds me of the photographs from Mary's book, which showed nighttime scenes of Coney Island during its glory days.

But Disney's Victorian theme has a violator tonight, . . . and that violator is Mary. She is leaning casually against a wrought iron column, and her party dress shows far more flesh than would have been acceptable in that earlier time. Her manner is both confident and carefree, and her easy sway sings like an anthem to the hard-won freedoms of the past century.

Whooooo! A train whistle cries in the distance, and before long, Steam Engine No. 2—the *Lilly Belle*—chugs into the station, pulling a linkage of passenger cars. Tonight, we'll be shuttled to Toontown by the locomotive named for Walt Disney's wife.

We select an empty bench and climb aboard.

The conductor signals the engineer, and the Lilly Belle rolls from the station. Balmy air washes across us, as the clickety-clack of the wheels picks up speed, and we enter a stand of trees.

At the far end of Adventureland, our train turns northward and eventually crosses the exit road for the parade, where the first float has yet to arrive. But Merryweather was correct to keep us on this train past Frontierland. We can see that our route to the castle is blocked from here as well.

Our train lurches forward and leaves the Frontierland Station. Next stop: Toontown.

We enter a thickly wooded area, which opens briefly to a small body of water. Its surface shines with a blush of moonlight, and I'm reminded of the young Walt Disney on his journey back to California with Lilly after their loss of Oswald.

My *Story of Walter* gave credit to Lilly for naming Mickey Mouse. Yet, according to Mary's book, Walt himself told several different versions of the tale.

I begin imitating the sound of a train: "Chug, chug, mouse . . . chug, chug, mouse . . . *m—m—mowa-ouse*," I reach under the seat and pull out an imaginary pad of paper, then draw on it with a make-believe pencil I've found behind my ear.

"Lilly, I think I've got something," I say. "It's a mouse. . . . I've named him Mortimer. I like that, don't you?"

Mary's mind is a steel trap; I'm sure she knows her part.

She looks at me as though she's thinking. "I like the mouse idea," she says. "But Mortimer sounds wrong. Too sissy."

"What's wrong with it?" I say. "*Mortimer-Mouse, Mortimer-Mouse.* —It swings, Lilly."

Mary shakes her head.

"All right, then," I say. "How about Mickey . . . Mickey Mouse?"

She nods her agreement, and I tuck away the sketch pad, returning the pencil to my ear. I then put my arm around Mary, and she rests her head on my shoulder.

Upon our approach to the Toontown Station, I see that the land beyond it is sparsely populated at this hour. I guess that's to be expected because this region is geared to youngsters. There's virtually no line of guests at the station, and the walkway is almost completely clear.

Mary sits up. "I don't see Roy and Edna."

We hop from the train and expect an easy five minutes to the castle. There's a good chance we'll even be early.

As we climb the hill toward the houses of Mickey and Minnie, a red theater curtain—hanging from a circular rod—forms an enclosure that is rolling across a nearby cul-de-sac. It continues forward until it intercepts with our path, then it stops about twenty feet in front of us. The attending cast member draws open the curtain.

From inside, two figures raise their hands to their cheeks and express excitement at seeing us. They are Mickey and Minnie.

Mary looks at me with suspicion, but my surprise is almost as genuine as hers. It seems my Event Manager has found a better way to promote my service, trading the castle guards for the ultimate in Disney icons. We'll certainly be getting to the alcove in style.

Minnie wears a polka-dotted dress of red and white, and Mickey dons a black tuxedo coat with a yellow bow tie and bright red pants. They give each of us a Hollywood hug and then fuss over our outfits.

Minnie takes Mary by the hand and ushers her away toward the castle. Mickey turns me around and brings me into his own house. I wonder what Merryweather is planning.

Mickey's bedroom is the first door on our left, and he halts me beside his bed, where a red jacket is draped over it. He holds up the garment to me, then pantomimes that I should carry it and follow him.

He leads me through his house and into the back yard, where an opening in the fence brings us backstage. He delivers me to a dressing room and places me in the care of a cast member, who fits me into the costume of a prince.

I reemerge from the room and find Mickey in a new outfit as well. He is now my Majordomo in full regalia. He celebrates my transformation with a flurry of last-minute touch-ups: he polishes the gold buttons on my jacket; he combs the tassels over my shoulders; and he adjusts the hilt of my sword.

We backtrack through his house and join four castle guards on his front porch. They escort us through Toontown, where I see no sign of Mary.

We approach the Central Plaza and stop at the base of the ramp to the alcove. A fifth guard is there and clearing our path.

During our pause, a nearby guest points to the cable that runs between the castle tower and Tomorrowland. He asks a cast member if the wire carries Tinker Bell on her "flight."

"No," says the cast member, who is equipped like a Secret Service agent. "That cable brings ESPN to the prince. Tinker Bell has wings."

At the mention of the prince, the two men look in my direction, and I give them a lordly nod.

The ramp is now open and we're traveling once again, but as we approach the alcove, I can see that it's not yet prepared for tonight's service. Uncle Albert is not there, nor is the chapel of flowers. In fact, the alcove remains full of people who seem to be holding positions for the fireworks show. Perhaps dinner will be first after all.

As my entourage reaches the castle, I sense something big brewing behind it. Floodlights spill onto my path, and colorful banners mark the entrance to the rear courtyard. I'm beginning to suspect this is all for me.

Trumpeters begin a fanfare, and a sergeant barks commands to his regiment. Mickey and I wait while a company of guards marches from the castle breezeway and creates an aisle for us. We then walk to the base of the stairs at the back of the castle.

Mickey bows to me deeply and gestures me to climb. I glance up the wall at the balcony, but I can't see past the trumpeters moving along the railing.

I mount the stairway, which brings me to the turret at the top. And from there, the balcony opens up, revealing a lineup of my family, standing in absurd costumes.

Instantly, the whole thing becomes clear to me. I was not the *Mr. Alfred* Merryweather was expecting today; she was expecting my father. And the Disney staff probably never liked my wedding idea from the beginning; they simply went along with it to keep me fooled. But I have to hand it to Merryweather; she certainly showed some boldness today, taking me to the room filled with all these costumes.

Ferguson is dressed like a sea captain of the royal navy, and his two sleepy-eyed cabin boys, Dorsey and Sanders, rest peacefully in his arms. His chest erupts through his coat, and white powder falls from his wig down to his stockings, as he tips his head to acknowledge my presence.

Elsa and Nellie stand beyond him, wearing luxurious gowns of the French court. Each of them has their hair whipped up tight and tall, and they try to club me with these towers when they curtsy.

Jane and Tom . . . hallelujah! It's no wonder Jane stopped complaining about this vacation; Dad has delivered her a mega-dose of magic. The only way to describe her and Tom is as *vanity pirates*. They are sparsely clad in cotton fabrics and leather strapping, and their skin is gleaming with oil. Jane wears a silver hook on her left hand, and Tom wears an eye patch. Neither of them bows to me or salutes. Instead, they simply lower their three available eyelids and show me the stenciled artwork painted there.

And their daughter Angelica—she is unquestionably the curse imposed on my father. Her outfit is a complete departure from the eighteenth-century theme. She wears a modern-day cheerleading uniform and carries colorful pompoms. She stomps her feet and strikes a pose for me.

My mom, the queen mother, comes next, standing between Prince Michael and Princess Maryjane.

"Look, Daddy, look," says MJ. She steps forward and twirls in her dress.

"You're so beautiful," I say. "Especially with your hair down."

Uncle Albert is the last one to greet me. He is garbed in the silly cleric's costume I rejected earlier today, and he lays down his scepter in order to give me a hearty handshake. "So glad you could make it, my boy. Please forgive the get-ups."

I turn and face the courtyard, where castle guards have taken new positions. They've created a narrow aisleway from the base of the castle stairs to the carousel.

Music sweeps through the courtyard, and all eyes turn to a video screen on a nearby rooftop. A glass carriage, pulled by four white ponies and attended by three footmen, is making its way slowly across Fantasyland from the direction of Toontown. Its running gear is pure white, and its transparent coach is shaped like a pumpkin. Mary is the Cinderella seated inside. She is smiling and waving to the crowd.

Mary has on a white gown and long white gloves, and she glitters from top to bottom. There's a jeweled tiara in her hair, and I'm guessing she's wearing glass slippers.

The carriage enters the courtyard and halts beside the carousel. Two coachmen help Mary out onto the first step, and a momentary exposure of her legs sends up a howl from the spectators.

My father enters the courtyard from below, walking within the corridor of soldiers to the carriage. He is clearly our king, and he takes Mary by the hand for her final step to the ground.

As Mary's foot touches down, a runway of light unfurls beneath her, extending along the aisle to the castle. No wonder Mary didn't know of this feature in the pavement today. Dad probably designed it and had it built just for tonight.

Dad and Mary walk along together, looking up into the balcony and laughing. Mary seems to be enjoying herself, despite being on such patent display.

They disappear below the wall, then reappear a short time later in the doorway of the turret. They work their way through the reception line.

"Look, Mommy, look," says MJ. "I'm in a dress."

"Yes you are," says Mary. "And me too. Don't we look grand?"

I hold my hand out to Mary, and the two of us find our places in front of Uncle Albert.

The music of the courtyard fades, leaving behind just the quiet melody of the carousel's calliope.

Albert holds in his hand the paper with our wedding vows, but he doesn't begin speaking. Instead, he leans forward until his face is within inches of ours.

"Quite a circus," he says. "Shall we fake the vows?"

Mary and I nod.

"And guess what," he continues. "I have some good news. Your mother found my toast, Mary. It was tucked in her program all these years." Albert slides an envelope into my pocket.

"So, what now?" I say.

"I know," says Mary. "I've got a joke. I've been saving this one. *Which of King Arthur's knights established the Round Table?*"

"Heaven help us," says Albert.

"No stopping it," I say.

"Sir Cumference."

Albert groans and takes a step back. He then removes a small box from his robe. "And now," he says loudly, ". . . THE RING!"

Mary and I exchange glances, then look along the lineup of family. Everyone seems surprised.

Albert opens the box and reveals a diamond ring of impressive proportion—the stone is almost as big as Mom's and twice the size of Jane's. Only one person could be behind such a purchase, though my father maintains a look of innocence.

I brush my hand across Mary's cheek—tenderly, like the impassioned man of a jewelry commercial—then remove the white glove from her left hand and fling it down to the crowd. The new ring fits her perfectly, and I hold out her hand for Dad's inspection.

"Nicely done," he says. "It's about time."

Albert places a golden key around each of our necks and proclaims us *Disney-hitched.* "You may kiss the bride," he says.

Mary grabs me by the lapels and presses her lips against mine, kissing me so aggressively that I feel the heat rush to my face.

Music returns to the courtyard, and soap bubbles fill the air. Albert turns us around to face the railing, where we accept the applause of our throngs.

An instant later, the lights of the courtyard are extinguished, and we hear a low *booming* sound. Into the sky, a thin ribbon of red traces its way overhead, eventually exploding with splinters of color. The evening's fireworks show has begun.

Mary and I are whisked to the bottom of the stairs and brought directly into the castle hallway, where we are rushed through an unmarked door and into an awaiting elevator. The cast member accompanying us presses a button marked *P,* and the doors of the elevator close.

I recognize this elevator's interior; I rode it this afternoon with Merryweather down to Utilidors. Mary and I are no doubt headed to the restaurant's dining room to enter it the back way.

"Reginald is my name," says the cast member. "I'll be your server tonight."

The elevator doors slide open, and I'm expecting to see the restaurant's busy staging area. But instead, we're confronted with a dimly-lit foyer that contains a single door.

"Please," says Reginald, "step this way."

We exit the elevator and stand in the small foyer. "Are you ready?" he says. "You've got the best table in the house." He grips the fancy handle and gives the door a push.

Laid out before us is a dark and dusty old room stacked with boxes and crates along the walls. Splashed in the center, however, is an elegant table for two set with candles and white linens. Fireworks flash through the windows, illuminating the room in quick bursts.

"This was Walt's penthouse apartment," says Reginald, "never finished, of course."

Reginald seats us at the table, then lifts the stainless steel covers from our plates. Steam rises from buttered potatoes, and a candied roast soaks in a brine. He pops the cork on our carbonated grape juice, then returns the bottle to its pail of ice.

"I'll be right outside the door if you need me," he says. "Just ring the little bell."

Reginald exits the room, leaving Mary and I alone in this secluded chamber of the castle.

The Call of Coney Island

I lift my empty goblet from the table and hold it out to Mary. "Does Poor-girl pour out?"

"Poor-girl who?" says Mary, and she admires herself in her diamond ring. "I think I'm one of the Princess Collection now."

Mary compares her two hands, one of which still wears a white glove. "Is it bad form to eat with this on?" she says. "I'm just a country girl, you know."

As we dig into our meals, I reach into my pocket and pull out the envelope from Uncle Albert. "Would you like to do the honors?" I say.

"No-no," says Mary. "You do a much better impression of Albert."

I gargle some fake champagne and rehearse a mild lisp, then begin reading Albert's toast.

> Hello, everyone. For those of you who don't know me, I'm Mary's Uncle Albert. I'm the one who introduced these two some six years ago. It was at my house that Bert and Mary first laid eyes on each other. And let me tell you, the sparks were flying.
>
> Each Friday, as the three of us sipped tea together, I watched their mutual attraction prove itself with

every word and gesture. There was no mistaking their desire for a closer relationship.

But, as many of you may also know, Bert and Mary are the independent sorts—perhaps independent to a fault. Neither of them seemed capable of asking the other for a date. The situation soon grew comical.

I kept them in contact by employing Bert at needless jobs around my house. I was sure he'd quit before polishing my silver another time. But of course, he didn't; he wanted to see Mary.

And Mary . . . she was even more transparent. She stepped up her visits from monthly to weekly.

But still, after six months of teetotaling, the two of them had yet to start dating. So I took matters into my own hands and forced the issue.

On one particular Friday, I assigned Bert the ridiculous task of washing the ceiling in my basement. His proximity to the duct-work would allow him to hear any conversations going on upstairs. When Mary arrived on time, as she always did, I deliberately refrained from asking Bert to the table. Bert would either have to come upstairs on his own, or Mary would have to ask for him. Either action would be a strong signal to the other that their relationship was ready to start rolling.

It was Mary who asked for Bert. And the two of them have been inseparable ever since.

Now, some of you might also be aware that Bert and Mary have pet names for each other; they claim that I'm the one who coined them. Apparently, I introduced Bert as *my resident artist and philosopher,* and

I introduced Mary as *my devoted student of science* . . . not really such embarrassing pet names, as pet names go.

So here's my toast to the newlywed couple: To Mary, *my devoted student of science,* and to Bert, *my resident artist and philosopher,* your union is truly magical. May your life together be the greatest marriage of science, art, and philosophy the world has ever known. Here's to your happily ever after.

◆ ◆ ◆

I lean back in my chair after cleaning my plate. "This waistband's too tight," I say.

"Try wearing a corset," says Mary.

I rise up and strut to the window.

"Where are you going?" she says.

"To get us some new clothes," I say. "I'll shout down to some young lad and offer him half a crown—"

"You can't," says Mary, and she places a hand on her tiara.

"But you'll still have half a crown," I say.

"No, that's not it. You can't put your head out that window, Bert. You'll scare the dickens out of anyone who sees you."

I clutch at my face and hunt for a mirror. "Is it that bad?"

"Oh, no, Bert. You're beautiful. It's the castle that's the problem. Remember the scaling? If you lean out that window, you'll look like an ogre. The villagers will rise up. They'll storm the castle. You'll be slain!"

I reach for my sword and tug at the hilt. "Damn!" I say. "It's a fake."

I pace the floor until a carrot from Mary's salad hits me on the back of the head. "There's just one thing to do," I say.

"What?" says Mary, acting breathless.

I lift her from her chair and pull her close. "We'll go to

the bathroom and retrieve our clothes . . . because that's where I saw them."

Mary and I change back into our original outfits, though Mary continues to wear her crown and diamond ring. She returns to the table and picks up the bell that will summon Reginald, and just at that moment I happen to be stealing one of her glass slippers.

"You wouldn't," I say.

"I have a confession to make. My transformation into Cinderella was not without embarrassment. Minnie had to cover her eyes. You see, Poor-girl wasn't wearing any underwear . . . and she still isn't. I was going to tell you in the restaurant tonight, when you couldn't do anything about it."

I step toward her, and she rings the bell.

Reginald opens the door and escorts us to the elevator, where he returns us to the central corridor of the castle and reminds us that our *Keys to the Kingdom* are a universal fast-pass to every ride. He then sets us free to play.

Mary and I cruise through Fantasyland, stopping at *Snow White's Scary Adventure* for our first ride. We howl with blood-curdling screams at each sighting of the wicked queen.

Next, we stop at the *Mad Hatter's Tea Party,* where we manage the staggering feat of 150 revolutions in our teacup . . . or so we think. How can we really be sure? All we really know is that our staggering feet can't carry us from the ride. We fall to our knees and crawl to the exit.

At the noisy indoor roller coaster, *Space Mountain,* we cling to each other through the darkness, trying to keep hold of our personal possessions. I shout to Mary, "Is this where you lost you're underwear?"

Our next destination is Exposition Hall on the Town Square, where we intend to view the film *The Story of Walt*

Disney. This was where we began our honeymoon in 1991, and we want to see the film again for old time's sake.

But as we're crossing the Central Plaza and making our way to Main Street, I stop us in front of the Partners statue and await Mary's reaction. "Anything?" I say.

She stares blankly at the bronze casting of Walt Disney and Mickey Mouse. "Nothing," she replies.

During our walk down Main Street, I formulate a plan. If the theater in Exposition Hall is empty—like it was on our honeymoon—I'll bribe the projectionist to play the film without sound. I'll then stand at the front, like an exhibitor of old, and spin a yarn from the passing images. With my newly gained knowledge from Mary's book, I'll weave a tale of truth and humor that both honors Walt Disney while poking fun at his legend.

We enter Exposition Hall and learn that the film stopped showing in the year after our honeymoon. The building is now devoted almost exclusively to merchandising. "But you're in luck," says the cast member helping us. "The seven dwarves are currently greeting guests in the area of character cutouts. There's still time to see them."

"Is that so?" I say, punching my fist into an open hand. "Two of those goons tackled my sister and niece today, and I'm still pretty pissed off about it."

"Easy, tiger," says Mary.

"And I heard one of them's doing Snow White."

Mary grabs me by the bridge of the nose and pulls me toward the door. "I'll not have you brawling all seven at once," she says.

We backtrack up Main Street, and this time it is Mary who delivers us to the Partners statue. She stands us in front of it with her eyes closed, then slowly opens them.

"Ha-ha!" she says, using the sprightly voice of Mickey

Mouse. "Hey you goofs. You know what Uncle Walt says: *As long as there's imagination left in the world, Disneyland will never be completed.* Enjoy your night."

Mary hurries us away in the direction of Adventureland.

"Did you hear that?" I say.

"Yeah. What of it?"

"He's telling us the park will never be finished. That's why the film doesn't show anymore."

"You're tripping all over yourself, Bert. That remark was made about Disneyland, not *this* place. Leave it to one of the hired hands to screw it up."

As we cross the bridge into Adventureland, Mary lists for me the shops that have closed on Main Street since the park's opening. Gone is the penny arcade, where we could have cranked a motion picture viewer from the last century. Gone is the Main Street Cinema, where we could have watched a silent cartoon. And gone are the shops of the candle-maker, the magician, and the tobacconist. Only the barbershop remains.

Near the entrance to the *Jungle Cruise,* I point at it with an offensive finger.

"If I had my way," I say, "I'd overhaul that thing."

"How so?"

"Glad you asked . . . but hardly relevant. Did I ever tell you of the letter I sent to Disney when I was in high school? I had an idea for a product, but they wouldn't even hear of it because I wasn't an employee. The invention was a ceiling fan painted with a cartoon sequence at the end of the paddles that could be animated by a strobe light. I suppose it's for the best that they snubbed me, though. The last thing we need is another way to etch the Disney domain into our babies."

"Feisty," says Mary.

At the *Pirates of the Caribbean,* we use our *Keys to the Kingdom* and board the first boat without waiting. We watch with delight as the mechanical pirates plunder a village . . . plunder, that is, until the townswomen gain the upper hand. The women swing their broomsticks and rolling pins at the scurvy knaves, putting them on the run. Mary gains a measure of inspiration from this, and she chases me around our seat with unmercifully poking fingers. *Arghh!*

Our next stop is *Splash Mountain,* where Mary chooses the rear-most bench of our log. She then loosens the strap of her dress and slides it off her shoulder as we near the climb up Chickapin Hill. She's preparing for an overexposure, so I wrestle her for the duration, ultimately shielding her during the plunge and preserving our park attendance. Our photograph at the exit has not been *washed away,* though it clearly shows me as a hog of the picture.

We take a quick tussle on *Big Thunder Mountain Railroad,* then follow the Rivers of America to Liberty Square.

On our way, I ask a cast member if there's somewhere we can buy popcorn. He directs us to Sleepy Hollow at the far end of Liberty Square.

As Mary and I turn the corner beside the Liberty Tree Tavern, I bring us to a sudden halt. Framed perfectly on the horizon of our colonial setting is the futuristic Contemporary hotel outside the park.

"Hey! What the—"

"Theming violation?" says Mary. "Maybe not."

Mary places her right hand over her heart and stands a little straighter, if that's possible. "The founding fathers were forward thinkers," she says. "With eyes fixed to the future, they forged the greatest constitution ever written. The Contemporary hotel, then, is Disney's nod to that spirit."

"Wow," I say. "Your blue eyes never looked so brown."

"Or, here's another possibility," she says. "Maybe there

used to be trees in the way. So take a chill pill, Ichabod. It ain't worth losing your head over."

We enter the snack shop called Sleepy Hollow and return outside with a bag of caramel corn. Mary then leads me on a small expedition while we eat. We are snooping around the outside of the *Hall of Presidents* in search of an artifact.

"There!" she says, and she points to a slab of stone behind a metal railing. "That marble doorstep came from Monticello . . . if you believe the rumors, that is."

"Who cares," I say. "What a buffoon."

Mary and I lock pinkies, consoling ourselves over the loss of our heroes: Thomas Jefferson and Albert Einstein.

Mary then glances over my shoulder and slowly backs us away into the shadows.

Walking beside the Rivers of America are Jane and Tom headed toward Frontierland. They are still dressed as vanity pirates, though their cheerleading daughter is nowhere to be seen.

"It's Captain Hook," I whisper. "Cover your ring."

We watch for several minutes, as guests intercept our pirate relatives and engage them in conversation. Jane moves about as if she's loosely-hinged or drunk, and Tom crawls around on the ground as though he's chasing something. By the end of their encounter, the two pirates have posed for pictures and signed autographs. They then resume their walk into Frontierland.

"That was a close one," I say.

We wait a few minutes more, then cross Liberty Square toward the *Haunted Mansion.*

"Now, didn't you say a young bride was thrown from a window there?"

"Yes," mumbles Mary, "by her crazed husband . . . leaving room for one more ghost."

"Which window was it?" I say.

"Attic," she murmurs.

We finish our popcorn and hurry to the entrance, where a ghoulish butler escorts us to the front of the line.

As our *doom* buggy rattles through the noisy attic, I hold tight to my bride and shout, "If *you* go, *I'm* going. We'll give them a thousand and one."

Returning to Liberty Square, we take a breather at the railing beside Rivers of America. The paddle-wheeler is just now steaming toward the dock.

Above its three main decks is the bridge, where a captain and a copilot are stationed. However, one of them is a ghostly transparent.

I look to Mary for confirmation, but she is busy waving at the illusion.

"Do we know him?" I say.

"Of course we do," she answers. "That's Uncle Walt. He can finally haunt his own park, now that the mustache ban's been lifted."

Mary and I enter Fantasyland through the cross-fade gateway, then sail over a nighttime London on *Peter Pan's Flight*.

At *Cinderella's Golden Carrousel,* I rally my nerve and ask Mary to ride alone so I can watch her.

"That's what I'm here for," she says.

I take a position on the crimson runway of earlier and await the startup of the carousel.

Mary selects a horse with a gold ribbon tied to its tail, then climbs aboard to ride it sidesaddle. She never once looks in my direction.

The merry-go-round begins turning, and Mary rises and falls . . . advances and retreats . . . appears and disappears . . . like a mesmerizing music box dancer. She revolves in an endless stream of scrolling lights and flickering poles, and I can't take my eyes off of her.

Raindrops now strike the pavement, and guests are scrambling for cover. But not me. I remain where I am, waiting for Mary to find me.

The carousel eventually stops, and Mary steps away from it into the rain. She locates me on the path and saunters toward me. Water drags down her hair and soaks her dress, and her skin becomes wet and shiny.

The shower escalates into a downpour, and the calliope's melody changes to a waltz. Mary enters my arms, and we dance together within a curtain of rain.

Before long, however, a bright flash and a trailing rumble of thunder change our dance step to a Tango, and I point us at the castle hallway.

But the hallway is overflowing with guests, so I dash us down the path to the alcove and turn left into the Fairytale Garden across the way. This tiny outdoor theater is surrounded by high walls, which afford us great privacy, though little protection from the rain.

I press Mary against the wall and reach beneath her dress. It's only a short time before her legs are around my waist and we are violating a code far more serious than the *nipple policy*.

CHAPTER 25

The Moments to Savor

As the cloudburst comes to an end, Mary and I stand weak-kneed against the wall. I eventually lead us across the path to the alcove of my earlier plans, where we rest against the railing and survey the majestic view.

My wish at the fountain in Madison—the one I later rejected—seems to have come true, in an adult sort of way. Over the past twenty-four hours I've experienced numerous moments that I can now see as enchanted. The first came last night, when Mary and I stepped from the van into the jazz music of Port Orleans. The second happened this morning, as we spied the castle with MJ and Michael from the Transportation Plaza. And the third has been this entire evening.

Yet still, I can hear the muffled voices of Logic and Reason, as they try to argue with me through the duct tape I've placed over their mouths. They're calling me a numskull, though I really don't care. Somehow, I've reached into the well of my mind and pulled out the key to the trunk in my tower. I've rescued the chrome-plated sugar bowl of my childhood and now coddle it in my arms.

It must have been Feeling who did the work down in the well. But what force was it that guided her hand? Was it music? Was it the beauty of this place? Was it Mary's book and tour? Or was it something else?

I tear the tape off the mouths of Logic and Reason, freeing

them to make their case. They want me to believe that my success was due to *preparation* meeting *opportunity,* though I don't truly trust them anymore. Nor do I fully trust MJ's *luck* or Michael's notion that wishes really *do* work. There must be another explanation.

The clouds have drifted eastward, and they unveil a full moon. Its light casts a glow down the castle walls and spreads out across the moat.

I return my gaze to the sky and search for a bright star. If a fountain in Madison can fulfill a wish, then certainly a star over Disney can too. I silently wish for the courage to return to college; I want this to be the next chapter of my life. In the meantime, however, I want to know the secret behind the Disney Magic, and I feel I'm getting close to discovering it. It is buried somewhere in the details of the park, I just know it.

Mary looks at me with a smile. "You were right, Bert," she says. "Adventureland has a terrible waste of real estate. The *Jungle Cruise* is long overdue for a redesign."

PART III

The
Misery

CHAPTER 26

The Worth of the Ring

"Hey!" comes a shout from behind us. "*There* you are!"

I turn and see Jane hustling up the ramp to the alcove with Tom trailing her. She walks like a rag doll, staggering and waving her hook.

"I knew you could do it," she says. "There's hope for you yet, Bert. Let's see it, Mary."

Jane grabs Mary's hand and studies the ring. "Tiffany solitaire . . . princess cut, of course . . . invisible mounting . . . four—"

Jane leans forward for a closer look. "One stone?" She looks at me suspiciously.

"Oh, it's real all right," I say. "I love her that much."

Jane shrugs me off and conjures a half-hearted smile. She taps the diamond with her hook. "You deserve it," she says to Mary. "But don't expect a tennis bracelet anytime soon."

Mary shakes her head and flutters her eyelashes.

"Park's closing, folks!" says a voice from the ramp. "Please make your way to the exit."

The cast member waits for us to clear the alcove, then follows us to the Central Plaza, where we join a grand processional of other guests along Main Street.

"Why did you take off your costumes?" says Jane. "You could have been celebrities all night."

Jane explains that she and Tom posed as two of the

characters from Disney's new release, *Pirates of the Caribbean*. She was Anamaria, claiming the hook as her prize from the battle for the Black Pearl. And Tom was Ragetti, constantly losing his wooden eyeball and trying to retrieve it.

We exit the park and take Jane's sage advice to ride the shuttles to Port Orleans. Our bus is quite crowded, so we must stand at the front.

Jane and Tom revert to their Disney roles and "parley" with guests, ignoring any relationship with Mary and me. "The Pirate's Code?" says Jane. "It's actually more of a guide-line, really."

My attention turns to the bus driver, who is speaking with a passenger and sounding rather agitated.

"The morning drivers should know better," she says. "Do you remember his name?"

"I don't recall," says the passenger.

"This route divides at the end of the day: twelve goes to French Quarter; thirteen goes to Riverside. You're on the wrong bus. . . . But don't worry. I've cleaned up this mess before. Let me know if you think of his name."

I can't believe what I'm hearing. This cast member is disparaging a fellow worker. It's a behavior I've never before witnessed in Disney World.

Our bus approaches its one and only scheduled stop—at the French Quarter of Port Orleans. There, two other shut-tles are already parked and unloading. However, there's not enough space between them for our driver to squeeze in, so she angles our bus across the driveway and boxes in the rear driver.

She flings open the doors and wishes us well.

Mary and I step off into the road and wait for Jane and Tom at the bus shelters. But our performing duo is in no hurry to end their charade. They remain on the bus with the Riverside guests, apparently planning to escort them home.

Meanwhile, the rear driver walks from his empty bus and scolds our driver through her open front door. He upbraids her for blocking the road and then for letting her passengers off away from the curb. She slams the door in his face and drives away.

The whole episode is absurd, though rather amusing.

Mary and I cross the grounds and approach Building One, where we find my mom pacing the perimeter of the courtyard.

"I couldn't sleep," she says to us. "Your father was way out of line. I didn't know about the ring."

"No harm done," says Mary. "I'm actually glad for it. It was the perfect touch to a perfect evening. Thanks for the wonderful ceremony."

"Yeah, thanks," I say. "It was a surprise for me too."

Mom smiles and breathes a sigh. "I'm glad you both enjoyed it. But don't feel you have to keep the ring, Mary. He'll do whatever I tell him."

Mary twists off the ring and hands it to Mom. "Let him know he picked a lovely setting—simple, just like I would have wanted."

"Done," says Mom.

♦ ♦ ♦

In the morning, we eat a quick breakfast in the room, then prepare for our day at the water-park. I pack the prototype Flume Shooter t-shirts, and we're off to catch a bus for Blizzard Beach.

Much of the family is already there when we arrive, and they've commandeered a shelter beside the wave pool, known as *Melt-Away Bay*. Mom, Elsa, and Uncle Albert occupy deck chairs beside the coolers, and Ferguson stands in the pool teaching Dorsey and Sanders to tackle waves. Dad is farther out, floating on two innertubes in the vicinity of Nellie and Angelica. The only two family members not present are Jane and Tom.

Dad sees us approaching and paddles ashore. He hands off his inner tubes to MJ and Michael, then proceeds directly to Mary.

"I should have guessed he wouldn't let you keep it," he says.

"Right," says Mary. "Too proud . . . just like his father."

Dad reaches into his pocket and pulls out the diamond ring. "I hedged my bets, you know. This was just a place-holder for the real thing. Got it for thirty bucks on eBay."

"It was worth every penny," says Mary.

"Nah," says Dad, and he pitches the ring far out into the pool.

"Well *now* you've done it," says Mary, as she marches into the water, where she begins a slow search of the bottom.

"Do you suppose we should help her?" says Elsa.

"What, and leave the shade?" says Mom.

We all laugh.

A few minutes later, Jane and Tom make their way across the pool area. Jane wears a leopard-skin bikini and kicks up "surf" like a party chick in a music video. Tom walks beside her in his spandex shorts that are way too tight.

"Hey there, Beef-jerkies," says Dad. "It's about time you two showed. I see you're doing your part to save the planet."

Jane strides over to Dad and gets in his face. "Okay, Funnyman. Finish it."

"Is that a rabbit skin you're wearing?" he says. "I guess only one had to die."

"Yeah," says Elsa, "but she owns twenty suits."

Jane scans the shelter. "Where's Mary? I want to see that ring in the daylight."

"Out there," says Dad.

Jane looks toward the pool. "What's she doing?"

"Looking for the ring," he says. "But don't go out there. She's afraid someone'll step on it."

"Well I don't weigh anything," says Jane, and she tromps out into the water.

Mary and Jane sweep back and forth across the pool, eventually emerging with the ring.

"Caught it under my toe," says Jane.

"You mean, you stepped on it," says Dad.

Jane ties a towel around her waist and plops herself down onto Dad's lap. She then holds out the ring and dries it.

"An amazing forgery, isn't it?" says Dad.

"*I'll* be the judge of that," she replies. Jane brings the ring close to her mouth and steams it with her breath. She then pulls it away and inspects it. She repeats the procedure several times.

"It's real all right," she says. "It even has an inclusion. You really outdid yourself, Bert; I expected four stones and glue. This must be three carats."

"Three point two," says Dad.

"Tell her what you paid for it," I say.

"I know," says Jane. "Mary told me. But sellers make mistakes, you know. I wouldn't go throwing it in the pool anymore until you have it looked at."

Jane is no doubt toying with us. But she makes a good point. How do any of us really know when a diamond is genuine or not? None of us is an expert.

Though, at a deeper level, why should it really matter? If two gemstones are indistinguishable to the naked eye, then why aren't they worth the same thing? But I know there's a simple answer to my question. Just like the two sugar bowls of the Holiday Spirit and the Disney Magic, clear stones come in a variety of materials.

Mary slides the recovered ring back onto her finger and admires herself in it.

"Time's awastin'," says Jane. "Who's got the guts to do Summit Plummit?" She roots through her bag and pulls out a one-piece swimsuit.

◆ ◆ ◆

Noon rolls around, and the family reconvenes for a picnic lunch at the shelter. The four older children arrive as a group, all of them wearing my Flume Shooter t-shirts.

"Uncle Bert's invention worked," says Angelica.

"Will miracles never cease?" says Jane. "Kudos to you, Bert. You can put this one beside the Oddball in your trophy case."

"Wobble-bearing," I say.

Jane pours two extra cups of store-bought milk and serves them to MJ and Michael. She knows very well our ban against such milk, and the kids look at Mary and me with confusion.

It's said that politics and religion are two subjects that should be avoided in social situations. Well, I'd like to add food and finance to the list. But one of these topics is easier to avoid than the other.

Family gatherings almost invariably involve meals, so issues involving food are hard to sidestep. And to make matters worse, Jane is a nutritionist who thinks she knows all the answers. She routinely imposes her ideas on MJ and Michael, ignoring the wishes of their parents.

"Oh, come on," says Dad. "They've gotta have milk."

"Hey," I say, "I'm on vacation. Do you really want to start this?"

"But it's organic," says Jane. "How can you possibly object?"

Jane knows full well my objection. I've told her half a dozen times; organic is fine, but it misses the point. It's the pasteurization and homogenization that make the milk unfit to drink. Jane simply disagrees with the evidence I supply.

"Do you have any potatoes for Mary?" I say, going on the offensive. "Or maybe some *nuts*?"

Jane closes her mouth; even *she* can't argue with results.

Last Summer, Mary's doctor measured low levels of potassium in her bloodstream, subsequently recommending she take a supplement and find a nutritionist. Jane stepped forward to help, creating a special meal plan, which Mary followed faithfully for a while. But Mary's health declined swiftly on the diet: her weight dropped to 98 pounds; her heartbeat became irregular; and she paced the floors each night with terrible insomnia. Jane agreed with the doctor's diagnosis that *stress* was the cause of Mary's problems, and Jane further supported his advice that she (1) eat more calories to recover her weight, (2) take a beta-blocker to stop the heart arrhythmia, and (3) grant herself a much needed vacation. But my intuition told me that the problem had to be biological rather than psychological, and I was lucky to find the solution before something more serious developed.

I learned that the human body is like an airplane in flight. If you could see into the cockpit, you'd find meters and dials revealing every detail of how the plane is performing. I've discovered that Mary's body is a *fast oxidizer dominant – sympathetic – catabolic – thyroid type*. She needs to eat the foods that counter these leanings to her dials. Potassium and magnesium were just two of the micro-nutrients Jane and the doctor were blindly pumping into Mary's system that were causing the nosedive in her chemistry. The greatest culprit of all, however, was the insidious protein known as gluten, and it was milk that gave me the needed clue by stressing her digestion. I immediately revised Mary's diet, doing exactly the opposite of what our nutritional and medical "experts" were telling us: I eliminated wheat and other gluten-containing grains; I cut her intake of nuts, fruit, and root vegetables; I eventually upped her consumption of red meat and animal fat; and I eliminated all dairy products except for butter. Like magic, Mary began to feel better after the first meal, and her health has been improving ever since.

But Jane, to this day, refuses to believe that food had anything to do with Mary's recovery. She assumes that some other problem simply came and went undetected. And I guess I'm not surprised by her reluctance to heed my explanations. I'm essentially telling her that her higher education is flawed—that her expert status has fallen into question. How will she feel if she one day discovers that her life's work has been inconsequential, or worse, harmful?

"So, Ferguson," says Jane, "how's the stock market doing? Still roaring?"

"Tanked," he says.

Ferguson is another of the family experts I've inadvertently challenged in the past two years. He's a financial planner, with millions of dollars in his care, and he was advising my parents about where they should invest their fortune.

But the stakes were too high and too personal for me to sit idly by. I pulled Mom aside and explained to her how demographics drive the performance of an economy—how the investments that had made her and Dad rich over the past twenty years were now set to begin tumbling by decade's end and remain low for many years to come. I gave her a book to read, which she studied carefully. Then, she and I persuaded Dad to embrace a defensive strategy that would eventually pull them from the stock market and put them at odds with the conventional wisdom of investing.

Ferguson learned of my intervention and phoned me at home, calling me "irresponsible" and a "rank amateur." I confessed to his correctness on the second point, but then argued that I was not being irresponsible. I implored him to listen to the evidence I had to share, but he tuned me out. Needless to say, the topic of finance isn't openly discussed in our family anymore.

"Thanks for packing the gluten-free bread, Mom," I say. "It's nice to have someone who humors us."

Elsa inspects the shoulder pads on one of the Flume Shooter t-shirts. "You did a nice job, Bert. Where did you learn to sew like that?"

I point to Dad. "The old man taught me everything I know. I'm pretty sure he made Mary's wedding dress."

Dad smirks. "At least I got her *into* a dress."

"Yes," says Mary. "You're my Good Fairy Fauna."

◆ ◆ ◆

By mid-afternoon, Mary and I are on duty to watch the children, while the remainder of the adults return to the hotel and prepare for an evening out. Jane and Tom will be heading to the clubs of Pleasure Island, and the other five will be finding dinner and entertainment at the Boardwalk.

Come five o'clock, Mary and I pile our charges into a bus for our return trip to the resort, and Nellie supplies the activity for our ride. She teaches us a game that reminds me of Aunt Poppi during those final days of her life when she could sing but not talk. The objective of the game is to speak the lyrics of a song without allowing any rhythm or melody to creep in, and then to do the reverse—apply rhythm and melody to what would normally be plainly spoken words. It's not so easy to do. I can feel the regions of my brain struggling to work together. It takes all of my concentration to assign pitch and cadence to standard speech, and it takes a similar effort to do the opposite. Nellie, however, has been practicing and is quite good at it.

Michael begins speaking the lyrics of a song named *Tony Chestnut,* and Dorsey and Sanders can't help but start to sing it. The rest of us join in, and we point to our body parts as indicated.

> Toe knee chest nut [head] nose eye love you.
> Toe knee nose. . . . Toe knee nose.
> Toe knee chest nut nose eye love you.
> That's what toe knee nose.

We reach Port Orleans and enter the food court for dinner, where Angelica persuades MJ to be a vegetarian for the night. The two girls load their trays with all manner of derivatives of corn, wheat, potato, and sugar cane.

Back at Building One, I open the connecting door to the grandparents' room and create a baby-sitting suite. By eight-thirty, Dorsey and Sanders are snoozing in the other room, while the rest of us get comfortable on the beds to watch a movie.

Tonight's feature is the "sweetest story ever told"—Disney's *Cinderella.* I'm not worried about this one causing nightmares for Michael or Nellie; the cruelty of Cinderella's stepmother is tame relative to the wickedness of the queen in *Snow White,* and the imagery isn't nearly so dark.

Nellie and Michael drift off to sleep during the soap bubble scene, as Cinderella sings to herself while washing the hall floor.

Angelica and MJ remain awake for most of the film, though they, too, succumb during a lull in the action, when Cinderella and the prince meet beside the ballroom and dance together in the moonlight.

Upon the film's conclusion, Mary and I step outside onto

the balcony-hallway and wait for the return of the other adults.

At the center of the courtyard is the fountain where Mary cried the other night, and it reminds me of my favorite scene from *Cinderella.*

There comes a moment in Cinderella's story when her hopes for going to the ball have been dashed. She rushes off in despair, fleeing into the yard of her estate and finding a bench, where she kneels and sobs. This bench is just beyond a bird bath that stands at the center of a watering trough for the animals. The look of that bird bath and trough is similar to the look of the fountain in this courtyard.

Mary acknowledges the comparison and also finds that particular scene of the film appealing. We conclude that Cinderella is at her lowest point while crying at the bench: she has lost all faith that her wishes and dreams can come true. It is at this pivotal moment that her fairy godmother arrives and delivers the magic Cinderella needs to pick herself up and believe in her dreams once more.

I've often thought it would be nice to have a fairy god-mother on call to help me solve my problems. Magic is a far easier solution than looking inside one's self for answers.

This notion of looking inward is exactly the point I've been trying to make with MJ and Michael. What is the force that makes a dream or wish come true? Is it the magic of a star, or the toss of a coin? Or is it something found deep within each one of us? MJ and Michael aren't ready yet to accept the concept of internal magic; *external* magic remains the only solution they can see. And Mary and I have to confess, we seem to want to see it too. How else do we explain our attraction to the fairy godmother scene in *Cinderella?*

But perhaps it's not the magic of the good fairy that attracts us after all. Maybe it's Cinderella's wondrous transformation—no matter how it occurs—that captures our imaginations. Maybe the power to *change* ourselves is the magic we seek, and we yearn for any hints or clues or promises to the whereabouts of this magic.

Mary and I know in our hearts that the true magic of the world resides within; the evidence that confirms it is all around us. We can find no magic wand to explain why Uncle Albert lives out his life with a cheery disposition in a world that took his wife and baby when he was a young man. And we can blame no incantation for the demons summoned within the likes of Adolf Hitler to inspire the murder of innocent millions. No, the magic to change is definitely internal. The question that matters now is, who controls this extremely powerful magic? What guides the hand in the depths of our wells to fill our mental buckets with so much elixir or so much poison?

Mary and I want the answer, so we jointly make a wish to find it. We each hurl a coin halfway across the courtyard to register our wish with the fountain.

As we stand there at the railing, Mary reaches into her pocket and withdraws two vials of bubble solution from last night. She hands me one while she hums a sweet melody from the movie. The two of us then blow bubbles off the balcony in salute of the Disney artistry.

"Don't you have kids to watch?" says Elsa from below.

Everyone has returned except for Jane and Tom, so we rearrange the children and head off to bed ourselves, leaving Angelica with my parents.

Before shutting off the light, Mary picks up the phone and dials the front desk for a 6:30 wake-up call.

"What gives?" I say.

"Gift Four. —It's for me, too: a behind-the-scenes tour of the Magic Kingdom. I'll actually get to see the Utilidors."

As I lie awake in bed, listening to Mary's breathing, I'm enthusiastic about tomorrow's tour. It will be my greatest chance yet to discover the secret behind the Disney Magic, because our tour guide will be a Disney expert—

But what does this really mean? Jane and Ferguson are experts too, yet their abilities are now suspect in my mind.

I wonder if experts are like fairy godmothers. We turn to them for help, and when their help gets results, these results seem like magic if we don't fully understand what they did. A financial expert, then, is a fairy godmother who transforms

a small investment into a large one. And a nutritionist is a fairy godmother who transforms illness into health.

Yet experts are also like diamonds: some of them are counterfeits. Ferguson is not preparing his clients for the next Great Depression, and Jane's nutritional protocols are making some people sicker.

I stare into the facets of Mary's diamond and watch the lights of the digital clock refract through them. I wonder what the sparkly-eyed woman from the library would say about experts.

CHAPTER 27

The "Keys to the Kingdom" Tour

Mary and I are up with the sun and out the door by 7am. We've left MJ and Michael to wake up with Grandma and Grandpa, who will then take them to Epcot with the rest of the family.

As we cross Port Orleans toward the bus shelters, the burner of a hot air balloon ignites high above us. That silly lava lamp was right again.

Mary and I board the first bus of the day to the Magic Kingdom, planning to arrive more than an hour before opening time. Our shuttle is occupied by just one other couple and their tired child.

"Where are *you* going?" says the woman to Mary.

"We're—"

"*We* have a character breakfast at Cinderella's Royal Table," she says. "It's not easy to get tickets, you know. I had to call at exactly 5am ninety days ago using repeat-dial to reach Reservations. The only other way to get tickets is through a package deal, but those are a rip-off. . . ."

The woman's male partner stares blankly out the window; I suppose it's his job to breathe for her. Her mouth clips along, rattling off the details of her family's week-long vacation—specifying which parks on which days, by what routes and for what reasons. It's a dizzying monologue that sets my mind to wandering.

I feel like I'm listening to MJ, whose mental voice tends to flow without filter. Doesn't this woman have a second voice inside her head, like I do? —One that questions and edits her thoughts before allowing them to escape? It's my second voice that keeps me quiet much of the time, limiting my remarks to those that might be helpful or humorous to my immediate audience. Nine-year-old MJ is already developing *her* second voice; I hear traces of it occasionally. "*You* don't care about that," she'll say; or, "Gee, *that* was a stupid thing to say." Certainly this woman has a second voice too. I simply wish it was on duty.

We reach the Magic Kingdom, and the woman hurries her family off the bus. Mary and I give them plenty of room to get ahead of us.

We are moving around the Disney property off-peak, and the walkways and shelters outside the Magic Kingdom are nearly vacant. There's an empty monorail train sitting mid-track, and a cast member flits between lampposts, cleaning the light fixtures with a long-handled feather-duster.

Mary halts our progress near the boat dock. "I'm sorry for the abbreviated tour the other day," she says. "It just didn't feel right."

"No problem," I say. "Lay it on me."

"Well, I bet you didn't know that the early plans for Disney World called for five hotels around Bay Lake and the Seven Seas Lagoon. Two of them were built—the Polynesian and the Contemporary—but the other three never made it off the drawing board. The Persian Resort was to be located along the shores of Bay Lake behind what is now Toontown, and the monorail serving it was going to have a special stop in Tomorrowland. Imagine that . . . a second access point to the Magic Kingdom. Just think of the congestion problems it would have solved on Main Street—"

"And without a theming violation," I say.

Mary describes the other two resorts as the Venetian and the Asian. The Venetian was going to sit directly east of the Transportation Plaza, and the Asian was going to occupy the site where the Grand Floridian sits now. "The Asian would have mirrored the exotic theme of Adventureland just inside the park, like the Contemporary does for Tomorrowland."

So much for my notion that the Grand Floridian was part of some master scheme to match the Victorian architecture at the park's entrance. Lord kill me if I become a Disneyphile.

Mary and I enter the Magic Kingdom and find the so-called Tour Garden beside City Hall. We're too early to check in, however, so we loiter next to a cast member who is polishing a brass handrail to a wonderful shine. He shares with us some examples of the Disney Company's strict practices regarding maintenance and cleanliness: he explains that the horse-shaped hitching posts along Main Street are completely scraped and repainted every two weeks; he describes how the nightly work crews place giant pans under their trucks to prevent oil-drippings from soiling the pavement; and he boasts that it is the duty of every cast member to pick up any litter they see. "And do you know why the sidewalks are red?" he asks.

Mary and I both shake our heads because we want to hear the answer from *him*.

"—To enhance the color of the grass," he says. "It works because green and red are opposites on the color wheel. Please come back to City Hall if you have any questions. We're here to serve."

Mary and I stroll back to the Tour Garden, doubting that the Main Street hitching posts are actually overhauled biweekly. Mary hopes that today's tour will lay to rest some of the wild claims she has read.

A total of twelve guests are registered for the tour, and we're required to stow our cameras and other electronic devices behind a counter. The only items we're permitted to carry for recording information are notepads and pens, of which Mary has both. Each guest is issued an official-looking Disney name tag and an earpiece-microphone to facilitate communication. The tour will begin in ten minutes at the flagpole in the Town Square, so Mary and I venture over to wait there.

Near the flagpole is a sculpture like the Partners statue in the Central Plaza, but this one portrays Walt Disney's brother Roy sitting on a park bench next to Minnie Mouse. At Roy's feet is a dedication plaque from the park's opening celebration. I read it aloud: *"Walt Disney World is a tribute to the philosophy and life of Walter Elias Disney . . . and to the talents, the dedication, and the loyalty of the entire Disney organization that made Walt Disney's dream come true—"*

"Well intended prose, I'm sure," says Mary, "but hardly accurate. Walt's dream was the model city of Epcot, not this carbon copy of Disneyland."

I read the rest silently:

> May Walt Disney World bring Joy and Inspiration
> and New Knowledge to all who come to this happy
> place . . . a Magic Kingdom where the young at heart
> of all ages can laugh and play and learn – together.
> Dedicated this 25th day of October, 1971
> Roy O. Disney

These aspirations seem so honorable, but I wonder what *joy* the Native Americans have found in Frontierland . . . and I wonder what *inspiration* our African American citizens have found in Liberty Square. —The thirteen black lanterns that hang from the Liberty Tree might represent something quite different to them.

Our guide's name is Erin, and she begins our tour with some facts we already know: the Magic Kingdom is a theater, where guests are part of the show; the train station provides the opening curtain; Main Street rolls with the credits on its second story windows; and the Cinderella Castle is the main feature. The one surprise, however, involves the color of the sidewalks. We now have a third explanation. The sidewalks are red to simulate the carpets of a theater.

Erin instructs us to turn off our communicators while we follow her to the next point of interest.

"But there's more she should be telling us," says Mary.

Mary explains to me that the buildings of the Town Square are not part of the illusion to make the castle look taller, so they are actually full size. And Main Street slopes gently upward toward the Central Plaza to further enhance the stature of the castle. "Walt Disney learned from Disneyland," she says. "He was disappointed that the Sleeping Beauty Castle didn't appear more prominent."

Erin leads us halfway up Main Street and turns us at the stub street. She then signals us to switch on our transmitters.

"Did you ever notice," she says, "that people tend to stay right when they walk? Well, the Disney imagineers noticed. You'll find film, food, and entertainment on your right as you enter the park, and souvenir shops on your right as you leave. —Greater convenience for guests . . . greater sales for Disney . . . a win-win."

We return to Main Street with our electronics off and continue toward the Central Plaza.

Mary points with two fingers at a storefront. "Walt wasn't afraid to violate *period correctness*," she says. "He put the shop windows closer to the ground so small children could see in."

Just before the bridge at the top of Main Street, Erin halts our group and signals us again.

"The Central Plaza is an island in the moat of the castle," she says. "A fleet of swan boats once carried passengers around it, but they were decommissioned in 1974 due to high operating costs."

We switch off our headgear and follow Erin across the bridge. Mary now has a scowl on her face. "Someone's got it wrong," she says. "The swan boats made it into the 1980s—I'm almost sure of it. They probably *began* in '74."

"You can't believe everything you read," I say.

Erin gathers us in front of the Partners statue and directs our attention back down Main Street. She gives us the full lecture on forced perspective, but her details don't match with the ones Mary gave me. Erin claims that the ground floors are full scale, while the upper stories are reduced by a third. Mary's research, however, indicated that first floor façades are at ninety percent and that the upper stories shrink by an eighth. Again, someone's got it wrong. Certainly our guide should know the truth; she works for Disney, after all.

Erin then asserts that Main Street gets narrower toward the hub as part of Disney's trick for heightening the castle. Yet this is exactly the common misconception Mary was careful to dispel for me. Mary declared that Main Street remains the same width all the way along.

So who should I believe? Which one of these people is the truer Disney expert? The decision turns out to be easier than I expected. Erin loses her credibility in a single remark. "Notice how the train station looks farther away," she says.

Her observation is exactly the opposite of what it should be if Main Street indeed narrows as she said. The train station in the Town Square should actually look nearer, not farther away. Our tour guide is proving to be a disappointment. She's a wholesale counterfeit.

Mary opens her notepad and draws a frown.

Erin brings us into Adventureland and seats us within a semi-enclosed corral of benches. She then presents a brief chronology of Walt Disney's life. ". . . He released *Snow White and the Seven Dwarfs* in 1935," she says.

I know that's not true. *Snow White* premiered in December of 1937—I read it just a few days ago off a video case.

During the ten-minute break that follows, Mary points out several other errors for me. Erin claimed that *Snow White* was the second highest grossing film of all time, when in fact it ranks something on the order of tenth behind the likes of *Gone With the Wind, Star Wars,* and *The Sound of Music* "even after adjusting for inflation," says Mary. And Walt Disney's 1941 vacation—billed by Erin as a goodwill tour of South America—was, in truth, motivated by the labor strike at his studio that was causing him so much grief.

Our group reassembles and makes its way over to the *Pirates of the Caribbean.* Before entering the ride, Erin explains the term Hidden Mickeys and gives us each the task of finding one in the attraction. Oh boy.

It is then Mary who tells me what I really want to know.

The *Pirates of the Caribbean* was one of the last attractions Walt Disney worked on before his death. It opened in Disneyland shortly thereafter and was copied into the Florida park by popular demand. But over the years, the ride has drawn criticisms for its less than liberated portrayals of women. So, in 1999, the Disney imagineers made a change. They reversed the roles in one of the lesser scenes—arming the maidens with broomsticks and rolling pins, and placing them in hot pursuit of a few pirates.

"Why bother?" says Mary.

And she's right. The script for this attraction still includes the auctioning off of a shackled woman into slavery, where the pirate who is selling her peels off such politically incorrect statements as *Shift your cargo, dearie! Show 'em your larboard side!* and *Strike your colors, you brazen wench! No need to expose your superstructure!* There isn't a healthy role model in the bunch.

On our walk to Frontierland, Mary explains to me that Disneyland provided Walt with a valuable education. His original park didn't allow for foot traffic between adjacent lands, meaning that each transition required a return to the Central Plaza. But guests found a way around this inconvenience; they trampled his plant beds to get where they wanted to go. Walt Disney didn't react by erecting fences. Instead, he simply paved the footpaths his guests had already created.

Upon our arrival in Frontierland, Erin crosses a barricade and leads us along the parade route's exit road. We climb to the top of the hill, cross the train tracks, and pass through an opening in a tall wooden fence. On the other side, she reassembles us for another lecture.

Mary's face brightens, and she pulls out her paper and pen. She ignores Erin's lengthy explanation of Disney's high-tech system for monitoring floats during parades and instead copies the text of a sign we see on the back of the fence. It's titled *The 7 Rules of a Cast Member,* and Mary writes furiously to get them all down. They are a Disney creation all the way. Each rule references one of the seven dwarfs before rendering its dictate.

Mary is thrilled to finally have them. She knew of their existence before we came here, but she hadn't found a copy of them.

At the wooden bridge between Frontierland and Liberty Square, Erin asks if anyone can guess which performers on the Disney property don't have to follow *The 7 Rules of a Cast Member*. She gives us a clue. She walks like a zombie and turns slowly toward the *Haunted Mansion*, performing the two-armed point of the undead.

In the center of Liberty Square, Erin calls our attention to the crooked shutters on the nearby buildings. "That's no mistake," she says.

Erin explains that our colonial ancestors needed bullets for the Revolutionary War, so they harvested their metal hinges, replacing them with leather straps that eventually stretched and caused the shutters to sag. According to Erin, this subtle detail is testimony to Disney's integrity when recreating an authentic historic scene. She then notes that the white swath across the pavement is there to represent the open sewers of the colonial era. How ironic, then, that the colonial tavern in which we're about to eat lunch doesn't serve beer.

"The Magic Kingdom is a dry province," says Mary, "—a magical land of perpetual prohibition. I guess historical accuracy depends on the historian."

We seat ourselves in the area sectioned off for our tour group. Mary and I entertain ourselves during the meal by rewriting *The 7 Rules of a Cast Member* as they might apply to the maids and butlers of the *Haunted Mansion*.

Following lunch, Erin returns us outside and stops us at the *Hall of Presidents*. She claims that this attraction is the one place in the world that has permission to use the official United States Presidential Seal outside of Washington. And she also boasts that *two* presidents have taken time out of their busy schedules to supply recordings for the show.

We turn off our electronics.

"How embarrassing," says Mary. "Can that really be true?"

Erin leads us toward the Central Plaza, then turns left at the ramp that climbs behind the castle. She halts us at the top, beside the four drinking fountains that encircle the Cinderella statue. "Two years from now, in 2005," she says, "Disneyland will celebrate its 50th birthday. We, here in Florida, will be participating too. You won't want to miss this Happiest Celebration on Earth. The castle will be trimmed out in gold."

Mary chuckles as we switch off our communicators. "Yeah, tell that to the brides and grooms of '96."

In 1996, Disney World celebrated its 25th anniversary by decorating the castle like a birthday cake. It was painted pink and garnished with frosting, lollipops, candy canes, gum drops, and colorful sprinkles. But not everyone liked the new look. It is rumored that more than two hundred weddings were cancelled during that time, which might explain why the castle was restored to its original look after only four months.

"Don't mess with the magic," I say.

"Indeed," says Mary, and she redirects my attention to an attraction named *The Many Adventures of Winnie the Pooh*. "That building used to be the home of *Mr. Toad's Wild Ride*—one of the park's originals from 1971."

"I loved that ride!" I say.

"Didn't we all. But in 1997, Disney announced plans to replace it. Fans went up in arms . . . and frogs' legs. They printed up t-shirts and paid their admission to stage protests here in Fantasyland, calling them *toad-ins*. Woe to the deed-holder of this hallowed ground. Disney shareholders are not the only ones with something at stake here. It's just like you said, Bert: don't mess with the magic."

◆ ◆ ◆

The tour takes us into Utilidors, then returns us outside to the backstage area behind Tomorrowland and Main Street.

"Are there any final questions?" says Erin.

A man raises his hand. "Is it true that the largest castle tower can be removed before storms?"

To my and Mary's surprise, Erin confirms this notion, even going so far as to say that "yes, in fact *all* of the castle towers can be lowered."

"How is it done?" says Mary. "Have you ever seen them down?"

Erin claims no knowledge of the procedure and has never seen the castle in pieces, yet she promises to find an answer for us at the conclusion of the tour.

We enter Town Square through an opening in the fence and return to the Tour Garden where we started our day. We hand in our communicators and retrieve our belongings, then locate Erin beside City Hall.

She apologizes to our group, saying that none of the castle towers can in fact be removed; only the tiny flags can be detached. "Thanks for teaching me something new today," she says. "I hope you've enjoyed your *Keys to the Kingdom* tour. Have a magical day."

Our group disbands, and Mary and I hurry to the main gate. It is one-thirty in the afternoon, and we're longing to reunite with the family in Epcot. We exit the Magic Kingdom and enter the line for the express monorail.

"I can't believe it," says Mary, "—a place this scripted, and they can't even put together a decent tour. How pathetic. They might as well give the job to a Disney biographer. Did you wonder why there was only one book on the shelf at the library the other day? I moved all the others to the reshelving cart so you wouldn't find them; they were all junk."

"You're my go-to girl for all things Disney," I say. "I'm guessing you could get a job at City Hall."

CHAPTER 28

The Blue Room Session

Mary and I board the first monorail and notice that many of the passengers are staring at us and whispering. We no doubt look like cast members out on assignment. Each of us wears a Mickey baseball cap and an authentic-looking Disney name tag, and Mary is carrying a notepad and pen.

"Excuse me," says a man. "I'm wondering if you can tell me what those white buildings are over there?" He is pointing to the island beyond the Grand Floridian resort.

"Sure," I say. "That's the Fairy Tale Wedding Pavilion and Bride's Vestibule." I place my elbow on Mary's shoulder. "My partner and I were hoping to get married there, but the price was too steep."

"You two are married?" says a woman. "And you both work for Disney?"

"Yup," says Mary. "—Married to each other . . . and married to the mouse."

People snicker at Mary's comment.

"But we decided to skip the pavilion," says Mary, "and pay for a Justice of the Peace in the Magic Kingdom. We're saving our pennies for what we *really* want: a house in Celebration—Disney's model town. Though I'm afraid we'll never be able to afford one."

"Not without a raise," I say.

"So how long have you worked for Disney?" asks the same

woman. She is eyeing the diamond ring on Mary's finger. I'm sensing that our jig is up, and I'm ready to confess.

"Well done!" says Mary, and she pulls off the ring. "This is the Disney device that removes all doubt. Congratulations." Mary gives the ring to the woman. "Welcome to the Disney test-kitchen, where today *you* are the lucky taste-testers who will sample Disney's latest recipes for entertainment. Leave it to the Disney Company to be the tireless experimenters . . . the proving-ground for the next generation of theme park thrills. Disney will once again raise the bar and introduce a new kind of fun, called *self-parody*. Imagine it: a magical land stocked with cast members who treat guests with indifference, irreverence, or outright disdain . . . or a place where guests enjoy rampaging characters, disagreeable waiters, and whiny princesses. . . . Hmm. But perhaps you're not ready for something so shocking. Well, then how about a place where waiters simply can't recommend anything on the menu? Or a place where street-sweepers have back-trouble and ask their guests to pick up their own litter."

I join Mary in her improv. "Or where princes are always on the make and flirting with guests." I wink and blow kisses to passengers.

Mary and I have energized this carload of people. Before long, we're brainstorming a new offering for the Disney lineup—an evening in the Magic Kingdom, called Vagabond Nights.

Vagabond Nights is an adult get-away, where roving fairies cast funny spells on guests . . . where bootleggers dispense booze before fleeing from the constable . . . where gamblers award fast-passes to winners at cards and dice . . . where matchmakers bring singles together for games and dares . . . and where Cinderella's servants wander the grounds, stealing people away and giving them make-overs.

By the time our train passes the Great Ceremonial House of the Polynesian Resort, Mary is entertaining the riders with a reading of our parody on *The 7 Rules of a Cast Member*.

One: Don't be HAPPY...avoid eye contact and scowl.

Two: Be like SNEEZY...spread the spirit of hostility...it's contagious.

Three: Don't be BASHFUL...level guests with full-body contact.

Four: Don't be like DOC...pull the plug on service and prevent all hope of recovery.

Five: Be GRUMPY...always point with the most offensive finger.

Six: Don't be like SLEEPY...shatter dreams and dispel the magic of guest experience everywhere.

Seven: Be DOPEY...expect each and every guest to take unrelenting abuse.

As we pull into the Transportation Plaza, Mary thanks everyone for participating in today's Blue Room Session, "where the sky's the limit."

We shake hands with our guests—young and old—and cheerfully bid them a "tragical day." We then follow them down the ramp.

CHAPTER 29

The Monorail to Epcot

Mary and I proceed to the neighboring platform for the monorail to Epcot, though we are careful to put some distance between ourselves and our former passengers.

As the current train boards, we reach the front of the line just as the chain is lifted. We'll be the first riders onto the next train.

"This is our punishment," I say, "for duping all those people."

The train leaves the station, and the platform becomes quiet.

"Hey," says the attending cast member, "this is your lucky day. Being first in line means you get to sit up front with the driver."

Perhaps partly out of guilt, Mary and I forfeit our ride up front to the family behind us with children. We enter the second car of the next train and make room for entering passengers.

Our train leaves the station and is just barely up to speed when there's the smell of something burning. Soon, the floor has become warm, and there's smoke outside the windows. An alarm sounds, and the train quickly stops.

Almost without thinking, I'm up through the escape hatch and pulling Mary out. She crawls along the rooftop of the train as I lift out more passengers, instructing them to follow her toward the back. We're positioned about twenty-five feet above the ground.

Our car is the only one on fire, so I follow the last of the evacuees away from the smoke. But my progress is slow, as passengers climb from the other compartments.

At the far end of the train, I see that Mary and many others have slid down the rear nose to the beam and are either walking or crawling along it to make room for those behind them.

At the front of the train, the pilot has fastened a rope-ladder down to the beam and is now crawling behind his four passengers. The two young children are crying.

A fleet of emergency vehicles and specialized equipment has arrived along World Drive and is now traveling the grass strip below the track. An army of cast members accompanies them on foot.

Firefighters douse the burning car and lower the escaped passengers to the ground with lift trucks and ladders. We are marched away under the beam and told to keep all cameras and electronic devices switched off and concealed so that nothing can interfere with emergency communications.

Once we've walked a fair distance, we are turned through the trees and led to the road, where more Disney personnel meet with us. Mary and I are given clearance by a paramedic and then directed to a bus. We are handed free park passes as we board.

While the bus slowly fills, I'm disturbed by the scene outside. World Drive has been closed to traffic, and we're far enough from the burnt-out train that we can't see it through the trees. And come to think of it, I don't see any news reporters out there either.

The strong arm of Disney seems to have a long reach, and it's making me uneasy.

"We'll probably never know what really happened here today," says Mary. "Remember, this is forty-three square miles of private property—"

"With swamps to keep out trespassers," I say.

"Right. Just go ahead and dial 9-1-1; you'll get Mickey Mouse."

I stare out the window at the offending trees, which block our view of the train. If the Disney Magic has an evil twin brother, it's surely the Disney Misery.

CHAPTER 30

The Park Farewell

On our last morning in Disney World, we're off to the Magic Kingdom for a half day of fun before heading to the airport.

We ride *The Magic Carpets of Aladdin* and also the *Jungle Cruise,* then take one final plunge down *Trash-Flash-&-Splash Fanny-Mountain.*

We cross the Central Plaza at about noon for our departure, where Mary stops us in front of the Partners statue for a special surprise.

The kids never completed their activity cards, meaning they couldn't show them to the hotel clerk and collect their gift. Thus, Mary has devised a new plan for giving them the Disney quote book.

"Did you hear something?" she says. Mary closes her eyes, and we wait expectantly.

"Hey guys!" she chirps with the lively voice of Mickey Mouse. "Leavin' so soon? Awe. I hope you come back to see me. But before you go, I have something for you. Close your eyes now. Are they closed?"

I remove the gift from my bag and toss it into the plant bed that surrounds the pedestal.

"Oops," says Mickey. "Dropped it. Ha-ha. Best wishes. Bye for now."

MJ and Michael open their eyes and easily spot the gift. They retrieve it and rip through the paper, finding four red

Mickey lollipops and a store-bought book called *The Quotable Walt Disney*. I should have guessed it; Mary's refusal to let me see her work should have been my tip-off that she was actually doing something else.

The kids pass me the book and fawn over their suckers. "Can we eat them?" says MJ.

"Of course you can, but not now," says Mary. "Let's save them for the airplane."

The four of us wave goodbye to Walt and Mickey, then travel down Main Street.

Once outside the gates, we choose the ferry for our return to the Transportation Plaza, hoping to get stranded in the lagoon and miss our flight.

As I watch a monorail train glide into the Contemporary's atrium, Mary puts her hand on my shoulder. "You know what, Bert?" she says. "Erin was wrong about something else. The *Haunted Mansion* is not the only place where *The 7 Rules of a Cast Member* don't apply. In fact, the whole Disney property is a city under martial law, with costumed cops wearing Mickey Mouse badges."

I stare across the water, watching the sunlight splinter off the ripples. These searing shards of silver leave an impression on my vision, which lingers without form, until a picture suddenly assembles itself in great detail. I am kneeling beside the trunk in my tower with a hammer and chisel in my hands. I've chipped off the chrome plating of the Disney sugar bowl, only to find that its inner casting is not lead, as I had supposed. Rather, the Disney Magic is sterling silver, just like the Holiday Spirit. It is shiny when polished and tarnished when neglected, meaning the Magic and the Misery are common to both. My child-within was right all along: the Disney Magic belongs to the tea set in my parlor; it deserves to be displayed beside the Holiday Spirit.

At the Transportation Plaza, we take one last look at the Cinderella Castle before passing beneath the canopy and finding Grandma and Grandpa waiting for us in the van.

We shower them with our thanks for this terrific vacation. And Dad, as usual, deflects our gratitude by crediting the fine weather for our good time. We thank him for that too.

CHAPTER 31

The Trip Home

As we sit in the Orlando airport, waiting to board our plane, Mary places a wrapped package in my lap. "Gift Five, I think; I've lost track."

Inside is a second book about Disney World that picks up where the first one left off—at the death of Walt Disney in 1966. Mary again entertains the children so that I may read while we travel.

Like before, the first chapter offers a helpful historical context. Walt Disney's dream of building a model city was an ambition far older than George Pullman's or Robert Owen's. In fact, the notion of creating a model city stretches all the way back to Plato in the fourth century BC—and some say even earlier, to the stories of Hesiod.

In chapter two, Mary returns me to Florida in 1966 for the preparations being made to develop the Disney property. I discover that Walt Disney died about a month after making his film about Epcot, meaning that the planning for his property was to proceed without his guiding hand.

The remaining chapters of Mary's book tell a troubling tale of a corporation forging ahead without a visionary leader. The industrial park and airport never developed, and the Epcot Center that opened in the early 1980s was just another amusement park. Yet, from the outset, Walt's successors actively pursued the governmental powers they argued were necessary to build their model city. And Florida lawmakers granted them these powers. The result has been a decades-long struggle between Disney's private interests and the public interests of Florida residents. For instance, the Disney Company has rejected public transit solutions between Disney World and the Orlando International Airport when intermediate stops have been proposed; it has also won for itself governmental subsidies that were intended for public purposes; and Disney World's private security force has routinely guarded the release of information that would mar the company's image. It is difficult for me to respect a corporation with such a dismal track record.

◆ ◆ ◆

On the last leg of our journey home—the flight from Chicago to Madison—the children sit together and enjoy their *dissolving* Hidden Mickey lollipops. Mary and I do the same from the row behind them.

"It makes me sad," I say. "The Disney Company under Walt was about quality and innovation. Now, it's just another profit-chaser."

"Yeah," says Mary. "Walt wasn't afraid to gamble on a far-fetched idea."

"Where's the integrity?" I say. "Didn't he leave anyone like himself behind?"

My words hang in the air, and Mary lowers her eyes.

"There's something I didn't tell you, Bert. Walt had skeletons in his closet."

Mary explains that Walt Disney was an informant for the FBI during the Red Scare. He was one of those people who named suspected "subversives" and "communists" in Hollywood, and he testified at the congressional hearings that trampled First Amendment protections. All in all, ten people went to prison, and hundreds more were blacklisted.

These were the events that pre-dated the McCarthy trials, and Walt Disney played a role in them. "It's quite a bitter pill to take," she says.

Disney and *McCarthyism*: these are two words I never imagined I would be placing in the same sentence. I feel a mood-change sweeping through me. My cynical self is awakening to dissect Mr. Disney, and I share my first thoughts with Mary.

"Perhaps Epcot wasn't such a great idea after all," I say. "His model city would have certainly faced many of the same issues as today's Disney World. How would he have handled things differently? Would he have endorsed public transit solutions that might lower his profits? Would he have given free access to the press to cover disasters? Would he have refrained from using his municipal status to win public funds?"

"Right," says Mary. "How civic-minded would he have been?"

"And tell me *this*," I begin to rave. "How can a model city solve the problems of slums if it never actually has any to begin with? . . . And why would voters be such a threat to good development if the company was going to own all the property?"

I fall silent, recognizing that voters could certainly impose themselves in ways that might alter the character of the city and decrease the overall value of Disney World. I can understand Walt's reluctance to give any measure of public control to his dream city.

However, I wonder if Walt recognized the irony of his proposal. He was suggesting better living through centralized control—more like a dictatorship than a democracy. Did he see the parallels with the Soviet Union and Nazi Germany? Would he have employed a secret police to root out violators of a dress code, or to evict residents engaging in unacceptable life-styles? Would he have maintained a private security force, like the one in Disney World today, which denies free access to the media and limits the release of information to outside authorities?

"I think you're right," says Mary. "If Walt had lived to build his model city, we might have discovered a man we're not so fond of."

Mary reaches into her carry-on bag and pulls out a sheet of paper. "Here's what someone once wrote about the Town of Pullman during its heyday. The same things might have been said about Epcot if Walt had managed to build it."

Mary gives me an excerpt from an 1885 article by Richard T. Ely from HARPER'S MAGAZINE. It's called *Pullman: A Social Study.*

> . . . In looking over all the facts of the case the conclusion is unavoidable that the idea of Pullman is un-American. It is a nearer approach than anything the writer has seen to what appears to be the ideal of the great German Chancellor. It is not the American ideal. It is benevolent, well wishing feudalism, which desires the happiness of the people, but in such way as shall please the authorities. One can not avoid thinking of the late Czar of Russia, Alexander II, to whom the welfare of his subjects was truly a matter of concern. He wanted them to be happy, but desired their happiness to proceed from him, in whom everything should centre. Serfs were freed, the knout abolished, and no insuperable objection raised to reforms, until his people showed a decided determination to take matters in their own hands, to govern themselves, and to seek their own happi-

ness in their own way. Then he stopped the work of
reform, and considered himself deeply aggrieved.
The loss of authority and distrust of the people is
the fatal weakness of many systems of reform and
well-intentioned projects of benevolence.

A wave of disenchantment rolls through me. My admiration for Walt Disney quickly fades.

Unfortunately, this is a feeling I know all too well. A
number of years ago, another famous American lost my
respect in much the same way.

Thomas Jefferson became a role model for me when I
was fourteen years old. My family had visited Washington,
D.C. and toured the Jefferson Memorial, where I first read
his quotation engraved inside the dome:

> I have sworn upon the altar of God eternal hostility
> against every form of tyranny over the mind of man.

Those words made a lasting impression on me, and I hung
a copy of them on my wall. Thomas Jefferson remained one
of my heroes well into adulthood.

But following the commemorations of his 250th birthday
in 1993, a new generation of historians was forwarding more
complete disclosures of his life. I was dismayed to learn that
the man who endorsed an end to slavery owned more than
two hundred slaves himself—never managing to free them
as some other slave-owners were doing at the time. And I
was also disillusioned to learn that the man who wrote the
words "all men are created equal" also professed a hierarchy
among humans, concluding that blacks were inferior to whites
in the endowments of both body and mind.

These contradictions in Thomas Jefferson's thinking still weigh on me today. How can I hold this man in high esteem when his core principles run so counter to my own?

And now, it seems Walt Disney faces a similar fate. He, too, presents me with some disturbing contradictions. The man who created Disneyland for wholesome family entertainment was also willing to blacklist those whose political ideas differed from his own. And the man who planned to build a model city to demonstrate a better way to live was also capable of denying certain citizens their constitutional protections.

"Another hero bites the dust," says Mary.

"Is Abraham Lincoln the only one left?" I say. "Damn the documentaries. Hand me my rose-colored glasses."

"Let's put Abe off limits," says Mary, "—no studying his life. That way we'll always love him."

Mary pulls out a magazine and reads to herself, so I stare out the window at the evening sky.

Why have my heroes contradicted themselves? Surely I must be missing some shred of evidence that reconciles their behaviors.

I reach into my bag and pull out the Disney quote-book Mary gave the children. Perhaps Walt's own words can redeem him.

I breeze through the book and earmark a few pages. His quotations fall short of redemption, but four of them speak well to my situation: two offering hope, one giving advice, and one supplying motivation.

> All the adversity I've had in my life, all my troubles and obstacles, have strengthened me... You may not realize it when it happens, but a kick in the teeth may be the best thing in the world for you.

We keep moving forward, opening new doors, and doing new things, because we're curious and curiosity keeps leading us down new paths.

When we consider a project, we really study it—not just the surface idea, but everything about it. And when we go into that new project, we believe in it all the way. We have confidence in our ability to do it right. And we work hard to do the best possible job.

It's kind of fun to do the impossible.

I close the book and return to staring out the window. The sun has just set, and two worlds exist side by side—one day and one night. The sky remains lit by the hues of twilight, while the ground lies blanketed in darkness. Cities and towns sparkle like scattered diamonds across the landscape.

My heroes, it seems, occupy two worlds as well—one dark and one light. If I keep my eyes to the light, however, I might miss a dazzling city there in the darkness. *Don't be afraid of the dark,* I tell myself. *Study the dark sides of Walt Disney and Thomas Jefferson so you don't miss a dazzling city.*

The next chapter of my life, at least until school starts, will be an attempt to rescue my fallen heroes . . . because *it's kind of fun to do the impossible.*

I explore the eastern sky for a star and hum to myself the theme song from *Pinocchio.* Perhaps fate will be kind and deliver me a bolt out of the blue. My first order of business when I get home is to go to the library and find a book on the Red Scare.

PART IV

The
Odyssey

CHAPTER 32

The Real Walt Disney

During the Great Depression of the 1930s, capitalism looked like a failure. Bankruptcies, unemployment, and breadlines plagued the democracies of Europe and America. Many people craved a better, fairer social system. And Joseph Stalin of the Soviet Union claimed to offer one.

Communism promised a utopian world of peace, prosperity, and freedom . . . where governments, police, and militia were destined to dissolve away naturally. The Soviet Union claimed to be just one mere step away from pure communism—on the verge of completing the evolutionary path from feudalism to capitalism to socialism to communism. Stalin insisted that his socialist dictatorship would remain in power until the threat of capitalism was defeated by revolutionary uprisings around the world. Then, communism could finally take hold.

Stalin's Scientific Socialism was a seductive vision for populations under stress. But the vision, it turns out, was an illusion.

Stalin welcomed foreign visitors to glimpse his ideal world. Tours were carefully staged to portray a Russia rich in housing, food, employment, and education. Even the fronts of buildings were phony in some cases.

People from around the world praised Stalin for his achievements. And it was the American journalist, Lincoln

Steffens, who wrote the now famous quote: "I have been over into the future, and it works."

Stalin's many supporters also defended him against accusations that he was committing enormous atrocities against his own people, like tortured confessions, mass executions, and a planned famine.

Yet there were other writers who presented an opposing view. For instance, the Russian-born American, Ayn Rand, wrote, "the Russian people live in constant terror under a bloody, monstrous dictatorship."

Who were the world's readers supposed to believe, when prize-winning journalists argued convincingly from each side of the aisle? The literal truth was difficult to validate. It was poetic truth, then—the ability to persuade—that achieved results. In fact, poetic truth grew even more influential with the aid of widely disseminated print and film media.

Poetic truth acquired a new name around this time: *propaganda*. Propaganda was obscuring the unbelievable literal truth that Stalin was killing thousands of his own citizens every day, conducting a holocaust that would last a quarter century and claim four times as many lives as Adolf Hitler's.

Stalin funded and controlled Communist parties in nations around the world, hoping to convert these countries to communism. Party members in foreign nations were considered by the Kremlin to be Soviet citizens living abroad. Orders came from Moscow and were to be obeyed without question.

The COMMUNIST PARTY USA had the following preamble to its constitution:

> The Communist Party of the United States of America is a working class political party carrying forward today the traditions of Jefferson, Paine, Jackson, and Lincoln, and of the Declaration of Independence; it

upholds the achievements of democracy, the right of "life, liberty, and the pursuit of happiness," and defends the United States Constitution against its reactionary enemies who would destroy democracy and all popular liberties; it is devoted to the defense of the immediate interests of workers, farmers, and all toilers against capitalist exploitation, and to preparation of the working class for its historic mission to unite and lead the American people to extend these democratic principles to their necessary and logical conclusions.

By establishing common ownership of the national economy, through a government of the people, by the people, and for the people; the abolition of class divisions in society; that is, by the establishment of socialism according to the scientific principles enunciated by the greatest teachers of mankind, Marx, Engels, Lenin, and Stalin, and the free cooperation of the American people with those of other lands, striving toward a world without oppression and war, a world brotherhood of man.

The Communist Party attracted young, idealistic New York playwrights during the 1920s. Then, as film cinema replaced stage entertainment during the depression of the 1930s, Broadway writers seeking work migrated to Hollywood to be screenwriters. Hollywood's Communist Party offered these talent-guild members a social life, employment connections, and the promise that their art would naturally benefit from its rooting in the morally superior principles of communism.

Hollywood was a primary target for America's Communist Party because of film's great power to persuade.

In the 1920s, Vladimir Lenin of Russia sent cinema trains into the countryside, believing that "of all the arts the motion picture is the most important." Lenin's successor, Stalin, agreed: "The cinema is not only a vital agitprop device for the education and political indoctrination of the workers, but also a fluent channel through which to reach the minds and shape the desires of people everywhere."

Hollywood's Communist Party members seemed to toe the party line, writing scripts favorable to communist principles—endorsing labor unrest and negatively portraying capitalist business owners. Communists rejected intellectual films that might suggest people should look within themselves for the solutions to social problems: capitalism should be blamed; communism should be praised.

During the 1930s, as Adolf Hitler rose to power in Germany, America's Communist Party was instructed to endorse a military buildup against this growing fascist threat beside Mother Russia.

Then, in 1939, Stalin signed an alliance with Hitler and began invading his allotted share of Europe. Suddenly, Stalin reversed the communist party line in America, calling for an end to the U.S. military buildup and an end to U.S. aid to Britain and France in their fight against Hitler. American communists joined the anti-war effort, and party labor leaders called strikes in the defense industries. Stalin gathered strategic information from Communist Party members in Europe and passed it along to Hitler.

In June 1941, Hitler violated his alliance with Stalin and invaded Russia. This event marked another reversal in the stance of America's Communist Party—Americans should once again endorse U.S. involvement in the war. Communist labor leaders made "no-strike" pledges in the defense industries and advocated that the Soviet Union be considered an ally.

Following the war, Stalin's party line reverted to its original call for class struggle and revolution, ushering in the start of the Cold War. Hollywood labor unions provided a fertile battleground for the Communist Party, as the independent guilds maneuvered for turf. America's Communist Party backed Herb Sorrell in his fight to win control of the Hollywood trade unions.

Sorrell had led a strike against the Disney studio back in 1941, before the war. Now, in 1945 and 1946, he waged violent strikes at the major film studios.

In March 1947, President Truman set up the Federal Employee Loyalty Program—with its loyalty review boards—to investigate and dismiss government employees suspected of posing a threat to national security.

In September of that year, the HOUSE COMMITTEE ON UN-AMERICAN ACTIVITIES (HUAC) subpoenaed forty-three witnesses from the Hollywood film industry to address suspicions that movies were being used to spread communist propaganda. Twenty-four of the witnesses were classified as "friendly," and Walt Disney was one of them.

My history lesson gives me a feel for the times. Now, I want to get a glimpse into the workings of Walt Disney's mind; I want to know what he was thinking.

I discover a full-page advertisement Walt Disney placed in Variety Magazine on July 2, 1941. His studio artists had been on strike for about a month, and the ad was a direct appeal to them to reconsider their position. Walt seems convinced that communist influences were responsible for the strike and preventing its timely resolution.

TO MY EMPLOYEES ON STRIKE:

I believe you are entitled to know why you are not working today. I offered your leaders the following terms:

1. All employees to be reinstated to former positions.
2. No discrimination.
3. Recognition of your union.
4. Closed shop.
5. 50 percent retroactive pay for the time on strike—something without precedent in the American Labor movement.
6. Increase in wages to make yours the highest salary scale in the cartoon industry.
7. Two weeks' vacation with pay.

I believe that you have been misled and misinformed about the real issues underlying the strike at the studio. I am positively convinced that Communistic agitation, leadership, and activities have brought about this strike, and has persuaded you to reject this fair and equitable settlement.

I address you in this manner because I have no other means of reaching you.

Walt Disney
Hollywood, California
July 2, 1941

Three years later, in 1944, Walt Disney formalized his sentiments when he and other Hollywood notables formed the MOTION PICTURE ALLIANCE FOR THE PRESERVATION OF AMERICAN IDEALS. Walt Disney was the organization's vice president.

Much like the preamble to the COMMUNIST PARTY USA's constitution, the MOTION PICTURE ALLIANCE's *Statement of*

Principles reads like the Declaration of Independence.

> We believe in, and like, the American way of life;
> the liberty and freedom which generations before
> us have fought to create and preserve; the freedom
> to speak, to think, to live, to worship, to work and
> to govern ourselves, as individuals, as free men; the
> right to succeed or fail as free men, according to the
> measure of our ability and our strength.
>
> Believing in these things, we find ourselves in
> sharp revolt against a rising tide of Communism,
> Fascism, and kindred beliefs, that seek by subversive
> means to undermine and change this way of life;
> groups that have forfeited their right to exist in this
> country of ours, because they seek to achieve their
> change by means other than the vested procedure
> of the ballot and to deny the right of the majority
> opinion of the people to rule.
>
> In our special field of motion pictures, we resent
> the growing impression that this industry is made of,
> and dominated by, Communists, radicals and crack-
> pots. We believe that we represent the vast majority
> of the people who serve this great medium of expres-
> sion. But unfortunately it has been an unorganized
> majority. This has been almost inevitable. The very
> love of freedom, of the rights of the individual, make
> this great majority reluctant to organize. But now
> we must, or we shall meanly lose "the last, best hope
> on earth."
>
> As Americans, we have no new plan to offer. We
> want no new plan, we want only to defend against
> its enemy that which is our priceless heritage; that
> freedom which has given man, in this country, the

fullest life and the richest expression the world has ever known; that system which, in the present emergency, has fathered an effort that, more than any other single factor, will make possible the winning of this war.

As members of the motion picture industry, we must face and accept an especial responsibility. Motion pictures are inescapably one of the world's great forces for influencing public thought and opinion, both at home and abroad. In this fact lies solemn obligation. We refuse to permit the effort of Communist, Fascist, and other totalitarian-minded groups to pervert this powerful medium into an instrument for the dissemination of un-American ideas and beliefs. We pledge ourselves to fight, with every means at our organized command, any effort of any group or individual, to divert the loyalty of the screen from the free America that gave it birth. And to dedicate our own work, in the fullest possible measure, to the presentation of the American scene, its standards and its freedoms, its beliefs and its ideals, as we know them and believe in them.

During my search for a transcript of Walt Disney's testimony from the 1947 congressional hearings, I stumble upon a 1933 article in OVERLAND MONTHLY MAGAZINE titled, *The Cartoon's Contribution to Children.* Mickey Mouse was just five years old at the time of its printing, and Walt Disney was a young man of thirty-one. The article appears at the height of the Great Depression, yet Walt Disney conveys a mood that is both compassionate and optimistic. He is just like I remember him from his television appearances when I was a child. I can't help but love the man who can string together the following words:

> It would be presumptuous of me to speak for the entire motion picture cartoon industry. You will think me immodest to limit this discussion to Mickey Mouse. I seem to be on the spot!
>
> Standing on the spot, I will make three guesses as to the nature of Cartoon Pictures' contribution to children. I will do it blindfolded. I fear no man!
>
> To be honest about the matter, when our gang goes into a huddle and comes out with a new Mickey Mouse story, we will not have worried one bit as to whether the picture will make the children better men and women, or whether it will conform with the enlightened theories of child psychology.
>
> And yet, if Mickey were to say or do one thing to hurt the child audience in any way, he would die of shame; and we, all of us who work and play with Mickey, would sneak off to the unexplored recesses of New Guinea . . . and there . . . imagine our mortification . . . the New Guinea cannibals would refuse to eat us; we being lothesome things: we being the depraved souls who made Mickey do a thing which hurt children.
>
> But this will never happen. Mickey would never stand for it. If our gang ever put Mickey in a situation less wholesome than sunshine, Mickey would take Minnie by the hand and move to some other studio. Then, how would we eat, conditions being as they are, the wolf eating the Fuller Brush Man at the door and good men sleeping three deep on the benches of Pershing Square?

No, Mickey would never stand for it. He is never mean or ugly. He never lies nor cheats nor steals. He is a clean, happy, little fellow who loves life and folk. He never takes advantage of the weak and we see to it that nothing ever happens that will cure his faith in the transcendent destiny of one Mickey Mouse or his convictions that the world is just a big apple pie. Our animators and gag men having rescued Mickey from every conceivable predicament, the young fellow knows not fear save when he sees a friend in danger. When, on occasions, as boys will, the lad becomes too cocky and struts vaingloriously before admiring Minnie, Fate in the gag department kicks him from the rear and rolls him ignobly in the dust of gentle ridicule. Sex [gender] is just another work to Mickey, and the story of the traveling salesman of no more interest than the ladies' lingerie department. He is not a little mouse. He only looks like one. He is Youth, the Great Unlicked and Uncontaminated.

Now how could a fine, upstanding lad like Mickey ever do or say anything to hurt a child?

Nope! We have too much confidence in Mickey to worry about his effect on the growing child. In fact, we never think and build in terms of either child or adult audience. Mickey Mouse pictures are gauged to only one audience: the Mickey audience. The Mickey audience is not made up of people; it has no racial, national, political, religious or social differences or affiliations; the Mickey audience is made up of parts of people, of that deathless, precious, ageless, absolutely primitive remnant of something in every world-wracked human being which makes us play with children's toys and laugh without self-consciousness at silly things, and sing in bathtubs, and dream and believe that our babies are uniquely beautiful. You know . . . the Mickey in us.

Mr. Mussolini takes his family to see every Mickey picture. Mr. King George and Mrs. Queen Mary give him a right royal welcome; while Mr. President F. Roosevelt and family have lots of Mickey in them, too. Doug Fairbanks took Mickey with him to savage South Sea islands and won the natives over to his project. Mickey is one matter upon which the Chinese and the Japanese agree.

Of course there must be millions of people who have a downright feeling of animosity for our M. Mouse. Mr. A. Hitler, the Nazi old thing, says that Mickey's silly. Imagine that! Well, Mickey is going to save Mr. A. Hitler from drowning or something some day. Just wait and see if he doesn't. Then won't Mr. A. Hitler be ashamed!

What do animated cartoons contribute to children? Well, what do they give you? Wholesome entertainment? A clean laugh? A chance to spread the tattered wings of your imagination and soar to a realm where trees dance and you forget to shout, "Aw, neurts!"?

It is not our job to teach, implant morals or improve anything except our pictures. If Mickey has a bit of practical philosophy to offer the younger generation, it is to keep on trying. That's what we do who make animated cartoons. In the United States, there are fifty million children enrolled in Mickey Mouse Clubs. It is our hope and ambition to keep on trying so that the hundred million children of these fifty million children will have the Mickey

in them released and nourished by better cartoons
than we make today.

"THAT'S OUR JOB. . . . WE LOVE IT!"

I return to my search for Walt Disney's HUAC testimony
and uncover another artifact I wasn't expecting to find—the
testimony of another famous American, one who would eventually become the president of the United States. Like Disney,
Ronald Reagan was called to testify before the House committee as a "friendly" witness.

At the time of the hearings in 1947, Reagan was an actor
and the head of a labor union called the Screen Actors Guild.
He was well acquainted with the tactics of communist-led
labor. At union meetings, suspected party members sat in
the "diamond" formation so that their opinions seemed
to reflect the majority around the room. Party members
dragged out meetings until late into the night, hoping to delay
the vote until non-party members went home. Sometimes,
party members prevented the vote altogether by abandoning
meetings to eliminate the union's necessary quorum. In one
instance, Reagan witnessed a gathering where the reserved
hall was too small to hold all of the voting members. The
communist minority—who knew to arrive early and get seats
inside—voted to support a studio picket line.

Reagan's testimony on October 23, 1947 included the following statements, which impressed me with their candor
and decency:

[...]

ROBERT E. STRIPLING, CHIEF INVESTIGATOR – Has
it ever been reported to you that certain members
of the guild were communists?

RONALD REAGAN – Yes, sir; I have heard different discussions and some of them tagged as communists...

STRIPLING – Would you say that this clique has attempted to dominate the guild?

REAGAN – Well, sir, by attempting to put their own particular views on various issues, I guess in regard to that you would have to say that our side was attempting to dominate, too, because we were fighting just as hard to put over our views, in which we sincerely believed, and I think, we were proven correct by the figures—Mr. Murphy gave the figures—and those figures were always approximately the same, an average of ninety percent or better of the Screen Actors Guild voted in favor of those matters now guild policy.

[...]

STRIPLING – Mr. Reagan, what is your feeling about what steps should be taken to rid the motion-picture industry of any communist influences, if they are there?

REAGAN – Well, sir . . . 99 percent of us are pretty well aware of what is going on, and I think within the bounds of our democratic rights, and never once stepping over the rights given us by democracy, we have done a pretty good job in our business of keeping those people's activities curtailed. After all, we must recognize them at present as a political party. On that basis we have exposed their lies when we came across them, we have opposed their propaganda, and I can certainly testify that in the case of the Screen Actors Guild we have been eminently successful in preventing them from, with their usual tactics, trying to run a majority of an organization with a well organized minority.

So that fundamentally I would say in opposing those people that the best thing to do is to make democracy work. In the Screen Actors Guild we make it work by insuring everyone a vote and by keeping everyone informed. I believe that, as Thomas Jefferson put it, if all the American people know all of the facts they will never make a mistake.

Whether the party should be outlawed, I agree with the gentlemen that preceded me that that is a matter for the Government to decide. As a citizen I would hesitate, or not like, to see any political party outlawed on the basis of its political ideology. We have spent 170 years in this country on the basis that democracy is strong enough to stand up and fight against the inroads of any ideology. However, if it is proven that an organization is an agent of a power, a foreign power, or in any way not a legitimate political party, and I think the Government is capable of proving that, if the proof is there, then that is another matter...

I happen to be very proud of the industry in which I work; I happen to be very proud of the way in which we conducted the fight. I do not believe the communists have ever at any time been able to use the motion-picture screen as a sounding board for their philosophy or ideology...

J. Parnell Thomas, Chairman – There is one thing that you said that interested me very much. That was the quotation from Jefferson. That is just why this committee was created by the House of Representatives, to acquaint the American people with the facts. Once the American people are acquainted with the facts there is no question but what the American people will do a job, the kind of a job that they want done; that is, to make America just as pure as we can possibly make it.

We want to thank you very much for coming here today.

Reagan – Sir, if I might, in regard to that, say that what I was trying to express, and didn't do very well, was also this other fear. I detest, I abhor their philosophy, but I detest more than that their tactics, which are those of the fifth column, and are dishonest, but at the same time I never as a citizen want to see our country become urged, by either fear or resentment of this group, that we ever compromise with any of our democratic principles through that fear or resentment. I still think that democracy can do it.

The following day, Walt Disney took his place at the table and testified before the committee. I'm grateful to have found the entire transcript, because I don't want someone else feeding me their biases in the form of selected excerpts. I want to judge for myself every statement.

Stripling – Mr. Disney, will you state your full name and present address, please?

Walt Disney – Walter E. Disney, Los Angeles, California.

Stripling – When and where were you born, Mr. Disney?

Disney – Chicago, Illinois, December 5, 1901.

Stripling – December 5, 1901?

Disney – Yes, sir.

Stripling – What is your occupation?

Disney – Well, I am a producer of motion-picture cartoons.

Stripling – Mr. Chairman, the interrogation of Mr. Disney will be done by Mr. Smith.

Thomas – Mr. Smith.

H. A. Smith – Mr. Disney, how long have you been in that business?

Disney – Since 1920.

Smith – You have been in Hollywood during this time?

Disney – I have been in Hollywood since 1923.

SMITH – At the present time you own and operate the Walt Disney Studio at Burbank, California?

DISNEY – Well, I am one of the owners. Part owner.

SMITH – How many people are employed there, approximately?

DISNEY – At the present time about six hundred.

SMITH – And what is the approximate largest number of employees you have had in the studio?

DISNEY – Well, close to 1,400 at times.

SMITH – Will you tell us a little about the nature of this particular studio, the type of pictures you make, and approximately how many per year?

DISNEY – Well, mainly cartoon films. We make about twenty short subjects and about two features a year.

SMITH – Will you talk just a little louder, Mr. Disney?

DISNEY – Yes, sir.

SMITH – How many, did you say?

DISNEY – About twenty short subject cartoons and about two features per year.

SMITH – And some of the characters in the films consist of . . .

DISNEY – You mean such as Mickey Mouse and Donald Duck and Snow White and the Seven Dwarfs, and things of that sort.

SMITH – Where are these films distributed?

DISNEY – All over the world.

SMITH – In all countries of the world?

DISNEY – Well, except the Russian countries.

SMITH – Why aren't they distributed in Russia, Mr. Disney?

DISNEY – Well, we can't do business with them.

SMITH – What do you mean by that?

DISNEY – Oh, well, we have sold them some films a good many years ago. They bought the *Three Little Pigs* [1933] and used it through Russia. And they looked at a lot of our pictures, and I think they ran a lot of them in Russia, but then turned them back to us and said they didn't want them, they didn't suit their purposes.

SMITH – Is the dialogue in these films translated into the various foreign languages?

DISNEY – Yes. On one film we did ten foreign versions. That was *Snow White and the Seven Dwarfs* [1938].*

*February 4, 1938 was the official release date to U.S. theaters by RKO Radio Pictures following the film's premiere on December 21, 1937 at Carthay Circle Theatre.

SMITH – Have you ever made any pictures in your studio that contained propaganda and that were propaganda films?

DISNEY – Well, during the war we did. We made quite a few—working with different government agencies. We did one for the Treasury on taxes and I did four anti-Hitler films. And I did one on my own for air power.

SMITH – From those pictures that you made, have you any opinion as to whether or not the films can be used effectively to disseminate propaganda?

DISNEY – Yes, I think they proved that.

SMITH – How do you arrive at that conclusion?

DISNEY – Well, on the one for the Treasury on taxes, it was to let the people know that taxes were important in the war effort. As they explained to me, they had thirteen million new taxpayers, people who had never paid taxes, and they explained that it would be impossible to prosecute all those that were delinquent, and they wanted to put this story before those people so they would get their taxes in early. I made the film, and after the film had its run, the Gallup poll organization polled the public, and the findings were that twenty-nine percent of the people admitted that it had influenced them in getting their taxes in early and giving them a picture of what taxes will do.

SMITH – Aside from those pictures you made during

the war, have you made any other pictures, or do you permit pictures to be made at your studio containing propaganda?

DISNEY — No; we never have. During the war we thought it was a different thing. It was the first time we ever allowed anything like that to go in the films. We watch so that nothing gets into the films that would be harmful in any way to any group or any country. We have large audiences of children and different groups, and we try to keep them as free from anything that would offend anybody as possible. We work hard to see that nothing of that sort creeps in.

SMITH — Do you have any people in your studio at the present time that you believe are communist or fascist, employed there?

DISNEY — No; at the present time I feel that everybody in my studio is one hundred percent American.

SMITH — Have you had at any time, in your opinion, in the past, have you at any time in the past had any communists employed at your studio?

DISNEY — Yes; in the past I had some people that I definitely feel were communists.

SMITH — As a matter of fact, Mr. Disney, you experienced a strike at your studio, did you not?

DISNEY — Yes.

SMITH — And is it your opinion that that strike was instituted by members of the Communist Party to serve their purposes?

DISNEY — Well, it proved itself so with time, and I definitely feel it was a communist group trying to take over my artists and they did take them over.

THOMAS — Do you say they did take them over?

DISNEY — They did take them over.

SMITH — Will you explain that to the committee, please?

DISNEY — It came to my attention when a delegation of my boys, my artists, came to me and told me that Mr. Herbert Sorrell—

Smith — Is that Herbert K. Sorrell?

DISNEY — Herbert K. Sorrell, was trying to take them over. I explained to them that it was none of my concern, that I had been cautioned to not even talk with any of my boys on labor. They said it was not a matter of labor, it was just a matter of them not wanting to go with Sorrell, and they had heard that I was going to sign with Sorrell, and they said that they wanted an election to prove that Sorrell didn't have the majority, and I said that I had a right to demand an election. So when Sorrell came, I demanded an election.

Sorrell wanted me to sign on a bunch of cards

that he had there that he claimed were the majority, but the other side had claimed the same thing. I told Mr. Sorrell that there is only one way for me to go and that was an election, and that is what the law had set up—the National Labor Relations Board was for that purpose. He laughed at me, and he said that he would use the Labor Board as it suited his purposes and that he had been sucker enough to go for that Labor Board ballot and he had lost some election—I can't remember the name of the place—by one vote. He said it took him two years to get it back. He said he would strike, that that was his weapon. He said, "I have all of the tools of the trade sharpened," that I couldn't stand the ridicule or the smear of a strike. I told him that it was a matter of principle with me, that I couldn't go on working with my boys feeling that I had sold them down the river to him on his say-so, and he laughed at me and told me I was naïve and foolish. He said, "You can't stand this strike. I will smear you, and I will make a dust bowl out of your plant."

THOMAS – What was that?

DISNEY – He said he would make a dust bowl out of my plant if he chose to. I told him I would have to go that way, sorry, that he might be able to do all that, but I would have to stand on that. The result was that he struck.

I believed at that time that Mr. Sorrell was a communist because of all the things that I had heard, and having seen his name appearing on a number of commie front things.

When he pulled the strike, the first people to smear me and put me on the unfair list were all of the commie front organizations. I can't remember them all, they change so often, but one that is clear in my mind is the LEAGUE OF WOMEN SHOPPERS, THE PEOPLE'S WORLD, THE DAILY WORKER, and the PM MAGAZINE in New York. They smeared me. Nobody came near to find out what the true facts of the thing were. And I even went through the same smear in South America, through some commie periodicals in South America, and generally throughout the world all of the commie groups began smear campaigns against me and my pictures.

JOHN MCDOWELL – In what fashion was that smear, Mr. Disney? What type of smear?

DISNEY – Well, they distorted everything, they lied; there was no way you could ever counteract anything that they did; they formed picket lines in front of the theaters, and, well, they called my plant a sweatshop, and that is not true, and anybody in Hollywood would prove it otherwise. They claimed things that were not true at all, and there was no way you could fight it back. It was not a labor problem at all because—I mean—I have never had labor trouble, and I think that would be backed up by anybody in Hollywood.

SMITH – As a matter of fact, you have how many unions operating in your plant?

THOMAS – Excuse me just a minute. I would like to ask a question.

SMITH – Pardon me.

THOMAS – In other words, Mr. Disney, communists out there smeared you because you wouldn't knuckle under?

DISNEY – I wouldn't go along with their way of operating. I insisted on it going through the National Labor Relations Board. And he told me outright that he used them as it suited his purposes.

THOMAS – Supposing you had given in to him, then what would have been the outcome?

DISNEY – Well, I would never have given in to him, because it was a matter of principle with me, and I fight for principles. My boys have been there, have grown up in the business with me, and I didn't feel like I could sign them over to anybody. They were vulnerable at that time. They were not organized. It is a new industry.

THOMAS – Go ahead, Mr. Smith.

SMITH – How many labor unions, approximately, do you have operating in your studios at the present time?

DISNEY – Well, we operate with around thirty-five . . . I think we have contacts with thirty.

SMITH — At the time of this strike you didn't have any grievances or labor troubles whatsoever in your plant?

DISNEY — No. The only real grievance was between Sorrell and the boys within my plant—they demanding an election, and they never got it.

SMITH — Do you recall having had any conversations with Mr. Sorrell relative to communism?

DISNEY — Yes, I do.

SMITH — Will you relate that conversation?

DISNEY — Well, I didn't pull my punches on how I felt. He evidently heard that I had called them all a bunch of communists—and I believe they are. At the meeting he leaned over and he said, "You think I am a communist, don't you," and I told him that all I knew was what I heard and what I had seen. And he laughed and said, "Well, I used their money to finance my strike of 1937," and he said that he had gotten the money through the personal check of some actor, but he didn't name the actor. I didn't go into it any further. I just listened.

SMITH — Can you name any other individuals that were active at the time of the strike that you believe in your opinion are communists?

DISNEY — Well, I feel that there is one artist in my plant that came in there, he came in about 1938, and he sort of stayed in the background—he wasn't too active—but he was the real brains of this, and I believe he is a communist. His name is David Hilberman.

SMITH – How is it spelled?

DISNEY – H-i-l-b-e-r-m-a-n, I believe. I looked into his record and I found that, number one, that he had no religion and, number two, that he had spent considerable time at the Moscow Art Theatre studying art direction, or something.

SMITH – Any others, Mr. Disney?

DISNEY – Well, I think Sorrell is sure tied up with them. If he isn't a communist, he sure should be one.

SMITH – Do you remember the name of William Pomerance? Did he have anything to do with it?

DISNEY – Yes, sir. He came in later. Sorrell put him in charge as business manager of cartoonists, and later he went to the Screen Actors as their business agent, and in turn he put in another man by the name of Maurice Howard—the present business agent. And they are all tied up with the same outfit.

SMITH – What is your opinion of Mr. Pomerance and Mr. Howard as to whether or not they are or are not communists?

DISNEY – In my opinion they are communists. No one has any way of proving those things.

SMITH – Were you able to produce during the strike?

DISNEY – Yes, I did, because there was a very few—very small majority—that was on the outside, and all the other unions ignored all the lines because of the setup of the thing.

SMITH – What is your personal opinion of the Communist Party, Mr. Disney, as to whether or not it is a political party?

DISNEY – Well, I don't believe it is a political party. I believe it is an un-American thing. The thing that I resent the most is that they are able to get into these unions, take them over, and represent to the world that a group of people that are in my plant, that I know are good, one hundred percent Americans, are trapped by this group, and they are represented to the world as supporting all of those ideologies, and it is not so, and I feel that they really ought to be smoked out and shown up for what they are, so that all of the good, free causes in this country, all the liberalisms that really are American, can go out without the taint of communism. That is my sincere feeling on it.

SMITH – Do you feel that there is a threat of communism in the motion-picture industry?

DISNEY – Yes, there is, and there are many reasons

why they would like to take it over or get in and control it, or disrupt it, but I don't think they have gotten very far, and I think the industry is made up of good Americans, just like in my plant, good, solid Americans. My boys have been fighting it longer than I have. They are trying to get out from under it, and they will in time if we can just show them up.

SMITH – There are presently pending before this committee two bills relative to outlawing the Communist Party. What thoughts have you as to whether or not those bills should be passed?

DISNEY – Well, I don't know as I qualify to speak on that. I feel if the thing can be proven un-American that it ought to be outlawed. I think in some way it should be done without interfering with the rights of the people. I think that will be done—I have that faith—without interfering, I mean, with the good, American rights that we all have now, and we want to preserve.

SMITH – Have you any suggestions to offer as to how the industry can be helped in fighting this menace?

DISNEY – Well, I think there is a good start toward it. I know that I have been handicapped out there in fighting it, because they have been hiding behind this labor setup—they get themselves closely tied up in the labor thing, so that if you try to get rid of them they make a labor case out of it. We must keep the American labor unions clean. We have got to fight for them.

SMITH – That is all of the questions I have, Mr. Chairman.

THOMAS – Mr. Vail.

VAIL – No questions.

THOMAS – Mr. McDowell.

McDOWELL – No questions.

DISNEY – Sir?

McDOWELL – I have no questions. You have been a good witness.

DISNEY – Thank you.

THOMAS – Mr. Disney, you are the fourth producer we have had as a witness, and each one of those four producers said, generally speaking, the same thing, and that is that the communists have made inroads, have attempted inroads. I just want to point that out because there seems to be a very strong unanimity among the producers that have testified before us. In addition to producers, we have had actors and writers testify to the same. There is no doubt but what the movies are probably the greatest medium for entertainment in the United States and in the world. I think you, as a creator of entertainment, probably are one of the greatest examples in the profession. I want to congratulate you on the form of entertainment which you have given the American people and given the world, and congratulate you for taking time out to come here and testify before this committee. He has been very helpful. Do you have any more questions, Mr. Stripling?

SMITH – I am sure he does not have any more, Mr. Chairman.

STRIPLING – No; I have no more questions.

THOMAS – Thank you very much, Mr. Disney.

Walt Disney's testimony reminds me of my grandfather, who owned and operated a seed company in the small Indiana town of Crawfordsville, where my father grew up. Like Walt Disney, my grandfather referred to his workers as "my boys," and he spoke to them quite differently than he did to his office worker, named Betty. I think Walt Disney and my grandfather had a few things in common.

When I was a boy, my family would vacation in Crawfordsville for a week each summer and stay at my grandparents' house. Summer was the slow time at the plant, so Grandfather would bring me to work with him, where I could climb the empty boxcar out back and throw stones into the woods and creek below. I would observe my grandfather and his small crew doing projects and tinkering with equipment. He showed me how everything worked, and proudly explained his latest, greatest inventions. Everyone at the plant was quick to make a joke, and Grandfather loved to tell the story of the morning he arrived at the shop and found that a hole had been blown in the back of his safe. The safe was for fire protection only—he never kept it locked. He repaired the panel and posted a sign on the safe's door for the next burglar:

"Pull handle to open."

There were occasions, however, when I overheard my grandfather speaking callously. One day, he was sharing a story about the Second World War and referred to Japanese-Americans as Japs, supporting their detention during the conflict. And he used other words of prejudice too, like Commie, Kraut, Polack, Nigger, and Wop. Kids in my school who used such words were sent to the naughty bench, so it was exciting for me to hear him saying these things without getting in trouble.

I loved my grandfather. He teased and tickled me; he showed me off to his friends in town; he gave me batting and fielding practice every evening after dinner; and he used to drive my mom crazy by teaching me how to bare-fist box. "The boy's got to know how to fight," he'd tell her.

My grandfather was a good-hearted, well-meaning person who loved me always. And I always loved and respected him, despite his prejudices. He was loyal to his family, his employees, and his country; he was generous with his money for causes he believed in; he took pride in doing a quality job, always working harder than everyone else in his plant; and he would do any task, no matter how menial. But most of all, he loved new ideas, he loved to tinker, and he loved a good laugh.

I get a sense that Walt Disney and my grandfather were kindred spirits. And although I can't explain their varied prejudices, I believe that each of them truly meant well. Somehow, I feel that the explanation for their behaviors is based on the time and circumstances in which they lived rather than any particular flaws in their characters. I can't help but think that I would have grown up to be just like one of them if I had been born during the first decade of the 1900s.

These are my thoughts as I turn my attention to Thomas Jefferson.

CHAPTER 33

The Real Thomas Jefferson

I find a reprint of Jefferson's 1787 book, *Notes on the State of Virginia*, and read the full passage explaining his ideas about African Americans.

To my surprise, I discover a Jefferson sincerely struggling to address the issue of slavery. In fact, he describes slavery as such an injustice, that simply freeing the Africans is not good enough. He believes that white prejudice and black retaliation will surely lead to the extermination of one or the other race. Jefferson's solution calls for public funds to educate young blacks, supply them with equipment, and then ship them off to another part of the world to establish themselves as "a free and independent people" allied with the United States.

But Jefferson explains another reason blacks should be relocated rather than set free in America. Jefferson devotes five pages of his book to detailing the differences he has observed between the races. He compares such characteristics as appearance, biology, sleep requirements, sexual behavior, bravery, the handling of grief, and the mental powers of memory, reason, and imagination. He compares aptitude for the arts—specifically painting, sculpture, poetry, and music—and he makes the observation that both races prefer the company of whites over blacks. Jefferson concludes his lengthy analysis with the suspicion that whites rank higher than blacks in the animal kingdom's natural order. He determines that each race of people should live and breed independently "to preserve its dignity and beauty."

Jefferson's analysis reminds me of MJ and her current practice of ranking her fourth grade classmates. She'll rank them for anything: friendliness, fashion sense, singing skills, academic ability. It amazes me that she finds order in such a chaos of inconclusive evidence. Yet I believe MJ's effort, like Jefferson's, is a striving to be purely objective and scientific. She places herself within her lists somewhat honestly.

Both MJ and Jefferson seem to be assessing their situations as truthfully as they can. I don't believe their false statements and false conclusions reflect malice. Rather, I think their mistaken ideas reflect inaccurate and incomplete information.

In Jefferson's case, this is entirely understandable. Jefferson is writing a century before Charles Darwin's theory of evolution, and two centuries before the cataloging of the human genetic code. Jefferson has no way to know that blacks and whites are actually cut from exactly the same cloth.

But what's MJ's motivation to rank people without having all the facts? Certainly the facts are available to her if she's willing to learn them. But *willing,* she's not. When I try to supply her with information, she shuts me out. My help only aggravates her task, making her rankings more difficult to create. So she doesn't allow it.

It's a curious comparison I'm making between MJ and Thomas Jefferson. Both of them feel compelled to create "scientific" rankings, and both of them seem bent on forcing order onto a complex world.

I locate a biography of Jefferson and turn to the pages on slavery. I'm soon faced with another contradiction I'll have to reconcile.

In 1786, Jefferson wrote to a fellow statesman explaining a strategy for preventing a slave from declaring his freedom

on foreign soil. This strategy was most likely the same one
Jefferson himself used to retain his own slave, James Hemings,
while living in France. Here's what his letter said:

> I have made enquiries on the subject of the negro
> boy you brought, and find that the laws of France
> give him freedom if he claims it, and that it will be
> difficult, if not impossible, to interrupt the course
> of the law. . . . I have known an instance where a
> person bringing in a slave, and saying nothing about
> it, has not been disturbed in his possession. . . . the
> young negro will not probably . . . think of claiming
> his freedom.

Two years later, Jefferson wrote another letter from
Paris that included the following statements about his own
viewpoint.

> . . . that nobody wishes more ardently [than myself]
> to see an abolition not only of the trade but of the
> condition of slavery: and certainly nobody will be
> more willing to encounter every sacrifice for that
> object. . . .

Jefferson claims to be committed to making every possible
sacrifice to eradicate slavery, yet his actions prove otherwise.
Most notably, he maintains such a lavish lifestyle that even
upon his death his estate can't afford to free his plantation
slaves. And following his retreat from politics, he fails to
become an outspoken abolitionist.

Did Jefferson see these inconsistencies in his behavior?
How could he not have?

But then again, what about MJ? My daughter displays

similar inconsistencies all the time. She argues that people should be treated fairly, yet she's willing to take more than her share whenever possible. She calls for the reduction in carbon emissions, but can't manage to turn off any lights in our house. MJ doesn't see these inconsistencies, and my attempts to point them out to her are greeted with hostility. It seems Jefferson had similar blind spots.

In 1791, Jefferson received a letter from a 59-year-old free-born African-American named Benjamin Banneker. Banneker was a self-taught astronomer and mathematician preparing an almanac for publication. He sent Jefferson a hand-written manuscript hoping for Jefferson's endorsement.

Jefferson, as the former Minister to France, used his connections to forward the paper to the prestigious Academy of Sciences in Paris. A favorable review from this body would fuel the strong pro-African and antislavery movements in France, while generating prestige for the United States and publicity for Banneker. Yet here, right under his nose, was a sampling of African blood having abilities beyond those of many whites. Why didn't this evidence change the course of Jefferson's life? Why couldn't he commit himself to freeing his own slaves as soon as possible? Why didn't he take up the cause of abolition? How do I explain Jefferson's and MJ's tendencies to overlook seemingly obvious information?

These questions form a suffocating veil over my research as I continue to read the Jefferson biographies, hoping to find some answers. In the process, however, I get a welcome education in the history of my country, and it puts Jefferson's life in a better perspective.

◆ ◆ ◆

Thomas Jefferson wrote the Declaration of Independence in 1776 at a dire and hectic time in American history. The Revolutionary War was a year old at this point, and reports of defeat seemed likely from battles in New York and Canada. The delegates to the Continental Congress worked long days managing the war effort and drafting their respective state constitutions. Jefferson was doing some of this work as a junior member of the Virginia delegation.

At that time, the break from England was all but official. A small committee, including Jefferson, John Adams, and Benjamin Franklin, was assigned the task of drafting a declaration of independence, hoping to win French support for the war. Jefferson was chosen to write it because he was from Virginia—the state leading the initiative—and because he had authored two earlier papers arguing for separation from England. There was no notion that the document to be created would become a defining parchment of the new nation.

Jefferson drafted the document in just three days, and originality was definitely not a priority. Jefferson borrowed liberally from his earlier works and from the preamble of the Virginia constitution, which had been adopted just a few days earlier.

Virginia's preamble was written by George Mason and read: *"All men are created equally free and independent and have certain inherent and natural rights . . . , among which are the enjoyment of life and liberty . . . , and pursuing and obtaining happiness and safety."* But even Mason's words were not truly original—he was paraphrasing a still earlier work. Mason, like Jefferson and the other founding fathers, was heavily influenced by the writings of the 1600s English philosopher, John Locke.

Jefferson's gift in writing the Declaration of Independence was his ability to grant enduring poetic beauty to John Locke's principles. Jefferson reworked Mason's language for his first draft, writing: *"We hold these truths to be sacred and undeniable; that all men are created equal; that they are endowed by their creator with certain [inherent and] inalienable rights; that among these are life, liberty and the pursuit of happiness; . . ."* It was perhaps Benjamin Franklin or John Adams who reviewed the draft and suggested simplifying *"sacred and undeniable"* to *"self-evident."*

On the day the Continental Congress met to edit Jefferson's draft, it was the 70-year-old Benjamin Franklin who comforted this sensitive 33 year old, as the delegates hacked at his prose. Franklin consoled Jefferson with a story about a hatter who was trying to design a sign for his shop. The hatter's initial idea was to have a picture of a hat beside an inscription: *John Thompson, hatter, makes and sells hats for ready money.* The hatter presented his idea to several friends for comment, and by the time they were finished revising it, the sign had been reduced to *John Thompson* and the picture of the hat.

◆ ◆ ◆

My further studies of Jefferson shed no light on his inconsistencies. I still can't answer why he didn't rethink his views on African Americans based on the manuscript of Benjamin Banneker. Yet my reading has not been a waste of time; it has given me a great appreciation and fondness for two other founding fathers.

James Madison is a name I barely remember from my eighth-grade social studies class. Other names tended to capture the spotlight, like George Washington, Thomas Jefferson, Patrick Henry, and Paul Revere. But now, James Madison sits proudly at the front of the pack, for it was his monumental effort that was largely responsible for the simple yet elegant design of the United States Constitution. I never even made the connection before, that my home city of Madison was named for this man.

James Madison shares this front position with another colonial statesman—Benjamin Franklin. It was the elderly Franklin who, through his supreme finesse as an ambassador to France, single-handedly won French support for the war against Great Britain. And it was the Benjamin Franklin of ailing health who made the eloquent plea to his fellow delegates to set aside their differences and ratify the new constitution. I shift my reading to the biographies of these two men and eventually strike upon a startling comparison between Franklin and Jefferson.

When Franklin observed black children in a school, who were performing with the same abilities as white children, he overturned his opinion that blacks were inferior to whites. By his sunset years, Franklin had freed his two slaves and had become a leader in the nation's first abolitionist society, while Jefferson managed no such turnaround from similar evidence.

Why did Franklin have the power—or perhaps the will—to change his mind and Jefferson not? How do I explain this difference in their abilities? Both men were avid readers and students of the world. And both men prided themselves on scientific achievement and philosophical inquiry. Must I conclude that Franklin's powers of intellect were markedly superior to Jefferson's? It seems I must, but I don't like the feeling of ranking people—for certainly, if I can rank *them*, then I can rank everyone else, too. This notion smacks of Jefferson's ranking of the races and of MJ's ranking of her classmates. I've witnessed the errors and perilous oversimplifications that such exercises can yield. And to what end? What noble purpose is served by placing individual humans in a hierarchy?

Without further thought, I reject the idea of ranking intellectual abilities. I conclude that Jefferson and Franklin, just like Disney and my grandfather, meant well, and that their prejudices, whether resolved or not, were somehow a product of the times and places in which they lived.

My conclusion does not completely satisfy me, though. I still have no idea why prejudice exists at all.

I end my studies of Walt Disney and Thomas Jefferson with a modicum of renewed admiration for these two men. But I hold out little hope of ever redeeming them further.

With only a few days left until school starts, I have one last avenue to explore.

CHAPTER 34

The Beauty of Jazz

Our Disney vacation was interwoven with music, and it always seemed to be present during my more enchanted moments. Music and the Disney Magic seem to go hand in hand, and I want to understand this connection. What's so special about music? Perhaps the history of jazz will give me a clue.

The first book I find at the library begins with a quotation by the writer Gerald Early.

> . . . when they study our civilization two thousand years from now, there will only be three things that Americans will be known for: the Constitution, baseball and jazz music. They're the three most beautiful things Americans have ever created.

Baseball!

When Mary and I walked through the Fort Wilderness Campground, the smell of a brand of pipe tobacco took me back to a summer's day at the ballpark. Baseball is like music—it can generate a warm feeling.

But Gerald Early's quotation catches my attention for another reason. I am surprised by his use of the word "beautiful" to describe baseball and the U.S. Constitution. I've never thought of these things as *beautiful* before.

It's an interesting start to my study of jazz.

♦ ♦ ♦

During the 1800s, New Orleans was a cosmopolitan city known as the "Paris of America." It was a melting pot of world cultures, including Africans, Europeans, Native Americans, Caribbean islanders, and untold hybrids. Music was everywhere.

By the year 1850, the city's 116,000 inhabitants supported two symphony orchestras and three opera houses, and eighty public ballrooms employed orchestras and ensembles to meet the citizens' insatiable demand for dancing. Minstrel shows performed plantation melodies. Brass bands paraded through the streets, playing military marches. Groups practiced in parks and along the waterfront in competition for passing listeners. People sang folk songs from the sidewalks. Mourners chanted hymns during funeral processions. Black churches resonated with African spirituals and the blues.

Even the slaves were granted access to music. They could attend music halls with permission from their masters, and they were permitted several hours of singing and dancing in Congo Square on Sundays. It was in New Orleans that jazz music was born.

Following the Civil War and Reconstruction, federal troops abandoned the South. Suddenly, the Creoles of Color lost their white status and were grouped with the blacks, placing them under the fist of Jim Crow laws. Classically trained Creole musicians were forced to find work performing in black ensembles, where the music was raw and improvised. The mutual influences of these two groups, in combination with the 1890s' arrival of ragtime from the Midwest, produced the first sounds of jazz around 1898, with New Orleans trumpeter Buddy Bolden.

♦ ♦ ♦

My research into jazz prompts me to make a simple, yet startling observation. I realize that black Americans dominate
the list of twentieth century music pioneers. From ragtime
to blues, and from jazz to rock and rap, many of the names
I know best are held by people of a darker skin.

Why have prejudiced white Americans accepted so many
of these black artists, letting their music go mainstream?
Why were the slaves of New Orleans allowed to attend con-
certs and spend time singing and dancing in Congo Square?
What is the power of music to permit exceptions to the usual
prejudices and oppressions? On a hunch, I turn my attention
to sports.

In baseball, I learn that a black ballplayer named Jackie
Robinson entered the white major leagues in 1947, during a
time of widespread segregation. I learn also that during the
1936 Olympic Games in Berlin, white German spectators
cheered for black-American Jesse Owens and other colored
athletes from around the world, despite Adolf Hitler's propaganda of Aryan superiority. I learn that in 1908, whites finally
permitted a black boxer named Jack Johnson to contend
for the heavyweight title. I learn that in ancient Greece, the
original Olympic games were so sacred that athletes—often
soldiers—could leave the fighting and cross enemy territory
to reach the games. Sports clearly exhibit the same power as
music; they can cause exceptions to behavior.

So what is it that music and sports have in common? Again,
I recall the quotation by Gerald Early.

> . . . when they study our civilization two thousand
> years from now, there will only be three things that
> Americans will be known for: the Constitution, base-
> ball and jazz music. They're the three most beautiful
> things Americans have ever created.

Beauty! Gerald Early calls jazz and baseball beautiful. Is *beauty* the common thread between music and sports? Can *beauty* be a force that affects human behavior? I think it can.

I grab a book on human evolution and discover that rhythmic sounds and athletic rituals date back 2.5 million years to the earliest of the human species. Such group activities developed long before the modern Homo sapien of 0.1 million years ago. Music and athletics are deeply ingrained in all human beings. These activities speak a language far older than words.

That's it! A language!

Perhaps *beauty* is a language without words: a language so basic and common to all human beings that it has no vocabulary for cultural biases or prejudices.

As I consider this notion, I realize an interesting contradiction in my own grandfather's behavior.

My grandfather loved baseball, and he loved jazz music. I can remember how his usual words of prejudice softened when he spoke of his favorite black athletes and black musicians. It seems that even *he* could make an exception in his usual thinking when the beauty of sports or music was involved. I wonder if he recognized the contradiction.

I recall the words of Robert Owen:

> . . . where there is inconsistency there must be error.

Yes, error. My grandfather was making an error. Why couldn't he see it? It was so obvious; it was as plain as the nose on his face.

Like a bolt out of the blue, I picture my grandfather with the nose of Pinocchio. His words of prejudice are all lies, and the exceptions he makes for sports and music are the proof.

CHAPTER 35

The Conscience of Pinocchio

A scene from *Pinocchio* fills my mind. It's the one Mary and I know so well—the one where Pinocchio is trapped in the bird cage and lying to the Blue Fairy to win his release. But the scene I'm witnessing has a new cast of characters. Thomas Jefferson plays the part of Pinocchio, and I am the Blue Fairy standing beside the cage with the power to set him free. I watch Jefferson's nose grow longer with each of his lies about African Americans.

> They are at least as brave, and more adventuresome [than whites]. But this may perhaps proceed from a want of forethought, which prevents their seeing a danger till it be present.

> They are more ardent after their female: but love seems with them to be more an eager desire, than a tender delicate mixture of sentiment and sensation.

> Their griefs are transient.

> Comparing them by their faculties of memory, reason, and imagination, it appears to me, that in memory they are equal to the whites; in reason

much inferior, as I think one could scarcely be found capable of tracing and comprehending the investigations of Euclid; and that in imagination they are dull, tasteless, and anomalous.

But never yet could I find that a black had uttered a thought above the level of plain narration; never see even an elementary trait of painting or sculpture. In music they are more generally gifted than the whites with accurate ears for tune and time, and they have been found capable of imagining a small catch. Whether they will be equal to the composition of a more extensive run of melody, or of complicated harmony, is yet to be proved.

The improvement of the blacks in body and mind, in the first instance of their mixture with the whites, has been observed by every one, and proves that their inferiority is not the effect merely of their condition of life.

I remember, from this scene in *Pinocchio,* that Mary and I had judged the young puppet to be innocent. He was too naïve to understand and prevent the situation that led to his capture. He could not see the falseness of the information given to him by Honest John the Fox. Pinocchio proclaimed his innocence as best he could, spinning a yarn of poetic truths that sounded like lies to the Blue Fairy.

It seems Thomas Jefferson is like Pinocchio: he, too, is innocent because he couldn't see the falseness of his information. He was doing his best to be truthful, but still, his truths sound poetic to this Blue Fairy of the twenty-first century.

And what about *me*? Am I like Pinocchio too? Will future generations lock me in a cage and call me a liar for my beliefs? Or will they understand my innocence and set me free?

I don't like to see any living thing caged up. Perhaps everyone is innocent and worthy of freedom. But how can this be true? What about the worst offenders in history, like Adolf Hitler and Joseph Stalin? It's hard to think of *them* as innocent and worthy of release from the cages they forged in life. I note, however, that their cages hold them as adults, not as children. What about when they were young? Did they belong in cages *then*?

I simply can't believe that young Adolf and young Joseph were born pre-programmed to lead murderous lives. Somehow they *learned* this awful approach to the world. But *who* taught it to them? *Who* can I finger as the culprit? —A parent? A teacher? A friend? . . . And if I find the guilty parties, then *who* might I find responsible for teaching *them*? How many generations back must I go before I find the mastermind behind all of the evil in the world?

But I know in my heart there's no mastermind lurking in the shadows of history. There can't be. Every remote culture of the world has a long track record of bloody savagery and oppression. I must therefore conclude that nature is the schoolmaster, and that evolution is our passing from grade to grade.

Hitler and Stalin, then, were like children on a playground carrying weapons. They had to be stopped, of course, but their crime was nothing more than a simple ignorance of the truth—that peace and love are a better social arrangement than war and hate. Certainly their classmates were ignorant too, willing to follow their lead. Why were all of these people so naïve? Why couldn't they see the truth?

I think back to Pinocchio, who failed to see the truth too. His conscience, Jiminy Cricket, could do little to help him, just as Walt Disney had intended.

The original tale of Pinocchio, published in 1883 by Carlo Collodi, tells of a misbehaving puppet who gradually learns to be a good boy. But the puppet's long string of misbehaviors posed a problem for Walt Disney, as he tried to adapt the story to film. Walt wanted audiences of all ages to love his puppet throughout the entire story. He needed Pinocchio to have an excuse to misbehave.

Walt's solution was to recast Collodi's shadowy cricket-character in a more prominent role as Jiminy Cricket. Jiminy would serve as Pinocchio's conscience while the young puppet developed his own. When Jiminy was absent, the innocent Pinocchio was not responsible for his actions.

In essence, Walt gave Pinocchio a second, more skilled conscience. Jiminy could detect the deceptions of Honest John the Fox, whereas Pinocchio could not. With great frustration, Jiminy tried to warn Pinocchio of the treacheries befalling him, but Pinocchio simply could not see them.

We modern Jiminy Crickets look in frustration at Thomas Jefferson's inability to be swayed by the evidence of Benjamin Banneker. How could his conscience miss such clear information? And Mary and I are amazed that our own two children are so slow to learn our lessons of personal responsibility and the Golden Rule. And what about those people that we, ourselves, might be frustrating on a regular basis . . . people who can see truths that we cannot?

My mind wanders back to the theme song from *Pinocchio*. Fate has been kind and delivered my bolt out of the blue. And ironically, that bolt has come from the very same film that sings of it. *Pinocchio* has shown me that the world is innocent—that I should free Thomas Jefferson, Walt Disney, and, indeed, all of humanity from the cages I may hold them in. I can even free myself.

And more amazing still, *Pinocchio* points my way to the information that will help me to secure all of these freedoms. It is Walt Disney's Jiminy Cricket who sings, "always let your conscience be your guide." Jiminy Cricket is pointing my way into the study of human consciousness, promising me a reconciliation of all the contradictions I've found.

But there's just one problem now facing me. I've enrolled at the university on a scholarship, and my classes begin on Tuesday.

CHAPTER 36

The Labor Day Picnic

The side yard of my parents' house has a home-made pig-roaster fizzling in the rain, and beside it there's a canvas tent sheltering some picnic tables.

Dad rings the dinner bell, and fifteen hungry mouths converge on the tables for a feast. We squish through wet grass and must raise our voices to speak over the pitter-patter of droplets on the canopy overhead. Everyone is commenting on the same thing: Uncle Albert's birthday cake.

Today is the day we'll be celebrating Albert's eightieth birthday, and his sheet cake holds a full eighty candles on it. It is over-arched by a contraption of Dad's construction that will light all of the candles at once. It's an engineering marvel of wires and wicks, all curling to a point at the top, making it look like the dome of the Taj Mahal. Dad assures us that the framework holding it all together will lift off easily once the candles are lit.

After the meal, Dad tells the kids to run along. "The cake is for later," he says.

The four oldest children return to the house for video games, while Dorsey and Sanders label Ferguson as the Big Bad Wolf and taunt him until he chases them across the yard to the clubhouse. Jane proposes a game of croquet for the rest of us.

"I'm in," says Dad, and he scoops up the blue ball.

"Second," says Jane, and she snatches up the red.

"Too wet for me," says Elsa.

She and Mom carry two chairs to the drip-edge of the tent and seat themselves behind it.

Tom and Mary communicate in sign language and agree that I should follow Jane. They give me the black ball and hand the green one to Uncle Albert.

Dad lines up his first shot. "Perfect weather," he says, ". . . for building a garage, that is." His ball rolls through the first two wickets. "Mary tells me *you're* the hold up now, Bert. —Something about Disney?" He laughs.

Dad prepares for his second shot while I stand behind him, holding up my mallet over his head as if I'm planning to club him.

"Hey, Fairy Fauna," says Elsa, "why don't you cut Bert some slacks? He starts school tomorrow."

"School, shmool," says Dad.

"Good comeback," replies Jane, and she begins her turn. "Do you have your laptop yet, Bert? You're up against the whiz kids, you know."

"Don't waste your time, Bert," says Dad. "Go back to construction."

"But he has a scholarship," says Mary. "Why *wouldn't* he go back to school?"

I place my black ball next to the stake and dry my hands on Jane's sweatshirt. It's funny that everyone here is so willing to argue about my future without even consulting me. I take a practice swing, then wind up for my hit.

"Disney?" says Jane into my ear.

"Foul," cries Mom from the sidelines.

"Hey, that reminds me," says Jane, "has anyone read *The Da Vinci Code* yet? It talks about Disney."

My ball cruises through the first two wickets and into the

open lawn. I snicker at Jane. "Your tactics of the fifth column don't work on me."

Jane looks around. "Does that even mean anything?"

My second bonus shot bounces off Jane's ball, and I'm awarded two more strokes. I extend my lead by advancing through the third and fourth hoops before my turn finally ends.

"What does it say about Disney?" says Mary. "I'd like to read it."

Jane explains that Walt Disney belonged to a secret society and that he filled his fairy-tale cartoons with clues to the greatest coverup ever perpetrated by the Catholic church: that Jesus of Nazareth was actually the husband of Mary Magdalene, and that she was pregnant with his baby at the time of the crucifixion.

"I've heard enough," says Dad. "You're no professor. Set her straight, Albert."

Uncle Albert faces forward and separates his legs over his ball. His third stroke puts him in contact with Jane's.

"Send her!" says Mom.

"Hmm," says Albert, "I probably should . . . but I'm a bit unsteady, you know."

Mary places her foot on Albert's ball. "Do be careful, won't you?"

Albert turns sideways and prepares a golf swing. He launches Jane's ball, though it stops almost immediately in a soggy patch of grass.

"Now, I'm no expert," says Albert, "but the fairy tales are probably older than Jesus Christ."

"Listen up, Janey," says Dad.

"Stories like *Snow White* and *Sleeping Beauty* have come down through the ages by way of the oral tradition, only recently having been put into writing. They are believed by some to

be allegories to the lost sacred feminine . . . you know, the
fall of Eve in the Garden of Eden and that sort of thing. It
is said that women once enjoyed parity with men . . . and
they've been waiting a long time to get it back."

"Amen," says Elsa.

"Walt Disney?" I say. "—In a secret society? He doesn't
strike me as that deep."

"I'm not asking you to believe me," says Jane. "Read it
for yourself."

"I'd like to," I say. "But I won't have any time . . . with
school and all."

"Oh, that reminds me," says Albert. "Did I ever tell you
about Dexter?"

"What reminds you?" says Jane.

"When I was a professor at Minnesota in the late '60s, a
student boycott emptied my classrooms. Dexter stopped by
my office and asked if I would hold lectures off campus so
that he and some others could secretly attend. I denied his
request, though, telling him I couldn't allow him to compromise his principles."

Uncle Albert stops talking and takes his next swing. His
green ball hits a wicket and springs backward. His turn is
over, and he leans against his mallet as though there's nothing more to say.

"So?" says Jane. "Go on. What's the point?"

"Oh my, yes, the point," says Albert. "You see, the university didn't offer any courses on civil disobedience and
peaceful protest. We were all learning these things from the
television through teachers like Martin Luther King Jr."

Albert pauses again, and we continue to stare at him.

"The point!" he says. "The point is that professors can't
teach what they don't know. The *Theory of Relativity* didn't

enter college curriculums until a young patent clerk put it there. Some of the best ideas come from beyond academia. That's why I'm offering to double Bert's scholarship if he'll postpone school for a year."

"What?" says Jane. "—Pay him to quit school?"

I look around, and everyone appears shocked by the proposal . . . well, everyone except Dad, that is. He is smiling and nodding.

"Professors wear blinders," continues Albert. "They can't always be trusted. That's why I want you to go it alone, Bert. I want you to pursue your own education and see where it leads you."

Dad laughs. "Any words of wisdom from the graduates?" he says. "Speak now, or forever hold your peace. You'll have to put your money where your mouth is, though. I'm guessing Bert's smart enough to take the highest bidder."

"But Albert," says Tom, "you're setting him up for failure . . . no offense, Bert."

"Tom's right," says Jane. "Bert's no Einstein."

"So," says Elsa, "what will you study, Bert?" She's trying to show me some support.

But I'm not sure how to answer her question without sounding like a dope. "Consciousness," I blurt out, sounding like a dope anyway, "—the history of human thinking."

"Whoops," says Jane. "Sounds like psychology to me. Maybe your first day should be an interview with Elsa over there."

Elsa shakes her head. "Oh, Bert. Don't do this. The world is full of PhDs already working on the subject. What can you possibly hope to add to their work?"

"I'm not trying to add anything," I say. "I just want to understand it."

"Then change your major," she says.

"Blah, blah, blah," says Dad. "Leave him alone and let's play. My underwear's starting to droop."

The rain falls harder now, and I'm just a few strokes from victory when Jane calls it quits.

"Oh boo hoo," says Dad. "Is the sacred feminine made of sugar?"

Dad grabs Jane by the arms and signals Tom to lift her feet. The two men then carry her to the wading pool and dunk her in.

Meanwhile, Elsa and Mary hurry there too, carrying plastic cups full of water. They pour the contents over Dad and Tom, initiating a water fight that soon spreads to every member of the family. Even the children inside the house hear the commotion and race outside to join us.

Mom eventually rings the dinner bell and brings the soak-fest to a halt, announcing that it's time for the birthday cake.

We gather under the tent—all fifteen of us, tired and breathless—and watch Dad perform his preparations.

He equips the garden hose with a nozzle and hands it to me. "Put me out if I catch fire," he says.

"When I get around to it," I answer.

Dad finds his matches and stands beside his creation. "No singing until the candles are lit," he says. "Everyone stand back."

Dad lights the bundle of wicks at the top, which burn like sparklers. I can't imagine we'll be able to eat this cake after all the fallout.

As the eighty little fires move down their respective ropes, they hit the candles and instantly change to red jets of flame. These flames then dive down into the cake.

"Oops," says Dad, and he takes a step back.

Blam! Blam! . . Blam! Blam! Blam! . . Blam! Blam!—

Explosions rip through the cake like a machine gun, spewing frosting and devil's food in every direction like shrapnel.

Dorsey and Sanders wail in terror, while Nellie and Michael hover somewhere between laughter and tears.

One thing's for sure; none of us will ever forget Uncle Albert's eightieth birthday.

CHAPTER 37

The Ascent into Darkness

On Tuesday morning, I begin my day at the registrar's office and drop out of college for the second time in my life. Uncle Albert is paying me to study on my own, though I share in my family's concern that this arrangement might not be the best thing for me. Why am I forsaking the conventional route to a career and employment for such a questionable enterprise? The answer is simple: because Albert is sanctioning it with his credentials and his resources. And inwardly, the whole endeavor excites me. I've already formulated a plan for my first day.

Instead of leaving the campus right away, I locate a freshman psychology class and seat myself at the back of the lecture hall.

College is just like I remember it: too far into the details too fast. It's an endless treadmill of memorization, where every closer look into a topic reveals more and more to learn. There's no end to the minutiae that can be cataloged, and as far as I can tell, the cataloging never adds up to anything meaningful.

I wait until the end of the hour, then exit the room and smartly eavesdrop on subsequent classes from the hallway rather than being trapped inside for the duration. I want the freedom to move around as I see fit. I roam from building to building, sampling lectures on psychology, history, archaeology, and anthropology. I feel like a stow-away of the university system—unable to earn a degree, but also unbeholden to any department that might impose its curriculum upon me. I'm at liberty to follow my instincts and intuitions, wherever they may lead.

By the second afternoon, I've abandoned the lecture halls and found a remote region in the north stacks of the university's main library. This place quickly becomes my favorite haunt for reading. Each day, I trek here with a book or two from the public library and sit alone at a table.

The stacks of any library are a mystical place for me. They are a dark and cool catacomb, where dusty old tomes whisper their lost and fading messages. No author calls out to be heard more than any others because all of them know their ultimate fate—they are on a long and slow march into obscurity, and they are grateful to anyone who might chance upon them and listen to their words, if only briefly.

For three months, I scour the popular literature in search of a definitive work on the subject of human consciousness. But I can't seem to find one. Rather, I endure a gradual accumulation of details that seem impossible to sort through. My education is stalling once again, and I wonder if perhaps school was never really the cause of my earlier college failure. Maybe the problem was *me*.

Mary assures me that the pile of details I'm gathering is a natural consequence of a job well done. "You must persist with the struggle," she says, "because that's the way to find the patterns. Your work will become fun once you separate the primary details from the secondary ones."

Mary is proud of my progress so far, though I'm deaf to her praise. My mood continues to blacken.

Unlike Snow White, who stood at the top of her well and drew up fresh water, I'm hauling up buckets of puzzle pieces.

I carry each load into my castle and dump it on the floor. I've managed to do some minor sorting—to separate out a few secondary details—but the pile left behind is huge. I can't seem to wade through it, and even the edge pieces confound me. It seems there are too many pieces here for a single puzzle. And to make matters worse, I'm working without a picture of the final product. I can only guess at what the finished puzzle should look like.

The Thanksgiving holiday comes and goes, and the weather turns colder. The outside world becomes a dreary reflection of my soul.

My roles as husband and father reduce themselves to a mere business arrangement. I keep the schedules and do the dishes, but I'm no fun to be around. If Mary and the children are the teacups in my parlor, then I've clearly consigned them to a corner shelf, where they now sit tarnishing while I work on the puzzle at the table. My despair only deepens with the onset of Christmas.

On December 15th—the Monday of the last week of school before winter recess—I trudge, as usual, to the university library with my books. I take my notes, eat my lunch, and begin my departure at two o'clock to pick up the kids from school.

As I walk the dark aisles of the stacks toward the exit, my steps become slow and heavy, and my eyes fill with tears. I'm failing at my education for a second time, and there seems to be nothing I can do to stop it. School or no school—it doesn't seem to matter: there's a deficit in my mind that I can't overcome.

I stop at a bookshelf and lean against it to cry.

But my sobs are soon interrupted by a similar sound coming from somewhere else in the stacks. I decide to investigate in case someone needs my help.

I follow the voice, which is now plainly speaking, and it leads me toward a pool of light. There, seated between the shelves, is an elderly woman reading to herself from a book open on her lap.

I recognize this woman right away. She's the little old lady I encountered beside the drinking fountain last summer—the one who laughed and said "nonsense" at the bulletin announcing a lecture on human origins. I don't think she has noticed me, so I take up a position in the next aisle and spy on her.

Snap! She closes the book in her lap and bursts out laughing. "High marks for you. Stopped at page two." The woman puts the book on the shelf and pulls out the next one in the row.

She reads from this second book for less than a minute, then again snaps it shut and laughs. "So sorry, sir. Done at page one."

This woman is not sad or in trouble, and it's time for me to be leaving to meet MJ and Michael. But I wish I could stay longer and try to understand what this woman is doing. I linger a few minutes more.

The woman withdraws another book, but the binding on this one never cracks. "Category worst! Lost from the first."

I'm on my way out the door and must jog to the school. I arrive just in time to greet the children as they exit the building.

On Tuesday morning, I return to the stacks and investigate the aisle where the woman was sitting. The topic under her scrutiny was Ancient Egypt, though I can't seem to find anything amusing about the books she was reading.

I stake out a location where I can observe her if she happens to return today.

Sure enough, shortly before two o'clock, I hear footsteps. She arrives to the same row as yesterday and stows her shoulderbag on an empty shelf. I remain out of sight and watch her as she builds a nest on the floor with her coat and then sits on it with a book.

For ten minutes I stay and listen. And during this time, she opens and shuts four books, giving each one a laugh and a curious rhyme. I wonder what's causing her to stop reading so abruptly. She seems to be halted by certain words or phrases, but I can't understand why. I guess I don't know enough about Ancient Egypt.

I run to school and find the kids waiting for me outside.

On both Wednesday and Thursday, the old woman arrives a little later, granting me just one observation each day before I have to leave.

Mary is as curious as I am about the habits of this woman, so she arranges to leave work early on Friday and pick up the children so that I can stay at the library as long as I want to.

The old woman returns at two o'clock on Friday, and again, she stows her bag on the shelf and builds a nest with her coat.

The hours slip by, with the woman snapping, laughing, and rhyming much of the time. All but two of the many volumes she pulls from the shelf get this treatment.

The first book to win an exception is one where even *I* can tell that the words are flowing beautifully. When she eventually snaps this one closed at page three, she sighs, "Ahh. So much poetry."

The second book to earn a distinction is one that achieves an unprecedented milestone—a full half hour of her unbroken reading. I listen intently for the debilitating words that will ultimately snap the book closed, but they never come. Eventually, her reading trails off, and she tenderly shuts the book. She wraps her arms around it and sways from side to side, murmuring, "An early arrival."

At seven o'clock, the old woman gathers her things and makes her way to the elevator.

I dash down the stairs and position myself in the hallway beside the drinking fountain. I want to know what this woman has been doing, though I'm not exactly sure how I can ask her. If I speak to her on the matter, she'll rightly conclude that I've been stalking her and possibly scream for my arrest.

She turns the corner and advances toward me through the hallway. I have no more time to think. Her eyes meet with mine, and again, I feel that tingle down to my toes. I open my mouth, as if to speak, but no words come out.

"Excuse me," she says, and she steps to the drinking fountain. Her shoulderbag flips down to her side, as before, revealing its monogram: *L.N. Smith.*

She finishes her drink and shuffles to the north door, opening it and disappearing into the darkness.

So *now* what?

I exit the west doors and emerge onto the wind-swept Library Mall, where powdery snowflakes swirl around me and hammer at my face like the details I can't cope with. They bite at my nose and sting my eyes, bringing back the tears I'd forgotten since Monday.

As I climb Bascom Hill, I see the statue of Abraham Lincoln assessing my progress from his seat at the top. He is no doubt disappointed in me, as he should be. Thankfully, though, he keeps staring forward as I pass.

I approach the Jeffersonian-style building behind him, where I find a large plaque mounted to the wall beside the doors. I stop and read it, because I've got nothing better to do.

> Whatever may be the limitations which trammel inquiry elsewhere, we believe that the great state

university of Wisconsin should ever encourage that
continual and fearless sifting and winnowing by
which alone the truth can be found.

Sifting and *winnowing?* These sound like the things I should
be doing with my puzzle pieces right now. But how? How
do I find the right sifters and winnowers for the job? And
now that I think of it, I don't even know what a winnower is.

My sadness escalates into self-pity, and I feel no desire to
see Mary or the children. I want to punish myself in every
way possible, so I decide to remain outside in the wintry ele-
ments for an extended period by taking a meandering route
home—one that will hide me from the disapproving eyes
of drivers and pedestrians alike, while keeping me out until
long after the kids have gone to bed. I want to be alone, so
very alone.

CHAPTER 38

The 2003 Holiday Gathering

My parents' home is an oasis for me—a sanctuary that nourishes my spirit. Its windbreak of century-old pines is self-pruned so high that it resembles a Dr. Seuss illustration, and the fires within Ketchell Oven still warm me from afar as long as I know Mom and Dad are there to stoke them. The house and yard, together, connect me to my childhood like no other place in the world.

It's the night of Christmas Eve, and Mary is holding the flashlight for me as I read *The Polar Express* to the children. One by one, all of us take our turns at the window, scratching *I believe* into the frost . . . even Mary. When the story has ended and the kids are quiet, Mary and I head downstairs to rejoin the adults.

The baking is all done and the gifts have been wrapped. The television is now playing the Alistair Sim version of *A Christmas Carol,* and the card table is set for our annual game of Scrabble.

Ferguson carries Uncle Albert's 150 pound crate as though it's a toy and lays it on the desk behind Albert's chair.

Albert's 1933 Oxford English Dictionary includes twelve volumes of fine print, plus a supplement containing the changes and additions that accrued during the half century it took to compile the main set. Mom and Dad have offered to update the series for him, but Albert has always refused, saying "the new edition is almost as inaccurate as mine, and I don't want to lose all my notes in the margins."

Albert opens the locker and withdraws a Merriam-Webster's Collegiate Dictionary. "For the referee," he says, and he hands the book to Dad.

Dad opens it and finds the copyright page. "1998?" he says. "That's five years old." He tosses the book onto the couch and walks over to the Christmas tree. He crawls under it and returns with a book wrapped in a ribbon. "An early Christmas present," he says. "Your next edition, sir."

"Goodness," says Albert. "You *do* know my weaknesses. Thanks ever so much."

"I can ref for you this year, Dad," says Jane. "Wouldn't you rather play, Wheelbarrel Man?"

Dad grimaces. "I hope Albert and my better half whip you this year. . . . Oh wait. —They whip you *every* year."

Mom and Uncle Albert are the undefeated champs in this tradition. We three younger couples pose little threat to them.

Dad walks around the table and lets each team pull a tile to determine who will go first. Mary and I win the draw, and every team loads its rack with seven tiles.

Mary and I place the word STAND across the center square and earn 16 points.

Play passes to our left, where Elsa and Ferguson add ING to the ending of our word.

"Wow," says Dad, "30 points for junk. You're just *giving* away the game, Bert."

"Hey," I say, "isn't Mary on my team too?"

Albert and Mom take their turn, adding UNDER in front of STANDING.

"We couldn't resist," says Albert.

"Oh, way to throw the game, Bert," says Elsa.

Albert rotates in his chair and faces the many spines of

his Oxford Dictionary. The fabric of each book is scuffed and faded to a light brown. He slides Volume XI from the grouping and lowers it onto his lap. "I want to look this one up," he says. He reaches for his magnifying glass.

While Jane and Tom set down the word QUEER and earn 25 points, Albert reads the entry for *understand*. *"To stand under,"* he says, *"—to stand beneath."*

"Incredible," says Jane.

"To stand beneath *who*?" I say.

"Your wife," says Mary. "Who else?"

Albert buries his head in another volume. "Ah," he says. "The entry for *queer* says *'of doubtful origin,'* so there's no point in reading further." He returns the book to the shelf and pulls out one more. "But let's try *faggot* instead. Maybe *that* one has something to offer." His finger moves down the page, then stops. *"Faggot*: a *bundle of firewood*. Isn't that interesting? The word jumped from the firewood to the servant who was carrying it. And just look how the meaning has changed since then."

"Hmm," says Mary, "I'm feeling a chill. Can you throw a faggot on the fire for me, Grandpa?"

"My pleasure," says Dad. "Which one? Tom or Bert?"

Mary and I begin Round Two with the word DESTINY for 22 points. Albert retrieves Volume III and thumbs to the correct page. "My Oxford is worthless on this one too," he says. He then reads from a slip of paper tucked into the seam of the book. *"Destiny* derives from the Greek word meaning *tendency*, so your destiny is more of a likelihood than an inevitability."

Elsa places a blank tile on the board and declares it an H. She plays the word PSYCH around the Y in *destiny*. No one has the guts to challenge that the word might actually need an E on the end, so she and Ferguson collect 34 points.

"Splendid," says Albert. "The E-ended version of the word used to mean *breathing* . . . just like *thinking* was akin to *sexual alertness*. These are two great examples of the visceral start."

"That decides it," says Jane, "—men invented language. *Sexual alertness* is where they do most of their thinking."

Tom has been following the conversation through Mary's signing. He grabs Jane around the rib cage. "I'll squeeze the *psyche* out of you if you don't obey me."

"What better place to think?" says Albert. "The brain started as a throw-away, you know." He pulls out Volume I and finds a page with lots of handwriting in the margins. He rotates the book and reads aloud: *"Brain: rejected matter; rubbish; the paste that leaks from a cracked skull."*

Albert returns to helping Mom study the board, then the two of them place the word DEXTER for 30 points.

"Isn't anyone going to challenge us?" says Mom. "*Dexter* is a proper name."

Albert is drumming his fingers together with delight. "I don't even have to look this one up," he says. "*Dexter* means *to the right,* and *sinister* means *to the left.*"

"Play moves *sinister,*" says Dad. "It's Tarzan and Jane's turn."

Jane and Tom study their tiles and eventually play the word XENON for 14.

"And that brings us to the end of Round Two," says Dad, "Elsa and Ferguson are in the lead with 64 points."

"Not for long," I say. "Read'em and weep."

Mary and I gather all seven of our tiles and form the word GOODBYES along the right edge of the board, scoring 116 points for the move—a game clincher.

"Challenge!" calls Mom.

"Excellent choice," says Albert. "It might need a hyphen."

Dad opens the new Webster's Dictionary, but delays

his verdict by reading the neighboring words on the page: *"Goofball . . . goose bumps . . ."*

"I need a drink," says Jane, and she snaps her fingers in Dad's direction. "Bring us another round, Wife."

"Good-for-nothing," Dad reads another word from the book. "And by the way, the challenge stands. The E at the end of *goodbye* is optional, but the hyphen *isn't*. Losers take their chips and forfeit their turn."

Albert opens his Oxford dictionary. "Ooh, tough luck you two. I see that *goodbye* doesn't need a hyphen in *this* dictionary. Did you know it's a contraction of the phrase *God be with you?*"

"You're kidding," says Elsa. "And all this time I thought I was being so secular."

"Happy holy-days," says Mom.

"Yes," says Albert, "the Christian references are hard to avoid . . . unless, of course, you pick a clever word like *Catholic*."

"What?" says Jane.

"It meant *universal* in early Greek," continues Albert. "The original Christians were a fragmented group, and the name just happened to stick when the followers were reigned together under a universal orthodoxy."

"That reminds me," says Mary. "I need to return your copy of *The Da Vinci Code,* Jane. Thanks for letting me borrow it."

"And what did you think?" says Jane.

Mary pauses. "It certainly was an eye-opener. But I think Dan Brown is a knucklehead. He stated on his first page that the facts would be accurate, but that simply wasn't true. There's no hard evidence that Jesus and Mary Magdalene were married and had children. And Jesus was more likely to have been single and celibate—"

"Truth!" says Albert, and he pulls out Volume XI while Elsa and Ferguson take their turn.

"The word *truth* originally meant *faith, trust, loyalty,* and *confidence.* The truth was not a *fact,* it was a *faith.* I would say that Mr. Brown violated Mary's *trust,* but not Jane's. I suspect both of you could pass a lie detector test while giving opposite answers."

Mom lays out the tiles for HAZARD and collects 46 points for her team. Albert thumbs through Volume V while Jane and Tom play WIZ for 30.

"*Hazard,*" says Albert, "—and keep in mind that answers can be seductive. According to the archbishop, William of Tyre, *hazard* was the name of a dice game invented during a siege in Palestine of a castle named Hasart. But our Sir William was writing this history two generations after the Christians of the First Crusade coined the term. It turns out that the castle's real name was probably *Ain Zarba* and that *hazard* actually derived from the Arabic word *az-zahr,* meaning *one of the dice.*"

"Well done, Professor," says Dad. "And at the end of Round Three, Albert and his darling teammate are in the lead with 93 points, while Bert and Mary swim in the toilet with 38."

I make a flushing sound, then announce that Mary and I are waiving our fourth turn so that we can exchange five of our tiles. Play passes to Elsa and Ferguson, who place the word IDIOT on the board.

"Terrific," says Albert. "If I call you an *idiot,* you might get upset with me. But what I'm really saying is that you're a *private person—a common man.* The word has obviously morphed into a label for lay ignorance, departing from its brethren of the *idio* root, like *idiom* and *idiosyncrasy,* which don't carry the negative connotation."

Mom and Albert play VIEW for 54 points, extending their lead dramatically. Jane and Tom put down GULL for 17 to end Round Four.

Mary and I have yet to play a high-scoring word this game, and our prospects aren't looking good. I stall for time.

"Hey, Wife," I say to Dad. "My drink needs a recharge. Hop to it, Princess."

Dad raises an eyebrow. "Right you are, Skippy. Yours is coming back with a can of whoop-ass."

Mom and Dad travel into the kitchen and return with snacks and beverages.

"*Wife*," reads Albert, "—yet another one with a negative connotation to modern ears. *Wife-man* is Old English for *woman*. And it just so happens that *weapon-man* dropped the *weapon* to become simply *man*. Therefore, *man* comes in two genders: a *wife-man* and a *weapon-man*. There was no ill intent in the evolution of language; the word *mankind* is not sexist."

I stare at our rack of tiles, and a word finally comes to mind. We play SHERIFF for 48 points.

"—The *shire's royal official*," says Albert. "And his horse was in the care of the stable's head groom—the *constable* or the *marshal*."

Elsa and Ferguson play the word PUN. Then Mom and Albert place OMEN.

"Ah, yes," says Albert, "another one which echoes of the visceral start. *Omen* once meant *to hear* or *to listen*."

Jane and Tom lay out the word LADY, and Albert switches books. "*Lady* meant *bread-kneader*, and *lord* meant *bread-keeper*. The servants of the house ranked higher than the faggots outside."

"Attention pitiful Lords and Ladies," says Dad. "You're no match for d'Governor and d'Governess. At the conclusion of Round Five, 156 is the score to beat, and none of you rats is even close. It's 110 for Elsa, 108 for Jane, and a sorry showing of 86 for Bert."

Mary places CLOCK on the board for 45 points.

"*Clock* comes from *bell*," reads Albert, "and so does the name of a bell-shaped garment, called a *cloak*."

Bong! There's a ringing sound from the television set. Scrooge is meeting with the Ghost of Christmas Yet to Come, and the menacing spectre is covered from head to toe in a black cloak. The only visible flesh on his body is that of his outstretched hand, which indicates the direction the two of them are to travel.

"Look," says Mary. "The Grim Reaper is a Disney cast member. He's doing a mixed-finger point."

"—And with his left hand," says Albert. "A sinister apparition, to be sure."

◆ ◆ ◆

The Scrabble game ends as usual, with Mom and Uncle Albert coming away with an easy victory. Mary and I manage a come back to third place, finishing ahead of Elsa and Ferguson.

Dad picks up his drink. "You coming?" he says to Ferguson.

The two men leave the room and find their coats, then head out onto the front porch for their annual cigars.

Tom punches me in the arm. "You're such a girl," he says.

I hit him back. "No, *you're* a girl."

"*Girl*," says Uncle Albert, and he pulls out Volume IV. "—*A child or animal of either gender; something worthless. A knave girl is a young male. A gay girl is a young female.*"

I put my arm around Tom's shoulder. "Well, at least we're not gay."

"And what's wrong with being gay?" says Elsa.

Tom frowns. "You can't say anything anymore."

"Hey," says Mary, who's been studying Dad's score sheet, "check this out. The last five plays make a sentence. *Job has two boob god.*"

"You're such a *gay girl*," says Elsa.

"Not *job*," says Albert, "—think Holy Bible and *Book of Job*. It's telling us that Job of the Old Testament had a two-boobed god."

"Now we're getting somewhere," says Jane.

"Yes, God is a woman," says Elsa. "We all know it."

"You mean a *wife-man*," I say.

Albert raises his finger. "*Man* meant *human*, and many of the pagan gods were female. But go back even further, and the term *man* gets dicey. *Man* once referred to ghosts and other paranormals, absent of any human form. A *man* was a poltergeist swarming through the spirit world, wreaking havoc. It took awhile for these spirits to settle down and take on human traits, becoming the forebears of *man-kind*. The worshippers of *man* eventually *became* man. Check out the Bible sometime. Jesus refers to himself as the *Son of Man* . . . in other words, a *human*."

"Exactly the point in *The Da Vinci Code*," says Jane. "The divinity of Jesus was decided long after he was dead. He was known to be just a man when he was alive."

"Well," says Albert, "that's one way to see it, but there's another. Jesus was a deity to the early Christians, and so was *God the Father*, and so was the *Holy Ghost*. The problem for the Council of Nicea was to consolidate the Christians and make them less pagan. The solution that won the vote was to declare Jesus and the Holy Ghost as *one in substance with God the Father* so that the trinity could merge into a single god. It was religion by committee—a camel instead of a horse."

Mom sets a Bible on the table, and I open it to a random page, finding the start of the Gospel of John.

> In the beginning was the Word, and the Word was
> with God, and the Word was God.

How can the people of today make any sense of such a passage without a translator?

"What do you get when you cross a sheep with a bumblebee?" says Mary.

"Dear god," says Albert.

"A bah-humbug."

♦ ♦ ♦

After everyone has gone to bed and the house is quiet, I sneak back downstairs and turn on the lights of the Christmas tree. I make myself comfortable on the couch and restart the film *A Christmas Carol.*

On this particular Christmas Eve, I feel an acute pity for one Ebenezer Scrooge, as his predicament actually reminds me somewhat of my own.

His ghost of Jacob Marley is warning me to change the course of my life or else repeat my college failure, and he informs me that my chain of despair is now a ponderous one. The only hope for my salvation is to accept the three visitations he has procured for me.

The clock tolls one, and I recognize the Ghost of Christmas Past as the old woman from the library stacks, appearing in a pool of light. We travel together, exploring the shadows of history.

At the second chime, I meet Uncle Albert as my Ghost of Christmas Present, but instead of arriving with a feast, he arrives with a Scrabble board and a crate full of books. He breathes new life into words and tells me to know them better.

With the ringing of the third bell, I'm brought face to face with the Ghost of Christmas Yet To Come. But he has no surrogate in my mind, so I must simply watch him as he shows the future to Ebenezer Scrooge. I'm surprised by Scrooge's inability to put together the clues of his own death being presented to him. He watches as his laundress, his charlady, and the undertaker all converge on Joe's pawn shop and sell his worldly possessions, discussing the dead man they've taken them from. And Scrooge wonders at the identity of the deceased man who his business associates are joking about, while also noticing his own absence from the seat under the clock of the London Exchange. But still, Scrooge does not connect these observations to himself.

In fact, it is not until Scrooge is looking upon the letters of his own name on a tombstone that he falls to his knees and repents, swearing he'll change if it's not too late.

What is the power of his name on a grave marker to finally drive home the other clues? Why wasn't he equally capable of gleaning the truth from the words and actions of the people he knew? Wouldn't *they* be more reliable than the words on a headstone, which could easily belong to some other person named Ebenezer Scrooge. Printed words are inherently a poetry that might or might not be true.

That's it. *So much poetry, so little truth.* This was the phrase the old woman was abbreviating when she read the one book for longer than the others. The truth was what she was after, and any perceived violation was an amusement to her. Only one author enjoyed her complete approval, winning the utterance "an early arrival," which must have meant *an early arrival to the truth.*

My parlor table is indeed stacked with too many puzzle pieces. There must be at least three or four puzzles represented here, and each one portrays consciousness with a slightly different look. The pieces of each puzzle are hard to tell apart, and many of them can interlock with the others. Consciousness has been unfolding and changing with time; I should have guessed it all along: there are multiple versions of the puzzle. Consciousness is an ever-changing lens through which all things are studied, including consciousness itself.

I must learn to spot the pieces of the truest picture and set the others aside.

I detect a pattern right away. The most famous *early arrivals* in history were those people who sparked revolutions in science, art, philosophy, and religion. It can't be a coincidence that these great transitions also align themselves with well-documented stages of psychology. Aristotle's universe of childlike simplicity fits the *literal psychology* of the modern four-year-old. Isaac Newton's later application of math fits the *abstract psychology* of a modern adolescent. And the relative universe of Albert Einstein, presented in the early twentieth century, fits the *relativistic psychology* of the modern adult.

And the subject of art seems little different. Why has art advanced through stages that seem to match the capacities of a growing child in today's world? And what about philosophy and religion? Surely they, too, have advanced in measurable degrees that relate to an evolving human intellect.

I'm suddenly impatient for the holidays to be over; I'm ready to return to my studies. No longer will I be spending my days in the stacks of the library, because my new strategy will be to gather a large sampling of books on a single topic, then compare them closely and try to spot the inconsistencies between them. Only those authors who prove themselves most precise will earn my trust . . . although my trust will never be blind. To the best of my ability, I will remain skeptical at all times, chasing into footnotes and bibliographies for sources whenever I sense an error or contradiction might be at hand. I will follow any lead into any topic, no matter how strange or tangential, for whatever insights it might offer me. And I vow not to fear dead ends or to shy away from challenging new ideas. My quest for a higher truth is about to begin.

CHAPTER 39

The Great Awakening

My research consumes me throughout the winter and spring months of 2004. Mary and the children—my three silver tea cups—sit neglected and tarnishing on the parlor shelf while I work at the table on the puzzle.

Mary is a good sport. She does many of the household chores for me, and she makes light of our home-maintenance projects that are going undone. For instance, Mary calls the icicles on the ceiling of our screened-in porch "a geologic wonder," and she claims that she has always wanted a carport, now that our garage door has finally crumbled away. But Mary saves her best humor for my family; she tells them that living with me is like living with a corpse.

In truth, however, I have Mary's full blessing for what I'm doing. She wants me to take as much time as I need because she recognizes this project as an equivalent to her *Story of Poppi*.

Each night, Mary and I review my day's work, and she helps me to sift through the puzzle pieces. Mary is benefiting as much as I am.

The two of us are no longer frustrated and dismayed by the madness in the world. Even humanity's current headlong hurl toward self-destruction is perfectly natural: it's nobody's fault, and it might just be unstoppable. Yet, we still find cause for hope. The means for reversing current trends are at hand. The emerging picture of consciousness holds the answer.

Mary and I have discovered that my earlier notion to rank intellect was, in fact, correct and supported by more than a century of research. Human intellect unfolds in stages: history demonstrates it; our children demonstrate it.

We've learned that people see the truth with varying degrees of clarity. Human perception is like a picture taken from a camera: whatever shows up on the film is seen as the truth. People spend their childhood grinding better lenses and improving their film sensitivity, ultimately enabling them to capture the truth with better accuracy. Parents and teachers do what they can to help, limited by the capabilities of their own camera equipment. With each successive generation, picture quality tends to improve.

As it should be, Mary and I see the truth more clearly than MJ and Michael, at least for now. We also see truths that were not evident to our forebears—Jefferson, Disney, and my grandfather. And we have no doubts that there are truths we see less clearly than some of our contemporaries. Yet *all* people, no matter how clearly or unclearly they see the world, deserve our respect and compassion. Picture quality is more a product of circumstances than free will. It is not a measure of worth, but rather, a measure of awareness. Picture quality does not bestow shame or glory; it indicates a stage of intellect.

The intellectual stages are marked by big jumps in picture resolution. Evolutionary forces drive these jumps, putting humankind on a natural path toward higher consciousness.

Our human history, then, is a record of exactly what should have happened given the intellectual capacities of the times. Likewise, the present is exactly as it should be, because the intellect of today dictates it. And the future will be no different. The intellect of tomorrow will dictate it, too.

The words of Robert Owen ring truer for me now than ever before.

> . . . that Power which governs and pervades the universe has evidently so formed man, that he must progressively pass from a state of ignorance to intelligence, the limits of which it is not for man himself to define; . . .

PART V

The
Jungle
Cruise

CHAPTER 40

The Anniversary Dinner

My research is mostly finished by the end of the school year, and I'm a changed man because of it. No longer do I crave a college degree, because I know that the universities don't teach what I've learned. Instead, I'm restless to share my newfound knowledge with the world.

But how can I do it? A lecture series or a textbook seem doomed from the start, because these were exactly the kinds of sources I used for gathering the information, and they obviously haven't reached much of an audience yet, even among the experts. No, I need a way to present this information that appeals to the general public: a novel perhaps, or maybe a screenplay.

I'm just beginning to pen some ideas when school lets out for the summer, and I place the project on hold. Our calendar fills quickly with kids' activities, weekend excursions, farmers' markets, cookouts, and one particular dinner outing for Mary and me—courtesy of Uncle Albert.

In late June, Albert sent us a gift card with a note, saying he would come to Madison and watch our children so Mary and I could go out to celebrate our first Disney wedding anniversary.

On the prearranged July afternoon, he arrives with a teenage niece, and the two of them take over playing with MJ and Michael in our back yard. Mary and I say goodbye to them and head for the bus stop.

Mary wears the same poor-girl outfit she surprised me with last year, including the suntan lotion for cologne. I haven't yet determined if she's got anything on underneath.

♦ ♦ ♦

Madison's downtown is a pleasure to behold on a fine summer's evening such as this. And when that evening also

coincides with one of six special Wednesdays in June and July, the air is truly electric.

Mary and I are among some twenty thousand people who have descended upon the Capitol Square for an outdoor performance of the Wisconsin Chamber Orchestra. The ensemble is now warming up, and the surrounding lawns are filled with people sharing wine and food on picnic blankets.

"Finally," says Mary, "our wedding reception."

"Better late than never, I suppose."

"But let's blow it off," she says.

We turn at King Street and walk the one block to our favorite restaurant in the old Fess Hotel. There's no waiting for a table on the patio, and we request a seat near one of the planters. Mortimer Mouse is already there, scavenging among the vines.

We collect our drinks and raise them in toast, honoring the people responsible for last year's ceremony: Mom and Dad as our generous benefactors; Uncle Albert as the goofy bishop, and Merryweather as the mad organizer of it all.

"And let's not forget Mickey Mouse," I say.

"Who can forget *him*?"

Mary stares into her glass of hard apple cider, watching the bubbles lose their grip from the sides and rise to the top. She whispers something to herself, then looks thoughtfully at me. "Walt Disney wanted to put Epcot between a parking lot and an amusement park. There's your answer, Bert."

I pick up Mary's drink and taste it. "I'm checking this for poison," I say. "I don't remember asking you a question."

"Your book," she says. "It belongs between a parking lot and an amusement park. The answer couldn't be simpler, Bert."

"Are you sure you're okay? What's the date today?"

"Education and entertainment go hand in hand, don't you see? People were going to learn about Walt's model city on their way to the Magic Kingdom. Amusement was the lure. That's what *you* need, Bert. A book isn't your answer, and neither is a movie. You need to design a ride for Disney World."

I ponder the idea. "Edutainment," I say. "Not bad."

Over the course of dinner and drinks, Mary and I abandon the real world and escape to a land of creative imagination. Our first breakthrough is the idea of the *Virtual Reality*

Coaster, or *VRC*—the world's next generation of thrill-ride. The VRC is a dark indoor roller coaster with four passengers to a car. They are seated in a single row that faces forward, with each person secured by a pull-down padded restraint. Riders watch a large video screen mounted in front of them and listen to an on-board sound system. Motors and brakes add acceleration and stopping to the usual freewheeling of the coaster, while special effects, like wind and spray, are blown through the car. All of this activity is synchronized by computers, making the VRC a simulator ride of extreme capability.

Mary and I become so engrossed in our brainstorming that the visits by our waitress fail to bring us fully back to reality. We stop short in the world of *Alice in Wonderland:* we introduce ourselves as Tweedledum and Tweedledee, then argue incessantly; we repeatedly ask her the whereabouts of the White Rabbit, then tell her we're late; and we point into the nearby tree and wonder why she can't see the Cheshire Cat. By the end of the evening, I'm impersonating the Mad Hatter and declaring this our un-anniversary. Our waitress is a good sport; she helps us celebrate by bringing us a special treat.

While Mary takes care of the bill, I thank Mortimer Mouse for tonight's Blue Room Session. I now have something to occupy my mind for the rest of the summer. I'm well on my way to redesigning Disney's Jungle Cruise.

CHAPTER 41

The Launch

By the end of summer, I've completed the script, and I can imagine the new Jungle Cruise from start to finish.

In my mind, I stand with my back to the Cinderella Castle of Disney's Magic Kingdom. I am looking southwest into Adventureland, where a mammoth ten-story Maya pyramid now looms over the trees. A tangle of vines climb its weathered and crumbling sides. The ruin is the new home for the Jungle Cruise.

As I enter Adventureland, the pyramid vanishes behind some trees. A waterway eventually appears alongside the path, turning inland through the vegetation and granting a small glimpse of the pyramid's massive base. I can hear a waterfall in the distance.

Farther along the path, the horizon opens up, revealing an enormous acropolis at the foot of the pyramid. An open-air pavilion sits before it, sheltering an imposing stone wall.

The pavilion is built of raw timbers that are fastened together by vines of seaweed. Lesser limbs and branches form the trusses that support the grass roof. Television monitors hang from the framework overhead, all playing the same program, and the stone wall is etched with hieroglyphics. A line of people stand waiting to reach the wall, yet the edifice shows no signs of having a door.

The line for the Jungle Cruise is an hour-long attraction

of its own. It begins here under this pavilion, where the television screens present a test-drive of the newly theorized
"smallest particle in the universe." Then, guests head into
the acropolis for three consecutive rooms of entertainment,
showcasing the history of the cosmos and of the Planet Earth.
The first room explains the creation of the universe and of
our small blue planet. The second describes the seeds of life,
which evolved over the next 3.6 billion years. And the final
room presents the earth's current billion years of history in
spectacular fashion—from before the Cambrian explosion
to the arrival of modern humans—teaching that the human
species has swiftly become the greatest threat to life on earth.
And beyond these three rooms come two hallways, having
museum-like atmospheres. The first is a tall, sky-lit corridor
that presents a vivid timeline of the history just learned in
the previous three room, illustrating that the human presence on earth is no more than a single grain of sand in a
vast hourglass. The second hallway offers a dark gallery of
art, called *The Gray Room*, and the easel at its entrance holds
the following sign:

The Bridges of Intellect
– Assembling the Driftwood of Experience –

Dedicated
to All Explorers
on the River of Truth

I pull out my fast-pass and show it to the attendant. My
plan is to skip the line today and board right away. I follow a
separate aisle through the corridors and move quickly toward
a continuously-loading stream of vehicles.

Each vehicle is shaped like a hollowed-out human head,

with ears and cheeks missing to allow for boarding. The cars roll quietly on rubber wheels that sandwich steel rails, and these cars move apart from each other at the room's exit.

When I reach the front of my short line, I step onto the conveyor and walk to my vehicle. I take my seat beside three other people and pull down the restraint. Directly in front of me, on the backside of the vehicle's face, is a large video screen displaying a closed metal door.

The car is exceedingly quiet inside: the noise from the boarding area sounds muffled and distant. A cast member checks the shoulder harnesses and bids us farewell.

Our car exits the room, stopping for a moment in total darkness. A small motor begins to whine, and we start a slow ascent through a cool dark shaft. The metal door on the video screen slides open, revealing a cockpit having two seats, but only one pilot.

The pilot is a young woman with ebony skin and long braided hair. She wears the safari gear of an 1800s European explorer, including the wide-rimmed hat. She swivels in her chair and looks at us.

"Welcome to Disney's Jungle Cruise," she says. "My name is Sarah Bellum. I'll be your pilot and tour guide today. Now, I guess you might be wondering what we're doing in a contraption like this, instead of a boat, for a ride called the Jungle Cruise. Valid question. But as you'll soon see, this jungle cruise is something quite special." She bulges her eyes. "It's an ANALOGY.

"This cruise is a river-ride through the history of human intellect." Her voice has acquired an ominous tone. "It will survey the changing architecture of the human mind on its journey to greater understanding. Ours is the vehicle necessary to make that journey. . . . But of course," she slips back into common speech, "there's a disclaimer. No one knows for sure how the brain and its intellect evolved. It's premium guess-work at best. This jungle cruise simply offers one compelling possibility based on the evidence available at this time. Disney intends to keep the ride up to date. But one thing's for sure: we humans have come a long way since our beginnings."

Sarah swings back around to the front. "And that's just where I'm taking you now." She ignites some jet engines.

Through the cockpit window, we can see the elevator shaft brightening. Soon, we are perched in an open-air temple at the top of the Jungle Cruise's ten story stone pyramid. We have an excellent view of the Cinderella Castle and of the rest of the park.

Our craft rumbles, as it gently rises from the platform and floats free of the temple. Sarah yanks the throttle, and we launch forward, pressed firmly into our seats as the vehicle climbs into the sky and into the darkness of space.

Sarah looks over her shoulder at her passengers. "Here comes Venus," she says. "Watch this."

She accelerates the ship and veers toward the planet for a near miss. Its gravitational pull slingshots us around it.

"Did you like that?" she says. "Then I've got good news. We're about to do it again, but around the sun this time. You see, we've got to go back in time 5 million years, and the gravitational boomerang is how we're doing it. Five million years ago is the beginning of the hominids . . . or rather, the hominins, since scientists keep changing the name. The hominins were those furry monkey-like creatures that shared a common ancestor with the chimps, gorillas, and other primates. It was these hominins which ultimately gave rise to us humans."

Sarah points to the dashboard. "For those of you who like the numbers, note the display. We're at 160,000 BC right now; that's how far Venus just took us back. But the sun's gravity is thirty times stronger. It will take us the rest of the way . . . that is, if it doesn't tear us to pieces.

"I assume you all signed the liability waiver," she says in a business-like tone. "Too late now, I guess. Just sit back and relax. Your life is out of your hands."

Sarah places goggles over her eyes and tugs on the throttle. "Wee-yaa!" she hollers, as we accelerate toward the sun. Radiation warms my skin, and the front window becomes unbearably bright.

"Well, don't look right at it," she says. "Haven't you got any sense? Where are your goggles?"

We swing hard around the sun and streak back into the darkness of space.

"We did it," says Sarah. "If you look at the control panel, you'll see that we're back to 5 million BC. Next stop: Planet Earth."

Without delay, Sarah turns our ship and fires the engines. The earth drifts into view, showing swirls of blue and white in the sunshine, though I can't make out the continents.

Sarah points with two fingers. "See that white patch over there? That's the South Pole. Antarctica started piling up with ice after the extinction of the dinosaurs. By about 3 million BC, we'll be in a full-blown ice epoch. Glaciers will be growing and shrinking in intervals that last tens of thousands of years."

Sarah steers us to the dark side of the planet, where the earth appears as a black circle against a ring of light through the atmosphere. Darkness fills the front windshield as we fly closer.

"We'll be splashing down in the ocean at the mouth of a river named Truth. Yeah, you heard me right—the *River of Truth*. My instruments report clear skies and a full moon, so it should be a lovely landing. Brace yourselves for re-entry."

With no time to prepare, the ship decelerates and begins to heat up. A red glow fills the cabin.

The heat quickly dissipates, and soon we are gliding smoothly like an aircraft. Sarah opens a window in the cockpit to let in some fresh air.

Below us, the ground is dark except for a ribbon of reflected moonlight that meanders its way to the sea.

"That's the River of Truth," says Sarah. "And up ahead is the ocean it drains into. At the mouth of the river is a wide delta filled with sandbars, but you can't see them from here because they're enshrouded in fog, owing to where the cool ocean breezes meet the warm river air."

Sarah tips us into a shallow dive and skims the top of the fog. The ocean spreads out before us, and we continue our descent until we are gliding just above the water's surface.

Our speeding craft skips and skids across the ocean swells, splashing sea water into the cabin, until we finally settle to a stop. We sit for a moment, bobbing gently on the waves.

Sarah flips some switches and engages a new throttle. I feel a surge from beneath us, and our aircraft now performs like a speedboat. We bank around and cruise across the waves toward the coastline.

"Welcome to the official start of the Jungle Cruise," she says. "We are just about to enter the river's delta. It's full of sandbars, and the visibility is poor . . . so close your eyes if you get squeamish."

Sarah activates the headlights and charges into the delta at full speed. She swerves to avoid the many sandbars that flash into view.

CHAPTER 42

The First Hominins
5,000,000 BC

Sarah cranks the wheel and cuts the motor, bringing us to a quick halt. Our headlights can barely cut through the murky fog.

A trolling motor sputters to life, and Sarah guides us forward until we see a grassy sandbar up ahead. She idles the motor and throws an anchor out the window, which falls away completely because it's not connected with a chain or rope.

The sandbar features a human-like creature walking around on it, moving between pieces of driftwood it has laid out on the ground.

"That, my friends, is a hominin," says Sarah. "—Well, at least part of one. Do you remember when I said this ride was an analogy? Here's what I meant. The figure you see there is a representation of the hominin's emotions. The sandbar he is walking upon represents his physical body and brain. The sandbar is created and destroyed by the passing currents of time. Awesome, aye? As for the branches washed ashore, those are the hominin's only contact with the outside world. They are the experiences he feels through his senses, like sight, sound, smell, and touch. It is the job of his emotions to organize the riverwood, because . . . are you listening? . . . *Emotion* is the architect of intellect. And let me say it again. *Emotion* is the architect of intellect.

"I know it's already a heavy analogy, but it's about to get

heavier. When our drifting boat touches the sandbar, we'll enter the mind of this hominin. We're almost there."

As our boat bumps the beach, there's a brief sucking sound, and the view out the front windshield goes black. The calm drifting motion of the river is replaced by fits of bouncing, swinging, and spinning. The sounds of birds, insects, and other wildlife come and go sporadically, as do the sensations of wind and rain. There are fleeting moments of heart beat, breathing, and the gurgling sounds of digestion. Breezes blow across us, switching instantly from bitter cold to balmy hot. Odors shift randomly as well.

Sarah turns in her chair to face us. "You probably noticed that the front window went dark. This happened because we're exploring the mental world and not the physical one. In the mental world, 'seeing' means 'understanding.' This hominin does not see . . . I mean . . . *understand* the world it experiences. This creature is alert but not self-aware."

There's an awkward pause as Sarah turns to the console and flips through a notebook. "Here it is," she says, and she prepares to read. "This hominin walked upright on two legs, and carried a brain about one-third the size of a modern human's. It hunted and gathered its food in small family groups that followed a strict social hierarchy, with a dominant male at the top. Eye contact was a primary means for communicating the social order. Group survival relied on each member following the cues of its leader, like watching his body language to flee, fight, or travel to a new feeding ground."

Sarah snaps closed the notebook and says, "I've had enough of this hominin." She whips around in her chair and pulls a lever, lurching our boat off the beach. The chaotic movements and sounds dissipate into the quiet calm of the river, and the view of the sandbar returns to the headlights.

"Are you ready to jump forward in time?" she says.

Without waiting for a reply, she jettisons us from the water, and we enter a steep climb through the fog. I'm drawn into my seat while a mist flows over the windshield and through the cabin. We emerge from the haze into a star-filled sky.

But our rapid ascent quickly stalls, and we flip and fall backward like a stunt airplane. Our wings eventually catch air, and we glide back into the fog, where we splash down onto the river.

CHAPTER 43

The First Humans
2,500,000 BC

Sarah points to the display on the dashboard, which reads 2.5 million BC. "The sandbar of our first hominin-friend washed away long ago—some two and a half million years ago. We're approaching another sandbar now, one that belongs to a new breed of hominin, called a human."

A sandbar appears in the headlights. Its driftwood is better organized than the earlier one. In fact, some of the branches are driven into the sand along the shoreline to brace others that extend out into the water. There's a human figure moving around on the island, and I watch him go wading into the water alongside one of his anchored branches.

"The early humans pointed their riverwood upstream in the River of Truth and then used it to secure themselves while they ventured out. They were building on their experiences, and such learning carried considerable survival advantages. And notice something else. The creature there in front of us is immersed in the river, but the surrounding fog prevents him from seeing upstream or down. He feels the push of the water flowing past him, but he perceives no future or past; he lives entirely in the moment. All remembrances and all anticipations arrive uncontrollably in the here and now, triggering chemicals and causing emotions that affect immediate behavior. To these first humans there is only the present."

Sarah twirls in her chair with her arms outstretched, as

if gesturing to give us a hug. "Let's enter the mind of this base human," she says.

We hit the beach, and again the windshield goes dark. The experience is similar to the previous one—it's a bombardment of sounds and smells. However, there is slightly more order this time. There is a rhythmic quality to the noise, which now includes clicking stones, tapping sticks, and shuffling feet.

"These first humans excelled in something called *emotional signaling.* Perhaps you've never heard the term before—it's relatively new. Emotional signaling is the key to intellectual evolution. It is the long-sought missing link between humans and the rest of the animal kingdom. Emotional signaling is what organizes the driftwood."

Sarah pulls the lever and backs us off the sandbar. We bob peacefully on the water.

"Here's the history lesson," she says. "Following the extinction of the dinosaurs some 65 million years ago, mammals evolved to fill the niches left behind. But these mammals differed significantly from reptiles, amphibians, and birds when it came to child-rearing practices. Mammal mothers held their eggs inside their bodies, giving birth to live young, and they manufactured their own milk to feed their babies. These early steps toward greater care of the young introduced a new level of interaction between the generations. It was only a matter of time—about 60 million years—before the most advanced mammals, called primates, acquired the tools for the next leap in perception. The first hominin babies of 5 million BC snuggled up to their mothers for warmth and protection; they stared into mother's eyes while feeding from her breasts; and they engaged in short, unbroken interactions of touch, sight, and sound with caregivers. Such emotional connections became essential to survival, effectively programming an emergent culture into the new babies. We can finally discard the long-standing debate that pits *nature* versus *nurture*. It turns out that nature *causes* nurture.

"But this was just the beginning. The stage was set for further advances.

"The transition to walking upright shrank the female reproductive anatomy, such that large babies could no longer pass through the birth canal. Infants were born smaller and less developed, helplessly dependent on mother and family for a longer stretch of time, extending the period of intense emotional signaling.

"Yet the trump card leading to the first human species—the critical evolutionary jump separating humans from the other critters—was the loss of facial hair on the females. It was this disappearance of hair that sparked the creation of the world's first stone tools.

"Do you think I'm crazy?" says Sarah. "What could facial hair possibly have to do with stone tools? Please bear with me, because the connection is not so strange when you understand emotional signaling.

"An emotional signal is a mental cue that interrupts a biological call to action. Here's what I mean. Primates don't necessarily fight or flee at the first sign of danger. Rather, they automatically survey the signals bouncing around their group's social hierarchy before taking action. It is the number and complexity of these signals that determine a creature's intellect. —It is the stacking and sorting and patterning of such signals that ultimately lead to the higher forms of thought.

"Please look into my face," says Sarah, and she performs a silent display of over-dramatic expressions. "The human face is a canvas of unrivaled complexity in the animal kingdom.

It is the most potent signaler of emotions in the world. But this was not always the case, of course. The loss of facial hair was just an early step toward this complexity.

"Without hair on the face to obscure subtle movements, babies could engage in longer and more meaningful chains of back and forth emotional signals with mother and others. The advantages of such signaling granted 'human status' to the first species capable of ritual tool-making, music, dance, and athletic contests.

"But don't be fooled. These first humans—despite their elaborate displays of culture—were very much like the other primates: they had no written or spoken language; they were unaware of their existence; and they responded to the world by reflex."

Sarah suddenly thrusts us from the water and takes us into a vertical climb, this time spinning the ship in circles as we go. Again, we stall at the top and fall into a glide. She spirals us down through the fog.

After splashdown, Sarah stands up and stumbles around the cockpit as though she's dizzy. She crawls back to her chair and aims our headlights at the next sandbar.

CHAPTER 44

The First Modern Humans
150,000 BC

Sarah raises one eyebrow. "The modern human species is difficult to date. . . . Ain't that the truth! . . . but the evidence suggests that the first modern humans appeared in Africa more than 150,000 years ago."

Sarah directs our attention forward, where a frame of intertwined branches extends upstream from the beach of the approaching sandbar. A shadowy figure is out in the water, hanging on to the end of the frame while using his free hand to collect passing driftwood.

We coast ashore, and the windshield goes dark. The ride is once again more fluid and rhythmic than before.

"This creature has the best hardware yet," says Sarah. "Its face is equipped with a wealth of small muscles that broadcast the finest of emotional nuances to its neighbors. It's a change born of the stone age, when stone tools relieved the human jaw and front teeth of extreme cutting duties. Lighter duty meant facial features could become more refined and thus better at signaling subtle emotions. Signaling had fostered the technology of stone tools, and now stone tools were rewarding the signalers. Some things never change.

"And the trend toward better body-hardware included the speaking apparatus too: the human mouth and sinus cavity changed shape; the tongue became more agile; the voice box descended into the throat; and the nervous system took control of breathing to regulate airflow across the vocal cords. Sounds began to rival the complexity of facial cues.

"So what was the big break from the other human-type species inhabiting Africa and Eurasia at the time? Why can all of us trace our ancestry to a woman living in East Africa about 150,000 years ago? As you might have guessed it, the answer is emotional signaling. One tribe of humans was the first to reach the next intellectual platform: it could manage a social group numbering a hundred or more; it could manufacture an abundance of new tools and weapons; and it could ultimately produce sewn-clothing, jewelry, ornaments, and cave paintings. By 26,000 BC, this more adaptable group was the only one to survive the return of the glaciers."

Sarah backs off the island, and the sandbar returns to view.

"Quiz question!" she says. "How did modern humans reach the continents of America and Australia?" She pauses. "They walked, duh . . . well, mostly."

Sarah grabs an empty drinking glass and fills it with ice cubes from a machine under her dashboard. She grabs a cube and tosses it into the air, catching it in her mouth. With the ice bulging from her cheek, she tries to speak. "Around 25,000 years ago, glaciers trapped so much water in the form of ice that the oceans were several hundred feet lower than they are today. Huge areas of land were exposed off the world's current coastlines. Humans—who had been spilling out of Africa since about 60,000 BC—simply spread to wherever the land could support them. Some lived along the Bering Strait of Northeast Asia and thereby reached the Americas. Others thrived along the widened coastlines of India and Asia, drifting to the islands of Polynesia and Australia."

Sarah spits what's left of her ice into the glass. "After 18,000 BC, the earth's warming climate initiated a slow retreat of the ice sheets and produced a growing bounty of food, particularly near the equator. The human tribes around the Mediterranean Sea and across Asia—and likely those of Central and South America—were able to hunt and gather more food over less and less territory. By 10,000 BC, many tribes in these regions had settled into villages, and their populations grew.

"Now, we're ready to move on. Our next stop is 10,000 BC."

Sarah fires us from the delta and out over the ocean. I wonder what sort of tricks our time-travel will involve *this* time. I don't have to wait long to find out.

Sarah tips the plane forward into a dive, plunging us toward the water. We roll out just in time and fly upside down over the wave-tops. Sarah holds this position for a moment, then corrects the aircraft. She turns us around and races back to the delta.

Having returned to the fog, Sarah reduces our speed and flies us low over the sandbars. She eventually drops the plane on the water and trolls a short distance.

CHAPTER 45

The First Villagers
10,000 BC

The headlights cut through the fog and reveal a wooden frame of familiar construction, but longer than the previous one. It is obviously straining against the river's current.

"Before we enter the world of the ancient villager," says Sarah, "we need to talk a little more about language.

"Across thousands of years, vocal cues were developing into a storage system for tribal knowledge, just like music, dancing, and athletic contests had already done. Speech was just another language of emotional connection—a reaction to the world that could be passed from generation to generation. It didn't sound much like the speaking of today. Words of that time arrived in patterns and with cadence, forming chanted verses inseparable from the task at hand. Building shelters, moving heavy objects, making clothing and tools and weapons . . . these were among the activities carrying associated sounds. Such 'speech,' as we might call it, founded its own region of the unconscious brain, linked closely to hearing. But there was another region of the brain developing even farther behind the scenes."

A hologram of a human brain appears above the vacant seat in the cockpit. Regions glow within its two hemispheres, and a pipeline of light connects them.

"This new region of the brain was a decision-center that

was activated by the stress of an unfamiliar situation, where a superior member of the group was not present to lead the reaction. This decision-center sent its messages into the sound-processing area of the brain through the neural networks already established—those associated with hearing. The effect was . . . well, I'll let you see for yourself. Keep your eyes on the front window."

Our boat runs aground on the sandbar, and the window goes dark. The motion of the ride is gentle this time, with sounds reminiscent of people working.

"Our host is a young boy making pottery," says Sarah. "His father is away at the moment, and the boy is struggling with the clay."

The front window flickers with a dim light, as a voice speaks directly into my ears from my shoulder restraints. The voice belongs to a man, and it cycles through a chant in a language I don't understand.

"The boy is 'hearing' his father's reaction to the clay when it's too dry . . . but his father isn't really there. The boy is unaware that the sound is coming from within himself. His mind attributes the voice to perhaps a glimmer of light, or a rustle of leaves, or a trickle of water somewhere. The boy immediately responds to his father's command by adding water to the clay.

"By 10,000 BC, villagers were also acquiring individual names for themselves, effectively putting them into their own cultural narratives and causing them to be remembered by successive generations. This change dramatically altered the treatment of the dead, with ceremonial graves becoming more ritualized around this time. But make no mistake, the graves were not memorials to the dead. In fact, the dead remained quite alive—their voices could still be 'heard.' In some cultures, the dead were laid to rest twice, and depending on the person, such ceremonies could range from weeks to months to years apart. First and second burial rites marked the fading into silence of the voice. In some cultures, the skulls of the dead were actually cleaned, plastered, and painted for display in the home, often with sea shells inserted for the eyes. The dead were very much alive, regularly supplied with food, tools, and other worldly provisions.

"But when a tribal leader died, the situation was far more serious. Everyone in the tribe relied on him for commands; his voice must continue after his death to ensure the order of the group. The corpse was carefully prepared and enshrined in a great house at the village center. Daily deliveries of food and other comforts were common. The great house was built taller and grander than the surrounding homes so that it would serve as a visible trigger for the king's voice to all villagers. Sometimes, a holy fire burned in the tomb so that smoke would conjure the voice for those working at great distances. Successive leaders were laid to rest in this same central house.

"And leaders were ruled by the voices too. Kings heard past kings, and these became the commands to the tribe. The living king was merely a messenger, a servant, a priest of the former kings. These hallucinated voices from the other side of the brain told people what to do. They were the voices of the gods, and they spoke directly to them."

Sarah backs off the sandbar and drives away. She looks over her shoulder at us. "The voices of the gods: they were a hidden voice within the brain . . . they were the seeds of human consciousness beginning to germinate. Put that in your pipe and smoke it."

Sarah turns her head away slowly, then glances back

quickly, as if to catch us with shocked looks on our faces. She turns forward again and guns the engines.

Soon we're out over the ocean doing more tricks. We fly several loop-the-loops and then return to the delta with our wings rocking.

CHAPTER 46

The First Writing
8000 BC

We land in the fog, and Sarah reaches out her window. She aims her spotlight at the water. "Do you see that Floating Frame there?" she says.

A woven mesh of sticks leads away from the boat.

"It's now 8000 BC, and the frames are reaching farther upstream, aided by the brain's new tool."

Sarah tosses a small object from hand to hand. "*This* is a clay token," she says. "It is the world's first form of record-keeping. Such tokens of standard shape represented quantities of perhaps grain or cattle owed in a transaction. These tokens were the precursors to writing . . . but it would take several thousand years before humans would take the next big step.

"Clay envelopes were often used to store these tokens. The envelopes had to be broken to get into them. By 3500 BC, however, the containers were being spared by a clever practice of putting markings on the outside of the envelopes to denote their contents.

"Now think about it for a second. What's the point of having tokens when the etchings on the outside tell you how many are in there? By 3100 BC, the tokens were gone, and the clay containers had been flattened into tablets. This was the birth of writing in the Eastern Hemisphere. The Western Hemisphere had its *own* story, which has yet to be fully discovered, so the rest of my tale centers on the Middle East.

"But please keep in mind that such early writing didn't use alphabets in the way we use them today; characters didn't represent the sounds of speech. Rather, the symbols were pictures that conjured meanings within the minds of the readers, much like the icons on a computer screen do today. This picture-writing was an alternative form of memory, conveniently located outside the brain, where it could be reviewed, organized, and shared."

Sarah pilots our boat alongside the frame and parks on the sandbar. The front window goes dark, but again flashes with an occasional gray light.

We hear tools working in the dirt.

"By 7000 BC," says Sarah, "cultivating crops and raising livestock were the primary sources of food. Villages grew from a few hundred inhabitants into communities of more than a thousand. Food surpluses freed some villagers to specialize in other trades."

I hear voices in my ears while Sarah lectures.

"But it was more difficult to maintain social order in a larger community with a more diverse workforce. The human mind coped by developing a strict hierarchy of gods to handle the complexity. The gods spoke directly to the king and his priests and priestesses, regulating every detail of society. For instance, there was no such thing as bartering or haggling when making a trade. Rather, the terms of exchange were fully commanded by the gods.

"By 5000 BC, a few cities had upwards of ten thousand inhabitants. And for cities of this size, the central houses for the dead leaders became grand temples visible for miles. The mortal remains were entombed inside, while statues became the vehicle for conjuring the voices. The statues were treated like living things: they were bathed and dressed; they were carried outside for ceremonies; and they received daily

deliveries of food and drink to an altar beside them. Regardless of the culture, many of these statues had oversized eye
sockets filled with gems, quartz, or crystals . . . please recall
that eye contact was a powerful social cue dating back millions of years to the earliest hominins. And below the level
of the king, his holy officials maintained their own tier of
idols for conjuring the voices.

"Around 4000 BC, Sumer emerged as the world's first civilization in the Eastern Hemisphere, followed shortly thereafter
by Egypt and others around the Mediterranean Sea and
Asia. In the Western Hemisphere, it was along the coastline
of Peru in South America where the first civilization formed
centuries later.

"These giant kingdoms strained the organizational limits
of the gods. Many people had a personal idol enshrined in
their own home to assist. Nevertheless, on several occasions,
the authority of the gods simply unraveled, and the affected
populations dissolved back into smaller chiefdoms. It required
the emergence of another strong god-king to reorganize them.

"The rulers and their people were puppets to the mystical voices. They followed the commands without even the
capacity to question them. There was no concept of 'good'
or 'evil.' People simply did as they were told. They could not
know that the gods were, in fact, their forming consciences.

"You might find it interesting to note that the languages
of the time lacked words for the individual: there was no *I*
or *me* to speak of; there were no words of introspection, like
think, decide, mind, and *emotion*; and even the human body was
without a defining word, described instead by its many parts.
Without such defining words, none of these concepts could
exist within the minds of the people."

Sarah backs away from the sandbar and launches us from
the water. We soar through the mist and out into the clear

skies over the ocean. "Now," says Sarah, "we come to the humorous portion of the tour. I'm telling you that so you'll know."

She points to the year-counter on her dashboard and pushes some buttons. "Look," she says. "It's just a calculator." She types in **5317**. "Go ahead; read it upside down.

"You see, this time-travel stuff we've been doing . . . well . . . it's been based on a branch of science we here at Disney call 'fictional.' I think you're getting it. I've been deceiving you. This trick-flying stuff has been solely for the fun of it."

Sarah banks the aircraft and takes us back over the river. This time we remain above the fog and settle onto the water just beyond it.

CHAPTER 47

The Fall from Grace
2000 BC

As the boat idles, Sarah scans the water with her spotlight. "None of the Floating Frames are out of the fog yet, but some of them are right at the border.

"Around 2000 BC, a few kings began to chisel the commands of their gods onto walls, pillars, and tablets—putting the gods' words on display. Seeing these commands side-stepped the traditional channels of 'hearing' the gods. It was a new visual avenue for receiving instructions. Writing was quieting the voices. But another change was coming, one that would silence the gods more swiftly."

Sarah kills the engine, dims the lights, and flips up a large video screen in the cockpit. She stands beside it, holding a pointer at a stationary picture. "This is a map of the Eastern Mediterranean Sea around 1520 BC. At that time, the world's first technologically advanced civilization was at the height of its power. It was the Minoan culture centered on the island of Crete. These people ran a fleet of merchant ships second to none, with outposts on the nearby Cyclade islands and on the surrounding coastlines of the continents. The Minoans dominated the trade routes between the known world of Africa, Egypt, Asia, and Europe. Their island-isolation and naval superiority protected them from invasion, and their wealth afforded them a living standard unsurpassed for many centuries to come. Their major cities needed few defenses, freeing their resources for the development of two and three-story buildings, with multi-room homes for even the poorest of citizens. Buildings had clay pipes built into the walls, supplying running water to bathtubs and flush toilets. Similar pipes carried sewage into covered trenches under the streets that led to cesspits.

"The Minoans were the lost civilization of Atlantis described by Plato more than a thousand years later. Plato was not making them up. Until recently, his story has been viewed as a fiction by scholars, citing his gross factual inaccuracies regarding the age, location, and size of Atlantis. These scholars were convinced that the story was not a literal truth, as Plato claimed, but rather a poetic truth meant to inspire his Athenian readers to live more virtuously. But translation errors between the time of the Minoans and Plato can explain away the glaring inconsistencies. Furthermore, recent archaeological discoveries confirm many of the literal truths behind Plato's story."

The video picture goes into motion, doing a close fly-over of the island of Crete and focusing on a city along its northern coastline.

"The capital city of the Minoans was Knossos. This was the home of the legendary labyrinth—the enormous temple where priestesses performed rituals to the gods. In fact, the frescoes found so far show few signs of male dominance over this lost civilization. Such a gender bias should not be so surprising. Pre-conscious humans deified females for their life-giving abilities of birth and suckling. The numerous paintings and ornaments from the time, which showcase female anatomy, were *not* pornographic—of course they weren't, don't be ridiculous. They were created in reverence to the female as a source of life. Bare breasts were an integral part of sacred rituals. Those of you women with the urge to expose yourselves, please refrain . . . but recognize that this urge has a history deep within you. It would take the rise of self-awareness to bury this urge and switch the emphasis to male power and the ability to kill."

The video moves a short distance north across the Aegean Sea, to where a pillar of smoke and ash rises from a distant island. The ash plume seems to hover motionless in the sky, testimony to its colossal size.

"The wealthiest Minoan city was Akrotiri on the volcanic island of Thera, about sixty miles north of Crete. The volcano, as shown here, has been erupting for several days now . . . but don't let that fool you; it's only just clearing its throat."

The video zooms across the port city of Akrotiri, which sits knee-deep in ash. It then circles the island's mountain and climbs the dark column.

"The island was evacuated several years ago, following earthquakes and a discharge of pumice from the volcano. But the inhabitants have not moved far enough away to be safe from what's going to happen next."

The video image backs away from the volcano, as a section of the mountain breaks off and crumbles down.

Suddenly, there's a massive explosion, and a black cloud swells miles into the sky. It spreads out at high altitude, creating a thick canopy.

"The eruption of Thera was three times larger than that of Mount Pinatubo in 1991 and about thirty times larger than Mount St. Helens' in 1980. The eruption of Thera devastated the cradle of civilization.

"Under a rain of scorching dust and stone, day was turned to night for weeks on end. Earthquakes and the collapsing caldera caused tsunamis, destroying coastline cities and their fleets all around the Aegean. Thick ash blanketed everything, killing inhabitants, livestock, and crops. Farm ground was spoiled for years."

The camera backs away farther.

"As you can see, the ash cloud tracked south-westerly, sparing the Greek mainland while covering the cities of Crete. In Egypt, darkness loomed to the north, as ash polluted its soil and water. Even as far away as China, the sun fell dim, and there was a frost in July. Ash remained in the sky for several years, perhaps dropping the region's temperature by five degrees."

Sarah closes the video screen.

"When the nightmare finally ended, the giant mountain of Thera was reduced to a water-filled crater six miles across. The remains of its emerald city lay buried under yards of ash.

"The death toll from the Thera disaster was huge. For centuries to follow, refugee populations battled their way into neighboring civilizations. Disorder, famine, and slaughter were the norm. And for those people who blindly listened to the voices of their gods, *they* fared worst of all: their gods were getting them killed. The gods were instructing them to defend their families and villages, even when sorely outnumbered and out-weaponed. Those who were able to ignore, or at least postpone, acting on such commands had a better chance of survival. Treachery and deception became the new skills for winning the game of natural selection. Those who could betray their own people and feign allegiance to unfamiliar gods were being spared.

"Writings from the period support this notion of a shift away from an internal voice directing the action. Instead, behavior becomes associated with physical sensations, like heart rate and breathing."

Sarah points out the front window to the Floating Frame.

"Here on the River of Truth, intellect clings for dear life to its breaking and collapsing wooden frame. It clutches desperately at the water for anything that might offer some strength. It discovers the viney seaweed growing below on the river-bottom, and it uses these vines to reinforce the grass windings of its frame. The added strength allows these frames to get longer. Some even manage to reach the boundary of the fog.

"It's an awakening to reach the boundary," says Sarah. "These humans can at last see the glistening river stretching out ahead of them. The sight is as beautiful and empowering as it is terrifying. Humans can at once see the flow of time marching steadily toward them, across them, and behind them. They are able to order the events of the past and plan for the future. They are also aware of their mortality. It is during this time that the documenting of history begins."

Sarah drives the boat to the edge of the fog, where we ride alongside a Floating Frame to its originating sandbar. Sarah pulls ashore.

The windshield goes dark for a moment. Then gray patches remain fixed on the display. The image has no identifiable shape.

Our host is a man, and his voice rings through the cabin, speaking an unfamiliar language.

"In truth," says Sarah, "the voices of the gods were not being silenced. Rather, they were moving front and center. Languages were acquiring the vocabulary needed to put people in their own narratives. This simple change awakened people to the sound of their inner voice. Our host on this sandbar just barely knows he exists. He can take no respon-sibility for himself. He impulsively exploits whatever and whoever he can to generate feelings of power and pleasure."

Sarah pulls off the sandbar and trolls the boat upstream.

"So where do you handle your thoughts?" she says. "Most

people answer, 'in my head, of course.' This seems like the obvious answer . . . but it's not that obvious, really. Your thoughts are just a bunch of electrical impulses dashing around between cells. There's no specific location for them. People simply *imagine* such a place, and most people imagine this place behind their eyes. But this was not always the case.

"At the time of the transition to self-awareness, the imagined mind-space was in the chest, where the pumping and inflating was going on. This was the natural site for consciousness to emerge, because it was the location of strong physical sensations. It's no wonder the first glimpse inward occurred there, where lungs lost their breath from surprise, where the heart pounded with excitement, and where muscles trembled and the stomach ached with fear. But consciousness could not remain in the chest for long. The outer world causing these sensations was largely a visual experience. Eyesight became the channel through which these sensations were related and understood. Do you *see* where I'm going with this? Do you *see* my meaning? *Vision* is the analogy for consciousness: it gives us our mind's eye; it positions our thoughts in our heads behind our eyes. Imagine, if you will, a surgery that relocates your brain to the other end of your spinal column. Where will your mind-space be when you wake up? I would argue that it will remain behind your eyes. It doesn't matter where you put the processor; you do your work at the monitor."

Sarah changes the number on the display to 500 BC. "Get ready," she says, "because the Floating Frame is about to get a new look."

CHAPTER 48

The Ancient Greeks
500 BC

We motor out of the fog onto the open river, where Sarah directs the spotlight at a nearby structure that looks quite different from anything we've seen so far.

"Out here," she says. "the Floating Frames are braced by timbers driven down into the river's bottom. On top, a weave of grass and seaweed creates a platform for the creature to move around on. These Anchored Piers are far sturdier than the former design. These structures quickly advance upriver.

"The silencing of the gods was interpreted as abandonment by the newly self-aware minds. People could at last recognize wars, disasters, illnesses, and death . . . and they cited these occurrences as testimony to the anger of the gods. People scrambled to win back the lost favor, enhancing their ritual sacrifices and assembling their sacred scriptures.

"Artwork changed too. Humans, who once stood eye to eye and toe to toe with their gods, now knelt before empty thrones. The gods had flown into the sky, and their winged angels were the silent messengers operating between heaven and earth. It is God that you stand under . . . do you understand?

"It was during the time of this transition, between 2000 BC and 500 BC, that the world's oldest religions formed—Judaism in the Middle East, Hinduism in Central Asia, Buddhism in India, and Confucianism in China. Each recorded its own stories of awakening.

"The scriptures of Judaism are among the oldest, with the story of Abraham dating from between 1800 and 1500 BC. Its book of Genesis describes a man and a woman, Adam and Eve, eating from 'the tree of knowledge' against the command of their god. The fruit opens their eyes to the fact that they are naked. Their god acknowledges that the humans have 'become like one of us, knowing good and evil.' God banishes Adam and Eve from the Garden of Eden, cursing Eve with an awareness of the pain of childbirth and of the rule of men, and cursing Adam with an awareness of his endless toils to feed his family.

"But consciousness had its plus side too. A landslide of innovations swept across the culture centered around the city-state of Athens.

"Athens was a wealthy center for trade that unknowingly inherited much of its culture from the earlier Minoans. Athens was intellectually capable of conceiving a new form of government, called a democracy. It wasn't a democracy as we think of one today, however. Only male citizens participated: women and slaves had no voice.

"Democracy, coupled with a thriving entrepreneurial economy, yielded a moderate level of tolerance to new ideas, so intellectuals flourished. It was the ancient Greeks who founded such disciplines as mathematics, astronomy, philosophy, politics, and theater."

Sarah pulls our boat toward one of the Anchored Piers. "These structures are strong enough to tie onto; we don't have to go back to the sandbars anymore."

We inch closer, and Sarah lassos one of the piers with a rope. The front window flashes black for an instant, then areas of light return, this time appearing in bright white. Our host is again male, and he speaks a foreign language.

"Our human friend," says Sarah, "knows only the strictest

of rules for behavior, where obedience is rewarded and disobedience is punished. Pride and shame are the emotions
that bury his natural impulses deep within him so they don't
surface and violate his unyielding code of conduct. It's the
only way to keep social order."

Sarah reaches out the window and retrieves the rope. We
drift free, which brings the voice to a stop and returns our
view of the river.

"The people of this time didn't know they had just become
self-aware. Consequently, vestiges of their unconscious past
held a strong presence in their cultural narratives, telling
them of the golden age when the gods spoke directly to them
and granted them divine guidance. People lamented the loss
of their gods by plying their voices to hymns and psalms.
They desperately wanted to renew these connections and thus
turned to activities they believed were god-directed, such as
casting lots, looking for omens, observing the movements of
oil in water, and studying the organs of sacrificed animals.
They also pilgrimaged to oracles and prophets, who, through
ever more elaborate training and rituals, managed to bypass
the filters of their self-awareness and 'channel the gods'—in
essence, speaking from an unconscious region of the brain.

"Of these divining activities, it was those open to the most
interpretation that reveal what was truly happening. Take
the study of oil in water, for example. Observing the irregular
movements of these two non-mixing liquids provided a visual
foil for narrating solutions to problems. The shapes seen in
the oil conjured fresh words and ideas to keep the narration
moving. These rituals were the catalyst for a human brain
still lacking the tools of logic and reason for problem-solving.

"Eventually, however, logic and reason did develop, moving
these divining activities to the fringes of society and giving
them names like gambling, witchcraft, and superstition. But

the evidence of our longings for the gods remains strong today: we still look for *signs*; we still enjoy lava lamps; and we still seek out our horoscopes.

"The intellectual burst of the Greeks was short-lived, however, lasting only a handful of centuries. The subsequent Roman Empire borrowed from the Greek culture, but advanced it very little before its own collapse in 476 AD. Most of the Ancient Greek texts remained in the coastline cities of its former empire—in the grand libraries of the Middle East, from Alexandria to Constantinople.

"Ironically, it was during this same period that the isolated Western Hemisphere across the Atlantic ocean experienced *its* first awakening culture. Between 250 AD and 900 AD, the Maya civilization of Central America independently pioneered writing, mathematics, and astronomy. It remains unclear what caused this civilization's eventual collapse."

CHAPTER 49

The High Schoolers
1890 AD

Sarah adjusts the clock on the dashboard. "It's now 1300 AD," she says. "The past centuries have seen a slow advance of intellect, as two new religions, based on Judaism, branch out from the Mediterranean Sea—Christianity to the north, and Islam to the south and east. By the 1300s, however, circumstances are right for an intellectual breakout.

"Italy is now a wealthy center of commerce for the region. Its contact with ancient Greek and Roman writings sparks a revival of art and learning called the Renaissance. The Renaissance will sweep through Europe in the coming centuries."

Sarah hits the throttle and we speed upstream.

"Human intellect," she shouts over the noise of the motor, "advanced quickly for the privileged classes, especially after the year 1440, when Johannes Gutenberg introduced the moveable type printing press to Europe. Prior to this innovation, all writings had to be transcribed by hand or laboriously carved into blocks for printing, greatly limiting the volume of literature available. But the printing press spread information easily through the trading world. Literate people could build upon the ideas and discoveries of others. Books became the readily accessible storage device for pictures and words.

"Since their days near the fog, few humans had advanced beyond the Anchored Pier design. Those who *did* were the great thinkers and inventors of their time. But the printing press drew even more people forward on the River of Truth."

Sarah takes her hands off the steering wheel and aims the spotlight across the water as we zoom across it. "For several more centuries, the masses crept upstream, catching the intellectual trickle-down of the *Scientific Revolution,* the *Reformation,* the *Age of Reason,* and the first phase of the *Industrial Revolution.* Then, in 1870 AD, a monumental change occurred."

Sarah kills the engine, sending a large wave forward of the boat. "But we're not ready for 1870 just yet. I've stopped us at the year 1532 AD, when an interesting thing happens—the Spanish Conquistadors meet the Incas of South America. It's a classic clash of intellectual differences.

"Francisco Pizarro wanted to conquer the Incas of Peru, just as Hernando Cortés had easily conquered the Aztecs of Mexico eleven years earlier. The Inca leader poised to win the current civil war sent an envoy to meet Pizarro near the west coast. The envoy led Pizarro's small force of 168 men into the continent's interior along a treacherous trail to a valley in the Andes mountains. There, in the valley, lay a small town, with a battle-hardened Incan army camped out on the hillside. The army was estimated at thirty thousand men.

"A small detachment of Spaniards crossed the valley to meet with the Inca leader. They spoke to him with kind words, telling him of Pizarro's love for him. The Inca granted the Spaniards accommodations in three houses along the square of the nearby town, and agreed to meet Pizarro there later.

"The town had few inhabitants, and its central square was flanked on three sides by long buildings that offered many points of access. The Spanish hid their 62 horsemen in the openings of these buildings. They positioned their eight muskets and four small artillery in a fortification that allowed for a volley into the square, should that become necessary.

"The leaders of the Inca army staged their visit to Pizarro in the form of a grand parade. The leader and his high-ranking officials entered the town near sunset with an accompanying force of about five thousand soldiers. All were dressed in ceremonial clothing and were remarkably without weapons.

"The small Spanish force ambushed and slaughtered the group, while the giant Inca army looked on from outside the village without doing anything. These Spaniards captured the Inca leader and quickly conquered the Inca civilization.

"These events are not difficult to explain with an understanding of intellect. The Incas viewed the world from the boundary of the fog, clinging to their Floating Frames. They still relied on their gods for many of their decisions and were incapable of identifying or perpetrating a willful deception.

"The Spaniards, on the other hand, sat far upstream on their Anchored Piers. They made their own decisions and skillfully employed deceit and treachery to their advantage.

"Should we hold the Spaniards in contempt for their actions? —Their behavior was certainly brutal by today's standards. But that's the key here: the Spaniards of the 1500s did not live by today's standards. In their worldview, their behavior made perfect sense."

Sarah returns her hand to the throttle and speeds us upstream. She points to the clock. "We're finally headed to the 1870s and the end of the first phase of the industrial revolution."

Moonlight shines across the water, revealing a wide turn in the river up ahead. Sarah points forward. "The Anchored Piers can't make the bend. When they try to, the churning waters tear them apart. They can't move upstream without a new design. But until the late 1800s, the new design is almost exclusively the domain of the upper classes."

Sarah drives the boat around the bend and stops. She shines her light on a new kind of structure. This one sits high out of the water on its piers.

"This bridge design is called the Elevated Walkway. It has fewer but stouter posts into the river-bottom . . . and, most importantly, its walking platform is several feet above the water's surface to reduce drag."

Sarah ties us to a nearby post. The front window goes dark, and then a picture appears. This picture is dramatically better than the white image seen before; this one has a full complement of gray tones. But the picture is terribly out of focus, and I still can't decipher any forms.

The cabin fills with the sounds of a formal social gathering and a string quartet. Sarah explains that our host is a male servant delivering hors d'oeuvres to English-speaking guests at a party. He moves from conversation to conversation, allowing us to eavesdrop on them.

I hear phrases like "the ends justify the means" and "the world is a chess game I intend to win." The people at this party take themselves quite seriously, and they bask in the prestige of their affiliations with scientific societies, teaching academies, and new libraries. They vainly and unapologetically boast of their material purchases, musical evenings, and book collections. Their intellectual superiority over the general population is unquestioned in their own minds, as they speak of the commoners as so woefully ignorant that they must be told what to do at all times . . . like children.

Sarah reaches out the window and disconnects us from the Elevated Walkway. We drift free in silence.

"The industrialized world of the 1870s had a generation gap, but it wasn't based on age. Rather, the lines of this gap were drawn by money and privilege and gender, separating those who could achieve the Elevated Walkway design from those who could not. It was a significant source of friction in these populations. However, the gap was about to narrow.

"By 1870, the industrial revolution was entering a second phase. Its focus was expanding from textiles, iron, and coal to the more technical disciplines of chemicals, steel, and electricity. Wealthy industrialists needed laborers with basic skills in reading, writing, and math. Governments responded by removing working class children from the fields and factories, and placing them in schools. It was the first time in history that the masses, and not just the elite, could devote their childhood years to personal development. The consequences were felt by the 1890s, as young teens across the industrialized world rebelled against the authority of their parents. In 1904, G. Stanley Hall explained this crisis as part of the transition to a higher stage of intellect—one that moved beyond mere literal thinking and was capable of handling more abstract concepts.

"As for our analogy on the river, this rebellious behavior marked the period of instability during which these adolescents converted their Anchored Piers to Elevated Walkways. Viewing the world from these higher structures allowed this new generation to see beyond the concerns of their families and to identify with causes of a broader social group.

"I have something interesting to show you," says Sarah. "Hang on!"

She speeds back around the curve in the river and stops us beside an Anchored Pier. She aims the spotlight at a section of its lattice.

"Do you see that weave of sticks?" she says. "The pieces are bent and broken. Guess what that means."

Sarah pushes a button, causing our vehicle to grow a skin

and dive beneath the water's surface. Sarah shines the light through the murky water toward the anchored pier.

"Do you see that post? It's been twisted by the current. Such construction weaknesses in any bridge design limit its ability to climb the river unless strengthening can be performed. This particular Anchored Pier may be unable to make the transition to the Elevated Walkway design, meaning it will forever sit behind the bend in the river."

We return to the surface and discover flashlights searching in the distance.

"By the late 1800s, help is on the way. Psychologists are developing tools for exploring the workings of the mind. Through free-association and other such techniques, doctors are probing the human psyche for clues to its construction, hoping to explain and bring relief to those mentally suffering. Occasionally, the tools help make a needed repair, perhaps permitting the structure to extend farther upstream.

"Hall's 1904 insight regarding the widespread rebelliousness of youth prompted a flurry of research into child development. The results challenged many widely held notions about parenting and moved the Elevated Walkways steadily upstream for several decades, as teachers and parents helped their children build sturdier structures."

Sarah guns the engine, and we speed across the water. "By 1940," she shouts, "the stage is set for another major advance in bridge design. You see, after the bend in the river, there's another obstacle that even the Elevated Walkways can't overcome. The river gets too deep. The next design demands longer and stronger piers to reach the bottom."

CHAPTER 50

The Hippies
1960 AD

Sarah leaps our craft from the water and turns us skyward, climbing higher and higher over the river. She then levels us off, giving us a marvelous moon-lit view of the terrain below. She slows our airspeed and sets the cruise control.

"Now, sit back and relax," she says. "I'm going to share with you some history. At the start of the 1930s, the industrialized world entered a severe economic depression. For more than a decade, jobs were hard to find. But those with a college education fared better. The new crop of parents entering the 1940s saw value in a higher education. They ultimately encouraged their own children to attend colleges. These parents were unwittingly granting their kids four additional years of personal development.

"But that's not all. These new parents were raising their children from the intellectual viewpoint of the Elevated Walkway design, virtually assuring that their children would develop at least that far.

"Now, here's the exciting part. In 1944, near the end of the Second World War, there began a baby boom lasting twenty years. The population of young people entering universities during the 1960s swelled. College campuses became caldrons of unrest, as the students, who years earlier had rebelled against their parents, were now rebelling against society and its institutions of authority. In 1970, Kenneth

Keniston identified this phenomenon as the crisis period for yet another stage of intellectual development.

"The Elevated Walkways of this generation," continues Sarah, "could not enter the deepening river; these new young adults had to overhaul their designs. They uprooted many of their piers to strengthen those that remained, and they re-configured their frames into long-spanning arches. The resulting structures were taller and more beautiful than any that had come before, and the new vantage point atop the Marching Arches broadened the host's perspective once again. These people could see beyond their own social groups and cultures, viewing issues from multiple perspectives. They had moved beyond the limits of abstract thinking and into the realm of relativity."

Sarah pauses. "Let's go visit a flower child."

She puts the plane into a steep dive and races us toward the water. It appears she'll be smashing us into an arched bridge, but at the last moment, she levels the plane and reverses the engines. We settle gently on top of one of the wooden structures.

The front window goes dark, and then a full color image appears in tie-die: it is the same blurry image that appeared in black and white for the Elevated Walkway.

A medley of familiar songs is playing.

"The musical poets of the 1960s found a ready audience for their songs of liberation and defiance. The meaning of *freedom* broadened radically for this new generation."

Sarah hops our craft off the bridge down to the water.

"Now, you may be thinking to yourself, 'Which frame am *I* on?' That's an important question. But even more important is how you will feel about the answer. Will you feel inferior or disgraced if you are not on the highest bridge design possible? —You shouldn't. You see, you are not responsible for your current view of the world. You had no control over the circumstances that gave rise to it. You did not control the time, place, people, or genetics that produced you. And you had no idea you were following an intellectual path . . . until now, that is. Welcome to the downside of this ride."

"Now that you *do* know of the path, *you* become responsible for whether or not you continue to develop. *You* are the one who must choose to endure the upheavals of transitioning to a higher bridge design, or instead, sit in the relative comfort and stagnation of your current outlook.

"But just so you know, there's an incentive to reach the higher designs. People of the higher bridges are freer, more relaxed, and, most importantly, more peace loving. It's simply a matter of empathy. People of the higher bridges can see issues and problems from more perspectives. They can place themselves more fully into the shoes of another person 'to see how it feels.'

"So now, let's return to that all-important question, 'Which bridge are you on?' Perhaps you're thinking, 'I didn't go to college, so I'm probably stuck on the Elevated Walkway of my adolescence.' Or maybe you're thinking proudly, 'I went to college, so I must be on the Marching Arches.' Well, let me clue you in. This Jungle Cruise analogy outlines broad trends across large populations. What happens at the individual level varies tremendously. There are plenty of highly credentialed experts who have yet to engage in the crisis necessary to achieve the Marching Arches. Sadly, many of them stand little chance of moving forward because they are validated in their current thinking by educational degrees, financial success, and the esteem of their colleagues.

"On the other hand, there are plenty of people who never went to college, but who engaged in the crisis periods nonetheless. Their struggles were likely more challenging and stressful because they were undertaken while handling the responsibilities of career and family.

"Now, take my case, for example; I'm confident I stand on the Marching Arches. I remember in high school having a clique of friends. We used to criticize everybody not in our own group—a behavior I now understand as common to the Elevated Walkway design. I didn't go to college, but my life experiences eventually challenged those adolescent ideas. My work put me in contact with a wide variety of people, and for two years, an argument raged in my head, as I tried to determine whether all people were worthy of my respect. The struggle was grueling, but I feel fortunate with the outcome. In my case, the evidence furnished by my experiences tipped my worldview toward acceptance of these other groups, and I built the arched spans. If my experiences had turned out differently, however, I might have become even more deeply committed to defending my Elevated Walkway. Experience is the key. When all goes well, you get an Albert Einstein. When all goes to hell, you get an Adolf Hitler.

"But I'm not done developing my bridge . . . oh, no. Now that I'm on the Marching Arches, I have a new goal in sight. I want to keep climbing the river to the next obstacle and beyond."

Sarah starts the motor. "I'm going to take you there now."

CHAPTER 51

The Worldcentrics
1990 AD

We cruise upstream with the headlights shining in front of us, revealing a mist that rises in the distance. A waterfall spans the width of the river, and Sarah drives us into its churning waters at the bottom. She stops us, and we listen to the roar.

Sarah closes her window. "The Marching Arches cannot scale the falls. A new design is required. It's the 1990s, and a minuscule portion of the world's population has produced the next style of bridge.

"For some people, the transition to this next stage of intellect coincides with the mid-life crisis, as commitments to career and family begin to demand less attention. But for a fortunate few, the transition actually occurs earlier—during their 20s or early 30s—immediately following the youth rebellion.

"This new crisis is not a rebellion against parents or society. Instead, it's a rebellion against the authority and the contradictions of the individual's own narrator—that stream of consciousness that plays constantly in one's head. The struggle involves listening carefully and then questioning every viewpoint and examining every bias that might lie behind the words and judgments of the narrator.

"This crisis is an overhaul of the inner voice. It's the development of a second narrator whose job it is to scrutinize and revise the words of the first. It's a monumental task.

"And this new bridge design is far more precarious to build than the others. The period of instability during reconstruction is quite unsettling to the person undergoing the transformation. The person is 'out of sorts' and might even have medical symptoms."

Sarah aims her spotlight at the falls and raises its beam to a series of rock outcroppings at the top. A triangular truss extends from one of them, arching up into the dark sky overhead. She follows the structure with the light for as far as the eye can see.

"It's a single arch extending from the rock all the way back to the sandbar," she says. "To create it, the builder had to disconnect the arched spans from their piers, fasten the ends together, and hoist the whole thing up into place at once. There's a name for people who view the world from this Soaring Arch design; they're called Worldcentrics. Their behaviors are similar to those of the people who have reached the base of the falls on the Marching Arches: neither group is motivated by external affirmations, such as titles, awards, and material possessions; and neither group seeks status or personal glory. Instead, both are motivated to find the truth, regardless of how disruptive, unsettling, or painful it might prove to be. They are their own toughest critics, and when faced with a problem, they call upon an internal panel of experts who objectively evaluate it from all identifiable positions. The results are weighed carefully for trade-offs before a decision is reached. The difference, however, between a Soaring Arch and a person broaching the transition has to do with the skill-level of the panel of experts. The experts of a Soaring Arch can work together in a fully integrative fashion and optimize a whole system of variables, whereas those of the Marching Arches tend to work independently, narrowly optimizing individual components. The solutions of a Soaring Arch are vastly superior to those of the other designs, handily shattering the notions of *diminishing returns* and *unavoidable compromise.*

"The Soaring Arch is a powerful mental arrangement. It's the one I want for myself."

CHAPTER 52

The Wonderful World of Disney

Sarah moves her hand to the throttle. "Are you ready for the best news of the day?" she says.

Before answering, she launches us from the water and into a climb that takes us far over the river. She levels off our craft and rotates in her seat to face us.

"For all of human time, we have built our bridges in the dark of night, unaware of their very existence. It has only been in the past two centuries that our psychologists have gone exploring with their flashlights. . . . But now, look to the east." Sarah points out the window.

"The eastern horizon glows with the coming of dawn. Soon, the sky will brighten and illuminate the bridges on the river. We will at last be able to view the structures that guide our thinking, and with this new knowledge, be better equipped to build and mend our bridges. The veil of darkness is finally lifting from the River of Truth."

Sarah pauses. "Walt Disney had big plans for his Florida property—plans that were obscured by the poetic truths of his successors who didn't know how to implement his vision. The current park hardly resembles what Walt Disney intended. But take heart, because dawn is arriving. The Disney Company of today wants you to see the alternative destiny we all missed. They want you to see the Disney World of Walt's dream. So come with me now and fly over his park. The morning twilight is upon us; it's sunrise over Disney."

Sarah jets our plane higher before swinging east. We are above the atmosphere, in the black of space, with the glowing curve of the earth's horizon expanding. The ocean glimmers toward the peninsula of Florida, and city lights sparkle on the ground in gathered clusters. We are headed for one particular cluster near the center of the state.

Magically, the lights of Orlando begin to swirl and rise, forming a column of pixie dust into the sky. Tinker Bell flies out to greet us, and Sarah follows her with our craft into the plume of fairy dust, where each twinkle against our windshield rings like a little bell, playing the tune *It's a Small World After All.*

Our plane stops flying, held up by the droplets of light. We revolve slowly down to the ground while children's voices sing to the music.

When our plane touches down, we are sitting on an airport runway.

"This is Disney's *Jet Airport of the Future,*" says Sarah. "We'll be taking a short tour of Walt's design for the Disney property."

"Cleared for takeoff," announces a voice over the radio.

Sarah faces forward and engages the throttle. We take to the skies and swing east, where the sun is just barely peeking over the horizon. We then turn northward.

Computer generated lines overlay the view out front. "The lines you see on the ground indicate the borders of Disney World. They enclose about 28,000 acres."

The computer lines disappear, revealing that some of them were hardly necessary. Disney World is an immense natural area walled by development along its borders.

Sarah points to the ground. "That's the airport we just took off from. It sits beside Disney's Entrance Complex and giant parking lot. This is where all visitors were to arrive at the park, whether by ground or by air.

"Extending north through the swamps are two mono-rail tracks leading to the next node of development—the Industrial Park. Farther ahead, you can see Epcot's tower-ing thirty-story hotel glowing like a candle in the morning sunshine."

We fly past Epcot's grand hotel, looking down upon its seven acre patio that perches high above the downtown atrium. Cars can be seen circling the city on its main col-lector road, and PeopleMover tracks extend like the arms of an octopus into the outer neighborhoods. We continue north toward the amusement park, where the Magic Kingdom parking lot is conspicuously absent from the near side of the Seven Seas Lagoon—only monorail tracks, access roads, golf courses, and hotels sprinkle the ground.

Sarah slows our air speed and skims the lagoon. We swerve between the two islands and make a beeline for the Magic Kingdom. People on the ground take notice as our craft lifts over the train station and soars up Main Street. Sarah buzzes the towers of the Cinderella Castle, then banks hard left over Liberty Square. Walt Disney himself waves to us from the captain's bridge of the Liberty Belle paddle-wheeler on Rivers of America.

Sarah swings east and flies off the Disney property, then takes us out over the Atlantic Ocean.

"That was Disney World as Walt envisioned it," she says. "It's now time to explore another person's vision of the world. I want to show you the universe of Aristotle."

CHAPTER 53

The Shells of Ignorance

"In the 300s BC, the Greek thinker, Aristotle, struggled to explain the movements of the heavenly bodies. He did it, though. And here's how."

Sarah turns our plane skyward, and we fly straight up. But as we attempt to zoom past the moon, our ship suddenly decelerates as though caught in a giant rubber band. We are quickly thrown backward.

"Aristotle devised a system of 56 transparent spherical shells for the heavenly bodies to ride upon. These shells rotated like nested soap bubbles, with the earth on the innermost sphere. The stars rode together on the outermost one, while the rest of the spheres explained the complicated motions of the sun, moon, and the five known planets of the time. This theory of the universe prevailed until the 1500s AD."

Sarah corrects the position of our vehicle, seemingly preparing us for another run at the shell.

"And now I'm going to tell you a name you've probably never heard before: Aristarchus.

"Aristarchus was another Greek astronomer, and he lived in the century after Aristotle. Aristarchus proposed an alternative design for the universe, one that did away with the complicated spherical shells of Aristotle. But Aristarchus's idea was rejected. His theory suggested that the earth was in motion as a satellite of the sun. Outrageous! Everyone knew the earth didn't move—you could feel it was standing still.

"But Aristarchus was right. . . . Or was he? How do we really know the earth travels around the sun? Certainly our senses don't confirm an earth racing through space at thousands of miles per hour and spinning like a top on its axis. So why do we believe it?

"The answer is *experts*. Experts are the people we rely upon to validate or refute new ideas. The experts in Aristarchus's day favored Aristotle's theory. It would take nearly two thousand years before pioneers like Copernicus, Kepler, and Galileo would daringly challenge the conventional wisdom of the experts and once again propose Aristarchus's hypothesis.

"So, just who *were* these experts rejecting the new theory? Why didn't they consider the four men I just mentioned as experts of science alongside themselves?

"The answer is simple: there was no such thing as an 'expert of science.' The established panel of experts came from a single discipline, unable to recognize that it was in the process of dividing into three separate fields of study—Science, Philosophy, and Art. To the old experts, all three topics were intertwined under a single heading: that of Religion. Religion dictated that rain and a good harvest were rewards for good behavior, inspiring rituals of music, dance, chant, and sacrifice. Likewise, Religion dictated that famine and disease were punishments for bad behavior, inspiring more rituals of music, dance, chant, and sacrifice. The Science of rain . . . the Philosophy of good behavior . . . and the Art of rituals were all seamlessly fused. In fact, well into the 1800s, the human vocabulary continued to muddy the distinctions, calling Science both 'natural philosophy' and 'industrial art.'

"People did not see the transition happening before their eyes. They did not see their panel of experts dividing into three disciplines.

"The splitting of the panel inaugurated the long and painful struggle between Religion and Science, each vying for the chair of the presumed one-expert panel. Religion suffered most, losing control over governments and forcing itself into the seat with Philosophy. Poor Art wasn't even considered a contender.

"The experts of Science still dominate the panel. It is they who tell us the earth revolves around the sun, and we believe them because they supply a wealth of convincing evidence to support the claim."

Sarah fires the engines and launches us forward. "Our experts of Science have dispelled Aristotle's universe and shown us the view we hold today. But is there a more accurate view still?"

Our ship rips through the shell, continuing to accelerate as it tears through dozens more. The words of Robert Owen ring through the cabin.

> The history of humanity shows it to be an undeviating law of nature, that man shall not prematurely break the shell of ignorance; that he must patiently wait until the principle of knowledge has pervaded the whole mass of the interior, to give it life and strength sufficient to bear the light of day.

Sarah punches some numbers into the console and presses a red button.

With a sudden thrust, the starlight turns blue and then disappears. A blast of heat warms me.

As we fly through space in total darkness, a voice addresses Sarah on her radio. "Squadron Four, report to sector thirteen for a Code Blue."

Sarah hurriedly punches some new numbers into the instrument panel, and we take a new course.

"I apologize for the interruption," she says. She takes off her safari hat and replaces it with a high-tech helmet. She pushes more buttons, and the cockpit transforms into that of a fighter jet. Each and every surface becomes filled with instrument panels, monitors, and heads-up displays.

"Perhaps you remember the battle clause in the form you signed before boarding. It seems we have a dangerous situation, where the advanced technologies of the higher intellects have fallen into the hands of the lower ones. As expected, these technologies are being used without discretion."

Sarah faces forward, as our craft automatically slows to a normal cruising speed. The starlight returns.

"I've worked in this sector before," she says. "This species has been out of the fog for quite some time, yet most of them have not advanced beyond the Anchored Pier or Elevated Walkway designs. Their aim is always the same: to cleanse the universe of all other cultures. This time they've assembled a death star.

"As usual, our peace negotiations with them are a joke; our team of Marching Arches looks weak and foolish to them. We encourage them to tolerate and accept other cultures, which they know are inferior to their own. We are contemptible for our ignorance and should be annihilated as well. We defeat them easily with our superior weaponry, and then 'help' them establish a democracy to govern themselves. The democracies never last, though, because their cultures aren't ready for them. Each time our troops leave the scene, there's a bloody civil war between rival factions. Perhaps Plato's age-old wisdom was correct: the best route to peace and stability for a culture of this kind is via a strong philosopher-king."

Voices suddenly fill Sarah's radio. She moves our craft into formation with other fighters, and our squadron is assigned the task of destroying the death star.

A planet-sized globe of dark steel appears in the distance. Moments later, there are explosions ahead, and the first squadrons have engaged the enemy. Stressed voices stream across the radio, conveying the intensity of the dogfights.

Sarah's monitors light up, as our squadron enters the melee. I watch with amazement as she converts a tremendous volume of sensory data into immediate physical responses. Her skillful handling of our craft is automatic—mostly unconscious—the product of countless hours of thoughtful practice. Her extensive training frees her to focus her attention where it is needed most: on the overall mission.

Our squadron makes its way toward the surface of the death star, where anti-aircraft guns send pulses of energy ripping past us.

Sarah's job is to defend the forward cruiser carrying the destructive payload. She handles our craft with precision, knocking out every enemy ship that threatens. The forward fighter delivers a bomb, and we flee the scene.

As we accelerate away, we are hit in the wing by laser fire, which sets us slowly spinning. The Death Star comes into view just as fissures of fire erupt through its skin.

POW! the Death Star explodes. Its fireball races toward us and threatens to consume our ship if Sarah doesn't get us away in time. She turns the ship and presses the red button, bringing us to warp speed and ultimately preventing our destruction.

Sarah removes her helmet and restores the cockpit to its original layout. "Whew, that was a close one," she says, and she wipes a bead of sweat from her face before returning the safari hat to her head. "Let's get back to the ride."

She types in new coordinates.

Chapter 54

The Big Picture

Sarah slows the ship and parks it in outer space.

"I've taken us beyond the fringes of the Milky Way," she says. "And the bright clusters you see out front are the many other galaxies that share our universe. All told, scientists estimate there are ten billion trillion other stars besides our own. It seems likely there's other life out there, don't you suppose?"

Sarah lets our craft rotate until a spiral galaxy comes into view.

"Ain't she a beauty," she says. "That's our home—the Milky Way. Let's pause here for a minute."

Sarah opens her video screen once again. "It's time for a slide show," she says.

Sarah flips quickly through some familiar images: they are the pictures we saw through the windshield when connected to the sandbars and bridges. The images progress from solid black to blurry full color and back again.

"Think of the mind as a camera," she says. "This first picture suggests that the camera is without film, or that someone has forgotten to take off the lens cap. This is the intellect of the animal kingdom and of our early human ancestors—alert and responsive, but unable to see their own existence. It's the worldview from within the fog, the worldview of a human infant."

Sarah advances to the next frame, showing a screen with patches of hazy gray.

"At the edge of the fog, the mind wrestles with self-awareness. In the modern world, our powerful vocabulary achieves this milestone with the terrible twos, creating a world that teems with fairy-tale creatures, magical spirits, and powerful people. Happiness and pleasure are all that matter. There's no capacity for guilt, regret, or remorse."

The next picture finds the gray areas overexposed to bright white.

"Emerging from the fog, the world appears in sharp contrast—win and lose, reward and punishment, pleasure and pain, love and hate, good and evil, life and death, heaven and hell. In this worldview, personal responsibility does not exist because outcomes are controlled by a higher power. This is the world as seen by today's self-aware child at around the age of five."

Sarah rises from her seat and faces us from the cockpit. Her costume transforms into a long green robe with a white fur border. Her safari hat is replaced by a wreath of holly and shining icicles. She slowly opens the folds of her robe to reveal two huddled children clinging to her. They are wretched and starving.

"This boy," says Sarah, "is Ignorance. This girl is Want. Beware of them both. . . . But beware of the boy most of all, for on his brow is written Doom, unless the writing be erased. Deny it!"

Sarah closes her robe around the children, and the whole costume dissolves into her original safari outfit.

"Many of the world's people live in poverty," she says. "Intellectual development is a luxury they simply can't afford. Survival is their primary aim."

Sarah points to the white blobs on the screen. "This is how the world looks to them. —It is the view from the Anchored Pier. But you and I are more fortunate. We went to school as children. Our world looks at least this good."

She flips to the next image: the blurry black and white photograph, with its many shades of gray.

"The view from the Elevated Walkway delivers powerful new insights. It means the ability to consider science, philosophy, and art as separate disciplines. It means the ability to form hypotheses and then test them through experimentation. And it means the ability to see the world as a machine that can be manipulated. This is the first worldview to realize personal responsibility, where outcomes can be controlled to chart the course of one's existence. People who achieve the Elevated Walkway design view their earlier ideas—those conceived on the Anchored Pier—as simplistic and naïve."

Sarah points again at the picture. "As you can see, the picture-quality with the Elevated Walkway is still pretty poor; it's so out of focus that it's impossible to identify the forms. But it's a leap in perception nonetheless. The addition of gray shading reveals details unknown to the Anchored Pier design. No longer does the world appear in simple black and white. In modern industrialized countries, children achieve the Elevated Walkway design at around the age of middle school."

Sarah clicks to the next slide, transforming the black and white photograph to full color. It is still dreadfully out of focus, and the addition of color actually obscures the image, making the underlying forms that much more difficult to imagine.

"The Marching Arches see a world of infinite detail. They study the colors, cataloging new shades with every closer look they take. Their task is daunting but fruitful. It affords them greater command over their physical world, and it makes them aware of life's rich diversity. The Marching Arches view the ideas of their former selves on the Elevated Walkways as overly idealistic.

"Now, are you ready?" Sarah holds her finger over the button, preparing to advance the picture. "The next view will be the perspective from the Soaring Arch."

I stare at the blurry color photo, waiting for Sarah to push the button. I hear the click, and the picture on the screen swirls like a weather system, repeating a short sequence.

"Notice that the forms are still impossible to decipher," she says. "But the motion reveals some information. It shows which details are more important than others. This is a valuable advance in perception, permitting the mind to see past the details and to grasp the bigger picture. The mind of a Soaring Arch looks back on its days from the Marching Arches and sees ideas that were needlessly complicated.

"So what will the next picture of intellect look like? What will the next advance in perception bring? Better focus, perhaps? How about continuously streaming video? . . . Or maybe 3-D."

Sarah turns off the monitor and flips it closed. "You may have noticed that I told you how the higher bridge designs view the lower ones, but not vice versa. There's a good reason for that. You see, the view up from a lower design can take opposite extremes, depending on the situation. When two different bridge designs happen to agree on an issue, the higher design becomes the ally and champion of the lower one. However, when they oppose each other, the lower design views the higher one with a loathing and contempt that is difficult to articulate."

Sarah directs our attention out the front window to the Milky Way. "Keep your eyes on the spinning galaxy," she says, "for there lies your future.

"And what does your future look like? It looks like your kids. The earth's most advantaged children are growing up with parents and teachers who respond to them from the Marching Arches and higher. When these kids reach their crisis periods, their transitions will be smoothed by internal narrators already well-versed in the right phrasings. Consequently, more of the next generation will reach the Soaring Arch design.

"This transition will produce yet another generation gap. Count 'em: that's three in just over a century . . . certainly a current world's record, since the earlier transitions were separated by thousands of years.

"With this transition, it will be the baby-boomers, on their Marching Arches, who will be dismayed by a younger generation they don't fully understand. Their grown-up children will present a confusing mix of wonderful sensitivity and seemingly sexist, hierarchical, and authoritarian undertones. But perhaps the baby-boomers will appreciate the fruits of their labor. It was the baby-boom generation, arriving in large numbers to the Marching Arches, that made possible the sweeping social reforms of the past thirty years. The baby-boomers built a new world in which to raise their children, one largely free of earlier struggles. The next generation will move to the higher intellectual ground it has inherited.

"But there's more to the generation gap than issues of perception. Another difference involves the external storage of information. For centuries, the printing press has put words and pictures into libraries. But now, computers and telephones are putting whole libraries and more into hand-held devices. The next generation is mentally wired for a world of instant access to people and information.

"And the mind-melt doesn't end there. You know the old saying 'a picture is worth a thousand words?' Well, the kids of today are learning volumes. Computer animation delivers concepts with ease and accuracy—concepts that were previously unavailable except through painstaking study of written descriptions or hands-on experience. These kids today think less in words and more in graphics. It's a shift with long-term implications for grammar and dictionaries."

Sarah looks away from us and peers out at the Milky Way. "It's all about change," she says. "Change has been the rule since the beginning. It's frightening. It's humbling. And it's unstoppable.

"And just look at what change has done to God. Each intellectual advance has revealed an almighty creator more powerful and more mysterious than the one before. For instance, to our pre-conscious ancestors, the gods spoke directly to them, giving them practical instructions for daily living. What terror it must have been when self-awareness arrived, and the gods fled into the sky to rule with unbridled power and vengeance. But mathematicians were a savior of sorts. They came along and revealed a world not so angry—rather, a world functioning more like an intricate machine. Their insights revealed a god with much more to watch over than just we humans, as earth moved from center-stage to being just another satellite of the sun. The theory of evolution came next, explaining our creation as a product of chance, arising in a universe equipped for life but seemingly indifferent to its survival. God became an architect of genius to create such a self-sufficient system, undemanding of any divine attention or intervention. God's power continued to grow as astronomers pushed the boundaries of the universe ever farther away. And now, psychologists have revealed that humans follow a natural path of intellectual development—a path rooted firmly in both joy and suffering. God, it seems, has an interesting sense of humor.

"Intellect around our globe is at its greatest disparity ever. But mind you, this is a disparity reached purely by natural forces. And it is these natural forces that remain poised to take intellect even farther along the path. The question is, can the forces succeed? There's no guarantee against a long-term or permanent setback. The good news is that we humans are among the natural forces controlling the outcome. We can attempt to speed intellectual development around the world. I've been thinking about ways to do this. I hope you will too."

CHAPTER 55

The Skywalk

Sarah turns forward in her chair and grips the throttle. "Hello Milky Way," she says. "We're comin' home."

We zoom into the galaxy and dash between stars, eventually slowing toward one in particular.

Sarah races between the planets of our solar system, shouting the name of each as we pass. "Pluto! . . . Neptune! . . . Uranus!"

At Saturn, she swerves between the rings. Beyond Jupiter, she takes a joy ride through the asteroid belt.

When we enter the earth's atmosphere, we are over the Gulf of Mexico. Sarah leans back in her chair and puts her hands behind her head. She swivels around to face us. "There's something I haven't told you about this Jungle Cruise. Each of us has a sandbar, it's true. But what's *not* true is that we each have just one bridge extending from it. In fact, the number is more like three hundred. Each of us has a dozen or more sub-personalities we call upon in different situations, like our adult self, our parent self, our critical self, our ideal self, our lustful self, our underdog self, and so on. And each of these sub-personalities develops along some two dozen specialties of the big three—art, science, and philosophy. All in all, it's an intricate weave of intellect that places each one of us all over the River of Truth."

"Having said that . . ." Sarah returns to her controls. "We'll be flying over our modern-day Disney World from the south."

We enter Disney airspace, and I recognize it as the current version of the park. It's a spaghetti of roadways that connect regions of widely scattered development. We fly low over the Epcot amusement park and head toward the Magic Kingdom.

Our plane slows as we cross the Seven Seas Lagoon, then it angles toward the Maya ruin in Adventureland. We soon hover beside the top of the pyramid, moving gradually into its temple. Sarah sets us down on the landing platform and shuts off the engines. Motors from below begin to whine, and we descend into the dark elevator shaft that began our ride.

"I've enjoyed being your tour guide today," says Sarah. "I hope it's been fun for you too. Please see us again soon."

Sarah gives us a wink and closes the doors of the cockpit. Moments later, light streams into the car from the sides, and we've entered the unloading area. The safety bars lift and I climb from the vehicle.

The exiting hallway is dark at first, but there's a light up ahead from beneath the floor. The walkway becomes a clear acrylic skywalk over a giant diorama. The scene below is that of a jungle with a river running through it to the ocean, and the horizon is bathed in morning twilight. Bridges of every variety extend along the river to where the foggy delta meets the sea.

The walkway reaches the end of the diorama and becomes dark once again. Then, I'm released into Adventureland through a set of metal doors.

PART VI

The
Meaning

CHAPTER 56

The Poetry of Ghosts

Today is the first Saturday of September—Labor Day week-end. MJ and Michael began school last week . . . and so did I, reluctantly.

I decided that the Jungle Cruise was about as likely to reach a wide audience as my Oddball, so I re-enrolled at the university to get my teaching degree. I'm figuring that if I can become a high school history teacher, then maybe I can infuse my course material with some of what I've learned without rankling too many of the parents and teachers who might seek to defend the current orthodoxy. I need to inspire the next generation to do a reinterpretation of history.

This afternoon, Mary and I are planning to take our children downtown for a street festival, where we'll be delivering them to the rooftop of the Capitol building for a surprise rendezvous with my parents. The children will be shuttled away to a hotel and water-park, and Mary and I will then celebrate our real wedding anniversary together.

The four of us spend the morning doing chores and running errands. One of the errands is to go to a second hand store and buy school clothes for MJ and Michael. During our time there, I secretly make two purchases while Mary and the children are in the dressing rooms. The first is a gift for Ms. Forward, which I place in a long box and tie closed with a red ribbon. The second is a gift for the old woman in the library, which I merely stow unwrapped in my shoulderbag.

By eleven-thirty, we've arrived at our neighborhood pool for one last swim of the summer.

"I've added truth to her story," I tell Mary from my deck chair. "Today it's *my* turn at the statue. But you can forget the scrapbook."

Mary studies my face, no doubt trying to determine if I've figured something out about Aunt Poppi's story. I show her my self-satisfied grin and nothing more.

◆ ◆ ◆

Upon our return home, the four of us prepare to go downtown. Mary puts on a tank top and colorful shorts, and MJ wears her hair down.

I instruct the two children to pack the copper coins they acquired in Disney World last year, suggesting that the coins might actually perform some magic today.

"So," says Mary, "are we walking or taking the bus?"

"Walking," I answer. "No other options; I've planned a special route."

Since completing the design of the Jungle Cruise, I've been trying to conceive of a way to convince MJ and Michael that the true magic in the world comes from within—that people have the power to make their wishes and dreams come true. I think I've finally found the way to tell them, though I don't think they'll be ready to fully hear it until they're in high school or beyond. My plan is to make this walk a family ritual, one I intend to sprinkle with conversations that mature along with the children. Mary has her *story at the statue*, and now *I* have my *walking tour of Madison*. It's filled with details that I hope will one day convince them that *words* are the secret oppressors and liberators of humankind.

As we head out the door, our clock chimes for the one o'clock hour. I've become the Ghost of Christmas Past, here to take Mary and the children on a walk through the shadows of history.

I exit the house and tuck Ms. Forward's gift under my arm. I'll surely be late for my two o'clock appointment as her Ghost of Christmas Present.

We turn at the bottom of Birch Avenue and follow Glenway Street toward the Village Bar. Someday, when the kids are older, we'll stop there for lunch and I'll begin my spirited visitation.

Stop One: The Village Bar

You may be wondering why a drinking establishment is the appropriate place to begin an educational tour. *Won't alcohol cloud our thinking?* Exactly the point. Alcohol alters reality in the mind of the drinker, and if enough of it is consumed, the drinker can lose his conscious awareness altogether. Such an occurrence is called *blacking out* because the person won't later remember what happened during this time. But you don't have to over-drink to experience a *black out;* you do it every night when you go to bed.

Sleeping is similar to a black out because the body continues to function without anyone's deliberate attention. And the comparison proves even better for sleepwalkers and sleeptalkers. Such unconscious behaviors link us closely to the animal kingdom.

Almost all of the earth's creatures live in a reality similar to that of a sleepwalker; their highly skilled activities proceed without any self-awareness. The most interesting of these critters is probably the human baby.

Our young neighbor Andrew came into the

world making gurgling noises and moving on his own, and by the time of his first birthday, he could walk and talk and solve some basic problems. But even so, Andrew won't ultimately remember these first years of his life. They will reside in his mind as a foggy patchwork of images and feelings that fade into nothingness as childhood progresses.

The point I'm trying to make here is that the brain is like an enchanted musical instrument that can perform without an attending maestro. Did you ever have an idea that seemed to come out of nowhere? Did you ever have a feeling you just couldn't explain? These are the clues that the subconscious mind is at work on your behalf. Pay close attention to the insights it reveals to you. That's what Albert Einstein did.

Einstein studied the available physics of his day, so you might just assume that his most famous equation, $E=mc^2$, was derived carefully at his desk. Not so. Rather, the equation was already present in the scientific literature, so it was merely a moment of inspiration upon his waking one morning that convinced him that the equation had to be true in every frame of reference. This was the great insight that popped into his head unexpectedly. But where did it come from? The answer is simple: it came from the region of his brain that was working on the problem. All Albert Einstein had to do was to apply himself to the task with a relentless ambition, and his subconscious brain handled the rest, ultimately handing him the solution. But don't think for a moment that Einstein's case is an isolated one. Many of history's greatest thinkers tell similar stories, where ideas simply appeared before them while bathing, sleeping, or strolling.

So keep in mind that the brain is an organ of awesome ability, and that its aptitude for self-awareness is actually a relative newcomer to the circuitry. But don't take *my* word for it. See for yourself. Languages across the world are imbued with biases rooted in the subconscious past.

Case in point: Why are *left-handed compliments* considered dubious or insincere? Why did left-handed children face physical tortures for using the "wrong hand?" And indeed, why did the word *left* once mean *wrong, troublesome,* and *weak*? Likewise, why is the *right-hand man* considered indispensable? Why does the right hand take the oath of office and greet a stranger? And why does the word *right* derive from *right,* meaning *correct, proper,* and *strong*? I'm here to tell you that there's nothing mysterious about these prejudices. They were born of a common experience arising in an ultra-smart mammal with a lateralized brain.

"I bet you didn't know that your brain has two halves," I say to Mary and the children, as we wait at the traffic light along Mineral Point Road. "Each half controls one side of the body, and each half can think for itself."

I place my hands on my head. "So which side is *me*?"

The kids look confused.

"The answer is *both* because there's a pipeline running between them, carrying my thoughts back and forth. But what if that pipeline gets cut so that nothing can get across? Then, which side am I on? I'm not joking. My right hand might disagree with what my left hand is doing."

I relate to them the stories of the 1960s' split-brain studies, where epilepsy patients were carefully observed after
a surgery that disconnected the two hemispheres of their
brains. When a man was asked to arrange some blocks in
a pattern, his right hand took to the job but soon fumbled
in its efforts. As the left hand tried to help, the right hand
slapped it away. The man eventually sat on his left hand to
keep it out of trouble. But progress with the blocks remained
slow, so the researcher suggested that he let his left hand
participate. And this time, the right hand yielded, letting
the left hand arrange the blocks quickly and easily. The left
hand was able to do the job because it was hard-wired to
the side of the brain best suited for spatially-oriented tasks.
Then, there was the example of the smoker, whose left hand
uncontrollably snatched cigarettes from his mouth and extinguished them, trying to get the man to quit the habit. And
there was the woman who was awakened in bed by her left
hand, as it slapped her in the face to alert her that her alarm
clock was ringing.

"Imagine," I say. "What if you wanted to take a walk and
one of your legs refused to go?"

The four of us try to imitate how such a walk might look.

We continue along Glenway and climb the steep hill beside
Reservoir Park. We turn right at Ridge Road and stop just
short of the next corner.

From here, we get a glimpse of the Capitol dome on the
eastern horizon. And someday, I'll ask the kids to think about
that building's special appeal.

Stop Two: The Capitol View

> Why is the Capitol building the centerpiece of our
> city? Why do we shine lights on it at night?

Please think for a moment back to the Cinderella Castle in Disney World. It, too, is the centerpiece of a small city; it, too, is taller than all the other buildings around it; and it, too, is gently illuminated at night to make it beautiful.

Why are these two buildings like this, and what is our attraction to them? I suggest that their allure goes way back in time to when our human ancestors functioned more like sleepwalkers, and baby Andrew.

A long time ago, people had the maturity of a modern one-year-old. They were alert and responsive, like other animals, but they were entirely un-self-conscious. They had no idea they were alive, and they felt no responsibility for their actions. They did whatever their emotions dictated . . . and their emotions dictated an attraction to the voices of their parents and elders. And when such a voice was lost due to what we now know as *death*, it was still heard through charms, trinkets, and other devices that inspired what we now know as *memories*. In the case of a dead leader, the device was a temple at the center of town, visible for miles.

Madison's Capitol building and Disney's Cinderella Castle are modern versions of these sacred temples. We are still drawn to them despite our long-ago awakening from that primitive slumber. I believe that the popular appeal of these two places—Madison and the Magic Kingdom—is deeply rooted in their crowning structures: they link us to the past; they give us a sense of place; and they inspire feelings within us that are difficult to describe. Isn't it ironic that the mythology surrounding Walt Disney places him in a tomb within the Cinderella Castle?

People seem to want to believe that their dead king still resides in his town's central house.

We cross Franklin Avenue and enter Resurrection Cemetery, where there's a small enclosure to our left created by some bushes and trees.

"See if you can find the Young family monument in there," I say to MJ and Michael.

The children race ahead, and I know they won't have any difficulty finding it; it's the only monument in the space.

The kids climb onto a large block of cut stone and peer out over the shrubbery. They gaze across a rolling meadow of tombstones, which stand in ranks like soldiers.

Stop Three: The Young Family Monument

The current year is two thousand and four. But why? Why not two *million* and four? Why are we at such a small number when humans have been around for such a long time. What happened two thousand years ago that caused people to start counting their years over again from one?

The answer is, the birth of Jesus Christ. Early Christians began the practice of labeling the years before Jesus' birth as BC, meaning *before* Christ, and labeling the years after his birth as AD, meaning *after* his arrival. But these labels, BC and AD, are under pressure to be changed. A few scientists and historians are now substituting a new set of letters. Why are they doing such a thing? Are they trying to complicate our lives? What's wrong with BC and AD? Well, I'll tell you what's wrong.

For some people, the sight and sound of the letters

BC and AD cause negative feelings . . . and under-standably so. Not everyone in the world is Christian, so why should the world's calendar begin with Christ?

But the solution being offered for changing the letters is something of a joke. The new letters, BCE and CE, which stand for "before common era" and "common era," continue to place the pivotal year at the birth of Christ. I think there's a better year for marking zero—a year not tied to any particular religious tradition.

So, if one imagines that we are seriously going to change to new letters, then let's at least make the letters *mean* something. Here's my suggestion. Let's change the words "common era" to "conscious era," and change the transition date to the awakening of humankind at around 1000 BC. Under this new system, then, the birth of Christ would be in 1000 CE, and our walk today would be happening in the year 3004.

But do I really advocate such a change? Of course not. History is rife with examples of words and sym-bols that have changed in meaning over time. How many people know that the beloved torch relay of the modern Olympic games was a Nazi invention from 1936? And how many people know that the most sacred word for God in Judaism once meant nothing more than *I am who I am*? And how many people know that the word *Dixie* has an innocent origin not tied to any racial hatred?

BC and AD might indeed be headed for the waste-basket, but let's at least try to salvage the word *Dixie*.

I ask MJ and Michael to imagine this cemetery as a war

memorial, where each headstone marks the grave of a fallen soldier. Someday, I'm going to tell them the story of how the soldier named *Dixie* was chopped down.

The Disney organization renamed Dixie Landings for the same reason that some people want to change BC and AD to BCE and CE: the word *Dixie* can generate negative feelings.

You see, the word *Dixie* has a history . . . and that history put it on the side of the South during the Civil War—the side favoring the continuation of slavery. The meaning was then given new teeth in the 1960s, as angry whites sang the song *Dixie's Land* at civil rights marchers. To those who still remember the fight, the word *Dixie* can invoke rage. Yet the true origins of the word are entirely harmless, born of a simple mis-translation.

In the early 1800s, a New Orleans bank produced a ten dollar note that was known and trusted throughout the nation. The note was printed in both English and French to better serve the bank's local customers. The word for ten in French is *deece*, spelled d-i-x, but English-speaking citizens didn't know the correct French pronunciation. Gradually, people around the country began referring to their southern port-city at the end of the Mississippi River as *the land of Dixie*. By the time of the Civil War, the meaning of the word encompassed the entire South, and the celebrated tune *Dixie's Land* became the anthem for the Southern Cause during the war. It's ironic that this same song was one of Abraham Lincoln's favorites, and that *he* was the president who ultimately freed

the slaves. It just goes to show you that a word's true
meaning can be a moving target.

I pull three water bottles from my bag and instruct the
kids to find the nearby statue of Saint Joseph. I've prepared
a short demonstration.

Stop Four: The Statue of Saint Joseph

"I want you to pretend that this statue is our four-year-old
neighbor, Andrew. I have an experiment for us to try with
him the next time we see him. Here's what we'll do."
I place two of the water bottles side by side on the pedestal.
They are identical in size and shape, and equally filled with
water. I explain that Andrew would agree with us that each
bottle contains the same amount of liquid.
Then, I place my third bottle beside the other two. It is
shorter, fatter, and empty. I pour the contents of one of my
original bottles into this newcomer and ask, "What would
Andrew say now? Would he think that these two differently-
shaped bottles have the same amount of water in them?"
MJ and Michael both know that Andrew should answer *yes*
to this question, because no water was added or taken away in
the exchange. It doesn't matter that the shapes are different.
"But the shape *will* matter to Andrew," I say. "He'll think
one bottle has more. He'll see exactly the same events we saw,
yet he'll get the wrong answer anyway. How is this possible?"
I explain that Andrew is still too young to perceive the
bottles by more than one attribute at a time. He can't compare them by height and width simultaneously. He won't
understand that *short and fat* can hold the same amount as *tall
and thin*. He'll probably say that the skinny bottle has more,
because the surface of its water rides higher. It won't bother

him that water had to be created or destroyed magically to make his answer correct.

"Do you know what this tells us about the mind of a four year old? It explains why kids will believe almost anything you tell them." I point up at the statue. "And Joseph, here, was little different. The people of his time believed in magic and miracles too. Their world was like a preschool playground, with no adults in attendance to supervise."

> Our ancestors, who were just waking up to their inner voice, lived in a world of fantasy and high emotion. They accepted magical explanations for the world because their perception could conceive of no others. It would take many centuries for them to stumble upon the conclusions that seem so obvious to us now.
>
> As for young Andrew, he has the benefit of those fruitful centuries. We pass down the knowledge to him that differently-shaped bottles can hold the same amount of water, and we prove it by reversing the procedure—returning the water to its original vessel. With enough repetition, Andrew will master the concept at a young age and move on to greater skills.

I lead the family to the center of the cemetery and enter an outdoor mausoleum. Someday, we'll stop in this small courtyard for a discussion.

Stop Five: The Open-Air Mausoleum

> The crypts that surround us are memorials to the dead . . . and so are the words we speak of them.
> Have you ever heard of a guy named Aristotle?

He lived a long time ago, just after the great awakening. He is still very famous.

Like Saint Joseph, Aristotle's intellect resembled that of a modern four year old. Do you know what he was famous for? —This will make you laugh. Aristotle was famous for explaining how the world works. His ideas made good sense to the people of his time, just as they would make good sense to Andrew today.

Aristotle explained that the world is built in layers. The bottom layer is the ground—the earth. The next layer is the water of the oceans, lakes, and streams. Then comes the air. And finally, above all three, comes fire, most notably the sun. Each layer has its proper position among the four and is constantly striving to get there: fire reaches for the sky; air climbs through the water; streams seek the valleys; and rocks always return to the ground when thrown.

Did you notice my careful choice of words? —This is my memorial to the dead. The fire *reaches*, the bubbles *climb*, the streams *seek*, and the rocks *return*. Each of these actions is a human thing to do: It is *people* who reach, climb, seek, and return. People do these things on purpose. And so did Aristotle's fire, air, water, and earth. They behaved deliberately, just like people.

Here's the idea of Aristotle's time that lies dead and buried in history, merely echoed within the development of today's children. The people of Aristotle's time believed that everything which could move or change was alive. Stars, clouds, and boats were just as alive as animals and people. All of these objects had a life . . . a spirit . . . guiding them. For instance, it was the spirit in the tiny acorn that swelled it into a mighty oak tree, and it was this same spirit that changed the color of its leaves each year before casting them away. If an oak tree dropped an acorn on your head, it was trying to tell you something.

It sounds crazy, I know. But there's a good reason the people of Aristotle's day thought this way. The reason has to do with words. Words help us to make connections in our minds that allow us to consider things, like the height and width of a drinking glass. As for what it meant to be *alive* in the time of Aristotle, there were no distinct words to separate the concepts of *life*, *movement*, and *change*. All three ideas were helplessly wrapped together into the meaning of a single word: *motion*. It would take nearly two thousand years to finally unwrap the package. I bet you can't guess which machine helped to do the unwrapping. I'll give you a clue: it was the invention mentioned alongside the alphabet in Aunt Poppi's story as having done the most for humankind.

That's right, the printing press.

The printing press set the stage for the scientific revolution of the 1600s. It allowed for widespread distribution of information, ultimately splintering the concept of *motion* and shattering the worldview of Aristotle.

It's hard to grow up, but that's exactly what people were doing. That's exactly what our neighbor Andrew is doing today, but *he* has the added benefit of parents and teachers who already know some of the answers. He'll skate easily along to their level of understanding before joining the adult struggle to advance knowledge any further.

We exit the cemetery at its main entrance and take Farley Avenue straight ahead. Farley becomes University Bay Drive at the stoplight, and we climb the hill toward our place of worship.

At the sight of the Unitarian Meeting House, I ask MJ and Michael to state the name of our creator.

When the kids were younger, we coined the name *pirate* as a kid-friendly term for every form of villain in the world. Mary and I then sought a similarly generic term for God—one that wouldn't play favorites among the particular religions. Thus, *Allah, Brahman, God,* and *Yahweh* were out of the question. So, adhering to our nautical theme, we were tickled when we found a name that gently referenced the Big Bang Theory of our cosmic origins.

As we pass the old Meeting House auditorium, with its architectural element that resembles the prow of a ship, MJ and Michael call out the name: "Admiral Boom!"

Stop Six: The Unitarian Meeting House

Where do you go when you die?

It's an age-old question that no one can truly answer . . . yet plenty of people try. And I'm no different . . . well, a *little* different. You see, the answer I'm willing to offer is a lark—a muse . . . one I don't whole-heartedly believe in, yet one which appeals to me more than any other I've ever heard. See what you think.

As we all know, Admiral Boom is a real character. He lives for adventure and loves a good joke. He sails around the cosmos with his happy-go-lucky crew of sailors, occasionally stopping to enjoy what they all love most—extreme sports. They love the untamed competition of "natural selection" and "survival of the fittest." Admiral Boom sets up his stadium around a small blue planet that is blooming with life, then fills the stands with his sailors. As an added bonus, if intelligent creatures emerge and reach the stage of self-awareness, Admiral Boom sends his sailors onto the field to occupy the bodies. The sailors began arriving here on earth around 1000 BC.

The sailors know that eternal bliss is an infernal bore without the highs and lows of a worldly experience. They enjoy the wild ride they call *life*, then return to the stands to laugh with their chums and await their next turn. The stands are about as rowdy and as festive a place as you can imagine. Sailors pour drinks on each other and poke fun at the crazy circumstances that bring them back into the seats. They celebrate with gusto the heavens and hells they've created, then laugh uncontrollably when friends are returned to the field to live out new lives of poetic irony.

So, to answer the question: where do you go when you die? *the stands* is my answer. It is *there* that you came from, and it is *there* you will return. Your loved ones await you. They are your eternal pals for the eternal party.

We take the right fork onto Highland Avenue and follow it around to Walnut Street. Walnut delivers us to Marsh Lane and a wooded path that runs beside Lake Mendota.

"Do you know what a grotto is?" I ask MJ and Michael.

"*Ariel's* Grotto," says MJ.

Michael nods.

Both of them know the word *grotto* only in its association with the Disney film *The Little Mermaid.*

I ask them to imagine Ariel swimming in the lake beside us and entering a cave-like room built into the bank. "It is filled with her treasures," I say. "*That* is her grotto."

At the Porter Boathouse, we turn away from the lake and follow Babcock Drive for less than a block. We enter a formal garden and take a quick lap through it. Someday, I'll stop us beside the little pond and tell them about the grottoes of Saint-Germain-en-Laye.

Stop Seven: The Allen Centennial Gardens

The enchanted grottoes of Saint-Germain existed in France about 400 years ago. They were built into the tall face of a terraced garden along the Seine River. The grottoes were lit by torches and connected underground by vaulted galleries. These particular grottoes were quite amazing.

King Henry IV commissioned a skilled fountaineer to pipe gravity-fed water into the grottoes and use it to power sculptures. These sculptures were extraordinary: they played music on mechanical instruments; they simulated the sounds of birds and people; and most remarkably, they moved. One bronze statue, named Perseus, descended from the ceiling to slay a dragon rising from the pool. And some of the figures were activated by hidden plates on the floor . . . like the bathing Diana, who hid her nudity behind rose bushes when visitors approached.

These grottoes existed in the 1600s—a time when some people were growing restless with the ideas of Aristotle. The concept of *motion* was beginning its fateful split from the concepts of *life* and *change*. The split was far from clean, however. For instance, you may know of the scientific terms, *acceleration, force, inertia,* and *attraction.* Well, each one of these words began with a more human meaning: *acceleration* meant to quicken one's step; *force* referred to muscle strength; *inertia* described someone sitting idle; and *attraction* meant the same thing as it does today.

Likewise, the animal- and human-looking forms within the grottoes of Saint-Germain were an interesting mix of creature and machine. On the one hand, they could move and make noise, but on the other, they were obviously bronze and man made. How were these animated figures different from real animals and people? It was a question puzzling thinkers of the time, as more and more machines of all types appeared throughout Europe to do the work of men. The parallels between machines and creatures led to a logical conclusion that I'll share with you in a moment.

The important person who experienced the grottoes of Saint-Germain was eighteen year old René Descartes. Descartes concluded that everything in the world was a machine . . . well, everything, that is, except the human mind. The human mind, alone, was uniquely different from the world of matter: it could choose its own course of action. Everything else was governed by the cause and effect of physical forces. The *mental* force, however, was something else entirely.

Descartes elevated the status of the human mind. His was an awkward early step toward separating living and non-living things. He missed the mark, though. Descartes classified animals among the nonliving.

To Descartes, animals were simply hydraulic machines, driven by pull-cords, piping, valves, and ventricles. The screams from the animals on his dissection table were no different from the hisses and whistles from the water-driven birds in the grottoes. It would take time to weed out the distinctions between living and nonliving things.

And Descartes was not the only expert of his time doing bizarre experiments with animals. Other investigators were trying to locate the soul. They removed organs, one at a time, until a creature stopped moving, suspecting that the last organ pulled contained the soul. Imagine their confusion when they cut the head off a chicken and watched its decapitated body run and fly around the yard. Other people thought the soul might be in the blood, so one experimenter drained the blood of a cow and put it into a sheep to see if the sheep would then act like a cow.

Some researchers concluded that each part of an animal is independently alive, with the varied activities of each part organized by the animal's brain. Body-parts, to them, were like the musicians of an orchestra. In the case of the beheaded chicken, the conductor was missing, leaving the performers out of control.

As we exit the centennial garden and climb Observatory Drive, I read from a list created in Britain in the year 1650. It categorizes *causes of death* and certainly wasn't meant to be funny. But it's an excellent example of the muddled thinking of that time, relative to today.

aged
bleeding
executed
found dead in the streets
grief
killed by several accidents
lethargy
mother
plague
poisoned
suddenly
vomiting
wolf

Stop Eight: The Washburn Observatory

We've come a long way since Aristotle and Descartes. We've sharpened our language skills to such a degree that we now see very clear distinctions between *motion, change, life, mind,* and *body*. But language is a toolkit of limited ability. What great insights might our current rhetoric be hiding? Here's one possibility.

The words of science unknowingly constrain the answer to one of today's most important philosophical questions. The question is this: *Does our cosmic creator, Admiral Boom, play dice?* The famous Albert Einstein insisted *no, he does not,* while modern scientists answer that *yes, he most certainly does.*

Now, this question about whether or not the Admiral plays dice may sound pointless, but the two opposing answers given to us by Einstein and the current scientists have something strangely in common. Einstein's *no* answer suggests that Admiral Boom is in complete control of everything, while the scientists' *yes* answer suggests that our fate is left solely to chance. Both answers subtly ignore the human ability to make choices. Both answers subliminally imply that our destiny is out of our own hands.

It may be time for a new rhetoric—a new way to couch this compelling question of physics. Perhaps Albert Einstein was right when he said that Admiral Boom doesn't play dice. And perhaps the modern physicists are right too when they show evidence that probabilities govern the universe. What if, instead of playing dice, the Admiral plays cards? Perhaps this re-framing of the question could help the scientists as well as the philosophers. Here's how it goes.

The Admiral shuffles his deck and deals out the cards, but the outcome of the game is not entirely decided by the hands he deals. You see, the Admiral's deck contains jokers . . . and jokers are wild. We humans are the Admiral's jokers. We can change the course of the game. We might even win if we play ourselves wisely. The power to choose is the magic the Admiral has granted us to make our wishes and dreams come true.

For the scientists, then: the universe is a deck of cards randomly shuffled. For the philosophers: we humans are the jokers managing the odds. And for the artists out there, here's the true beauty of the analogy.

The human mind is a castle ruled by a tempestuous queen named Emotion. Emotion gathers the

Artifacts of Experience and then uses them to furnish the rooms of her castle. When an artifact fits the décor, Emotion feels pleasure. But when an artifact arrives that does *not* fit, Emotion gets upset. She banishes the offending item to the highest room of the tallest tower, then becomes more and more agitated as that room fills up. Once the tower chamber swells to overflowing, Emotion enters a crisis. She has no alternative but to force newly arriving artifacts into her lower rooms, where they sorely clash with the furnishings. This dissonance overwhelms her. She either surrenders in misery to the mess, or she rises to the occasion and redecorates. Redecorating means enduring, for as long as necessary, the clutter and disarray involved with an overhaul of the castle's interior. Once complete, however, the tower chamber is again clear of artifacts, because all of them have now found a suitable display in the living quarters below. Emotion does the work of a hero.

A hero, by definition, is someone with the courage to seek new themes among the Artifacts of Experience. Children are forced to be heroes several times as they grow up, pressured as they are by their parents and teachers to adopt the prevailing adult arrangement of furnishings. These same adults, however, face less pressure to redecorate their own castles. It often takes a calamity to get the job done. One such calamity is the arrival of an *epic* hero.

An epic hero is someone who stumbles upon a revolutionary new interior design—one that remedies the common clashes among the prevailing Artifacts of Experience. Aristotle, Newton, and Einstein were three of humanity's epic heroes. They challenged the established experts of their day and ultimately changed the way Emotion organizes her castle.

Emotion recently reordered *my* castle. Science and Religion now sit peacefully within the same display. And here's why.

Science tells us that the human mind is a soulless biological machine, while Religion insists that the soul must be in there somewhere. I believe both sides are correct, but that they've simply lacked the rhetoric to reconcile their misunderstanding. The word *soul* has been changing in meaning, and it's about to do so again. A few thousand years ago, the word for soul meant *breath*. It was *breath* that left a dying person, not a *soul*. In fact, the concept of death, itself, was unknown at the time. Death and the loss of breath were rolled into that single idea of *motion that has stopped.* It was a giant leap forward to become self-aware and implant the soul into the individual. But ownership of that soul is slated to be relinquished when a new and higher truth takes hold, one that reveals that the soul has a collective nature instead. Science shows us that death is final—a permanent slipping away of consciousness due to a physical world that can no longer support it. Science also shows us that the universe is persistently alive, allowing consciousness to resurface wherever conditions are right. Yes indeed, the soul is much bigger than any one individual person. It is something we all share, and it inhabits every speck of the cosmos.

Please take a moment to tour your own castle and see what your Emotion is doing right now. Is she storming the hallways after what I've just said?

Or is she sitting in quiet contemplation? To know the answer to my question, you must rely on another person who lives in your castle. Oh, didn't I tell you? Emotion has a stepdaughter named Feeling.

Feeling lives in the castle too. She was raised by Emotion, and she is the one who observes Emotion's moods. Feeling has always lived at the mercy of Emotion . . . at least, until now. Feeling's coming of age has brought to her a handsome suitor named Logic & Reason. He is the dashing prince who comes to call on her. The two of them together have the best chance of persuading Emotion to try out a new design scheme for the castle. But Emotion is a tough old bugger. She resists any new ideas unless they are presented in just the right way. And that's exactly my aim with this discussion of the *soul*—to present it in just the right way.

The new definition of *soul* is not really so surprising; it is merely a term that is coming full circle. It hearkens back to an earlier time, when life was seen as a circle rather than a straight line. And there was a good reason for this circular depiction. You see, *time* is another one of those concepts that was unknown to our distant ancestors. They could not perceive their own existence, let alone plot it on a timeline. Primitive people responded to the world by reflex, and their reflexes put them in harmony with nature as a matter of survival. These humans could not consciously choose to believe in reincarnation and the circle of life, so it was their experience with nature that forced such beliefs into their cultures. We would do well to revisit that earlier model of the world.

No one can say for sure whether life is a one-way passage or a revolving door, but the evidence definitely favors the latter notion. Life in this world is all we know, so why do we tend to dream up fantastic other-worlds for an afterlife? It seems more rational to assume a return to *this* world instead. But a fruitless debate of such unprovable ideas is not my objective here. There is a wholly practical reason to choose the *circle-of-life* philosophy over the *single-life* option. Just look at the motivational differences inherent with each.

A *single-lifer* is a fly-by-night operator who sweeps in to take profits during a brief stay, while the *circle-of-lifer* is here for the long haul, fully invested and protective of the future. So ask yourself the following questions: What's the harm in imagining yourself as the reincarnation of someone you admire—someone whose life's work you can continue to improve upon? And what's the harm in believing that your next life will return you into the heaven or hell you've created in *this* one? And tell me this, what's the harm in valuing every conscious creature as though it's a former loved one?

Your philosophy is a personal choice, of course, but why not make it work for you? Stop wandering alone through the cold and unforgiving night. Join the great circle of life and bask in its resplendent firelight under the portraits of your heroes.

My walking tour ends beside a sundial on the observatory's lawn. Mary notes that this analog clock needs to be reset for Daylight Savings Time.

CHAPTER 57

The True Magic Kingdom

The four of us enter Bascom Hall, where the kids stop at the washrooms. Mary and I wait for them in the hallway and browse a display case.

We learn that this building was named after John Bascom, a philosopher and clergyman who served as the president of the university from 1874 to 1887. We read that he was also a professor of mental and moral philosophy, publishing a number of books during his career. The title of one such book gives us both a chuckle.

Bascom's 1871 publication, *Science, Philosophy and Religion*, is a perfect example of the intellectual wrestling match between the experts coping with their split from a one- to three-member panel. It's funny that the third true member of the panel, *Art,* wasn't even mentioned. Mary and I suspect that the long-standing dispute will eventually resolve itself peacefully with a simple and agreeable change to the panel's letterhead: *Religion* will become the title for the organization, and *Science, Philosophy,* and *Art* will be named as the Board of Directors. Even Bascom's own words hint at this underlying truth. His book is open to page 292, where we find the following passage:

Theology, therefore, is simply gathering together, into

one presentation for practical ends, what pertains
to many departments of knowledge.

As the chimes of the university's carillon tower ring the
two o'clock hour, I realize I'll be exceedingly late as Ms.
Forward's Ghost of Christmas Present. She's still quite some
distance away.

When MJ and Michael emerge from the bathrooms, we
exit the building onto a hilltop terrace that overlooks a portion of Madison's downtown. A lawn slopes away from us,
bordered on each side by sidewalks and university buildings.
The statue of Abraham Lincoln sits in front of us, gazing
down the hill.

The kids scramble around to see him from the front, then
climb onto his lap with a little boost from me. They survey
their scene from this new and higher position.

Our location points us straight downtown toward the
Capitol building, yet our line of sight is obstructed by trees
at the bottom of the hill. Only the gold statue on top of the
dome is visible from here, though just barely so.

"What's he looking at?" says Michael.

"I was wondering the same thing," I say. "He should have
the best view in Madison. There must be something wrong."

Mary and I lower the kids to the ground, then walk about
fifty feet to the right. Again, we look down the hill, and this
time our view is considerably better; we can see around the
trees, all the way to the Capitol building. But the view is still
partly blocked by the upper stories of the university's main
library.

"Who put that building there?" says MJ.

I now recall the full history.

Last year, while frequenting the Memorial Library, I saw
a display commemorating the building's 50th anniversary. It

included a dramatic picture taken during the 1980s' renovation, when citizens discovered that the new addition was going to block the view from Bascom Hill. Public outcry halted construction, prompting politicians to make a compromise: they trimmed the addition from eight stories to seven, creating what we see here today.

"Note to self," says Mary. "Strike the words *Model City* from John Nolen's 1911 master plan."

MJ and Michael return to Lincoln's statue and kneel beside his pedestal, sifting through some fragments of broken tile on the ground. Each of them selects a piece of granite and carries it away as a souvenir.

"Do you know who broke that tile?" says Mary.

The kids look at her as though she's crazy; how could they possibly know who broke it?

Mary points to the statue of old Abe. "*He* did it," she says. "He bounced his pedestal when no one was looking, trying to get his view back. Poor Mr. Lincoln."

The four of us proceed down Bascom Hill and cross the footbridge over Park Street. I deliver us to the fountain of last year, at the center of the Library Mall, where we made our wishes before traveling to Disney World.

"Do you remember standing here last summer and wondering why people make wishes on stars, fountains, and birthday candles?" I say.

"And butts," adds MJ.

We revisit our list of wacky items to wish upon, then I return us to my discussion. "But we forgot the most basic one," I say, "—the wishing well."

"Of course," says Mary. "How could we forget that?"

MJ and Michael lean over the edge of the fountain and put their hands in the water.

"It turns out," I say, "that the wishing well was more

important than all the others because it taught me that you two were right. MJ, you said that *luck* is what makes wishes come true. And Michael, you said that wishes really *do* work. But I bet you can't remember *my* awful answer. I said that wishes come true *when preparation meets opportunity.* Yuck! Well, I've since learned that I was sadly mistaken, and it was you two who taught me, that with a little luck, wishes really *do* work. And the wishing well showed me how."

It's quite likely that the kids have stopped listening to me. But that's okay; most of what I have to say is for Mary anyway. I just hope they keep busy until I'm finished.

"When you make a wish or say a prayer, you lower a bucket into the well of your mind. With any luck at all, you don't pull up a shoe. But the rest of the wish is largely up to *you: you* can change the size and shape of the pail you lower down; *you* can lengthen and strengthen the rope; and *you* can pull and dip and swish the bucket around as much as you please. *Endless experimentation* is the key to snagging a gold nugget. And that's the lesson that you and the wishing well taught me. *Preparation* and *opportunity* are just complicated ways of saying *try. To try* is the key to success—*try* with all your heart, *try* with all your courage, *try* with all your curiosity, and *try* with all your humility. Never ever stop trying."

The kids scoop up water and bat at it with their hands.

"But don't be surprised," I continue, "if *trying* doesn't always work. There are no guarantees down in the well. You see, there's a hand down there that maneuvers the bucket, and our wishes on stars, fountains, and birthday candles are merely a plea to control it. But guess what. I've learned what has the power over that hand, though I'm not going to tell you just yet. You see, our statue friend, Ms. Forward, needs to hear the answer too."

At the mention of Ms. Forward, the kids turn and look at

me. They know that the package under my arm is for her, and they also know that it's going to be their job to open it for her.

"Let's go," says MJ, and she takes my hand.

The four of us walk along State Street, debating the proper pronunciation of the Brat Block and then coping with Mary as she calls the Double Block the *Double Bock* and the *Doppelbock*.

As we cross Gilman onto the Ice Cream Block, Mary points forward to the *Sacred Feather* hat shop and explains that it used to be a tea shop during prohibition, but that the tea shop was rumored to have housed a speakeasy in its basement. "I didn't find any evidence to support the claim," she says, "but it certainly is curious that the tea shop changed its name to *The Kopper Kettle* at about the right time. Maybe Ms. Taggart and her widowed mother were actually moonlighting in moonshine—brewing a little hooch, as it were."

"Geez," I say, "you'll drag *anyone* through the mud."

At the corner of State and Gorham, Mary parks us under a red awning that reads with the words *Madison's Happiest Corner.* "Do you remember the Good News Bakery Man?" she says. "He told us there were tunnels under the street between Shatki's bookstore and Quinton's patio. I've since learned that some of what he said was true."

Mary reaches into my bag and pulls out a piece of paper that I didn't know was in there. It's a photocopy of a newspaper photo from 1982.

Mary explains that the Hausmann Brewery once stood across the street from us and covered much of the block. The arrow in the photo points to the brewery's beer cellar under what is today's Quinton's patio, where young boys used to carry mini barrels up and down ladders. But the brewery was gone long before the Good News Bakery Man was born. His bakery opened and closed in just one year's time, during the late 1970s. He probably saw the excavation

Beer cellar uncovered

a few years later and imagined the tunnels he might have found in the basement of his store. But according to Mary, who questioned some of the city's oldest engineers, the hole in the wall he described was likely just an abandoned coal vault or an elevator shaft under the sidewalk."

"I guess Bootleggers Block is the wrong name," I say. "It's Brewers Block—"

"Or Good News Bakery Block," says MJ.

"Not so fast, 'ere mateys," says Mary. "There's still a chance that the real bootleggers used the old Hausmann cellars. The brewery burned down in 1923 during prohibition and was replaced by an auto service station—the perfect front for a bootlegging operation. Just think about it. There's nothing suspicious about vehicles coming and going from an auto shop. And there's no doubt from this photo that the cellars still existed at the time. I ain't saying it's true, but I ain't saying it ain't."

♦ ♦ ♦

We walk along the Theater Block and cross the barricades to the Museum Block. This 100 Block of State Street is truly a pedestrian mall today for the *Taste of Madison* festival. In fact, the entire Capitol Concourse is off limits to traffic for a full block in every direction.

We stop at Vic's Corn Popper, then carry our snacks toward some live music. I've got Michael on my shoulders.

Our favorite Madison ensemble, *Mama Digdown's Brass Band*, is wailing from a plaza between two museums along State Street. The music is New Orleans jazz, and it inspires a phrase to course through my mind: *the sweet sounds of dixie*. It's a shame the word *dixie* remains shackled to a negative connotation. I think the time has come to set this word free and let it celebrate the people and the music and the city that gave it birth.

Michael leans his head down. "It's Disney World," he says in my ear.

"Yeah," I answer, "—Port Orleans."

"No," he says. "It's Disney World. There's the castle." He is pointing to the Capitol building.

He's right. We're smack dab in the middle of the Magic Kingdom. We're standing along Main Street USA near the Central Plaza. And the Capitol building is clearly the Cinderella Castle.

Michael shares this comparison with Mary and MJ.

"And Ms. Forward is the Partners statue," says Mary.

I ask Michael and MJ to recall their disappointment when they learned we couldn't go exploring inside the castle at Disney World. "But *this* castle is open to the public," I say. "You can even climb into the tower."

When the band has finished playing, we weave our way between people and vendors to reach the statue, Ms. Forward. We quietly invoke the family ritual, cupping a hand behind one ear and reciting, "I can hear her talking. She has a story to tell."

I instruct Mary and the children to take the storyteller's

seat today and not to open the gift for Ms. Forward until I give the signal. I then move to the base of the steps in front of the statue.

Mary is looking at me searchingly, and I hope she's not disappointed by my presentation. I give her a quick smile as I pull out my speech.

A nearby church bell starts to ring three o'clock, and I wait for the sound to pass. I realize I'm exactly an hour late as her Ghost of Christmas Present.

"Good afternoon, Ms. Forward," I begin reading. "Today is a special day for you. You see, Mary and I have learned why people create statues like yourself. And we also know why people haven't heard you when you've tried to speak to them. The story begins long, long ago, during a time when people turned to their statues for advice. These statues delivered the voices of the gods, and you are a vestige of that past."

I reach into my bag and remove a box of sidewalk chalk, which I then give to the children.

"And there's more," I continue reading. "Before statues came along, people heard the gods in other ways: they heard them in the sounds of trickling water and rustling leaves, and they heard them in the sight of flickering flames, curling smoke, and towering temples. But their gods eventually fell silent, fleeing into the heavens to live among the stars. Yet we humans have persisted in some of those old habits. We still appeal to stars, fountains, and birthday candles with our wishes. But notice I didn't mention statues in my list. People don't often make wishes to statues anymore. So why are you here if people no longer listen to you or make wishes upon you? What purpose do you now serve?"

A few passersby have stopped and are listening to me.

"The human mind is like a deep well of thought," I say.

"Thoughts come to the surface like water hauled up in a bucket. For most of human time, we've stood beside this well in the darkness of night, unable to see the water we've withdrawn. Then came the moonrise, and a shadowy hand grew faintly visible, making fleeting appearances in the surface-waters of the well. These first glimmers of self-awareness revealed that a hand, called *Religion,* steered the pail in mysterious ways. But then came the morning twilight, casting its glow a little deeper into the well. The hand of *Religion* was clear to see when it worked at the surface, filling the bucket with machine-like reliability and precision. It took on the nickname of *Science* in this upper region, and the name *Philosophy* was adopted for the murky transition zone below it. The hand of *Philosophy* was less predictable than that of *Science;* it could fill the bucket with puzzling contradictions. Yet there's one more region of the well that needs to be discussed. That's where *you* come in, Ms. Forward.

"I have good news for you today; you serve a tremendous purpose—an indispensable purpose. You are *Art.* You are the nickname for the hand working in the blackness of the well. Yours is the hand that fills our buckets with truths we can *feel* but not yet see. You, Ms. Forward, are the truth of *Art* that cannot be denied by *Science* or *Philosophy.* You are the poetry of Thomas Jefferson's Declaration of Independence that speaks equally well to people of opposing ideology. You are the beauty of jazz and of baseball that allows people to bypass their racial and cultural prejudices. And you are the breathtaking animation of Walt Disney's *Pinocchio* that still plays some sixty years after its creation, and that miraculously pointed my way to all of these discoveries. You, Ms. Forward, are *Art.* You are the intuition . . . the inspiration . . . and the revelation responsible for every form of human emancipation."

I glance away from my notes and look at Mary. Tears are
running down her face because she knows I've uncovered
the lost name.

"You, Ms. Forward—as your name suggests—are the force
of *Art* pointing us to a brighter future. Allow me to share with
you some words by Robert Owen.

> . . . man is about to advance another important step
> towards that degree of intelligence which his natural
> powers seem capable of attaining.

> . . . a change must take place; a new era must com-
> mence; the human intellect, through the whole extent
> of the earth, . . . , must begin to be released from its
> state of darkness.

"It's no coincidence," I continue, "that athletes, musicians,
and artists of every kind are among the most celebrated
people on earth. Their achievements are often classified as
treasures, and two such treasures need singling out. First, *It's
a Wonderful Life* has taught me that my life is not in vain: that
my hometown of Bedford Falls is counting on me to prevent
its decline into Pottersville. And second, *A Christmas Carol* has
taught me that my life is mine to change: that my destiny is
largely of my own choosing. When MJ and Michael are a
little older, I plan to prove the magic of art to them with the
showing of two films. The first will be *The Architecture of Doom*,
revealing *Art* as the poison behind Adolf Hitler's war and
holocaust. The second will be Walt Disney's *Victory Through
Air Power*, showing the potential for *Art* to serve as the world's
greatest elixir—education. You, Ms. Forward, are *Art*: the
greatest educator of all time. You are the source of the Disney
Magic and of the Holiday Spirit that adorn my parlor table.

Indeed, you are the wandering alchemist who I suspect will one day reveal the formula for transforming my sterling tea set to pure gold. Yours is the awesome and humbling force at work within the well of my castle garden, and I'm grateful to finally know you."

I fold up my paper and discover Mary drying her eyes with her shirt.

"It's time for the present," I say to MJ and Michael.

The children put down their chalk and peel the ribbon off the box. Inside it, they find a black umbrella, which I instruct them to lean against the back of Ms. Forward's pedestal.

"This umbrella," I say, "is a token of our affection for you, Ms. Forward. I hope it will always remind you of us and of our dear Aunt Poppi. Goodbye, Beautiful."

"Goodbye, Beautiful," says Mary and the children.

I offer Mary my hand, and the four of us proceed along the sidewalk toward the Capitol building.

"In case you were wondering," I say to the children, "the rules of Rock-Paper-Scissors are changing. Pretty soon, the only way to win will be to get all three to come up at the same time."

"That sounds boring," says MJ.

"What will happen to the umbrella?" says Michael.

"I guess we'll just have to wait and see," says Mary.

We enter the Capitol building and head directly to the center for our usual stop: we lie down on the cool stone floor and stare up into the lofty dome.

At the nearby information counter, we ask our Madison cast member for directions to the observation deck. He points with a single finger at the North Wing, telling us to take the elevator. I resist the temptation to scold him for using such an offensive gesture.

We follow the route and reach a spiral staircase, which

climbs to the observation deck. MJ and Michael race ahead of us and are standing at the railing when we emerge. They are spying the dome-shaped fountains across the street.

"Hey, look! Boobs, Daddy!" they shout.

Mary snickers at me.

"But wait," I say, and I raise both of my hands to the children like a choir director. "I've made *Boobs Daddy* mean something," I say to Mary. "The *Boobs* are the serious part, and the *Daddy* is the punch line—the joke of it all."

"As it should be," says Mary.

I begin conducting, and the kids and I perform our rehearsed lyric.

> Build the **B**ridges of intellect.
> Save the **O**ceans
> and **O**zone.
> Slow the human **B**irthrate.
> Live in a utopian **S**pa.

> **D**isease,
> **A**ccident,
> **D**isaster, and
> **D**eath
> anywa**Y**.

Mary claps her hands for the children, then gives me a look of exasperation.

"But I did it for *you,* sweetie pie," I say, "and for women everywhere. Don't you see? It's the return of the goddess—the lost sacred feminine. The female breast is once again calling us to worship. Sojourner Truth was an early arrival."

"Well," says Mary, "I suppose half the population might

agree with you." She gives her breasts a quick lift, then smiles at me coyly.

The four of us stand at the railing and study our downtown from this overlook. The heart of our city resides on a narrow strip of land between two lakes, and we speculate that Lake Monona is actually Disney's Bay Lake, and that Lake Mendota is the Seven Seas Lagoon. Continuing our comparison, we find that Washington Avenue is the path to Liberty Square, and that Martin Luther King Jr. Boulevard leads to Tomorrowland. But the best match of all is King Street, which enters Fantasyland—the home of our favorite restaurant and Mortimer Mouse.

"I want to live in Disney World," says Michael.

"Me, too," says MJ.

I spread out my arms. "But we already do."

"No, I mean *really*," says Michael.

"Not possible," says Mary. "No one lives in Disney World."

Mary is lying, of course. She's neglecting to mention the community of Celebration.

I point across the railing into Fantasyland. "Do you kids remember my *Story of Walter*?" I say. "It ended with a big mistake on my part. Walt Disney's last big dream was not to build an amusement park. What he *really* wanted to do was build a great city that you and I could live in. But he died before he could do it. So we'll just have to deal with Madison, I guess. How do you suppose Walt would make our city a better place to live?"

"He'd give Abe Lincoln his view back," says Mary.

"Probably," I say, "—he was a planner all the way. But even more than that, Walt Disney was an early player of Rock-Paper-Scissors by the new rules. He combined Science, Philosophy, and Art into creations we still love today."

MJ and Michael stare out over the railing, surely tuning me out again. But I don't care. "If Walt was improving Madison, he'd do what he always did: he'd do his homework and he'd never give up. And one more thing. He'd motivate the people around him to share in his dream and apply their talents to it, for Walt Disney understood that life is a *TEAM* effort—that *Together Everyone Achieves Magic*."

I tap the children on the shoulders. "So," I say, "what will *you* do to make Madison a better place to live?"

There's a moment of silence, then MJ answers: "What can *I* do? I'm just a kid."

Mary snorts. "Just a kid? Just a kid? Why, you don't—"

"But you *shopped* today," I interrupt her. "Money is your great power. Every dollar you spend . . . or *don't* spend . . . is a vote you cast for the world you want. *Just a kid!* You bought used clothes today . . . and you walked downtown. What a great example you've set—wearing secondhand clothes and walking on empty sidewalks for all the world to see."

I close my eyes and copy the pose of Walt Disney in the Partners statue, then I recite two of his quotes.

> People look at you and me to see what they are supposed to be. And, if we don't disappoint them, maybe, just maybe, they won't disappoint us.

> The way to get started is to quit talking and begin doing.

MJ and Michael begin to shriek, and I open my eyes just in time to see them rushing past me and into the arms of Grandma and Grandpa. The kids desperately want to know the reason for their appearance.

"Let's see," says Grandma, and she pretends to be thinking. "Oh, yes. We want to take you two to the Dells, but first we need proof that you are brave, truthful, and unselfish."

MJ fumbles frantically to pull out her Disney coin, and Michael does the same. They show them to Grandma, whose face lights up.

"Disney tuppence!" she says. "There's no greater proof in the world."

We take my parents to the railing and show them our fair city of Madison, pointing out the parallels with the Magic Kingdom.

"And guess what?" says Dad. "We're taking you to a hotel named the *Polynesian,* just like in Disney World."

I flinch at Dad's likening of the Wisconsin Dells to Disney World. The Dells is one of the gaudiest commercial strips on the face of the planet. Walt's dead body is no doubt erupting with goose pimples right now, though they're probably going unnoticed by his castle guards, given that he's already frozen and all. But maybe Walt's not actually so offended by the comparison after all, because outside of the Magic Kingdom, Disney World is hardly his park.

Mary and I hug our children goodbye, then watch them enter the stairwell. We can hear my dad announcing the weather conditions of their hotel. "The pool temperature is seventy-eight degrees. The air temperature is "—

CHAPTER 58

The Keys to the Kingdom

Mary and I return to the railing of the observation deck and look out over Madison's Fantasyland. A horse-drawn carriage makes its way around the Capitol Square, reminding us of Mary's glass coach ride and our ceremony on the castle balcony last year. We wonder if we'll be whisked away to a hidden room inside this castle for dinner.

But the parallels are beginning to break down. It's mid-afternoon, so we can't expect a fireworks show, and there's no intimate dining inside the Capitol building. Furthermore, we know why Uncle Albert's not here because we're scheduled to meet with him for tea on the Union Terrace, beside the boat launch of the Seven Seas Lagoon.

Mary and I exit the castle and walk down Madison's Main Street USA. The Library Mall is clearly the Town Square, and we reach the terrace through the lower level of the Memorial Union. The terrace is a wide patio that steps down toward Lake Mendota and is filled with colorful tables and chairs.

We find Uncle Albert seated in the shade with his nose buried in a bright yellow book. The table beside him has a pitcher of iced tea on it and three plastic cups, all of which are covered by a newspaper.

"You're a messy eater," says Mary, sweeping the many acorn fragments off the table.

"Oh goodness gracious," says Albert, and he quickly tucks away his book. "Between you and the squirrels, I'm getting shell shock."

Mary pours us our drinks, and Albert places one of my prototype Oddballs on the table. It is scuffed and marred.

"I believe congratulations are in order, Bert," he says. "I hope you don't mind; Mary loaned this to me. It was a hit at the skate park. The kids called it a Skeeter Ball. Maybe a toy is the best way to spread your idea."

◆ ◆ ◆

At six o'clock, Mary and I walk Uncle Albert to the pier, where a sailboat belonging to his relatives from Maple Bluff is approaching to pick him up.

"Why does Ariel hide her breasts behind seashells?" says Mary.

"Ugh," says Albert. "Perhaps I should *swim* to the boat."

"Good idea," I say. "I think I'll join you."

"Because A-shells and B-shells are too small."

I put my arm around Uncle Albert, and the two of us commiserate.

He eventually boards the boat, and we watch him sail away.

"That was a risky joke," I say. "You might have made Albert seasick. Get it? —not A-sick or B-sick, but C-sick."

Mary rolls her eyes, and I can only hope that I've at last cured her of her corny joke-telling.

Mary and I return to Madison's Town Square and enter the Memorial Library at six-thirty, where I have another present to deliver. I lead Mary into the darkened stacks, and together we search every floor for a pool of light, hoping to spy the old woman doing her reading. My plan is for us to observe her until she leaves, then place a brass bell with a thank you note on the shelf where she keeps her bag.

But the woman is nowhere to be found, so I take Mary to

the original floor where I discovered her and investigate the aisles for any clues as to where she might be reading these days. Unfortunately, the only clue we find is a profoundly troubling one.

Sitting on a bookshelf is the old woman's shoulderbag covered with dust. It hasn't been moved for months.

Mary and I discuss what to do, then decide to take the bag home with us for safekeeping and leave a note behind with our phone number.

I brush the dust from the leather, exposing its monogram—*L.N. Smith*—then raise the strap to my shoulder. Instantly, I feel a rush of closeness to this woman who served as my teacher, and I yearn to hug her and call her *an early arrival.*

"Well," says Mary, "there's nothing more we can do here. I'm thirsty for a brewskie. Shall we go to Bootleggers Block?"

"Thank god it's not a dry town," I say.

We stop for a cold one at the Angelic Brewing Company, where Mary asks me why I'm still carrying Albert's newspaper. "Don't tell me you're not potty trained," she says.

"Not sure," I reply. "But if I don't soil it, the paper's going to help us make a decision tonight."

Mary downs her sorghum lager and wipes her mouth with her bare arm. "Let's go," she says.

We work our way past the booths and stages of the *Taste of Madison,* eventually reaching our favorite restaurant in Fantasyland. The hostess seats us at an outside table in the garden.

"What's on the agenda?" says Mary. "I hope you're not planning to feed the newspaper to Mortimer."

"Don't be ridiculous," I say. "We need to figure out if I'm going to submit the Jungle Cruise to Disney or not. The newspaper has our horoscopes."

"Hmm," says Mary. "I'll need more to drink. Let's wait on that."

During dinner, Mary and I hatch an idea for a new television series designed to teach the real differences between people. It turns out that Thomas Jefferson was not entirely incorrect when he grouped humanity according to biological differences. His mistake, however, was to group them by "skin pigment" rather than "metabolic profile." Perhaps an extreme make-over show could demonstrate the real potential for transforming people's health and appearance without leaving them hungry or putting them on diet pills or performing surgeries on them.

I finally open the newspaper to Mary's horoscope.

> Look for God in the big picture, then look for the devil in the details. Try to know God before you wrestle the devil.

"You can throw that one away," says Mary. "God is in the big picture, all right, but you can't really know him until you've wrestled the devil."

I slide my index finger along the page and read my own horoscope.

> Explore your thoughts and feelings with the critical eye of consciousness. The Age of Aquarius is upon us. It's up to you to lead the way.

"Aquarius?" says Mary.

"Sunrise on the River of Truth," I say, "—it's the dawn of a new age. The Jungle Cruise has a date with destiny. *Of course* I'll submit it to Disney."

"But you're a Pisces," says Mary. She looks into the plant bed. "Tell him, Mortimer. He's loopy."

"That's not Mortimer," I say. "We're in Fantasyland tonight. *This* is the Dumbo ride—"

"No argument *there*—"

"That's Timothy."

Mary and I make a toast to the past year and to the new paradigm that now informs us. Humankind's age-old desire to live in a paradise here on earth explains the long-standing attraction to places like Madison, the Magic Kingdom, Walt's Epcot, the Town of Pullman, and the 1893 World's Fair. But Mary and I are also quite sure of one other thing: that the promise of a utopian paradise is not found in the design of a city or town; rather, it is found in the design of a bridge. Intellect is the true construction project that leads to ever greater utopias.

For Mary and me, bridge construction has been fast and furious over the past handful of months. We seem to be ahead of many people on the River of Truth, at least in a few departments of knowledge. Almost no one would know the names we are now toasting, as we salute the future prize winners for medicine, economics, psychology, and anthropology. Another beer later, and I'm personally accepting the Nobel Prize for physics.

"The world of tomorrow exists today," says Mary, "but only for those who can spot the true experts."

"That's it!" I say, "—the redesign of Tomorrowland! That's the next chapter of my life . . . I mean, after I finish school, of course."

I tip my half-empty beer glass from side to side, dreaming up the headline: "From *retro*-future to *ready*-future, the new Tomorrowland introduces the ideas reshaping our world."

"And I know just the right person to stand at its entrance," says Mary. "Benjamin Franklin."

"But he's dead—"

"A statue, then," she says, "like the Partners. —Old Ben holding hands with Pinocchio."

We rework a famous Franklin proverb for the statue's plaque.

> Early to learn, and see truth through the lies, makes
> a person . . . a nation . . . a world . . . healthy, wealthy
> and wise.

♦ ♦ ♦

After dinner, Mary and I exit the restaurant and cross the Capitol Square toward State Street. We pass Ms. Forward and note that the umbrella is still leaning behind her.

As we walk the length of State Street, we observe that our surrounding revelers foreshadow a new Golden Age that will vaguely resemble the former one. Tattoos and body piercings that were once an act of innocence are now an act of choice. In fact, that's the significant difference between now and then. Consciousness has stripped away our innocence, showing us the beauty and horror of our natural tendencies. It has been a long and painful road to our current state of maturity, but we finally seem capable of indulging some of life's beauty without inciting some of its horrors. We cannot, however, return to that Golden Age of Innocence, nor should we want to: the next golden age will be far superior. It will begin with the recombination of science, art, and philosophy, this time under the direction of that extraordinary capacity known as self-awareness. It will be called the Golden Age of Consciousness, and it will be spectacular.

But there's another interesting parallel here on the street between the people of today and the people of long ago. Today's people carry cell phones, putting the voices of absent others into their ears. This is similar to the voices of the gods speaking directly to our pre-conscious ancestors. The difference, here again, is that the voices "heard" by our ancestors were generated within their own brains, whereas the voices heard today come from distinctly separate living beings. Consciousness is being shared like never before. Our growing connectedness reminds me of another statement by Robert Owen.

> Ere long there shall be but one action, one language, and one people.

Mary and I wonder how many generations it will take before the world-wide gap in human intellect begins to narrow, blending all of humankind into a single global culture that shares one common language. We wonder how long it will take for people to believe in the science of evolution that proves we are descended from animals. And we wonder how long it will take for people to accept the next big change to our vocabulary—the one that will blur the distinction between "life" and "machine," as genetics and robotics and neuroscience and computers become equal partners in the support of creatures that are self-aware. The word "soul" must once again migrate to a deeper meaning.

Mary and I stand beside the fountain on the Library Mall and fashion a joint wish. We pray that the natural forces advancing human intellect will win the race against those same natural forces destroying the planet. Mary and I want the human species to be one of the universe's success stories. We toss in our coin.

The two of us climb into the backstage area, known as Bascom Hill, and stop midway up to look out over our imperfect city. I can feel the eyes of Abe Lincoln upon me; he has words to share:

> There will be another Civil War, and this one will be global in its reach. But heed my words, you can't win this one with life-shattering guns and city-leveling bombs, for by now you must surely know that such weaponry merely strengthens the enemy. No, your next Great War must be fought with financial incentives, administrative advice, and tough-love accountability. And your warriors must be a peace corps well versed in human compassion and environmental stewardship, and they must be ready to face the enemy wherever he appears—even in the mirror, if necessary. The enemy of this conflict . . .

the villain to be disarmed at all costs . . . is none
other than Ignorance.

It will be a glorious war to end all wars, as the
world's richest private organizations and founda-
tions pool their talents and resources to accomplish
what your governments cannot . . . and as everyday
average citizens champion the cause as well through
their choices as consumers. Don't doubt that the
spoils of victory will be far sweeter than the fight,
creating a world of glistening cities and charming
small towns, rich in culture and history, and filled
with vibrant, healthy people. This must be the noble
cause that unites humankind and peels away the
shells of ignorance.

From the grassy slope of Bascom Hill overlooking the
Capitol building, Mary and I stretch out on the lawn and
gaze up at the stars.

At two o'clock this afternoon, I was not the Ghost of Christmas Present being foretold by the carillon's chimes. Rather, it
was Honest Abe Lincoln—sitting there, ready to show us our
home city of Madison as the Magic Kingdom. And then, at
three o'clock, it was actually Ms. Forward, in her dark robes,
who was *my* Ghost of Christmas Yet to Come, delivering the
greatest message of all.

I pose a philosophical question to Mary. "A few thousand
years ago, consciousness entered our torsos and then settled
behind our eyes. Where will the mind-space go next?"

"Our pockets," she answers simply.

True to form, my devoted student of science proposes that
electronic devices, which currently feed information into the
brain through the eyes and ears, may one day connect more
directly. Then, perhaps, the human mind-space will move

from a biological place to a cyberspace, hovering within an imagined library of instant access to every article on the shelves.

I, as Mary's resident artist and philosopher, remain true to form as well. I answer that she may be right, but that the library will be in the clouds. Ms. Forward was pointing the way with her right hand. The gods started in a hemisphere of our brains, then lured us across to take their places while they retreated into the skies. Humans are destined to follow them once again. The mind-space of the future will drift from the body and into the heavens in search of a common place—a library, perhaps—shared by all conscious creatures. Today's vocabulary, dominated by words for the individual, will be transcended by words for the collective, as greater and greater truths reveal that *self-interests* and the *common good* are actually one and the same thing. "The gods are clearly leading the way," I say. "It was *their* world of many gods that created *our* world of many individuals. And now, it is *our* world approaching a single god that will create the *new world* of a single humanity. There probably aren't words to describe such a world."

"On the contrary," says Mary, "there's a very good word. But please tell me, do you really think God is in the sky?"

"Heck, no," I say. "The chase won't end there. He'll dissolve into the stuff of the universe and become its pervading essence. We'll have traveled full circle from our pre-conscious roots, once again finding the Holy Spirit imbued in everything."

Mary pulls herself closer to me and rests her head on my chest.

As the moon sails high above us—just as it has done for thousands of years over our ancestors—Mary and I share this brief moment in time. It won't be long before the River of Truth washes our sandbars into the sea, yet we know that our short lives are not in vain. The remnants of our bridges will remain on the river long after our passing and serve as models for the newly arriving bridge builders. Mary and I will cheerfully devote our works and days to our earthly republic, pursuing our vision of utopia with each new sunrise. We will build the bridges of intellect in spirited fun and with purpose, freed by our newfound knowledge that the only true failure is *failure to try*.

Ms. Forward carries the banner of our march under her left arm. It reads, "All is right with the world; it always has been, and it always will be."

THE END

The 2004 Labor Day Picnic

On the Monday following our evening downtown, my entire family is gathered at my parents' home for another of Albert's birthday parties and the Labor Day picnic.

It is during this event that Albert shakes up the family for a second time. He gives me a yellow book—the one he was reading at the Union Terrace on Saturday—then hands me a check to buy me out of college once again. He wants me to write my personal story around the Jungle Cruise, and the yellow book is to serve as my instruction manual. It's called *Techniques of the Selling Writer* by Dwight Swain.

"You think he's cut out to be an author now?" says Elsa.

As expected, a contingent of my family is quite upset by Albert's proposal. But not Mary. She deflects their disparaging remarks and encourages me to accept the offer.

"Well," I say. "Do you mind, Uncle Albert, if I delay my start for a few months? There's something else I want to do first."

"Certainly," he says. "I'm paying for that too. Take all the time you need."

The redesign of Tomorrowland that Mary and I conceived of the other night is not the project that is currently pressing for my attention. Rather, it is the question of physics I dreamed up for my walking tour that has given me the spark of an idea.

I don't dare share the idea in present company, however. Tom has an undergraduate degree in physics and might not appreciate me treading upon his discipline. And even if my idea ultimately shows some promise, I'll still need to hire a professor and grad student to do the math, which will require a pile of money . . . perhaps from the sale of a book.

The Labor Day picnic ends with another of Dad's exploding birthday cakes, and this time everyone enjoys it.

Sources

Abravanel, Elliot, and Elizabeth King Morrison. *Dr. Abravanel's Body Type Diet and Lifetime Nutrition Plan.* Rev. ed. New York: Bantam Books, 1999.

Adler, David A. *B. Franklin, Printer.* New York: Holiday House, 2001.

AllEars.Net. http://allearsnet.com/

Anderson, Clifford. *The Stages of Life: a Groundbreaking Discovery : the Steps to Psychological Maturity.* New York: Atlantic Monthly Press, 1995.

Appelbaum, Stanley. *The Chicago World's Fair of 1893: a Photographic Record, Photos from the Collections of the Avery Library of Columbia University and the Chicago Historical Society.* New York: Dover Publications, 1980.

Barrett, Katherine, and Richard Greene. *The Man Behind the Magic: the Story of Walt Disney.* New York: Viking, 1991.

Barry, Kathleen, *Susan B. Anthony: a Biography of a Singular Feminist.* New York: New York University Press, 1988.

Bartlett, John, and Justin Kaplan, eds. *Familiar Quotations: a Collection of Passages, Phrases, and Proverbs Traced to their Sources in Ancient and Modern Literature.* 16th ed. Boston: Little, Brown, 1992.

Bascom, John. *Science, Philosophy and Religion: Lectures Delivered before the Lowell Institute, Boston.* New York: G.P. Putnam & Sons, 1871.

Bedini, Silvio. "The Role of Automata in the History of Technology." *Technology and Culture* 4 (1964): 24-42.

Bedini, Silvio. *The Life of Benjamin Banneker.* New York: Charles Scribner's Sons, 1972.

Berlin, Edward A. *King of Ragtime: Scott Joplin and His Era.* New York: Oxford University Press, 1994.

Billingsley, Kenneth Lloyd. *Hollywood Party: How Communism Seduced the American Film Industry in the 1930s and 1940s.* Roseville, Calif.: Forum, 2000.

Bloom, Paul. *Descartes' Baby: How the Science of Child Development Explains What Makes Us Human.* New York: Basic Books, 2004.

Braly, James, and Ron Hoggan. *Dangerous Grains: Why Gluten Cereal Grains May Be Hazardous to Your Health*. New York: Avery, 2002.

Brands, Henry William. *The First American: the Life and Times of Benjamin Franklin*. New York: Doubleday, 2000.

Broggie, Michael. *Walt Disney's Railroad Story: the Small-scale Fascination That Led to a Full-scale Kingdom*. Pasadena, Calif.: Pentrex, 1997.

Brown, Dan. *The Da Vinci Code: a Novel*. New York: Doubleday, 2003.

Buder, Stanley. *Pullman: an Experiment in Industrial Order and Community Planning, 1880-1930*. New York: Oxford University Press, 1967.

Burnham, Clara Louise. *Sweet Clover: a Romance of the White City*. Centennial ed. Caledonia, Mich.: Bigwater Pub., 1992.

Burns, Ken, dir. *Baseball: A Film by Ken Burns*. PBS Home Video, 1994.

Burns, Ken, dir. *Thomas Jefferson*. PBS Home Video, 1997.

Burns, Ken, dir. *Not for Ourselves Alone: the Story of Elizabeth Cady Stanton and Susan B. Anthony*. PBS Home Video, 1999.

Burns, Ken, dir. *Unforgivable Blackness: the Rise and Fall of Jack Johnson*. PBS Home Video, 2005.

Capra, Frank, dir. *It's a Wonderful Life*. RKO Radio Pictures, 1946.

Carlton, Donna. *Looking for Little Egypt*. Bloomington, Ind.: IDD Books, 1994.

Castleden, Rodney. *Atlantis Destroyed*. London: Routledge, 1998.

Ceplair, Larry, and Steven Englund. *The Inquisition in Hollywood: Politics in the Film Community, 1930-1960*. Garden City, N.Y.: Anchor Press/ Doubleday, 1980.

Clare, John D., ed. *Industrial Revolution*. San Diego, Calif.: Harcourt Brace & Co., 1994.

Cohen, Peter, dir. *The Architecture of Doom: The Nazi Philosophy of Beauty through Violence*. First Run Features, 1995.

Collodi, Carlo, and Troy Howell. *The Adventures of Pinocchio: Tale of a Puppet*. Translated by M. L. Rosenthal. New York: Lothrop, Lee & Shepard, 1983.

Cook, Diana. *Wisconsin Capitol: Fascinating Facts*. Madison, Wis.: Prairie Oak Press, 1991.

Costecalde, Claude-Bernard, and Peter Dennis. *The Illustrated Family Bible: Based on the New International Version Bible*. New York: DK Pub., 1997.

Cottingham, John, ed. *The Cambridge Companion to Descartes*. Cambridge: Cambridge University Press, 1992.

Creese, Walter L., and John S. Garner. *The Midwest in American Architecture*. Urbana: University of Illinois Press, 1991.

Dent, Harry S. *The Great Boom Ahead: Your Comprehensive Guide to Personal and Business Profit in the New Era of Prosperity.* New York: Hyperion, 1993.

Diamond, Jared M. *Guns, Germs, and Steel: the Fates of Human Societies.* New York: W.W. Norton, 1997.

Dickens, Charles, and Trina Schart Hyman. *A Christmas Carol: in Prose, Being a Ghost Story of Christmas.* New York: Holiday House, 1983.

Disney, Walt. "The Cartoon's Contribution to Children." *Overland Monthly and Out West Magazine* 91.8 (October 1933): 138.

Disney, Walt. "To my employees on strike: . . ." Advertisement. *Daily Variety* 2 July 1941: 5.

Disney, Walt, and Dave Smith. *The Quotable Walt Disney.* New York: Disney Editions, 2001.

Disney's Fairy Tale Weddings. Disney promotional video, 2004.

Disney's Fairy Tale Weddings & Honeymoons. http://disneyweddings.go.com/

Dinsmore, Antonina Paratore. *In Greenbush.* Madison, Wis.: A.P. Dinsmore, 2004.

Donald, Merlin. *Origins of the Modern Mind: Three Stages in the Evolution of Culture and Cognition.* Cambridge, Mass.: Harvard University Press, 1991.

Edwards, Betty. *The New Drawing on the Right Side of the Brain.* 2nd rev. ed. New York: Jeremy P. Tarcher/Putnam, 1999.

Ehrman, Bart D. *Truth and Fiction in The Da Vinci Code: a Historian Reveals What We Really Know about Jesus, Mary Magdalene, and Constantine.* Large print ed. Prince Frederick, Md.: RB Large Print, 2005.

Eliot, Marc. *Walt Disney: Hollywood's Dark Prince : a Biography.* Secaucus, N.J.: Carol Publishing Group, 1993.

Ellis, Joseph J. *American Sphinx: the Character of Thomas Jefferson.* New York: Alfred A. Knopf, 1997.

The Encyclopedia Americana: the International Reference Work. New York: Americana Corporation, 1957.

The New Encyclopaedia Britannica. 15th ed. Chicago: Encyclopaedia Britannica, 1998.

Fenster, Jay. *DisneyWorld With Kids.* 5th ed. Cold Spring Harbor, N.Y.: Open Road Pub., 2002.

Findlay, John M. *Magic Lands: Western Cityscapes and American Culture after 1940.* Berkeley: University of California Press, 1993.

Fleming, Candace. *Ben Franklin's Almanac: Being a True Account of the Good Gentleman's Life.* New York: Atheneum for Young Readers, 2003.

Fölsing, Albrecht. *Albert Einstein: a Biography.* Translated by Ewald Osers. New York: Viking, 1997.

Ford, Barbara. *Walt Disney: a Biography*. New York: Walker, 1989.

Fowler, James W. *Stages of Faith: the Psychology of Human Development and the Quest for Meaning*. San Francisco: Harper & Row, 1981.

Fried, Frederick. *A Pictorial History of the Carousel*. South Brunswick: A.S. Barnes, 1978.

Galvin, Irene Flum. *The Ancient Maya*. New York: Benchmark Books, 1997.

Geronimi, Clyde, dir. *Cinderella*. Walt Disney Productions, 1949.

Geronimi, Clyde, dir. *Alice in Wonderland*. Walt Disney Productions, 1951.

Geronimi, Clyde, dir. *Sleeping Beauty*. Walt Disney Productions, 1959.

Gilbert, James Burkhart. *Perfect Cities: Chicago's Utopias of 1893*. Chicago: University of Chicago Press, 1991.

Gilbert, Olive and Sojourner Truth. *Narrative of Sojourner Truth, a bondswoman of olden time: with a history of her labors and correspondence drawn from her "Book of Life"*. New York: Oxford University Press, 1991.

Green, Amy Boothe, and Howard E. Green. *Remembering Walt: Favorite Memories of Walt Disney*. New York: Hyperion, 1999.

Greenspan, Stanley I., and Stuart Shanker. *The First Idea: How Symbols, Language, and Intelligence Evolved from Our Early Primate Ancestors to Modern Humans*. Cambridge, Mass.: Da Capo Press, 2004.

Haas, Robert Bartlett. *Muybridge: Man in Motion*. Berkeley: University of California Press, 1976.

Haden-Guest, Anthony. *The Paradise Program; Travels through Muzak, Hilton, Coca-Cola, Texaco, Walt Disney, and Other World Empires*. New York: W. Morrow, 1973.

Hand, David, dir. *Snow White and the Seven Dwarfs*. Walt Disney Productions, 1937.

Hemming, John. *The Conquest of the Incas*. New York: Harcourt, Brace, Jovanovich, 1970.

Hendricks, Gordon. *Eadweard Muybridge: the Father of the Motion Picture*. New York: Grossman Pub., 1975.

Henle, Mary, Julian Jaynes, and John J. Sullivan. *Historical Conceptions of Psychology*. New York: Springer, 1973.

Hesiod. *The Works and Days. Theogony. The Shield of Herakles*. Translated by Richmond Lattimore. Ann Arbor: University of Michigan Press, 1959.

Hidden Mickeys of Disney. http://www.hiddenmickeys.org/

Hovde, Ellen, dir. *Benjamin Franklin*. PBS Home Video, 2002.

Hoyt, Austin, dir. *Chicago: City of the Century*. PBS Home Video, 2003.

Hurst, Brian Desmond, dir. *A Christmas Carol*. United Artists, 1951.

Isbouts, Jean-Pierre, dir. *Walt: the Man Behind the Myth*. Walt Disney Home Entertainment, 2001.

Jaynes, Julian. "The Evolution of Language in the Late Pleistocene." *Annals of the New York Academy of Sciences* 280 (1976): 312-25.

Jaynes, Julian. *The Origin of Consciousness in the Breakdown of the Bicameral Mind*. Boston: Houghton Mifflin, 1976.

Jones, Steve, Robert D. Martin, and David R. Pilbeam, eds. *The Cambridge Encyclopedia of Human Evolution*. Cambridge: Cambridge University Press, 1992.

Kimball, Ward, dir. *Walt Disney Treasures - Tomorrow Land: Disney in Space and Beyond*. Walt Disney Video, 2003.

Larson, Erik. *The Devil in the White City: Murder, Magic, and Madness at the Fair That Changed America*. New York: Crown Pub., 2003.

Laughlin, Rosemary. *The Pullman Strike of 1894: American Labor Comes of Age*. Greensboro, N.C.: Morgan Reynolds, 2000.

Lawson, Robert. *The Great Wheel*. New York: Scholastic, 1957.

Lemonick, Michael D., and Andrea Dorfman. "Who Were the First Americans?" *Time* 167.11 (13 March 2006): 42.

Levitan, Stuart D. *Madison: the Illustrated Sesquicentennial History, Volume 1, 1856-1931*. Madison: University of Wisconsin, 2006.

Liberman, Anatoly. *Word Origins . . . and How We Know Them: Etymology for Everyone*. Oxford: Oxford University Press, 2005.

Liberman, Anatoly, and J. Lawrence Mitchell. *An Analytic Dictionary of English Etymology: an Introduction*. Minneapolis: University of Minnesota Press, 2008.

Luske, Hamilton, dir. *Walt Disney Treasures - Disneyland USA: Special Historical Broadcasts*. Walt Disney Video, 2001.

MacDonnell, Kevin. *Eadweard Muybridge, the Man Who Invented the Moving Picture*. Boston: Little, Brown, 1972.

Manes, Stephen. *Pictures of Motion and Pictures that Move: Eadweard Muybridge and the Photography of Motion*. New York: Coward, McCann & Geoghegan, 1982.

Mann, Charles C. *1491: New Revelations of the Americas before Columbus*. New York: Alfred A. Knopf, 2005.

Marling, Karal Ann, ed. *Designing Disney's Theme Parks: the Architecture of Reassurance*. Montréal: Canadian Centre for Architecture; Paris; New York: Flammarion, 1997.

McCormick, Anita Louise. *The Industrial Revolution in American History*. Springfield, N.J.: Enslow Pub., 1998.

McManus, I. Chris. *Right Hand, Left Hand: the Origins of Asymmetry in Brains, Bodies, Atoms, and Cultures.* Cambridge, Mass.: Harvard University Press, 2002.

Meltzer, Milton. *Benjamin Franklin: the New American.* New York: Franklin Watts, 1988.

Meltzer, Milton. *Thomas Jefferson, the Revolutionary Aristocrat.* New York: Franklin Watts, 1991.

Merriam-Webster's Collegiate Dictionary. 11th ed. Springfield, Mass.: Merriam-Webster, 2003.

Miller, Diana Disney, and Pete Martin. *The Story of Walt Disney.* New York: Henry Holt, 1957.

More, Thomas, Tommaso Campanella, Francis Bacon, and James Harrington. *Ideal Commonwealths: Comprising More's Utopia, Bacon's New Atlantis, Campanella's City of the Sun, and Harrington's Oceana.* Edited by Henry Morley. Port Washington, N.Y.: Kennikat Press, 1968.

Mosley, Leonard. *Disney's World: a Biography.* New York: Stein and Day, 1985.

MousePlanet. http://www.mouseplanet.com/

Murray, J. A. H., Henry Bradley, W. A. Craigie, and C. T. Onions, eds. *Oxford English Dictionary.* Reissued 1st edn, 12 vols with one-volume *Supplement.* Oxford: Oxford University Press, 1933.

Nolen, John. *Madison: A Model City.* Boston, Mass., 1911.

O'Brien, Maureen, and Sherill Tippins. *Watch Me Grow, I'm One--two--three: a Parent's Essential Guide to the Extraordinary Toddler to Preschool Years.* New York: Quill, 2002.

Olson, Steve. *Mapping Human History: Genes, Race, and Our Common Origins.* Boston: Houghton Mifflin, 2002.

the-original-epcot.com. http://sites.google.com/site/theoriginalepcot/

Owen, Robert, and George Douglas Howard Cole. *A New View of Society and Other Writings.* London: J.M. Dent. New York: E.P. Dutton, 1966.

Painter, Nell Irvin. *Sojourner Truth: a Life, a Symbol.* New York: W.W. Norton, 1996.

Papalia, Diane E., and Sally Wendkos Olds. *Human Development.* 6th ed. New York: McGraw-Hill, 1995.

Pearson, Michael Parker. *The Archaeology of Death and Burial.* Stroud: Sutton, 1999.

Peary, Danny, and Gerald Peary, eds. *The American Animated Cartoon: a Critical Anthology.* New York: Dutton, 1980.

Perrault, Charles, and Sally Holmes. *The Complete Fairy Tales of Charles Perrault.* Translated by Neil Philip and Nicoletta Simborowski. New York: Clarion Books, 1993.

Plato. *The Republic*. Edited by Giovanni R. F. Ferrari, and translated by Tom Griffith. Cambridge: Cambridge University Press, 2000.

Principe, Lawrence. *Science and Religion*. The Teaching Company, 2006.

Roop, Peter and Connie Roop. *Sojourner Truth*. New York: Scholastic, 2002.

Ross, Stewart. *The Industrial Revolution*. New York: Franklin Watts, 2000.

"Save Mr. Toad's Wild Ride!" *University of Miami Department of Mathematics*. http://www.math.miami.edu/~jam/toad/

Schickel, Richard. *The Disney Version: the Life, Times, Art, and Commerce of Walt Disney*. 3rd ed. Chicago: Ivan R. Dee, 1997.

Schiffer, Fredric. *Of Two Minds: the Revolutionary Science of Dual-brain Psychology*. New York: Free Press, 1998.

Sehlinger, Bob. *The Unofficial Guide to Walt Disney World, 2003*. New York: Wiley Pub., 2002.

Sharpsteen, Ben, dir. *Pinocchio*. Walt Disney Productions, 1940.

Sharpsteen, Ben, dir. *Walt Disney Treasures – Walt Disney on the Front Lines: the War Years*. Walt Disney Video, 2003.

Shaw, Marian. *World's Fair Notes: a Woman Journalist Views Chicago's 1893 Columbian Exposition*. St. Paul, Minn.: Pogo Press, 1992.

Siegel, Alan A. *Smile: a Picture History of Olympic Park, 1887-1965*. Irvington, N.J.: Irvington Historical Society, 1983.

Siegel, Daniel J., and Mary Hartzell. *Parenting from the Inside Out: How a Deeper Self-understanding Can Help You Raise Children Who Thrive*. New York: J.P. Tarcher/Putnam, 2003.

Smith, Dave. *Disney A to Z: the Updated Official Encyclopedia*. New York: Hyperion, 1998.

Smith, L.N. (2004). *The Disney World Dream*. Unpublished manuscript, L.N. Smith Pub., Madison, Wis.

Smith, L.N. (2004). *The Disney World Reality*. Unpublished manuscript, L.N. Smith Pub., Madison, Wis.

Smith, L.N. (2004). *Disney's Jungle Cruise: The Line*. Unpublished manuscript, L.N. Smith Pub., Madison, Wis.

Smith, L.N. (2004). *Poppi's Story and Scrapbook from 1893: the Chicago World's Fair and the Model Town of Pullman*. Unpublished manuscript, L.N. Smith Pub., Madison, Wis.

Snodgrass, Mary Ellen. *Signs of the Zodiac: a Reference Guide to Historical, Mythological, and Cultural Associations*. Westport, Conn.: Greenwood Press, 1997.

Stanton, Elizabeth Cady. *Eighty Years and More: Reminiscences, 1815-1897*. Boston: Northeastern University Press, 1993.

Stevenson, Robert, dir. *Mary Poppins*. Walt Disney Productions, 1964.

Swain, Dwight V. *Techniques of the Selling Writer.* Norman: University of Oklahoma Press, 1973.

Teeple, John B. *Timelines of World History.* London: DK Pub., 2002.

Thomas, Bob. *Walt Disney: an American Original.* New York: Simon and Schuster, 1976.

Thomas, Bob. *Building a Company: Roy O. Disney and the Creation of an Entertainment Empire.* New York: Hyperion, 1998.

Travers, Pamela Lyndon. *Mary Poppins.* New York: Reynal & Hitchcock, 1934.

Vrooman, Jack Rochford. *René Descartes: a Biography.* New York: Putnam, 1970.

Ward, Geoffrey C., and Ken Burns. *Jazz: a History of America's Music.* New York: Alfred A. Knopf, 2000.

Weimann, Jeanne Madeline. *The Fair Women: The Story of the Woman's Building, World's Columbian Exposition, Chicago 1893.* Chicago, Ill.: Academy Chicago, 1981.

Wells, Ida B., Frederick Douglass, Irvine Garland Penn, and Ferdinand L. Barnett. *The Reason Why the Colored American Is Not in the World's Columbian Exposition: the Afro-American's Contribution to Columbian Literature.* Edited by Robert W. Rydell. Urbana: University of Illinois Press, 1999.

Wells, Spencer. *The Journey of Man: a Genetic Odyssey.* Princeton: Princeton University Press, 2002.

Wilber, Ken. *Integral Psychology: Consciousness, Spirit, Psychology, Therapy.* Boston: Shambhala, 2000.

Wilber, Ken. *A Theory of Everything: an Integral Vision for Business, Politics, Science, and Spirituality.* Boston: Shambhala, 2000.

Wiley, Kim Wright. *Walt Disney World With Kids, 2002.* Roseville, Calif.: Prima Pub., 2001.

Wolcott, William L., and Trish Fahey. *The Metabolic Typing Diet.* New York: Doubleday, 2000.

Wolf, Anthony E. *"Get Out of My Life, but First Could You Drive Me and Cheryl to the Mall?": a Parent's Guide to the New Teenager.* New York: Farrar, Straus and Giroux, 2002.

The World Book Encyclopedia. Chicago: World Book, 2004.

Wright, Robert. *The Evolution of God.* New York: Little, Brown, 2009.

Zipes, Jack, ed. *The Oxford Companion to Fairy Tales: the Western Fairy Tale Tradition from Medieval to Modern.* Oxford: Oxford University Press, 2000.

Other titles by L.N. Smith

Grand Unification and The New Look of the Atom (2004)

The Redesign of Tomorrowland (2009)